T0303002

ROCK VARNISH

ROCK VARNISH

a novel

BARRY KENNEDY

McArthur & Company

First published in Canada in 2005 by
McArthur & Company
322 King St., West, Suite 402
Toronto, Ontario
M5V 1J2
www.mcarthur-co.com

Library and Archives Canada Cataloguing in Publication

Kennedy, Barry (Barry G. J.)
    Rock varnish : a novel / Barry Kennedy.

ISBN 1-55278-546-7

    I. Title.
PS8571.E62725R62 2005   C813'.54   C2005-904769-0
The publisher would like to acknowledge the financial support of the
Government of Canada through the Book Publishing Industry Development
Program, The Canada Council for the Arts, and the Ontario Arts Council for
our publishing activities. We also acknowledge the Government of Ontario
through the Ontario Media Development Corporation Ontario Book Initiative.

Cover design and composition: Tania Craan
Printed in Canada by Friesens

10 9 8 7 6 5 4 3 2 1

For Marnie

The sea and the air are blameless, as is the rock on which generations have stood. Fog makes me tingle, wind makes me gasp, cliff and coast raise a smile. If there is a distinction between what is natural and human craft-work, the divide is at the exact point where we can or cannot deal with the repercussions. We rebound from natural disaster, while human injustices have effects from which we never fully recover. I have been the cause of so much, so very much.

—G.H. *Nuttall,* And the Sea Shook the Rock

PART ONE
LIES

CHAPTER 1

On my fifteenth birthday my father said, "Dare, be brave, and life will open to you like a flower." Later: "Hesitate and perish." Much later, after he forked in the last cabbage roll and washed it down with the heel of the rye bottle: "Take up the world in your two good hands and shake it!"

Plain-spoken under normal conditions, when drinking my dad often decorated the air with skywriting of that sort. And since he clattered in bewilderment through life, like a fawn fleeing across glare ice, his broadsides were contradictory and ornamental. Furthermore, his church flew the flag of predestination, directing its parishioners to seize next to nothing with their own hands—they barely had need of opposable thumbs. So as usual his advice found me too slick for a toehold and I heard it without listening.

I'm hardly one to judge. My own contradictions are so massive they can buckle my knees. But on this day courage is either required or unavoidable, and eventually I'll pick up the morning paper. Soon everyone will have their hands on Chas Cassidy's article and the jig will be up, but in the meantime I may as well continue editing what I have in front of me—whatever Cassidy's investigative-journalism expertise, he couldn't possibly have unearthed the whole sorry package I've kept buried all these years. Even I'm still digging up rotting fragments I'd forgotten about.

And so—I'm a liar.

I look back and around and into the mirror and realize what I used to consider my philosophy, my unique crank on the world, has gradually, almost imperceptibly, been transformed into bullshit. It no longer is philosophy, rather a collection of loose conclusions based on a rewriting of my own history, fungus between the toes of my footprints in the sands of time. Most disturbing is that I didn't see it coming. I simply awoke one morning, performed the same ablutions as every other day, pulled on the same pair of pants, then at some point while I was making coffee my ears began burning with the realization I was lying in one way or another about everything. It has scored and scarred and over time even defined who I am, and it all reached the point of failure this past year down in California. Although my forty-day walk in the desert mountains at year's end helped keep the structure from complete collapse, it's a flimsy edifice. If I can't find Roger now that we're home, the whole works might let go.

I'm staring out my apartment window at a dropcloth of cloud. Middle of August and the Vancouver streets are rain-stitched, pedestrians shuffling along as cheerlessly as a troupe of flagellants. Cold and miserable, in acute contrast to my skin, which suffered more than my feet from my desert wanderings.

When I was young I spent at least one week each summer in a similar state of sunburn, forced into walking around with my elbows held out to minimize friction. Agony for the first couple of days, though when the peeling began I gained much welcome attention—surrounded by neighborhood kids, I'd carefully tear away great sheets of epidermis and raise them overhead to cheers from the crowd before saving them on my bookshelf until they browned and curled like Qumran scrolls. Each molting gained my dad's approval, evidence I was acquiring buffers against a predatory world, on the path to toughness, resiliency. He could have been right. I've survived so far, though to be honest most of the problems, being self-induced, have been easy to see coming.

The brush fire on my shoulders has taken eight tubes of aloe gel and my forehead is particularly tender, the hairline having receded by a couple of fingers in the past year. The UV receptivity up top is heightened by a slight sagittal crest—a bony ridge running down the center of my skull—over which the hair is thinning, exposing my dome to full solar assault. I should have kept my shirt on, used sunscreen, climbed down and picked up my hat when I lost it off the trail . . . all good advice that now seems laughably trivial. Once I find Roger my world will spin aright. Until then I'm just cranky and hungry and exhausted and dreading the arrival of Chas Cassidy's article and burnt on my shoulders and my forehead and my lower lip, which is swollen and cracked, making it difficult to speak, the sound of one lip chapping, that's all.

I could head out and wander to the West End. A convenience store on Davie Street gets its newspapers so much earlier than any other place I'm certain they're bribing the delivery drivers. It's run by an old Korean who for some reason thinks I'm famous and scrambles every time I walk through the door to have me autograph his latest Asian skin magazine that he keeps under the counter distinct from the even more savage domestic offerings on rack display. I can't imagine he believes I'm a porn star; I put it down to his being impressed by my overall look of a substantial man, custodian of secrets and potent insights, when really I'm just beat-up. And beaten I am—straightened to my full height I'd top six feet, but even when not sitting slumped and cross-armed I spend much time looking at the ground, examining, pondering. Short beard until my face heals enough to shave. Damn good physical condition most of my life, but aging, and as much muscle mass as fat was incinerated on my big hike. No longer muscular, not yet bony.

It's still raining. I should wait it out. For that matter, it makes little difference whether I'm the first or last person on the coast to read the article. The exposé will be just the sealer coat on many layers of imprudence. I did it all, believe me, I know what I'm talking about.

Besides, it would be good to have Roger along when I face my shame in print and I still can't track him down. Roger Jeffcoate, my best friend, if you can use that term for someone who serves weak coffee in china cups with saucers. I thought he'd be waiting for me here in town, though given his state when he left California two months before I did, it was a baseless assumption. Our trip to the desert was supposed to be restorative. My life was a hash and Roger's mother had died and plunking ourselves down in the little desert suburban bungalow Mrs. Jeffcoate had left her son seemed just the thing. And now . . . well, two months is too long to be without him. Good man, Roger Jeffcoate, the best, met as kids when my family moved to Vancouver, tight ever since, thick-and-thin type of thing, yin-and-yang polarities, me doing anything to gain an edge, him so staid argyle socks make him look like a rodeo clown.

His absence has me truly worried. A practical punctual man with a botanist's ability to compartmentalize, Roger has a gift for being where he should be at the right time. It's one of the many things about him I count on. Another is his guiding hand—no telling how much more seriously I would have pissed in the pickles along the way without his constantly pointing to the proper fork in the road. His phone has been reconnected and I'm getting by on the money he left on my desk and working at a computer he set up for me, so he must be around somewhere. He'd mentioned coming home to look for a teaching job at one of the community colleges, but none of them has his application on file. I should continue my search of our old haunts—Vancouver Library, UBC Anthropology Museum, the Sylvia Hotel tap room and other bars we'd frequent when we either had a belly full or needed one. Until desperation kicks in I'll suppress the urge to set up surveillance on his apartment and troll his garbage for clues.

In any case, I have too much work to do. Since returning to Vancouver I've been keeping the hours of a marathon dancer, sifting through and collating my journal of the past year, compressing here, soldering there, cross-breeding birds of different feathers. Getting near the end and I don't know whether I'm happy about it or not. The end of something, whatever it is.

One calendar year ago I couldn't have anticipated the cock-up to come. Everything on that day went right, a confluence of good fortune and promises of sweet treats. I tried to reincorporate the feeling when I first got back by physically retracing my course only to find an emptiness more toxic for the comparison, unable to sniff the mildest aroma of good things cooking. Of course, I was no longer ignorant of the details of that day a year ago, the sneak preview of catastrophe that was so innocuous I can forgive myself for missing it—only shamans and lunatics are able to divine the future from such slender evidence.

This year's parade starts in a few hours and you never know, by then I may have survived Cassidy's article and Roger will have called and climbed the stairs and the two of us had a laugh and strolled out under cloudless skies. In that case there will be nothing to stop us from heading over to see what the Hari Krishnas are up to. Certainly it would be an attempt to recapture the past, perfectly natural, nothing wrong with trying to revisit what you've experienced unless you try to relive it. Catch and release, my sporting friends. And I do love a good parade.

Roger and I had just finished a graceless fried breakfast so greasy it left us sweating when we heard the clamor. Denman Street was chockablock so we took the alley down to English Bay. We arrived to see the seawall and greensward dense with people maneuvering for vantage points and avoided the crush by settling in beside a dumpster at the mouth of the lane. From the bay came splinters of light reflecting off sails, hulls, wave tops. Across the water in front of the nautical museum and planetarium was an air armada of kites looking like an unruly bunch of cut flowers on monofilament stems. Roger cuffed me with a grin for no good reason and I gave him one back.

In the Vedas, the Supreme Personality of Godhead, the original cause of all causes, is Krishna, who possesses unlimited transcendental qualities that attract all living beings. He was earning his pay as a headliner that day—there was a full house. Welling up Beach Avenue was an exultation of celebrants. At the fore were Devotees clashing finger cymbals and chanting, while those on the column's periphery passed out literature and flowers and indiscriminate goodwill. The feeling was happy, light. Generally, nothing terrifies me more than great numbers of people thinking the same way at the same time in the same place—the edge is keen between fifty-thousand throats shouting "Pull the pitcher" and "Kill the Jews"—but these saffron dingalings were having a good time.

The usual grab bag of West Enders was well into the spirit, along with mystified tourists and a double row of children on a school outing who were attached by the wrists to a flexible blue safety line. Or tumpline, rather, since their mission commander had the lead around his forehead and was straining to maintain momentum, shouting warnings at the kids to get a move on and not to talk to anyone and not even to look back, plainly terrified of some sort of Vedic evil infiltrating their minds while they were in his charge. The tykes wore identical green Eddie Bauer golf shirts, matching ball caps worn backward, interchangeable sunglasses, and were pulling at their fetters, looking desperate to join the celebration or even just to roll around in the dirt a little bit then dart out into traffic, anything.

Along the street the procession continued, fragmenting briefly on the near flank when a missile hurled from a condo balcony ripped the robe half off a pamphleteer and thundered into a basket of incense sticks. All heads pivoted, eyes turned up four stories, brief tension, but from the balcony a loud lament, and on inspection the projectile was simply a plastic bag full of rose petals that was probably designed to burst and flutter down but had become glued from the earlier rain into a matted wad. Much relieved singing and dancing while omnipotence myths formed on the spot and percolated among the revelers.

When the main attraction—a magnificent float disguised as a chariot bearing a plump smiling guru—drew abreast of the alley, it halted. The celebration, the Rathayatra, honors the Deity of Krishna in the form of Lord Jagannatha, who is pulled on his chariot by hand. But the haulers had crossed and tangled their lines like a detox center's macramé class. The enormous canopied affair, festooned with brass, fringe, beads and the stand-in Lord's attendants, shook and rolled and shimmied from the yanking but didn't gain a pace. Not far ahead was the south entrance to

Stanley Park. A quick sprint and they'd be inside and on their way to their campsite of cultural exhibits, entertainment stage and free-to-all-comers vegetarian feast, a diet that very likely was detracting from their ability to unstick the chariot by main force.

Abruptly, as if by unseen guidance, the heaving and tugging stopped. All was calm. I once attended a Shriners parade that suffered a mass collision of mini-bikes, and by the time they sorted out the mess the Grand Marshal was out of his fez with rage and sixty or more pantalooned ninnies were up to their sashes in a fistfight. So the Krishnas' sober restraint was nice.

From their midst, softly:

> *Hari Krishna, Hari Krishna*
> *Krishna Krishna, Hari Hari*

Hands lightly clapping, bare feet stomping. Louder, the entire parade in voice:

> *Hari Rama, Hari Rama*
> *Rama Rama, Hari Hari*

People on the sidewalks, tourists and locals alike:

> *Hari Krishna, Hari Krishna*
> *Krishna Krishna, Hari Hari*

Folks approaching from the beach, pulled by the promise of transcendence, towels and umbrellas abandoned, children in the water left unsupervised as lifeguards leaped from their towers and bolted for the street:

> *Hari Rama, Hari Rama*
> *Rama Rama, Hari Hari*

The chariot moved. Not a hand on a rope yet the chariot moved.

The old red Ford Falcon hit the back of the float going the speed of rumor. Lord Jagannatha had to step lively to avoid being thrown from the float's poopdeck into the laps of the driver and passenger, who were barefaced to the sky because the hardtop had been sheared from the body either by amateurish design or as a result of some previous mishap.

I grabbed Roger by the elbow and forced our way to the curb, trying for a better sightline. By then the Falcon was reversing away from the float. It stopped and started forward and lurched onto the grass strip paralleling the parade route. There was a scattering of gazelles before the predator as people leapt azaleas and boxwoods. Roger went down and was up faster than I've ever seen him move and running for the illusory safety of a front patio. Turf rocketed into the air behind the Falcon's wheels. So grimy and cracked was the windshield, it wasn't till the vehicle passed in front of us while mowing down a rhododendron that I caught a glimpse of the occupants—jet hair and dark dark eyes on the woman driving, then she was blocked from view as her companion, male, pissy blond, spun to the rear, kneeled on the seat, pointed up at the guru, who was trying mightily to retain his dignity, and screamed, "Hey, everybody—it's Santa!" before catching a finger cymbal edgewise in the ear and dropping in a spray of blood into the back seat, where he lay on his back and stuck his feet up, bicycling in the air and laughing madly.

Across the street the Falcon flew, over the sidewalk and down the grassy incline and along the seawall and just before it hit the lip and flipped over onto the rocks below, a vicious one-eighty, back over the sidewalk and left onto Beach. For some unfathomable reason I felt like waving.

"I wouldn't exactly call it an accident," I said to the waiter in the Sylvia Hotel twenty minutes after the Falcon had aced a popcorn cart and vanished into the depths of Stanley Park's forest, fifteen minutes after Roger and I had placed our order.

"I seen the red car crash into those guys in the yellow kimonos and all that out the door when I went out for a smoke," the waiter said. He dropped our beers and shrugged. "Kids having fun."

"They weren't kids," I said.

"No older than me."

"You got to be forty."

"About that."

"Anyway," I said, trying to vault off the topic, "thanks for the drinks."

"I like their music, them Hari Krishnas," the waiter said. "I was listening when I went out for a smoke. Easy lyrics."

"Yeah, four words by my count."

"Three," he said. "You're counting 'Hari' twice."

"No, I'm not."

"It repeats in each verse."

"Oh, yeah." I was tired. The adrenaline from watching the Falconian rampage couldn't be sustained. Like an addict, I needed either more action or oblivion.

The waiter was intent on following his point to a conclusion. "Any song I can remember the lyrics to is okay with me. I've been beating my brains out over the words to *American Pie* since I was twelve." He headed for the service area, already lowly singing, "Helter-skelter in a summer shelter, the birds flew off with the fallout welter . . . nine-feet high and . . . fuck!"

Roger was still shaken but would come around. "That accident or whatever you want to call it almost made me bring up breakfast. And this isn't helping."

"I know. The aftermath of something that great can't support small talk."

"Right," he said. "You think that was great."

We felt each other's impatience in a glance. When the waiter returned to check on our beer level I shook my head and Roger stood. "Have you been thinking about my proposal?"

It took me a minute to realize what he was talking about. "Oh. California? I don't think L.A. is my kind of place."

"Not the city, the Palm Springs area—two-hundred klicks away, off in the desert halfway to Arizona, perfect place for you to indulge your little geology hobby."

"Rocks are important," I said.

"You can collect them by the tonne down there."

"Palm Springs. Got to be forty-eleven thousand bloody golf courses. Stop to pick up a rock, good chance you'll take a three-wood off the skull."

"I'm going," he said. "My mum wanted me to have the house."

"What'll you do by yourself down there?"

"Phone you sixty times a day until I shame you into joining me. Think about it hard, I want to leave soon, Morty."

I ducked my head into my shoulders and scanned the room. "Careful."

Smith. That's the name I've been using since shortly after my novel hit the bookstands. You know me as Morty Cahoot and you know my novel, both creatures gaining much praise and more notoriety in a ridiculously short period of time. A name, a description of sorts that has been assigned without solicitation, can be a paralyzing stroke, but asinine as my legal name is—Morton Haig Cahoot, I mean, please—it's what my name became associated with, the identification with the novel, that led to the secrecy that was and has been necessary for my survival. Brief as the fame was, it cauterized me wholly, and once I disappeared underground the where-is-he-nows? and what-is-he-working-ons? eventually died out—their deaths I celebrate to this day with a quiet ongoing wake.

Smith. That's better, isn't it? No first, middle or initial. Smith, commonly associated with drunken couples checking in sans luggage at a midnight motel, yet with a solid pedigree of honesty and hard work. Smith, Cooper, Sawyer, Carpenter—hands-on handles smelling of candor and rectitude. My wife liked those kinds of names, once explaining that centuries back in Britain as the population increased to the point where people required a surname for identification they simply adopted or were given ones reflecting their professions. Well, I thought, when she had finished her speech, this is almost grade-schoolish information, and was about to twit her on it, when she said it was lucky the practice had begun so long ago or we'd be having dinner that night with our best friends John Forkliftoperator and Judy Checkoutclerk. She had me again. She could always make me laugh. Gone now, the dear woman, quite a few years since she died. Still makes me laugh, though.

"Nobody heard," Roger said, startling me. "Besides, you have the perfect opportunity to re-re-invent yourself. Come south with me and go back to your real name. They won't know you in the desert, you'll be home free."

I promised to seriously consider his proposal, and as we said our goodbyes outside and I watched him head up Gilford Street I concluded neither action nor oblivion was required. Just a walk, that's all, so I followed the petal trail to the park. At the end of the street, where high-density living met manicured forest, I diverted down to the seawall and spent the rest of the afternoon and early evening circumnavigating the park via the ten-kilometer path. Everything was in place. I felt good. Clearly, my past was a ruin archeologists wouldn't touch for grant money and free spades, but I was managing to keep it in its proper temporal slot. Hanging in.

On the Bruce Peninsula, which separates Georgian Bay from Lake Huron, a dead Eastern White Cedar was examined and found to have lived 1845 years. The kicker is that while alive the tree maxed-out in height at 1.5 meters. Rooted on that stark segment of the Niagara Escarpment in rocks 450 million years old, with minimal nutrients and savaged by the climate, the little five-foot bugger had been hanging in there almost as long as it's taken us to go from the custom-built year of Christ's birth to now. Holding no trumps, nothing in the crib, not even a Get-Out-Of-Jail-Free card. And still in the game.

Hanging in was easy that day, but something's been lost in the past year. It's still raining and I still can't find Roger. The library returned my call, informing me Mr. Jeffcoate had accumulated an actionable amount in fines and the UBC Anthropology Museum phoned to invite us to a lecture on the Palm Springs Cahuilla Indians, an ironic poke in the eye. I hope Roger's not following me down the shitter. But if he is, there you have it—all truly great historical figures end in defeat, so living happily ever after is a powerful form of failure.

Where now? Throughout my life each radical thing I've experienced initially had the appearance of a turning point. . . . Then nothing. No detectable order, no rebound, no redemption after a fall, no triumphs or tragedies happening in sets of three, not even good money being thrown after bad. What to do or should I even try? I'd throw up my hands if I hadn't torn both rotator cuffs from doing it so often.

My wife understood. My wife, the only person who never lied to me. Even Roger fibs now and again when he thinks it'll calm me down or shut me up. Never that from my wife, just truth till the day she died.

In any event, it's a shame my telling you all this won't be a catharsis, at least in the sense of it doing me any good. Going by the evidence of my ruinous foolishness there's no reason to suppose I'll learn overnight. The notion of a cleansing leading to a rebirth is unacceptable. Being born again would be to discredit both my actual past and my present reality, essentially meaning that none of it ever existed. I'll just keep bashing away at these notes and see what's what.

CHAPTER 2

I accepted Roger's proposal. He'd been growing disturbingly antsy since his mother died so for once I'd be doing something to give him a boost. The role reversal felt strange, as I've spent very little time going out of my way for Roger's benefit. Of course he doesn't believe it, doesn't see that almost everything he's done since we've known each other has been to prop me up and that I'm way behind in the count—he thinks we're even, perfect mutualism. He even spun the purpose of the trip, telling me of his concern and suggesting a change of venue for my benefit. Whatever the ultimate truth, I accepted his offer—that it triggered the most nauseating plummet of my life is hardly his fault.

Just over a year later here I am, back in the land of rain and bizarre governance, serving up my largest apology to date. And hurting. It feels as though my sunburn is more along the lines of deep-tissue damage. My wife would have chalked it up as karmic retribution, an explanation she used as a skeleton key, though if I understand the concept at all, karmic sunburn seems like a pretty small potato to serve with the rib roast of my misconduct. In any case, I should give my doctor a call.

Now. Anxious as I am to get to the body of my notes, I must take one small step back to cover my proving ground, the forty-day desert walkabout at the end of it all that allowed me to make my way home with at least a shred of dignity. Obviously I was trying to bake away the shame and the sorrow, seeking isolation and deprivation among the desert flora and fauna, the sky and the rock, now that my failed attempts with humans seemed final. The positive attributes of solitude were required, as there had been no perceptible learning curve during our year in California—nope, she flatlined till I hit the hills.

It was some walk. I headed out from Roger's house and kept moving. Once in the mountains I found what I needed. Not the pacific well-irrigated desert in which we'd been living, but the scratchy-bitey outlying area, the one home to spines and teeth and stingers and venom and barbs and rattles and pointy succulents and water so alkaline it leaves a ring in your colon; black widows and fire ants and scorpion and snakes and

Yosemite Sam stuff like great horny toads! I wanted to leap to avoid a diamondback, briefly impale myself on the spines of a cactus then tumble off a cliff onto an eight-inch ledge, a shattered tibia puncturing my jeans while vultures circled primping themselves and arguing over the dark meat. Well, I got it. At least the nondramatic part, the lost-and-hungry-and-thirsty-and-footsore part, the desperation and the cursing-yourself-for-undertraining-and-underthinking part. Let me tell you something—the next time anyone bends your ear about an ancient prophet removing himself to the desert and returning with a story about having been spoken to from On High, you believe it. It's an elementary equation: Desert + Distress − Provisions = Voices. All hardship cases hear things as they cast around for explanations, for coherency.

No scary critters though, at least none above the microscopic. All I did was run and hike and stroll and lose my hat and burn and fall a few times. The earth was open, void of no more than a sampling of vegetation so I could look right into its guts as it geologically reared and looped over and around me. Unashamed of its history of violent change, transparent and honest, it proffered itself for inspection. The desert formed only after the last ice age had raked the continent and played out its span, but these mountains, their sediments and eroded metamorphic caps and granitic cores—that's deep time, baby.

I like rocks. Rocks and minerals and crystals and gems and even big ugly boulders. I took much schoolyard abuse for my passion because most of my contemporaries believed rocks were good only for chucking through windows or at one another, though I gained a measure of vindication when news hit of a man who had stumbled across an entire mountain of jade in northern British Columbia. Even at that age everyone knew deviant behavior was justified by financial gain, and for as long as the story was in the newspapers I was besieged by kids who would prefer to kick my ass dumping pocketsful of stones, hardened mud, hunks of weathered glass and once a broken yo-yo on my desk, then standing around like characters from a Robert Service poem awaiting my expert assay. Unlike true prospectors who would have taken the bad news in stride and reloaded the mule for another trip to the streams, the schoolyard editions took umbrage and bashed me around for a day or so. Each event reaped my father's slow nod—another steel rod added to my spine, you see.

Damn, that was long ago. Not deep time, though. Even the ongoing uplift of the Santa Rosa Mountains I was hiking began only a million or two years ago. No, to go deep you must think in millions and millions of years, the running battle of buildup and teardown, erosion countering each mountain-building episode. Underneath? The Peninsular Batholith, a widespread mass of rock that was intruded while molten, metamorphosing the old sediments into the foundation for all the singular elements of the terrain.

Yes, I'm aware rock-talk can reduce the brain to the level of a cow's, which is why I usually keep it under my hat. But the evidence of deep time is what we rest upon, even if my rock collection and other examples of my marching out of step form a pretty unstable batholith in the short term.

By Week Three of my hike, after I had crossed the valley floor to the Mecca Hills and the Little San Bernardinos, as I was beginning to wonder whether I would ever stop hearing voices, it was my father's that stood out from the babble. My dad was a serious man, constantly troubled by the state of the world. According to one of our neighbors, my dad's only form of fun was proofreading hymnals, though this came from a witless martinet who drilled his children like army recruits and punctured all footballs, soccer balls and beach balls that flew over his eight-foot fence. I admit my father's humor seldom caught me between the eyes, though sadly that's true for most aspects of our relationship. He was remote, or I was, or together we were.

"The essence of human existence is a virgin," he said on one memorable Canadian Club night.

I had been trying to talk to him, achieving nothing more than shaking his foundation with what he considered my preoccupation with trivial matters.

"Separate the wheat from the chaff," he said next. "Wheat from chaff!"

I don't know what he followed up with because I couldn't concentrate through my anger and frustration. Years later I came across an article while waiting in Terminal 2 at Toronto's Pearson International—Kurt Franz, the last commandant of Treblinka, was being released from custody. The report stated he had been convicted of mass murder, depraved indifference and forcing the inmate band to play the camp song. Wheat and chaff both, but my dad wasn't there.

My father's voice held no humor as it cut through the desert air, though my wife's had me positively giddy. Pretty near every occasion drew a laugh from my wife and me in the old days, even the night I went down on one knee. Terrified and broke, I had no ring to accompany my marriage proposal, and after she said yes of course I love you she let drop that the rule of thumb on how much to spend on an engagement ring was two months' salary. Before I could get the quaver out of my stammer she said not to worry, we could move to Haiti. If I could pick up a good job there with plenty of overtime, in two months she'd have a perfectly good plywood ring.

Yeah, we laughed at everything, and I'm certain it was because there were no lies. No groundwork of deception meant none expected, affronts impossible. She never deceived me, and trust me when I say I never lied to her. The falsehoods and the whitewashing, the poison, started with her death. So as much as I say otherwise, I suppose I have had turning points, or at least that one instance of massive refraction. I'll have to think about it more. When not lying I'm frequently mistaken, which can have the same effect.

There was another voice, one I was accustomed to hearing without the hallucinations. So pervasive had it grown over the past year that it formed a latticework in my mind tight enough to provide structure. I could think of little without reference to it, and though I had never met the owner and most surely had the delivery and timbre of the voice wrong, it was real for all that.

I stole his book. That is, I wrote a book that was close to his story, and even to put it in those words is being precious for it was straight plagiarism, an act of piracy that wouldn't have been more obvious had I swung down from a set of rigging and ran a cutlass through his guts.

I published on the Internet, providing a certain anonymity enhanced by using my false name, Smith. The odds are vanishingly small he's stumbled across my bogus book, though somehow his ignorance is worse than the shame of discovery. So even when Chas Cassidy's article snaps off the stage lights on my masque anything the author does in retaliation will bring a ration of peace. And who knows—if the empathy in his words is the palest reflection of his heart I might even escape retribution entirely.

I learned nothing of G.H. Nuttall from his book's dust jacket because it was missing. I'd been rockhounding for a week in northern Ontario when I found the slim volume of memoirs in a used bookstore off the highway near Cobalt, and once back in Vancouver tossed it unread among my papers and books and forgot about it. The name on the spine must have been encoded by my brain to some extent, because for years after it would bark at me whenever I came across it. That wasn't often, by the way—once in *Canadian Geographic*, a couple of times in the *Globe and Mail*, another in a television guide on upcoming talk-show guests— just enough to make me want to dig out Nuttall's book and give it a go, each time putting it off till the next.

G.H. Nuttall's title: *And the Sea Shook the Rock*.

My title: *A Quake in Time*.

No plagiarism there, but peek inside:

The rock that quaked is Nuttall's island of Newfoundland. On July 12, 1981, in a small east-coast outport, a fishing boat went to the bottom of the sea. G.H. Nuttall, as had three generations of men in his family, fished the boat from deckhanding for his father at thirteen to the day before she went down. The vessel had always been kind to him, or at least benign, until its penultimate voyage, when a line parted, recoiled into the captain's face and plucked out an eye as neatly as if it had eyes of its own. As his underage son wrestled with the pickup's big steering wheel on the way to the hospital Nuttall enjoined the lad to call the neighbor and have him lay up the boat. The next day, with his dad bandaged and bedded down, armed with a spicy stew of exuberance, youthful pride and Newfoundland kissmyass, the boy took the boat out on his own. Well, not exactly his own—unable to dissuade her son and possibly proud of his determination, his mother went out with him that day. Observers recalled seeing them mucking about in waters not far offshore, so perhaps the mother had been wise to accompany the boy and restrain his display of independence by keeping him from deeper water. But wind and waves, storm and sea, care nothing for wisdom, and the boat went down on that awful day.

After his release from the hospital G.H. Nuttall tried to sequester himself in his dank leaky shanty perched on the rocks overlooking the sea. But his neighbors would have none of it. They kept him fed and cleaned up his mess and patched the holes and leaks and eased his heartache until a man emerged, a new man scarred and softer.

G.H. Nuttall began his book. Half sightless, he wrote of loss and hopelessness and anguish, and of things much stronger—togetherness, the hiving of the community around him, the power of the many working in concert. The writing was his salvation. His had not been a happy family, and Nuttall through the drowning and its aftermath came to accept his hand in affairs, a theme to which he has hewed these years since as an essayist and a teacher.

In 1994 an earthquake along the San Jacinto fault jolted the tiny town of Presidente, which is pinched between the Santa Rosa and San Ysidro Mountains north of California's Anza-Borrego Desert State Park. It occurred years before Roger and I drove down, yet almost immediately upon arrival in the region, more or less as soon as we had whooped ourselves into paralysis over the cheap American beer prices and I had read his memoir, I set my hat and created a version of G.H. Nuttall's experience.

I wrote the false remembrances as a half-blind blind survivor who had lost his mother, father and wife to the earthquake. Substituting the quake and rockslide for the ocean storm, morphing a Newfoundland outport into a small desert town, transforming dockside into central market, abusing the plenary powers of an author by skewing my research, I eventually had Presidente's hero—me, Smith—behaving and thinking precisely the way Nuttall had. So while tragic loss at sea aroused one man to respectfully examine himself, the 1994 Presidente quake merely set my liar liar pants on fire.

I had to dredge up all manner of twaddle to link the stories, but other than that the going was easy. Every emotion and insight and revelation of Nuttall's I reproduced almost word for word. His recovery, the physical loss of an eye, the total agonizing experience of re-evaluating his personal history, the whole magilla.

The robbery poisoned me, but worse was its catalytic effect, as though I had triggered a rockslide, and not inadvertently. Random events, in a scientific sense, involve unpredictability but certainly don't imply a falling apart at the seams. I fell into the other sense of randomness, the everyday slang meaning—the loosey-goosey breakdown into formlessness and fear. Then again, it's a bitch not to see a pattern even in that, which might indicate an encompassing order after all. And if randomness of either stripe can be quantified, is actually a form of order, there must be a way to beat it at its own game. But I had no idea where to start, how to stop the blender to allow the ingredients to stratify by weight.

CHAPTER 3

It's still cool and raining, not that it's fazing the addicts. Despite a bur-geoning needle-exchange program in Vancouver the lads down on the sidewalk are swapping spikes, showing determination akin to casters-away of condoms to simplify existence to the point of its elimination. In *Sea of Cortez*, John Steinbeck defined adventure as the satisfaction of atavistic urges toward danger. The point can be made that Steinbeck and his buddy Ed Ricketts were merely traveling around the Gulf of California picking up marine samples and now and again getting shit-faced, but is that any different from the junkies even in degree? True adventuring seems to be more closely allied with a restlessness of soul than anything else, an addiction plain and true, replete with the mental and chemical rewards that insist on its repetition.

Our transplantation to California wasn't motivated by adventure. Roger knows that on a base level I'm more of a hunter-gatherer than an agriculturalist, moving on when I've picked my home clean, or at least relocating temporarily to allow my campsite to regenerate. Necessity, always from necessity—adventure may be present, lurking, but my reward for actively seeking it is frustration. When I shut up and pay attention it pops up unannounced, much as Christmas Spirit does when given half a chance and not treed and bayed at.

On its face our destination was danger-free. I didn't know much about the Coachella Valley, just that at its head was Palm Springs—where old-time movie stars used to gambol away from Hollywood's prying eyes—and that it stretched down south-central California to Mexico. I knew nothing of the small interconnected cities beaded along the high-way, hadn't the foggiest notion of its bracketing mountains and their canyons, the elements away from resort development that of course made more development inevitable even while they provided me with the platform for my walkabout.

Roger and I figured it was a mild adventure—well-rested and in good health, car running fine, weather designed for safe motoring. Throw in Roger's childlike belief in the speed limit and the near impossibility of getting lost, and you can see why we felt there was nothing to worry about. A straightforward drive, illustrating the connectedness of our part of the Pacific Rim. So into Roger's Dodge Neon with us and south to California. It was my first trip to the Golden State if you don't count the times I made it in my mind in high school during the surf-movie craze. Dodge Neon, man—I should have held out for nothing less than a Woody.

Straight down Interstate 5 to Los Angeles until turning east onto I-10. The air cleared dramatically as we left the coast basin behind, and inside two hours we were climbing the grade through the San Gorgonio Pass. Scant transition to the desert. Rounding the corner and turning our backs to mountains upthrust along the Banning Fault, we ran down the windows and stuck out our heads like crazed spaniels to catch the rush of air that was parching the earth and spinning miles of power-generating windmills in their ranks up and down the hills.

A few miles past Palm Springs we turned off the freeway, and before my salivary glands could recover from their blasting and allow my tongue to comment, Roger had stopped and was fishing in the glove compartment.

"What you looking for?" A croak, trying to swallow.

"The clicker-thing."

I'd been absorbing the geography, wrestling with a sense of incongruity, and now refocused to the front at grillwork blocking the entrance into a walled compound. Roger found the remote control and the security gate slid smoothly aside. It look odd, like nothing less than a medieval portcullis that should have been lifted vertically to threaten with spikes wary visitors passing underneath.

"Didn't know your mum had this kind of money," I said.

"Hardly had any," Roger said. "Before the boom hit there was nothing past Palm Springs until you hit the farms farther south. Mum picked up this place for less than she would have paid for a summer cottage in B.C. Everybody has gates and walls around here."

A second clicker-thing failed to open the garage door, so we parked on the street and left the bags in the car. While Roger fumbled with his key ring I read the legend on a small terra-cotta plaque on the front door: *Aqui se acaba la tristeza.* Roger found the key and held it extended while he read the inscription and let his hand drop while looking as sad as he could look and I reached around him and removed the plaque and held it as he opened the door.

He gave me the nickel tour of the place. I followed behind, looking overtop his short well-groomed dome and flattening against the wall to let the little guy take the lead whenever he reversed course. A two-bedroom bungalow on one floor, no basement, modestly, even ascetically, appointed.

As though reading my mind, which I suspect he can do, Roger said, "Mum kept it plain. She wanted it plain, just a place to sit and read and walk outside and look at the beauty."

The beauty was there, framed by the craggy Santa Rosas to the west and the wrinkled Little San Bernardinos fronted by the Indio Hills across the valley, irregular mats of green-and-brown brush and sand interrupting the lush precision of the developed areas.

"That's what feels off." I moved closer to the sliding-glass patio doors. "It doesn't look like a desert once you get off the highway."

"People need reminders," Roger said. "A shrub or a plant from home, a familiar tree . . ."

"But this has been created from whole cloth."

Along with the standard-fare flora the community screamed with bougainvillea, jacaranda, hibiscus, providing visual splendor while being somewhat jarring.

"It's a little tropical, all right," Roger said.

"Don't get me wrong," I said. "I like it. And your mum must have felt safe inside these walls and gates. She never seemed to be afraid of anything, and this doesn't strike me as a high-crime area, but I guess it makes sense for anyone getting on in age who's only down here a few months of the year."

Roger looked at me strangely then opened the sliders and vanished around the side of the house. I put the plaque face-down on top of the fridge and followed.

Was there danger? Nothing predictable, providing a large enough margin of safety for relaxation. Or recovery. I'd known since before the Hari Krishna parade that Roger was afraid I was on the verge of taking off somewhere, despite the fact that whenever I did so it was only to a new apartment or underneath the covers at my old.

A few years back he figured I was lost for a month. Roger spent a rock star's ransom tracking me down, going so far as to hire a private investigator. The Dick—his term of self-reference during a subsequent interview in the *Globe and Mail*—followed my spoor through Lethbridge, Moose

Jaw, Portage la Prairie, Wawa, Val D'Or, New Minas, finally to St. John's, Newfoundland, where in a tiny bar he was properly screeched-in, a tradition that calls for one to kiss a dead cod on the lips then drink a shot of screech, a rum keg's dregs. So the Dick kissed the cod and drank the screech, several times, then switched to just the screech, incurring the usual partial paralysis and dropping a cigarette through the sound hole of a local musician's Martin guitar while the singer was on a break, scorching a tunnel through the forty-year-old instrument and earning a thumping from a couple of Newfs righteously convinced of his dickness, after which he dragged himself up Telegraph Hill and commenced taking haphazard shots with a .38 at the cargo ships a good half-mile up the harbor, missing them all but shooting the hat off a weekender visiting the big city from Joe Batt's Arm. At the trial, the Dick's attorney offered a novel defense—his client had been suffering from a form of brain disorder associated with paratyphoid fever induced by a species of *Salmonella* bacterium, all traced back to his being forced to kiss said cod. A dozen witnesses solemnly affirmed the Dick had kissed said cod willingly, of his own accord, and might even have slipped in a bit of tongue, which wouldn't be beyond a mainlander, and furthermore that that lawyer fella couldn't be from around there neither or he'd know the difference between a cod and a salmon. When all was said and done and the Dick, rather than stick around and do the community service time, had paid the fine with Roger's advance money, after all that and more, including the parading of my name in the media for a few weeks to a brief resurgence of the where-is-he-nows, I walked over to Roger's condo and informed him I'd been keeping to myself and wasn't answering the phone, that's all.

"I really do hope you like it here," Roger said after we had deposited the bags in bedrooms. "It might be a little resorty for you. Up the road in Palm Springs there's character, some soul. But pretty quickly the towns attached to it along the Highway turn country clubby, golf and tennis and spas mostly, until you get down-valley to the farms. Like any tourist area, I guess, the sprawl and the expansion, the small towns on the edges full of agricultural workers and tradesmen."

"Resorty and county clubby—did you forget how to speak?"

"Thanks again for coming," Roger said. "I had to get lost, that's all, and it might keep you from getting lost, and . . . I don't know. My mum going, well, I wish I had spent more time with her the last few years. My mum."

"You didn't know she was dying," I said.

"That's not really my point."

"We'll be going back some day anyhow," I said. "Before we left I read about a truck they found locked and abandoned somewhere in the desert this side of the Mexico border. When they broke into the back there were seventeen people dead. Some were only dying, I think, not all were dead. Can you even imagine being so desperate you'd pay a smuggler to get you into a country where you'll count yourself lucky to be given a hoe? You and I might be better off down here, maybe not, but it isn't necessary for our survival. You don't hear about a flood of Canadian refugees heading to the US border, climbing razor wire then packing fifty to a snowmobile to blast across a frozen river in the middle of the night."

"I think someone went over Niagara Falls in a barrel once and washed up on the American side."

I laughed and felt warm. "That's the first funny thing out of your mouth in a month. I'd say we're in the right place for now."

He grinned and perked up like a puppy, and that's not infantalizing him. "I'm starving," he said. "Do you want to order in? I haven't checked to see if the phone's working. If it's out we could drive up the street to Ralphs for groceries."

"I'm going to walk around."

"There goes you for two days."

Roger is helpless with the notion of walking for no reason. Or for a reason. If ever he found himself on a sidewalk under a plummeting office safe, before being atomized he'd be last seen hailing a cab. He can't comprehend walking's importance to observation, that when traveling it's the right pace for learning, no overload of the senses and thought-germination time to boot.

And I'm just talking about strolling around town. Head back a few million years and walking's importance jumps out at us with fire in its eye. When scientists and theologians—often the same beast until recent times—began amassing humanoid fossils from around the world, hinting that just maybe we hadn't emerged from either dust or ribs, those in charge of interpreting the evidence assumed that as it was the brain that had raised us up over the other animals, it must have evolved in lockstep with upright posture. Freeing the hands for making tools and weapons and hide couture prompted an increase in brain size to take advantage of the new niche, which in turn allowed the hands to be employed for ever more clever and mischievous tasks, and so on. And if we were wiser than the animals, placing us at the apex of development, was it not obvious that within humankind there were gradations based on the strength of one's mind? It was easily perceived that savages and women occupied their particular rungs because of inferior wit. That is, until the last half of the twentieth century when evidence surfaced that our hominid ancestors walked upright long before their brains increased appreciably in mass or complexity, that bipedalism and handy hands preceded the foggiest notion of forming committees to perpetuate the myth of natural dominance. We walked the walk before we talked the talk, and the one thing tying together the various factors that prodded our intelligence to increase was our dispersal. Relatively bugger-all happened when we stayed in one place. We learned when we dispersed, and we did so on foot.

I was barely to the road outside the compound and still four miles from the town center when I would have killed for a car with air-conditioning. Walking seemed to be the most asinine form of transportation conceivable.

I stopped at a convenience store to pick up a bottle of water and was told by the clerk it was closing in on 120°F. He'd seen me approaching along the sidewalk and guessed I was a tourist. "One hundred and twenty!" he barked with fierce pride. I recognized the intensity from my years on the Canadian prairies, when winter cold snaps would wring from us complaints and fury that immediately ceased once an outsider showed up. Then it was shrug the shoulders and what-do-you-do? and talk of how pitifully the cold spell stacked up against epic blizzards and subarctic temperatures of the past, everyone boasting of how many close relatives had lost body parts to frostbite or had fallen asleep on the side of the road and been consumed by snowblowers. Each of us has to be the best at something, by Jesus, even if it's just animalistic endurance, and I have to admit the first thing Canadian in me to go down there was the Celsius scale. There seems no point in bragging you walked ten miles with a pack in 45° heat when you can say it was 113°.

I finished the bottle and trudged back up the hill. Hot, very hot, and I could hardly wait till I acclimated enough to stretch out my walks, to seek further hardship in the mountains. Truly, though, the geography was incidental. The Old Testament seekers of revelation removed themselves to the desert because it was at hand. Had the Patriarchs set up shop in the Arctic, later prophets would have wandered out on the tundra for the same reasons, and its entirely possible Judaism's dietary laws would now include a proscription against ptarmigan.

I humped up the rise back to the compound and almost melted at the speaker box while I scrolled for the entry code. The phone at the house hadn't been connected, so I had to remove my T-shirt and wrap it around my hands to climb the iron gate. The top bar cauterized my pec just above the left nipple, but then I was over and had my shirt back on as I passed the community mailboxes on my way . . . home, let's call it for now.

Roger was stretched out asleep on his bed, wet hair shoved back over his ears. I stuck my head under the kitchen tap and stood under an air conditioning vent till I shivered. I hadn't brought much in the way of clothes and almost no personal effects, and those I quickly hung and tucked away in drawers. Then I started my notes.

Until then, keeping a journal in any form had never tempted me, just as taking pictures I find irritating, and the thought of dragging around a video recorder is too much even to address. My perceptions are compromised by fretting over light conditions and angles or by composing a diary entry. Whatever my brain does to process memory has to be enough.

It's possible my brain doesn't process it well at all. Learning from mistakes has never been my strong suit. Very early my adult life ossified into repeating the same behavior over and over and wondering why I kept getting the same results. In hindsight, it's obvious why I sat down and began writing—I could no longer forge ahead with life's house party before doing the dishes and giving the place a good vacuuming. The notes were to be my record, a conscious record, as if I had asked the police to tape a wire to my chest and leave it with me for a year.

And with the rain still coming down in Vancouver, I must say it's a good time for a final housecleaning, down on my hands and knees trying to reach the mess under the fridge.

The journal is all that's left. My website is gone for good, the bonfire of the verities deleted soon after I met the reporter. Counting on the anonymity of the Internet, I was innocent of its reach, and in a short time so many worms had gotten out of the can Roger's inherited house looked like a bait shop. So *A Quake in Time* is sleeping with the virtual fishes, and there's loss only in the sense that the book, though plagiarized, was born of inspiration. We're granted few instances in our lives of higher emotional and mental impulses and now I've wasted one. Then again, there are those who claim to be inspired to slaughter their entire families, so the concept of inspiration can be tricky.

G.H. Nuttall's memoir provided the main impetus for my writing, but after all, that I stole the substance and not the circumstance is significant—I shouldn't downplay the inspiration of the rocks. Remnants of ancient metamorphic layers high in the Santa Rosas, igneous intrusions in the Indian Canyons, the sheer brazenness of the desert mountains to appear in public without a forest, all of it was so open, so exposed, that it begged for speculation on what would happen if it came tumbling down and wiped out a family. It led to my researching the Presidente incident and everything that followed did so naturally, almost effortlessly. True, I could have aimed higher, maybe for honesty, but that was a daunting goal. New place, new country, Roger and I getting settled—the right way appeared impossible, though I'm well aware that with a sufficient string of fresh horses and an inexhaustible supply of lances, even windmills will go down right enough.

There were tangible obstacles. For example, the language stymied me. The population of Presidente was 91 percent Spanish speaking, and beautiful as I find the speech to the ear, I had no grasp of the content beyond *amigo* and *cerveza*. So I didn't actually do the research.

I know, I know, I'm springing it on you, what can I say? Research takes time and I couldn't very well go gallivanting around with an interpreter listening to tales of woe. Besides, I had already decided to plagiarize Nuttall and any research would unearth narratives incoherent with his personal tragedy, the main problem being that the Presidente earthquake didn't deliver much woe, including the fact that no one was killed. *Well, señor, the mountain fell down. ¿Qué? No, where I live just a few stones. Then my wife ask me to go to the Ralphs in La Quinta for tortillas.* Where the hell's the drama in that?

Sorry, I had to fake the whole shebang. I did some elementary background checking, which consisted mostly of hanging around the Blue Dog bar, a joint on a parched plot across the freeway away from the developed areas and a good sixty miles from Presidente, and asking the regulars what they recalled of local quakes. Other than a gnarly-handed drywaller who was inordinately proud of a forehead scar and old woman dressed like a deranged gypsy who seemed to know everything about the valley, there was no one able to contribute anything more than another story of a decanter falling off a shelf and the dishes rattling. The shabby bar helped my thought process. Support of some kind, I guess. The owner, Stan, treated me decently, and the locals palled up pretty well when I was buying, and whenever I drank a bit much and started complaining about one thing or another a helpful soul was always ready to tell me to "Shut my hole," good advice, given the environment.

Eliminating the research saved bags of time. Years ago after my wife died I wrote my novel with similar dispatch, but that was different—then I was driven by inspiration an order of magnitude greater than anything I experienced for the *Quake* writing. As well, the aching, the physical agony of loss, gave way to brief flashes of lucidity when all was clear and all was strong. I was a helpless whimpering ruin after my wife's death, yet paradoxically a very powerful man. There is danger in nothing when nothing has significance, and I was untouchable, fortified by a bereavement that separated me even from those who had survived far greater loss, proud of my suffering and its uniqueness, parading the sonofabitch. I can't recall when I lost the power. At some point I awoke realizing that over an indefinite period of time my mind had reorganized itself, leaving me unbelieving. I wasn't nihilistic, no, merely so mistrusting and skeptical as to be hyperaware of the faults and failings and weaknesses that suddenly were all around me. The novel became the catch basin for it all—the printed word was the only thing I could vomit without literally doing so.

I was still at the desk when Roger poked his head around the corner, hair flattened from his pillow. I left off and followed him to the kitchen and we stood at the sliders and looked out at the greenbelt.

"California," he said with a tone I was unable to read. "Not a bad place."

"A guy could live with it."

CHAPTER 4

I thought my notes were completely organized and figured this would be an easy job of cutting and pasting, but it's already frosting my ass. I'm trying here, I'm trying to fill in the gaps, but it isn't working the way I'd hoped. Already I've found an e-mail printout that belongs farther on, and because the message marks another one of those turning points in which I don't believe, it's hard to ignore. It appeared in my inbox almost six weeks after Roger and I had gotten squared away in his mum's old house, and after staring at it for the past twenty minutes I can understand why I punched three holes in the page and jammed it near the front of my hard-copy binder. It doesn't belong here quite yet, so I'll put it aside for the moment and try to concentrate on the narrative, no small task—the letter evokes such violent images I'm tempted to leap out the window onto Hastings and arm-wrestle a junkie for his kit.

Our first morning in California, Roger and I were up by six-thirty.

"Who's that at this hour?" Roger asked.

I put the coffee carafe on the table in front of him and went to the door.

"Good morning." Fifty, fifty-five. Plainly dressed but made up severely, with the sheen of a facelift victim. She touched the side of her hair and glanced at her hand as though afraid something had transferred. Maybe it had, because she wiped the palm on her woven shoulder bag.

"It is a good morning," I said.

"I'm Sarah Kolachuk."

I took her hand, the clean one. "Smith."

"Do you prefer Mr. Smith, or may I call you by your first name?"

"Smith does general duty."

"Oh." The sounds of Roger messing around in the kitchen made her lean so far sideways to see around me that her foot slipped off the concrete and crushed a baby aloe.

"He has the standard set of names," I said. "First, middle, last."

"The plaque is gone."

I looked at the door. "Right. A little remodeling."

She looked as if she had just tasted gamy bacon. "Are you renters?"

"Renters? No."

"Oooh, good. Renters are . . . well, you know what I mean."

"Not sure that I do."

She stepped back and appraised the front of the house. "Going to be another hot one," she said, and for an instant I thought she could tell by the stucco. "Do you have pets?"

"Pets? No."

"Some pets are fine," she said. "We used to have pets, Martin and I. Martin's my husband, Martin Kolachuk. It's the large dogs that cause the problems. Small dogs and cats are okay."

"How about large cats?"

"I mean small dogs are okay and cats are okay. Because really, how big can a cat get?"

"Very good point, Sarah." I looked behind me. "We're in the middle of—"

"—It's okay whatever you do." Her skin stretched tighter as her eyes went wider. "Mostly it goes on in Palm Springs, but you'll find we're very liberal about those things here, too. Martin and I. Everyone, really."

"So it's not like we're big dogs or anything."

"No, nothing like that."

"Whew." I dragged the back of my hand across my forehead.

"Is she here too?"

"Do you mean Willa?" I said. "She passed away. It's her son's house now."

Hers was a short bereavement. She rooted in her bag and handed me an envelope. "That's for Mr. Jeffcoate." Before I could speak she dove back into her woven sack and emerged with a pair of small plastic-coated dumbbells. "Welcome to the neighborhood." She checked her pulse at the carotid artery and strode off, crisply swinging the hand weights shoulder-high.

When I went in Roger was grinning.

"That was nice," I said. "And thanks, by the way, another city where my reputation's shot for hanging around with a fag."

"Wear the name or join the game."

"Where does that one live?" I said.

"Middle of the complex, right by the pool. She's head of the Home Owners Association. They run the neighborhood like a condo complex."

I opened the envelope. "What's this, Welcome Wagon coupons or something?"

"Very unlikely."

Dear Homeowner,

As those of you who attended the "Street Gala" know, for three years running our neighborhood has been voted "Tidiest Middle-Income Community" for the upper-central Coachella Valley. This year we also took the second-place ribbon for "Most Attractive Entrance Sign" and finished tied for third with Paseo Vista for "Best Perimeter-Wall Landscaping."

These "awards" and "ribbons" contribute to our reputation as one of the most "desirable" communities in the area and help maintain our property values. Standardizing wall and trim colors and submitting formal drawings for approval of any exterior alterations are the "watchwords" that keep our neighborhood "forward-moving" and "progressively conservative."

One of the things that helps keep us so attractive to prospective buyers is immediately disposing of any trash or "unnecessary objects" from the outside of our homes.

You are hereby notified forthwith and notwithstanding that the rolled-up carpet propped against the east side of your dwelling must be removed within 3 (three) calendar, not business, days.

Failure to do so with result in a fine of $35 (thirty-five dollars).

We are confident that this is just an oversight on your part, and are happy that you join us in our desire to make this the "neat-as-a-pinniest" community in the upper-central Coachella Valley.

Sincerely,
The Chairperson and Board of the HOA

God Bless America.

"You have a very nice reading voice," Roger said as I lowered the paper.

"You'd think there was a dead body rolled up in the carpet."

"They've flayed people here for having mismatched garage doors."

"Man," I said, "all the Kolachuks and other Ukes I grew up with in Manitoba just painted Easter eggs and threw great weddings. She's been bent along the way."

Roger went to refill his coffee then realized the carafe was still on the table and tipped some out. "Well, I definitely have to go on a grocery run and I wouldn't mind doing it before the store gets crowded. Why don't you just relax. Read or go for a dip."

"I owe you."

"Before I go, let's move the carpet inside."

That done, and now in full compliance with the neighborhood penal code, Roger went to Ralphs and stocked up and stood in line and lugged the groceries in the mounting heat back to the car and loaded the cheap beer and wine and perishables into the backup fridge in the garage while I sat on my ass and read.

And the Sea Shook the Rock. Here was a true-life hero. Not a policeman stopping a murder, a fireman with a child in his arms scrambling from a burning house, just a sincere middle-age fisherman surviving both his past and present realities and with the aid of a community family emerging redeemed. I read the book straight through. My journal doesn't record how many times I shook my head at Roger's polite offers to feed my body or brain. Done, I started in again. When I put down the book after the third read to let the pages cool off and to take stock of what was happening around me, having eaten twice and slept maybe ten hours over two days, Roger was changing his shirt to go to Ralphs.

"Again?" I said.

"I have nothing else to do," he said. "I'm like a retired farmer still listening to the grain report on the radio every day. I don't have to go if there's something you want to do."

"You go ahead," I said. "I think now I have to write."

Gentlemen, start your engines—I was off. Years ago I wrote the drafts of my novel longhand with a few dozen Bic medium-point pens on tablets of yellow paper and paid a college kid to prepare the typescript. Back then I enjoyed the painstaking process of transforming thought into written word, but I had changed—this time around both my patience and reflective insight were noticeably ragged and I couldn't tolerate the dawdling. As well, I had reached the point where I refused to fight with accepted methods. I had competed and failed, campaigned and lost, so I reversed my habits and procedures, parked myself in front of the computer and wrote fast and hard.

Roger didn't even ask what I was writing about. He faked unconcern, claiming my ignoring him was hand-crafted for peace of mind, for reflecting on his relationship with his mother over the years, allowing the remembrances gradually to advance along the light spectrum from the dark colors to the brights. That of course doesn't explain why he pampered me, feeding and watering the antisocial beast who cursed and grunted in front of a cathode-ray tube all day and passed out and fell from his desk chair after nightly fake-research trips to the Blue Dog. Roger went down to the compound's pool every day—for a swim only, he's so little the sun-worshipper he could be related to cave salamanders—and spent the rest of the time planning meals and watching untold-story and deep-mystery and alien-abduction shows on something they have the nerve to call The Learning Channel.

I figured I had the situation well in hand, maintaining balance. Sure, I was working the hours of an indentured servant, but I was never much one for resort zone vacations and felt the task was keeping me centered. Then one morning or afternoon or evening I violently shoved away from the desk and declaimed loudly to Roger that I was closing shop. I was pallid and bearded and weak in the joints and wouldn't have tried walking to the convenience store if Castro was there shooting a TV commercial for an investment firm. It was done. A sloppy piece of work containing elementary mistakes and slipshod grammar in those places I wasn't true to Nuttall's prose, it was good enough for my purposes. I didn't even bother with the computer's spellcheck function. By then I was up to speed on the Internet, and had visited sufficient sites and chat rooms to convince me that publishing on the web could be done by scanning in text written in crayon without anyone climbing on a soapbox to complain.

A Quake in Time – A Memoir at the top, Smith at the bottom.

A new start in California and still with the alias. Years back I used Morty Cahoot for the novel, and though I came to regret the fact I was proud enough of it at the time. That's not to claim I think the book measured up to its reputation—hype aggrandized it to a clownish extent—though it was praised deservedly for many things. It was honest, and while I had tried to avoid sentimentality it prompted an outpouring of love and tenderness. The letters and the phone calls and the fan club—fan club, if you can believe it—and even the unstinting praise from normally acerbic critics attested to the quality of the work in at least one category: Influence. Everyone was familiar with the model, the types of people and opinions and happenings in the small town on which the novel was based. They suffered with the victims of mischance, raged at the perpetrators of injustice, stormed at the social iniquities of the place and of the time. And it influenced. Behavior, appreciation of . . . well, let's not get into it here. Suffice to say there's a good chance you were influenced on some level if you are one of the many who read it.

On publication, the acclaim was instantaneous, and initially I was happy to tour as many levels of Hell as it took to get the thing in readers' hands and in gift baskets and Christmas stockings and even under table legs to keep them from wobbling, who gave a shit? Well, as it developed, I did.

The Presidente book was a horse of a different color, which makes sense given the animal was a freakish clone. The facts were faked, but with the aid of Nuttall's stencil I was able to take the measure of a man in the midst of loss, a man readjusting his apprehension of the past to fit a little better with life's fragility, learning to battle back from grief's isolation.

My wife wouldn't have understood what I did, and good for her. She strove her entire short life to be groundbreaking, to avoid recycling concepts, and believed originality could be generated from bare earth. The dear woman, my dear heart, loved literature and wrote voluminously but had the same trouble with fiction and poetry as I do with journals. The very act of recording interfered with her ability to receive, and in a short time her words were not her words and her thoughts not her thoughts and she'd shred the pages and smoke ten cigarettes and bitch till we both were laughing. So no, she would not be happy with what I did.

And then there was Roger. I sat him at the kitchen table, put Nuttall's book in front of him and arranged the printout of mine beside it. "Now it's your turn to read. Start with either one."

He stared at both. "Huh. It's that close, is it?"

"Well, closer than it started out."

"You're not going to tell me why?"

"Read," I said. "I'm trying to be honest with you."

"Just with me?" he said. "That's good enough?"

"Listen, I could really use your design suggestions for a cover page, and I need help transferring the document to my website."

"Great! Love to! Anything to help!" He leapt up. "Let's get right at it!" I don't think I even turned red.

That night, after Roger had promised to do all I'd asked of him, I was messing around with the home page when I felt his presence in the room.

"Forty days." The poor bugger looked hyped and desperate. "I don't care what you've done and what you will do. But I need a life. I've been waiting forty days and now I want to sit at a table in a restaurant and be served a rude blender drink by a gorgeous waiter and talk to you like a normal human being. Or not normal, I don't care, just talk about anything. Whether bell bottoms are really back in, why the sky is blue, why the good die young, why we can't tickle ourselves, why we don't get goosebumps on our faces, what the difference is between partly sunny and partly cloudy . . . I'd be happy just to trade funny animal stories and talk about people who have babies."

"You're starting to sweat," I said. "Give me a minute to wrap up."

"No, I won't," he said. "And don't slump your shoulders at me."

I rolled back from the desk and started stripping before I was out of the chair. "My turn?"

"I'll do it," he said.

"You've been doing everything around here." When I was clean and pressed and had gone through three blades scraping the beard from my face, I went to the garage and dragged the rolled-up carpet out and around the side and propped it against the wall.

"Baking soda," Roger said when I returned.

I looked down at the dirt smudge on my walking shorts. "We should get that rug cleaned if we're going to keep lugging it in and out all the time."

"Clean, shmean," Roger said. "Let's hit the town."

So that's that and what do you know—I've caught up to the e-mail.

CHAPTER 5

There it was first thing the next morning:

INBOX1(1 new)

Before I could click, the doorbell went. "Get that, will you, Roger?"

I had no cause to be irritated. Although it felt like first thing in the morning it was closing in on noon. I'd grown used to a clockless schedule and Roger had been rising earlier and earlier, but our celebration of the night before made us both sleep in and had us reeling around like toddlers on a duck punt. I held my click.

"Oh, good morning," I heard Roger say.

"Another day in paradise." Sarah Kolachuk, her tone variable, muffled when Roger had her blocked, clearing when she managed to sneak a look past him or weasel her way to the door frame. She'd been growing bolder each visit and last time got one foot and a shoulder inside when I let my guard down to watch a couple of male hummingbirds fight it out.

"Just a simple question then I'll be out of your hair. You and your . . . partner . . . wouldn't be running a business out of your home, would you?"

"What kind of business?"

"It seems like there are a lot of carpets coming and going. Running a business from your home is prohibited. We went through an awful time just last year with a young couple making and selling crafts. You know, birdhouses and those ceramic things. Then there was the added problem of the boxes the supplies came in that they'd put out with the trash. It's much less offensive when bags and other items are secured in the trash cans. Inside them, that is. The boxes just sort of hanging around on the curb beside the cans make the community look like a trailer park. I'm sure you know what I mean."

"It could effect property values."

"Exactly."

"The carpet will be gone today."

"Your cooperation means a lot to me. To us, Martin and I. And the Board."

Roger and I were beginning to sound like the same person when dealing with the Boardhead. He was still talking to himself as my e-mail opened, and later commented he could barely hear himself mutter over my grunts and expulsions of air as I read it:

Dear Smith,

Whoa! I'm blown away. Last night I was here in Vancouver consoling myself on the couch after my doctor told me my implants need to come out, and I found your website after entering Earth Shattering News in the Google search box.

I haven't slept since. I've been struggling with how I relate to the world, or at least fit in, and your book answered all my questions. Every one! I read and read from six or seven last night until just a few minutes ago. Your book would be perfect except for the rock stuff and the earthquakes and all the bad things that happened, but I know if it all hadn't happened you wouldn't have been able to write about it.

How anyone can survive their family being killed and actually end up feeling stronger is beyond me. But not beyond you, obviously—Ha!

Anyhow, I think I'm in love with you. You show such understanding in your book it makes my ex-husbands look ridiculous.

I'm 5' 6" tall, have black hair, am well-proportioned (until the implants come out—Ha!) and like short walks in the rain and bad movies.

I would have bought the book with my credit card, except whoever set up your website allowed access to the whole thing for free. Luckily, your address in California was included. Expect a cheque any day, just don't cash it until the 8th if you don't mind.

Sincerely,
Willo

p.s. There are several spelling mistakes in your book but I won't hold that against you—Ha!

What do you make of that? I read it through twice before printing it and reading it a half-dozen more. I suppose around then my noises tapered off, because Roger felt it safe to approach. I pushed away from the desk and pointed over his shoulder down the hall. "Go sit down and read this." When he was at the kitchen table I handed him the printout and stood back.

He scanned it and laid it face down. "Have her assassinated immediately."

"You had the site set up by six last night and she responded within eighteen hours. She must have been impressed to stay up reading something she wasn't looking for in the first place."

"I'll apologize for my error in setting up the billing, then that's it."

"I thought you were onside."

"You cheated. Never mind the passages lifted right from Nuttall's book, there's no such town as Presidente. And there wasn't even an earthquake in the area you describe."

"Wrong."

"It measured three point nine on the Richter scale," Roger said. "No wonder nobody was killed."

"There could have been. And if a man *had* lost his family? That's tragedy, man. Now go ahead and read the e-mail again. That's what's important, here."

He took longer this time and I nearly burst at the joints with anticipation. For all its piffle, the letter's openness sent my mind scorching back to the days when I first started seeing my future wife. She was similarly transparent, almost irresponsibly unguarded. Under a totalitarian regime she would have been tortured the minute she opened her mouth. I watched Roger finish and carefully set down the page, face up this time, and tell me I was nuts. I could taste the acidic saliva that gathers in my mouth whenever Roger and I disagree. I felt defeated already and obeyed his command to read it aloud.

Nearly every line was a monument to Roger's interpretation. The veins at my temples were turgid and my mouth went dry and all I wanted was to embrace the whole. Breaking down the woman's letter into its constituent parts seemed laughably reductionist. I said so when I had finished, but Roger forced me to pound away at it all over again, bit by bit. I'm quite good at that kind of thing, actually, at least with him, able to twist and distort, defending my point of view with thought-for-the-day psychology and scattergun nonsense, and when all else fails upping the speed and volume until I come out on top through sheer bullying and endurance. He looked uncertain at a couple of points and I had his eyes bugging at others, but in the end he remained undented.

"You're headed for a fall if you pursue this," he said.

"Fine, I'll tear it up and delete it from my inbox and we can spend the rest of our lives pulling juvenile pranks on the Boardhead and agreeing with everyone around here that we live in paradise."

"Do whatever you want."

"Is it the name?"

"My mother's name is legitimate. 'Willa' is a legitimate name. 'Willo' is silly."

"It'd be rude not to reply."

"Don't decide anything till after a long walk."

He didn't have to tell me that. When I had my water bottles packed and was ready to go I stopped at the sliders. "Roger, thanks. I mean, I know what you're doing and why, but . . ."

He was building a sandwich at the counter and didn't turn. "Bring the carpet in before you go."

I tried to walk it off, but the recent lack of activity soon had me muscle-weary and chafed on the feet from my new river sandals. Country club walls flanked most of the streets. Semi-tropical vegetation, exquisitely manicured central boulevards with their fan and date and queen palms, spiny sticks of ocotillo, curvilinear sidewalks sweeping in arcs around beavertail and prickly pear cactus, the mountains in cut-glass delineation against the sky. In such a pedestrian's heaven it felt odd not to encounter another human. From a distance I spied a few shuttling between stores across acres of paved parking outside the strip malls and service arteries, but the sidewalks were empty. With only rooftops visible over the gated ramparts, each compound gave the impression of a medieval town buttoned down for a siege, knights within preparing to sally forth in their Jags and BMWs to pepper-spray the encircling hordes.

It was near the end of September yet the atmosphere held no hint of autumn. According to a bank's LED display it was 112° at four in the afternoon. My hamstrings and Achilles tendons had been overworked by the time I hit the town center, so I stopped at a patio bar before heading home. It wasn't long till I was in conversation with the waitress, the bartender and three couples, all of whom were so friendly and enthusiastic I almost checked my ID to see whether I was someone important. An hour later, with nothing but booze in my famished carcass, I was sorely tempted to call Roger for a lift. Only thing stopping me was that I needed more time to assess our argument without hearing his side of it again. He's expert at recognizing my patterns around women, and men for that matter, though most people can recognize any number of natural phenomena without being able to tell you anything about them, so that talent alone isn't what makes him worth listening to. Trouble is, he usually makes so much sense it throws me out of whack awhile, which, amplified by beer and tequila, was the case at the moment.

Roger was beside me for the entire ride I took with my wife, from the first meeting to her death. He knows that period, just as he knows I've made little attempt to recapture it with anyone else. I tried again to decode the e-mail, unfolding and reading it up against the urinal and again after I washed my hands. I was impressed by its passion—okay, overly impressed—but there was nothing there behind or beyond or beneath the obvious that should have roused in Roger such a negative reaction. Just an impulsive declaration of affection, a little schoolgirlish at worst.

It was too important to wait on. On the first ring Roger picked up and lit into me as though I were interrupting hostage negotiations.

"Go easy," I said. "I called to see if you wanted to join me for a drink. I'm still hopeful we can salvage our relationship."

"Oh, that." A little strained, but at least he acknowledged the attempt at humor.

"What's that noise?" I said.

"The handyman's here."

"Same guy you phoned three weeks ago to install the fan?"

"The very same."

"Sounds like he's welding a bridge."

"Repairing the ceiling. He installed the fan over the kitchen table, and when I turned it on it ripped free and pulled the outlet box through the plaster. I'm cleaning up the blood."

"You okay?"

"He tried to catch it with the blades still turning. After I bandaged him he climbed into the attic to install a proper support, slipped off a joist and went through the ceiling to his waist. He's putting up a new sheet of drywall as we speak."

"I'll head right home."

"Are you okay to walk? You must have put some miles in and you know what cabs are like around here."

"I'll figure it out," I said. "And hey—"

"What?"

"Thanks for the advice."

"Wait till her check clears."

Back in the bar, the staff and my newfound friends acted as if I were leaving on a one-way space mission. Handshakes, hugs, a slobbery kiss. When they discovered I was walking there was near pandemonium—gasps of shock and sputters of protest, jaw-dropping indignation at the very thought I held their hospitality in such low regard I wouldn't ask for a ride. "I'm going right past there," a man said for the fifth time, though he didn't know my destination and earlier had claimed he was on his way over the mountains to the coast. Short of leaping the patio railing and losing him in traffic, in which case I'm sure he would have had a pair of hounds sniff my chair and bolt baying after me, I couldn't dodge his offer, but the least I could do was pay for his drinks. The others looked at me with the bulging eyes of rookie missionaries, wretched at having missed the opportunity to drive me to my door. "You can't say Americans aren't fucking helpful," I said half-drunkenly to applause and a chorus of cheers. I coughed up for everyone's drinks. "You can't say Americans aren't fucking friendly," I said two-thirds-drunkenly to applause, a chorus of cheers and a belch. I stayed for one more round five times and ended up taking a cab.

By the time I got home Roger was in the kitchen using a broom handle to tuck back the insulation protruding from the hole where the new drywall sheet had let go before splitting in two over a chairback.

"Experts," he said flatly.

CHAPTER 6

With the book done, I turned the computer over to Roger. Not exclusively, because I had transformed into something of a compulsive typer, not to mention the time I was spending on my correspondence with Willo, but he was back at work and couldn't hang around all day waiting for me to take a break.

October marks Roger's gear-up for tax season. It seems an odd time of year, but his clients participate in his need to stay a step ahead by faxing and e-mailing receipts and statements and whatever else in the way of paper hoops those with money must jump through. The pace gradually accelerates, peaking around New Year, leaving Roger and clients alike a four-month cushion on which to sit while they juggle their numbers trying to reach a consensus on the size of the past year's fiscal lie. Roger is Merlinesque when it comes to conjuring assets out of ashes and could use a bodyguard to repel corporate headhunters, yet has over the years cultivated a small group of wealthy individuals who, to be honest, don't lie much at all. That's just me again, suspecting everyone of being a sharp, when actually Roger's clients are good people who do much to redistribute wealth. Their tax shelters are constructed to keep the wind and the rain off charitable organizations, and their definition of an off-shore account is a savings plan in a Vancouver Island credit union.

As for my contribution to our money pool, it comes out of my allowance. After I pissed away the publisher's advance all those years ago Roger took charge and invested the royalties, which are still coming in, and though my balance bungees with the market the stipend is more than enough to meet my needs. I have no car and I dislike fine dining and expensive watering holes and I travel on the cheap. My everyday clothes are so old they're chic, and on the rare occasions I pull on my suit I'm frequently mistaken for William Pitt, the Elder.

Roger had cooled his jets a few degrees about my electronic romance, ever since our confrontation after Willo's second e-mail:

Dear Smith,

I can't say how sorry I am. Obviously I was wrong thinking you were the type of person to appreciate openness. Maybe I over-did the emotions, but I was excited by reading your memoir. That's not an excuse. I probably should have told you how much the book affected me and stopped there.

Too bad, I'm not built that way. When something grabs me I have to act. It's hurt people in the past but it's also helped them. I'm just confused. I thought maybe we could have had something together, something real, but now it's pretty plain you think I'm just a zonked-out groupie.

If I can say one thing, at least I put my honest emotions on the line. I thought I deserved better than a brush off.

Sorry,
Willo

What the hell? I hadn't replied to her first e-mail yet. What the hell? as I read it over and over trying to crack the code, tempted to print it and hold it over a candle in search of invisible ink between the lines. What the bloody hell? as I skated the mouse around, clicking on anything and everything. Finally, I scrolled down below her message and found the varmint:

Dear Willo,

Thank you very much. I'm glad you liked the book.

Sincerely,
Smith

You can bet I stared at that a good long while. Actually, it'd be a bad bet because I was out of the chair in two seconds. "Hey, Roger?" I said from halfway down the hall. "Rog?"

"I'm designing a container garden," he said as I hit the kitchen. "The HOA won't allow individual landscaping past six feet from the house so I thought pots and—"

"—Not what I'm talking about, my concerned friend."

He glanced up from his sketch pad. Had he been hooked up to a polygraph the needle would have jerked off the paper and imbedded itself in the wall. He penciled a spray of fronds on the paper and idly doodled a pot.

"Quit coloring," I said. "I know exactly what you're building up to say so let me beat you to it—'I was only trying to help.' Don't bother explaining. You've helped me every step of the way on my entire trip through this bloody life and you've done it the best possible way—by not interfering."

"This is different."

"You should hear how lame that sounds."

"You should hear your tone of voice," he said. "One simpering fan letter and you have your chest puffed out like a bantam rooster."

"You don't know how I would have responded on my own."

He looked wryly at me and leaned back in the chair. Just like that he'd gained the advantage, but it afforded him no pleasure. His face sagged. I apologized and told him it was okay.

"It's nothing like okay," he said. "I've been up all night thinking, and if you don't play this out you'll end up hating me as well as yourself. Write her back and blame it on me."

"I don't know that's it's technically blame if you actually did it."

It went no further. I immediately e-mailed Willo that her first message had scared me and asked her forgiveness, and that's all it took—by the end of the week we were exchanging messages three, four, five times a day. Often, I'd click SEND and immediately launch into a follow-up. Our messages overlapped and contradicted and we'd answer questions before they were asked, all of it grist for the madcap mill.

She started each letter with fluff and nonsense—the weather and what's-new-about-town pulp—and I didn't mind because I knew where she was heading, how quickly the weight would increase. I even began to experience geographical nostalgia. The naked magnificence of the desert and its mountains lost none of its power in comparison, it's simply that I found myself longing for moisture in the air and mountains decently clad in fir and spruce, rainpats on my head, sails and hulls on English Bay and planks on the Capilano suspension bridge and a tangle of deadfall in the temperate rainforest.

What I'm saying is that everything she wrote captivated me, each crumb held significance. When I learned she was from a small town in Saskatchewan roughly the same size as my birthplace in Manitoba, and moreover only a two-hour drive from the community featured in my novel, well, the clouds parted and a shaft of sunlight struck me full in the face and angels sang and I wanted to spend my fortune on donative candles. . . . All right, all right, since arriving in the Coachella Valley I hadn't seen one cloud, and there were no shafts of sunlight, just constant glare, and no angels would sing to a mendacious prick like me, and I had no fortune. But hey, I was infatuated out of my skull.

Lying is highly toxic to love, though come to think of it so is honesty when not handled with the proper safety equipment. Anyhow, the upshot was that with the underlying falsehood on my end and the truth on Willo's and my reasoning apparatus in need of repair, I was in no way capable of reaching a rational decision about any of it. Perfect. Who wants that chaff in the way when you're so enchanted you have to write reminder notes to blink?

Every day it was the same—Roger would take his turn at the computer and I'd hit the road to compose phantasmagoric situations in my head involving Willo and a more handsome confident Smith. Eventually, I'd rush back to the compound and made enough noise in the house to drive Roger from the desk, then sit down and come this close—this close—to telling Willo I was really Morty Cahoot and unloading a bunch of false humility concerning my famous first novel. I came very close, though each time decided to save such a large trump for a more critical point in the match, particularly as the game was going the way I wanted. My emotions were clean and honest and my only lies to her were of omission. But I didn't know, you see. Truthfulness is so much easier with no face across the table—no telling how I'd handle the immediate feedback of meeting in person.

"Enough," I said on entering the kitchen and taking in the mess.

Roger was sweeping up more insulation. A tattered remnant, compressed with age and impregnated with sand, was peeking from the garbage can.

"Get somebody else," I said. "It took almost three weeks for the guy to show up the first time, and it's been another two since he demolished the place."

"He's coming this afternoon."

"No, he said he's coming this afternoon."

Roger flicked the last bit of dirt into the dustpan. "With all the new construction in the valley, contractors are hard to nail down."

"I'd think a handyman would make an extra effort after plunging through a customer's ceiling and fixing it so it crashed down again the minute he left."

He glanced at the hole where the ceiling fan would have looked nice. "His daughter had a birthday."

"Who celebrates for this long?" I said.

"She has some type of heart disease, degenerative thing. He has to make special arrangements with the extended care staff when he wants to take her anywhere. She loves animals so they went down to San Diego, the zoo and aquarium. Complications . . . anyhow, they had to cut it short and he brought her back here to the hospital. He's just getting back to work."

"Oh."

He returned the broom and dustpan to the closet. "Everything okay with the stalker?"

"Her check cleared."

"Look, I cleaned up the website so the home address is deleted and made it impossible to download the book for free, and I'll handle any credit-card purchases, but that's it. I'm not interested in spin-offs or developments from your 'interpretation' of someone else's book." He grabbed a towel that had dried stiff as a terrycloth surfboard. "I'm going to the pool."

I followed in my street clothes. Although there were no sidewalks in the compound, it was safe to walk the streets. The roads were wide and most vehicles held a dead-slow speed on the way to and from the gates and the community mailboxes. We still hadn't met many folks in the neighborhood, though it didn't seem to matter—drivers and passengers and power walkers and cyclists grinned and waved, friendly enough to be cute.

"Any more hits on the site?" Roger said when the pool gate clanged shut behind us.

"A few," I said. "But who knows what they were really looking for."

"I've been wondering whether the love of your life has even read the book. Don't you find her references to it vague? Unless you're holding out on me."

"The only e-mails I don't show you are the boring ones. Well, and the exciting ones."

"I hope you're saving them all as future evidence."

"In her latest she told me her real name isn't Willo. Simple explanation, she's never done anything like this before and was shy and a bit afraid."

"She's shy," Roger said. "She's saying she's shy after telling you about her various addictions—yes, I know she's clean now, don't interrupt—and that she's fallen in love with you through a stolen book—"

"—She doesn't know it was plagiarized—"

"—and about her fake tits." He plunged in the pool and swam underwater.

I kept pace with him along the deck. "Juice," I said when he popped up like an eared seal and hung onto the edge. "That's her real name."

I admired his self-control. He pushed off the steps and breast-stroked submerged as I walked above him again, resisting the urge to stick my head in and talk to him underwater. When he surfaced in the shallow end and sat on the steps there I was.

Roger raked his fingers through his hair. "Let's quit arguing and have some fun."

It took me a second. "Yeah. Okay. Want to put the carpet outside again?"

"You just got your allowance. You're taking me into Palm Springs."

"Deal," I said.

"I don't feel very well. We've talked about our healthy contrasts and disagreements a thousand times, but lately it doesn't feel healthy. No conversations anymore, it's all edgy lines back and forth, two waspish old women or cranky old men or . . ."

"It'll be all right," I said. "Like always."

The cold shower was rejuvenating. Roger and I were ready at exactly the same moment, and I was thankful that at least our practical habits were still in harmony. I waited at the door to the garage while Roger checked for phone messages. His face was inscrutable as he lowered the receiver, pressed to repeat and handed it over.

"What's so important?" I said. "We have a whole city to destroy."

"At least your messages are full of love. Look what I get stuck with."

beep

Rog? Roger? You there? Sonny here from Right The First Time Home Repairs. Sorry the delay fixing that defective ceiling. New killer whale they got at the aquarium splashed my kid she had another of them heart seizures. Been driving back and forth to San Diego talking to a lawyer about suing their asses. Not the whales, the park and everything. The best for waiting this long, Rog, the best. Nobody's understanding anymore about natural calamities, probably don't have to tell you that with your line of work no matter what it is. Back at it now lean and mean, better than the kid anyway, drop by first thing tomorrow morning and be out of your hair. Maybe a little after first thing. This guy screwed me out of money on a remodel job, got to wait till he goes to work to even up the score. Just fair is all I ask. Buzz you from the gate around eight nine later sometime in the afternoon if another natural calamity out of my control happens. You got a check waiting for me that'd be great but cash always works good. The best, Rog, the best.

beep

I handed back the receiver. "Sounds like you hit it off."

"All I did was bandage him after the fan let loose and push up on his feet when he came through the ceiling."

"I'm going to start with one of those jumbo margaritas that come in a fish bowl."

He nodded vigorously. "Let's get out of here."

CHAPTER 7

Had Roger known Juice and I planned to meet it would have ruined the trip to Palm Springs, and though deflation would inevitable follow once I sprang it on him over dinner, at least he could enjoy the drive there.

Much of his frustration with me was diversion. Matching his approach to business, he was dealing with the loss of his mother as though following a twelve-step program, and after each stage took a break by worrying about me. Certainly I was aware of his right to select his method, but I was impatient for him to be healed. Furthermore—offensively selfish—I wanted him to be happy for me. I was flabbergasted complete strangers didn't approach me in public places and pump my hand in congratulation, so you can imagine how frustrating it was to have Roger cut me. When you're smiling the whole world may smile with you, but it's cold comfort if you suspect it's a forced grin. He was happy on the drive and that would do for now. We talked the whole way and made the restaurant just in time to wait forty-five minutes past our reservation.

"I hope you like it." Roger was holding a plastic torus with mini-bulbs that would light up when our table was ready so long as we kept within a sixty-foot radius of the hostess stand, source, I assumed, of whatever alien probe was targeting the device.

"I trust your taste," I said.

"The restaurant's changed. Used to be like one of those casual oyster bars you find on the end of a pier in Florida."

"It's a little theme-ish," I said, "but there you go. The city's built on tourism."

"We should go to a Mexican place."

"You don't have to worry about me," I said.

It was crowded as we wandered back and forth across Palm Canyon Drive waiting for the reservation thingy to illuminate. The Season was gearing up, snowbirds stealing a march on winter by hitting the interstates to avoid the slightest hint of snow and sleet at home. Not a bad decision. Persevere all your life, enduring everything that's chucked your way, and who can argue with wanting to let the sun bake the bones. Get old, kick back, hey. The area may have had one of the greatest concentrations of old farts on the continent, but also boasted the highest number of seniors in noticeably better shape than the glut of fat-assed teenagers around. Roger's mum was in her eighties when she died, smoked, had a rebuilt knee and drank rum like a Jamaican bootlegger, yet after each winter in the Valley came back to Vancouver in good enough shape to whip my ass in a triathlon.

Our reservation module started radiating so we ducked inside. Along a hollow square of benches in the foyer were a dozen people with their noses buried in the shopping bags of those already in line, a rank that stretched from the hostess stand to the heavy wood entrance doors. Even with our device legally flickering we had to endure snotty glances from those with inert ones. We were led through an arch of pegged wood.

Inside:

A flotilla of high-backed chairs. Booths of artificially aged wood lined the walls, fake portholes in the dividers framing the faces of children standing reversed on their seats and smearing the glass with saliva and goo from their hands. The walls were ornamented with plastic nautical and freebooter gear—hawsers, barometers, spars, helm instruments, cutlasses, matchlock pistols—and over the fireplace hung a kindergartnerish copy of *The Fighting Temeraire.* The staff were decked in pirate shirts and eye patches and pantaloons that looked pilfered from an Arabian surplus store. Huge brass loops dangled from earlobes, buckled shoes clomped on hardwood, billowy sleeves draped and absorbed soup from oversize tureens. The din was beyond belief, abetted by a chorus of waiters singing "Happy Birthday" to a man in his fifties who looked as happy as Nelson must have when his arm was blown off at Tenerife. I distinctly heard at least three "Ahar, mateys!" and without having to investigate knew the bathroom doors bore signs reading BUOYS and GULLS.

On a laminated treasure map at our table was a serving of tortilla chips and salsa that Roger and I polished off without drawing a breath. When the drinks arrived and we slowed down, sipping our margaritas and picking at the last tortilla crumbs, it was hard to tell we were in a seafood joint, confusion not wholly cleared up when the doors to the kitchen flew open, introducing to the room a large Japanese man with a glistening Chinese queue halfway down his back dressed as a nineteenth-century English Admiral.

"George Sameshima," Roger said.

The Admiral raised a spyglass to his eye—the one without a patch—and glassed the room, prompting guffaws from half the tables, the half not intent on digging their tablespoons into their crab claws. He played the room awhile, nodding at anyone who made eye contact, pointing and clicking his thumb down on his forefinger in the pistol-shot acknowledgment, sending around after-dinner shooters called Oyster Mammas. He paused in the aisle beside us, regarded Roger with uncertainty, then abruptly grunted and beckoned with the spyglass to a waitress. As she arrived with two shooters, the Admiral gunned us down with his finger and left.

"He never remembers my name," Roger said. "Or anything else." Before I could ask he added, "Friend of Mum's, sort of."

Hewing to the evening's theme of injecting some variety into our lives, we both ordered the Captain's Plate: shrimp, mussels, scallops, crab, salmon, little of this little of that. As we handed the waitress our menus—in Olde Englishe Fonte—a scream from around the fireplace penetrated the air.

Our server raised her eyes. "Someone's walking the plank," she said. "Don't ask."

We laughed with her like co-conspirators and she quickly moved off. I allowed Roger one more slug of his margarita before scotching his fun.

Juice and I. Two days from now. I gave him the goods three times in succession—the first nonchalantly, the second emphatically, the last apologetically—to give him the chance to ignore, accept or excuse the news as he chose. I stressed that we had picked a neutral site, no promises, no commitment either way, trial run type of thing to feel each other out just a date nothing more than a date what's wrong with a date, Roger? Vegas, I told him, explaining that Juice had never been there and was thrilled, and that on my part the overkill was perfect, enabling me to avoid the intimacy of a cozy restaurant or someplace where I could lose my head. What's wrong with that, Roger? Eh?

He found nothing wrong with it. Finished his margarita, pinched around the rim, sucked the salt off his fingers.

I couldn't wait for a response. "I found a cheapass motel outside of Vegas itself that has free shuttle service to the Strip."

"You don't have to appeal to the accountant in me," Roger said.

This time I waited.

"She seems all right," he said. "From what I've read."

"She's the best woman I've met in so long . . . okay, not met, but . . ."

We both were relieved when the waitress arrived.

"Here you are, gentlemen." Shrimp, mussels, scallops, crab, salmon, little of this little of that, every morsel breaded and deep-fried. "If you break out in a sweat just from eating, we've done our job."

Once she was out of sight we poked our forks at the crumbly rubble on our plates. Hunger won out and it wasn't till we were up to our foreheads and down to our sternums in grease and batter that another word was spoken.

"When?" Roger said.

"I told you. Day after tomorrow."

"I know you. You're thinking way beyond Vegas. I mean, when are you going to tell her? After all the tragedy in your memoir, all the soulsearching and honesty about how unfairly you treated your family before they were ripped from you in the earthquake . . . that's what she fell in love with."

"I've already started," I said.

"With what?"

"Well, I told her I made up the bit about losing an eye."

"Probably a wise maneuver."

"The rest will come out."

"It's as if you're deliberately designing the situation to explode in your face. Think about it—you stole a book. Almost immediately after that you fell in love with an Inbox. Every day you tell me how inspiring this woman's honesty is, but apparently all it inspires you to do is add more lies to the pile. I hope you don't expect me to help keep alive a fiction that can't possibly gain you a thing in the long term."

"I just have to go with my intuition on this one."

"Based on experience, dear, you should have figured out by now that your intuition is a fucking idiot. Why bother with the charade? Tell her now and put the whole thing behind you. Pretend it was a joke, beg her forgiveness, fake mental illness—well, not fake it, reveal it—or anything else so you two can start again clean."

"I'll tell her," I said. "Of course I will. Not immediately—I'm in too deep—but I'll tell her in good time."

"I hate that phrase. There's no such thing, no such thing as 'too deep.'"

"Too much," I said. "Too much chatter in my head to sort out. Let me, just allow me to stay with this. I need something solid, or at least what I know, a place to keep one foot still even if I'm using it to pivot on. For now."

"Are you guys done with your plates?"

Startled, we jerked back on our benches. It was easily the fastest I'd been served and quickest I'd finished eating in my life.

The waitress took our lack of response as a yes and began stacking the plates and cutlery on her forearm. "The owner wants to send you another round of Oyster Mammas."

"What's in those things?" Roger said.

"I don't know. Booze and some fishy stuff."

As she walked off, Roger starting laughing and lowly cursing at the same time. "What does she know about me?"

"Just that we're roomies. I've been trying to keep you out of it. You can pull out any time, blow the whistle and run."

Roger moved the condiments and his placemat and his crumpled napkin to the side. He ran his hand across the wood and looked at the clean varnished top of the table. "Be careful. I'm serious. With all that's gone on over the years, this is the first time that you've actively recruited me into a lie."

"Shows respect."

"I'm not sure, I'll have to think about it some more, but I have a strong hunch it shows lack of respect." He lightened and forced a smile. "I'll get back to you on that one."

Just like that I was shoved over on the bench by a Japanese English Admiral with a Chinese coolie's braid. He waited till we raised the shooters he slammed down in front of us before saying, "Gentlemen—the King!" and downing his own. Roger and I tipped ours as the owner wiped the moisture from his eyes and continued with: "I know you."

"How are you, George?" Roger said.

Another round of shooters appeared, and Roger stopped drinking after that. Not a bad move even if he hadn't been driving because they turned out to be vanilla rum and oyster juice. I was determined to acquire a taste so continued downing them like a college sophomore fortifying himself to call home for money.

Although everything was civilized enough, as the evening progressed George and I got on noticeably better than he and Roger. It leaked out that Mr. Sameshima had been carrying a torch for Mrs. Jeffcoate over the years, and while it seemed Roger held little animosity for his mum's old suitor, clearly he thought the pairing ludicrous. The deeper he got into his cups the more often George sadly shook his head, queue swishing his back like a horse's tail, and muttered, "She's gone and nothing ever happened. Nothing, not ever," at which Roger would nod smugly, as though he'd known all along. Mostly, he let the restaurant owner lead the conversation, only twice raising the matter of Willa and George's age difference. I didn't expect that kind of thing from him at all, though I guess when it comes to a mother a son's reasoning is useless, and I could identify with the images that must have been coursing through Roger's mind. It's against all logic, but to picture your old mum embracing a man twenty years younger causes the eyes to narrow and the nose to wrinkle in the way it does when envisioning the Queen of England on the toilet with six feet of gown gathered under her arms while she reaches for the roll.

Occasionally, I'd become aware of the crowd, which comprised all ages, even tots up way past bedtime as their parents hammered away trying to tenderize every fiber of vacation time. It kept expanding in both size and ferocity and the staff grew more frazzled with each new boarding party they had to fend off. George had stopped helping long before, wasn't even part of the proceedings, oblivious to the rumpus from the kids and the drunks and the fife-and-drum music blaring from the ceiling speakers. Glasses, whole trays, were dropped and smashed and George sat there drinking and swishing his braid. He stirred at one point, rising half out of his chair when a fight broke out near the front. Well, not really a fight, more of a titty-pull, two men in Hawaiian shirts ineffectually pawing and slapping at each other's faces till they tumbled over a coil of plastic rope onto the patio. George sat back down, and such was his lack of vigilance a youngster was able to snatch the spyglass from the table and whoop his way aloft on the rigging behind the salad bar before a bun hurled from across the room hit him square in the face and he fell screaming into the chowder.

Roger rose. "George, I appreciate the hospitality as well as all the kind words about my mother."

"You can't just go," George said. "We can stay after hours, I know all the cops. Let's talk about Willa some more. There's nobody around here who knows her, I mean, knew her, awww, I don't . . ."

Roger and I took one last look around us at the mayhem.

"You don't have to say it," George said. "How do we get where we are?

That's what I'd like to know. Know where I'm from? Bismarck, North Dakota, that's where. Never seen an ocean, right? So I come to California to go surfing just one time and I hurt my ankle and never even go in the water and then end up in the desert. With this. I should've just bought a fucking aquarium."

By the time we reached the car the dark and the quiet and the air had me so restored I could have walked the fifteen miles home. The spin of the tires on the pavement was the only sound as we drove, and we were satisfied to leave it at that. The breeze through the windows was pacific. Home and quietly through the security gates, the two of us wound down now, easy and light and limber. As we rounded the corner and Roger clicked open the garage door, the sound of it connecting with metal put an end to the interlude.

"Now what?" Roger said.

"It's in the driveway," I said, not adding much to the collective knowledge.

We were accustomed to seeing vintage and classic cars in town, machines lovingly restored by retired aficionados with time on their hands and money in them. The climate helped by preserving them in assembly-line condition, and they added color and a bit of fun to the streets. But this old thing looked nasty. A '60s Pontiac Bonneville stretching from the garage door almost to the curb, a sweep of metal with a trunk lid that could have launched a navy jet. The body was canary yellow splotched with rust-red primer, and though it was hard to tell in the lights of Roger's car, the black vinyl roof looked brush-painted.

A skinny guy levered himself from the vehicle and shaded his eyes from our headlights. When Roger shut them off, the man skittered over and was there before we knew it, the driver's door catching him on the knee as Roger got out.

Not a flinch. "Rog. Made it home."

"Yeah, Sonny. What are you doing here?"

"Always finish a job I start."

"It's quarter-to-two in the morning."

"The way home, thought I might catch you up late."

"Your message said tomorrow."

"Tomorrow's tied up," Sonny said. "Twenty minutes all it'll take, have a drink sit back watch a pro in action. You're Smith."

"Uh, that's right," I said.

"Sonny. Sonny Lemmatina."

"Sure." I was starting to completely zone out from the mixture of rum, oyster juice and now Sonny Lemmatina. "Can you move your car?"

He tossed me his key ring. "Should get right to work."

Roger sighed. "This better not take long. The only reason I'm letting you in is because I don't want to wait another three weeks for you to show up."

"Why would it?" Sonny said. "Take long I mean. Or any longer for me to show up, I mean too. Hey, that extra hunk of drywall still where I left it along the side by that carpet?"

Roger gave me the Neon's keys and followed Sonny up the sidewalk. The belly of the handyman's car barely cleared the ground. I wrenched the door closed then made out a hairy mass on the reclined seat beside me and froze. Sonny's face appeared in the open passenger window. Well, not open, nonexistent.

"Be fine long as I'm around," he said, referring to the brindled dog. It looked like a slightly scaled-down wolfhound that had been rescued from a hair-gel warehouse explosion. "Hand, give him the hand slow, real slow. He's a warrior."

I extended my hand to the thing. Nothing, neither sniff nor friendly lick. I kept trying, and due to lack of light rammed my hand into his nose, the tip of my forefinger entering a nostril. Still no sniff or friendly lick. No movement at all. I tried again then lightly scratched under his chin. Inert.

"Need protection," Sonny said. "Times the way they are."

"Scares off thieves, does he?" I inclined my head at the science-project version of a dog.

"Wouldn't believe."

The shooters had armed me with a belly full of brave so I experimentally poked the animal in the ass and lightly tugged his tail. Nothing. I could have drummed his ribcage with a rubber mallet to no more effect. "Maybe the old guy's just tired."

"Only sixteen, seventeen."

Sonny's gear was crammed into the back of the car, extending into the trunk through the opening where the rear seat had once been. Everything was coated with plaster and cement powder and looked welded together into a freeform sculpture, power cords and extensions entwined like snakes in their hibernaculum. He reached over the dog into the recycling yard and pulled out a cordless drill.

By the time I shuttled the cars and entered the house through the garage Sonny was wobbling on the kitchen table trying to fasten the replacement sheet of drywall, holding the four-by-four section in place with his head while trying to fit a screw onto his driver. Under most conditions I would have rushed to his aid, but he looked rebar-hard and seemed to be under no strain. Besides, given the time of night and all other factors, I felt under no obligation to be helpful. He dropped the screw and fished in his pocket for a replacement and dropped that and went for another and by then his sunken cheeks were starting to suck and blow so reluctantly I climbed beside him and held the panel in place for him to attach.

"That's not going to come loose again, is it?" Roger said over the sound of the drill.

"Wrong size screws last time, all I had. Be good now." He jumped off the table. Moving fast, he hung the ceiling fan and was done in the advertised time. "Yeah, okay, just the taping and mudding and texturing and painting to do on the drywall, nice as anything, won't even know I been here."

"How long will that take?" Roger looked at his watch.

Sonny laughed, actually doubling over and resting his hands on his knees. "Another day or two, Rog. You figure all this is a one-night job?"

"If you had come tomorrow morning you could have spent the whole day—"

"—Whole day! Hee!"

"Then when—"

"—Before you know it. The kid, get her fixed up first, everybody admits kids're more important than ceiling fans. Soon. Here I'll show you something you probably didn't know."

He pointed the remote control and the fan sped up then slowed down and the light dimmed, grew brighter and flicked off, then the fan sped up then slowed down and the light dimmed, grew brighter—

"Okay," I said. "We get it."

There was an inch-wide gap between the new drywall and the old and the sheet bulged in the middle. The fan was visibly askew, and I knew in my heart I'd never eat a meal at the table without expecting it to plunge like a stricken helicopter and carve me into slices of smoked meat. Sonny put the remote on the table and the three of us stood watching the new fixture rotate until Roger pulled out his checkbook.

Sonny avoided eye contact by peering at the fan as though reading runes. "Best you guys give me the full total, need supplies to finish her up."

"I should probably hold some back," Roger said. He hesitated with his pen over the check then scratched a figure. "I don't mean to be insulting, but until the job's done . . ."

"Heart goes on the kid," Sonny said, "there's me fucked."

Roger crumpled the check and wrote another one.

"The best, Rog, the best." Sonny tugged his wallet out by the chain and slid in the payment without looking.

"Do you have even a vague idea when you can finish?" Roger said as he walked him to the door.

"Whales threw my schedule out of whack. Funny world, got every-thing planned out then bam! hand of God there you are up the creek."

"Do your best, will you?"

Sonny turned at the door and raised a palm to me. I waved back. He kept his hand up until I dug in my pocket and fired the keys at him. He caught them with a flourish. "Good chuck, Smittybaby, good pitch!"

We watched from the doorway as Sonny worked his Bonneville through a five-point U-turn and pulled away. When he hit the speed bump directly in front of the picture window sparks jetted into the air as if he were towing a disc harrow.

"I'm tired," Roger said as he closed the door. "I mean it, I'm really tired."

"I'm not even going to brush my teeth." I started down the hall.

I had just flopped naked on the mattress and was hoping the breeze through the screen would pick up when Roger inserted the day's final punctuation: "This fan won't shut off!"

I feigned sleep, and sometime after nodded off for real despite the insane stridency of a mockingbird in the greenbelt.

CHAPTER 8

Many things squirrel in the brain's alcoves for the longest time until springing forth with a loud Ha! on bad breath. They exist as memory so presumably were prominent sometime in the past—unless they've been induced by therapy—yet they can feel brand new. In this case it was my appearance. I'm not revolting, though my squarish head with its moraine down the middle and lack of hair to cover it and my severely fissured face would earn me the role of the hard-times uncle in a romantic comedy—no one to flee from, just a little daffy and world-weary. I haven't often considered my looks since my early twenties. My wife found me good-looking, even magnetic, and that was enough for me. In truth, the phrase she normally used was "unconventionally handsome," but when you're in love the way I was that's easily enlarged in translation.

I found myself hoping Juice wasn't too attractive. I wanted no part of the inevitable comparisons, snide asides and what's-she-doing-with-a-poor-guy-like-him speculation. I like to think I could ignore that kind of fatuity, though not with the confidence to be tested. With the meeting imminent, I mentally willed Juice to have just the right amount of appeal for us to disappear from the public radar screen.

One thing I knew was that I couldn't wait another day to leave for Vegas, and I had to tell Roger so posthaste, if for no other reason than I needed the car. When I followed the scent of brewing coffee into the kitchen the morning after our seafood night, the first thing that struck me was the breeze from the fan. Autumn was starting to assert itself, and like most things in the desert wasn't doing so any too subtly. The last thing we needed was downdraft.

Roger had the coffee ready.

"How long you been up?" I said.

"I wanted to clean out the car," he said. "It's too hard to think about something important from a distance. Get there a day early so you have a chance to settle in."

"Just what I was thinking," I said. "Nothing you need it for?"

"I don't want to go anywhere after last night," he said. "Take it, get out of here. There's a top-up to your allowance in the glove compartment. I'd advise doing something like losing it all on the Strip, or buying a pair of lizard-skin cowboy boots and falling asleep to KENO numbers on the TV."

"You have to admit this is pretty brave of me." I couldn't keep a straight face, even though I believed what I'd just said.

"Take your coffee and go." He passed me the car keys. "Think of me while you're watching the white tigers."

There was more I wanted to add, but Roger shoved the remote control an inch from the fan and stabbed the buttons, air and spit jetting between his teeth.

The Neon had less than half a tank, so I stopped to fill up in Twenty-Nine Palms, forty minutes east of Palm Springs along Highway 62. The steep climb off the interstate, transitioning from the low Colorado Desert to the high Mojave, had already taken me through Morongo Valley and the towns of Yucca Valley and Joshua Tree. Well-separated houses scattered on the hillsides, communities at the stage of development where civic pride is saving up to buy some buttons to burst. Remnants of not long ago—modest pastel motels boasting COLOR TV signs and courtyard swimming pools; antique shops with false fronts selling cowboy paraphernalia and frontier craft work. Once past the marine base and heading north toward the National Preserve I began to have increasing appreciation for any community that was managing to maintain, that hadn't gone the way of the ghost towns I passed. . . . Amboy . . . Kelso . . . it grew achingly sad to see road signs promising something, anything, up ahead, only to have the anticipation shattered. Not even shattered, really, just slowly leached.

I was trying to make good time, holding eighty on the undulating pavement as it dipped into a wash then rose, hypnotically down again and up, ninety-plus on some stretches and still I would have killed for a school zone, been tickled to slow down for a kid or two. No children and no one else. Schoolhouses abandoned and sagging beside gas stations rusted and thirsty across from railway stations boarded and shot-up. It was haunting to think of the plans that had gone awry, the dreams blown away, the love that had been beaten by the elements and mischance into despair and sent packing down the road.

The land's beauty, the colors and the light, the miles of Joshua trees with their scales and grotesquery laughing at literal tree-huggers, inspired longing, a pull. At many points I could have parked and started walking in any direction with neither goal nor timeframe. At the same time, the air held a threatening eeriness urging me to roll up the windows and lock the doors and speed through the enchanted land. For many miles I fastened on the road and the power lines as symbols of civilized safety, convinced that by chancing even a short hike I would lose my way and have to crawl through the desert until coming upon a shack with a hermit who would resuscitate me and lay me on a cot with a cool washcloth on my forehead after which I would sleep until being sodomized and knifed as morning broke and years later having my skeleton discovered under a pile of creosote branches in an abandoned water trough by a natural history professor on sabbatical from Harvard. Good Christ—I needed a drink.

When I reached I-15, part of the main route between Los Angeles and Vegas, I was slammed back to earth as though my parachute had failed. I drove along the shoulder a ways, building up speed before merging with the lanes of manic motorists whistling east on their way to throw money down on gaming tables. Nevada drew us toward her, highway heat waves creating mirages of girls with eight feet of feathers atop their heads and Bedouins in corporate jets and pallid Minnesotans looking for a free breakfast at three in the morning. When I passed a sign that read: FOOD – GAS – CASTLE, I knew I was getting close, and could have sworn I saw through the shimmers a white tiger singing *Danke Shein.*

We forged ahead, we grim travelers. I felt part of a group, a single mass of driver ants, RVs and SUVs and semis and sedans and convertibles merely different body plans indicating distinct roles within the ant colony—fighters, groomers, scavengers, unlimited specialization. Road construction funneled us into the two left lanes, forcing us to a crawl. Surging and braking we crept along, impatience leaking from the vehicles and polluting the air. Late! We were going to be late for . . . well, just late! A spot of bad luck, not a good thing to run into on the way to Las Vegas. Slow as we were going, I missed the motel turnoff—farther from downtown than I had thought—and had to drive six miles through the construction zone to find a place to reverse course. Heading west, I zipped by the dumpy joint a second time, which I considered quite enough, and cut off a grader and mowed down a sequence of traffic cones after executing an illegal one-eighty across the median.

The maneuvering in the parking lot was no less hazardous. I had to swerve around two shuttle buses before stopping under the entrance canopy. A third bus crept nose-to-nose with me, so I reversed all the way to the edge of the property and parked by the motel's sign, which featured a caricature of a prospector replete with pick, pack, shovel, and wearing a king's crown indicating, presumably, he had struck the mother lode, or possibly had lost his grubstake and was reduced to shilling for Imperial Margarine. I slung my pack, dodged another shuttle bus and entered the lobby.

I could have done it worry-free. Right then I could have, standing in the lobby with my clothes and pack. It was the doorman's fault. He stuck his head inside and said, "You the asshole who parked by the sign?"

I went back out to move the car and there was overcome. Breathing deeply, I leaned against the Neon. Was this what I wanted? Maybe Roger was right, that there's no such thing as too deep. I could turn around and go home, no harm no foul. All my mistakes, the sum of the lies, I'm accustomed to regarding as a monolithic bloc, an enormous solitary lapse, but of course it's a series of minor miscalculations constituting the whole. Moreover, each one has been obvious—the defense of ignorance would be hooted out of a village idiots' kangaroo court. This was another step. Jesus. I had deliberately avoided fantasizing about the moment of impact, concentrating throughout the drive on the drive itself. After all, I had nothing to worry about, right? Just a blind date with someone I already loved—in Las Vegas, man, meeting my gal.

I heaved myself off the fender. Light-headed, feeling damned if I did or didn't, I regained a morsel of strength and hit the hotel.

Juice didn't show.

I checked in, climbed the stairs to the second-floor penthouse suite and spent the rest of the day and all night wide awake and alone. Phoned the airport every hour on the hour, the cops on the half-hours, checked the lounge eight times, my e-mail twelve. It wasn't till dawn that it dawned on me I'd arrived a day earlier than planned. In my state of anxious turmoil it would have been ill-advised to push my luck by bussing to the Strip, so I went for a short walk then parked in the lounge, checking the lobby every fifteen minutes. Night two of phone calls and feverish e-mailing and not a sausage, till finally I slept and woke at noon on day three. Downstairs shirtless, and at last, huddled over the miniature Internet access machine in the lobby, I saw her name bursting to get out of my inbox.

Dear Smith,

Oops! Something came up. Write when you get home.
  Love you, love you,
  Juice

A harsh stare from both the doorman and the front desk at my scream.

Dear Juice,

No sweat.

  Yours,
  Smith

After looping around the construction zone I wound the Neon out across the desert.

Years ago with the death of my wife I gained great power from having nothing to lose, and rampaged through the days wearing my sorrow and anger on my sleeve. All that did was strip me of membership in the world, and sometime later I sought to reclaim my standing via manufactured intimacy, attaching myself to anyone who crossed my path, trying to both fornicate and ingratiate my way back. My old friends I swiftly culled, then moved to a different area of town and spent and bragged my way into a group of male backslappers and women who laughed too loudly at too many things. I truly believed it was healthy, reveling in the alcoholic and coked-out bonhomie and the praise for how well adjusted I must have been to heal so quickly after my loss.

My loss, they said, mine, as though my wife's death hadn't cut down friends and family far more worthy of praise than I, as if her loss of life itself was of little moment compared to the distress it visited on me, the gang's new friend, the one who stayed to the end of every party and never bothered anyone with his burden. When finally I started to emerge from the grief—by myself, and I can hardly pat myself on the back considering I had no alternative—I almost dove right back into the shitpit, because even the old friends who returned when they saw the light of recovery in my eyes couldn't resist shaking their heads and saying such things as: "When something like this happens it makes you realize just how short life really is," then nodding sagely at one another.

I could have throttled them to an individual. Not one man-jack of them came to any such realization. All of them got up the next morning, pulled the same skirts and pants up over the same arses and commuted to jobs they hated while worrying themselves into knots over the dirt on their new cars and whether their belts matched their shoes and arguing about which Hawaiian resort had the cheapest drinks. So I shoved them off a second time, sick of their attempts to help me for my own good, wanting no part of anyone on a mission to get me back to normal. Normal, they said, normal, the idiots. Besides, no true friend would have allowed himself to be pushed away in the first place. Roger hadn't. He was the only person or thing during my years as a virtual recluse preventing me from biting the heads off live poultry and growing my fingernails three-feet long, and I blessed him for his support right the way through.

Two years later, when praise for my novel began to accumulate, I had nothing left to give and rejected everything that was offered, shut it all down. It takes no great expert on human nature to diagnose overcompensation in both cases, the difference being that the second period was darker, longer, more corrosive, much worse. Making the rounds as a drunken buffoon distorts; the absence of all social intercourse rapes.

The fantasies I'd passed up on the outbound leg couldn't be avoided on the way home. It had been so long, the physical, the sharing, the flush and flame. I gave myself up to the heat waves and dreamed. . . . Juice and I would have spent the night on bed, couch and floor sucking, licking, urgently squeezing and shuddering, stopping to talk a lot, eat a little. We'd have stayed up till the sun rose and watched it reflect off the desert and slash through the venetians into the room, and Juice would pull me up from between her legs and gently spin me on my back and straddle me and taste herself on my mouth, the striping of pink and yellow and shadow along our flanks straight from one of those dreams of a tropic isle—sun lancing through the matchstick blinds of a beach shack onto bronzed lovers under a palmetto fan, not another soul on the island yet the cottage mysteriously connected to a sewer line and a power source, with a full bar and plenty of towels and soap and tropical fruit as well as an indigenous population of wild pigs that daily roasted one of its members and left it as an offering on the verandah.

So strong were the inventions, I was more than content to cruise along the freeway doing forty in the center lane, the colorful flashes of paint as vehicles swerved and rocketed past on both sides pure delight, the repeated cries of "Stupid cocksucker!" as romantic as the call of the loon.

Since off-the-track sights and discoveries would have been wasted on me, I stuck to the interstate, after Barstow cutting through the national forest at San Bernardino and backtracking along I-10 to the valley. I spent every mile with no-show Juice in my daydreaming head, dissecting each glance and shift, word and moan, how she ate her food, drank her drinks, the confidence that allowed her to maintain eye-contact and a steady stream of chatter while she pissed and wiped herself, the effect she had on the room-service waiters, how she gently closed the louvers of the blinds to seal in the dark then later impulsively reefed them open, the brazenness of her lovemaking contrasting with her shyness when I took the lead. A truly magical and astonishing first meeting. I had acquitted myself like a knight, strong, honest, forthright.

By the time the mirage dissipated I was exhausted. I booted the car into a sprint, opened the window to clear out the last gasps of imagination and started thinking about what I'd tell Roger. I pulled through the gates and rounded the corner to the sight of a police car in the driveway.

Big beefy redneck cop, I thought as I entered the kitchen from the hall. I was disabused of my snap judgment the second he turned. Big and beefy all right, but kind-looking to the point of sadness. The type of man you want to hug just in case he needs it later when you're not around.

"I'm sorry," he said for no apparent reason. His features were relaxed, near to sliding off into the hat he held like a platter at waist height.

"I'm Smith."

He shuttled the hat between hands a couple of times until settling on the left and extending the right. It was like shaking a sandwich bag of gravy, though that was okay. My father had brainwashed me into believing a firm handshake was a sign of character, but once out of the house and experiencing the world on my own I could find no evidence it was anything more than manipulation learned at sales seminars. I tried not to burst the cop's gravy bag and hoped he was appreciative enough to cut us some slack on whatever trouble we were in.

"This is Martin," Roger said.

"What's up, Officer?" I said. "Not that old genocide charge again."

"He's kidding," Roger said quickly.

Martin was sweating. He edged closer to the fan—it had picked up much speed in my absence—and rubbed his brushcut. The air blast dispersed the droplets and Martin the Policeman almost crapped his handcuff pouch. "Gosh, that didn't get you boys, did it?"

"Anything I can help you with?" I said. "Or have you and Roger straightened it away?"

"No, this is just a social call."

"Martin Kolachuk," Roger said. "Our dear Sarah's husband."

"Oh, okay," I said. "The carpet will be gone next garbage day."

Martin looked at Roger.

"We got a notice from your wife," Roger said.

"She means well," Martin said. It wasn't the first time that had come out of his mouth.

"So we don't have to give a statement?" I said.

He smiled. "She takes her responsibilities very seriously."

"Well, I suppose we can sleep tonight knowing there's a policeman in the neighborhood."

"Gosh, I'm not with the sheriff's department." He hunched his shoulder so I could get a look at his patch—Honey Badger Security. "I've been with them two years now. Part time . . . business was slow . . . you know."

"What business is that?" The need to empty myself at Roger's feet was waning. Something Martin emitted had a damping effect and I was perfectly happy to make small talk.

"I have a golf car place. We call them golf *cars*, because they have a lot more stuff on them than your basic *cart.* We can custom order ones that look like anything you want—Jeeps, Jaguars, fifty-seven Chevies, even Hummers."

I would have been happy with his company for another hour, but he jammed on his hat and we said our goodbyes. Roger and I followed him out and waited till he pulled away, waving out the car window as though he were leaving behind his family to look for work overseas.

"Nice guy," I said. "Now sit down. I'll get us a drink."

"Why are you shouting?" Roger said.

The fan had broken out of its steady hum and was surging with a rhythmic throb. We maintained a safe distance.

"Let's go out to the patio," I said. "I'm sticking a broom handle into the blades if Sonny doesn't get here by tomorrow."

CHAPTER 9

The gardeners had pruned the olive trees to skeletons, allowing a perfect view of the Santa Rosas to the south. I had missed cutting day. The bucolic enterprises of planting and tending went on continually, but once a week the compound turned into a botanical abattoir as the machinery was cranked up. Mowers and chainsaws and trimmers surged through the community like a neap tide, lapping against the houses, driving the weak, lame and elderly indoors. When the tide ebbed, taking with it the major detritus from lawns and palm trees and ficus hedges, sandwich wrappers and lost shoes and mulched dry dog turds, the leaf blowers darted in to scavenge. One-hundred-pound workers with Volkswagen engines strapped to their backs scoured the community, blasting leaves and stray clippings off patios and driveways onto the grass, followed by fresh recruits who drove the leavings into the gutters, after which the mop-up crew finished at their leisure, casually blowing the debris down the streets to collectors with waiting burlap sacks. Only then would the residents cautiously emerge to note missed patches and brown spots on the lawns, collecting fodder for the next HOA meeting.

"How do you decide whether to pay the price?" I said after Roger and I had finished half our bloody marys.

"I don't know that it's a conscious decision."

The drink was so fiery I kept my mouth open between sips. I jerked my chin at the mountains. Meeting Martin had thrown me off and I was thankful Roger had the good grace to stare at the scenery and let me set the pace. We were quiet awhile, but once I got rolling it came out easily. Nothing to worry about. It wasn't the first time Roger had chucked rocks at me from the other side of the fence, and I knew from experience all we had to do was keep walking down the line till arriving at a gap where a rail was down or the wire had been cut and we'd rejoin on the same side. I talked about Juice at some length without Roger interrupting, even at those points I created in the monologue for exactly that.

Eventually, with the squeaking of his plastic patio chair attesting his restlessness, I finished with: "We'll meet eventually, and when we do I'm going to tell her the truth."

"Because it's the right thing to do or because you're scared silly you won't be able to pull it off?"

His hands gripped the arms of the chair and I watched his expression change in time-lapse from puzzled to astonished. I had no time to check behind me before the fan blade hit the slider and cracked it top to bottom. I was on the edge of the patio, holding my knee where I had slammed it on the underside of the table, when Sonny carefully slid open the door and nodded hello.

"Easy enough to fix," he said. He was holding a broom with a chipped and gouged handle.

"Where the hell did you come from?" I said.

He waved in the direction of the houses at the end of the greenbelt. By then Roger was on his way inside.

We followed and Sonny lightly kicked the fan blade. "You guys got her stuck full-on somehow."

She was still stuck full-on. Only one blade had let go and the fan was cavitating wildly. I looked again at the broom Sonny had rammed into the apparatus, and felt a fleck of pride at having merely threatened the wetbrain maneuver. Before Roger or I could react Sonny was on the table and again had the broom—straw end this time, learning from experience—rammed into the hub. He popped off the cover plate at the ceiling and jerked the wires.

"Stopped," he said, satisfied with the dicey bit of surgery.

Roger finally caught up to the speed of Sonny's world. "You know, this is getting to be a bit much."

"Yeah," Sonny said. "Homeowning's a bitch."

"Well, now that you're here . . ."

Sonny shook his head. "No time, on the way home. Doing a remodel for some blonde job the next street from you guys. Pretty good-looking. Tall job, nice frame. If I do good work who knows what? Single now sort of. Wife lives in New Mexico, place called Mountainair. I got stuck with the kids, not stuck, I love them, but so did she. Funny, that's all she liked, the kids. Even her work, she was in the daycare racket, always the kids till off she bolted. Great kids. There's Saxon fourteen, high school next year, good for him. Delilah the one with the bum heart, twelve, funny how time flies. And another one."

"Another one," Roger said.

"Yeah." He pulled a grimy envelope from the wallet pocket of his carpenter's shorts and handed it to me. On the front was my name in a dainty hand.

"What is it?" I said.

"Private letter," Sonny said. "Wouldn't peek with a gun to my head."

"What I mean is where'd you get it?"

"You talk like an Irishman or something. Irishman or that Australian crocodile guy."

"I'm from Canada. Same with Roger."

His eyes went wide and he stepped back to keep both of us in his field of view. "Both you guys, get out of here, both? It's where I come from, I come from Canada. Not a Canadian, not really a Canadian, three days only. My momma was carrying me visiting her boyfriend in Deetroyit, went across the river to the Canada side and I was born by mistake over there. Right there a place called Windsor, Canada, the state of Ontario, probably means I can't run for president of the US or something, but that's okay, I like working with my hands anyhow. Canada, that's just the best, I always love a good coincidence. That's it—I was giving you a break on the fan all along, you bet it's wholesale cost now."

"We'll be glad to pay full price," Roger said, "if you can give us a time-frame."

"No timeframe for you guys, not for countrymen. Right away, two three days at the outside." He picked up the broom again and leaned it against the wall. "Where's Boston Charlie?"

I unfolded the letter just as Sonny wheeled off down the hall. When I caught up he was dragging the warrior dog off my bed. So much hair was left behind on the duvet I could have compressed it into a dog of my own.

"Heel B.C.," Sonny said. "Heel."

I trailed behind as the animal got up to a mile-a-month racing after Sonny. By the time they reached the car out front Boston Charlie was heeled nearly to death.

"Hold it," I said. "This is from someone called Dowser—who is she?"

Sonny leaned in and peered. "Just a note she sent, probably a hope-you're-okay-to-the-new-home type of business."

"I don't know a Mrs. Dowser or any woman by that name. I don't know anyone around here beyond waving terms."

"The Dowser," Sonny said. "Not a missus anything, just the Dowser. And besides, she don't live around here."

"Oh," I said. "Thanks for clearing that up."

"Don't know, Smitty, that it's such a big deal to give me that look." There he was, leaning against the Bonneville, dog jammed behind his legs in the shade. Nothing in the world had the capacity to shake the two animals from their assurance. "Get the water into you before you go all goofy in the head, I mean it. Canada you're not used of the heat, awful things happen you get dehydrated down here. Don't pay attention to them TV ads neither about drinking milk will quench your thirst. Dairies are crazy, refreshing milk will quench your thirst they tell you. Walk around the desert a hour-and-a-half and drink milk, you'll die. Might as well stuff that pink insulation in your throat 'cause you're going down mister, and not coming up." He hammered a fist on the front fender panel and Boston Charlie sort of woke up. I heard the Bonneville scrape down the driveway as I cut across the grass.

Inside, Roger was swinging the fan. As it pivoted on the ball socket he took the nearest blade between his fingertips and lightly propelled it, watching as the motor assembly reached its gimbal limit and returned. Again and again. Unnatural.

"This was Mum's place," he said.

It knocked me just far enough off center to delay my response, and in the time it took, there was a scurrying at the door followed by fading footsteps. On the horsehair mat outside was a flat unmarked cardboard box.

I handed it to Roger. "One surprise each."

As he was peeling the tape off the box I started in on the letter:

Dear Smith,

Welcome. Welcome to the desert, welcome to my home.

Are you still asking questions? Changed them? Had the leisure time to realize that doing so is an end in itself?

You're not being stalked and your line isn't tapped. This is a simple case of someone—me—wanting to connect with a new friend— you—without the gimmick of a fruit basket.

Say yes. Yes, you will attend your housewarming, even though it's at my house. I enjoyed meeting you. We had a good talk. The second

time you were under more pressure than you were the first and we
hadn't the chance to delve into anything of importance. The third
time you were drunk and the fourth I was. Let's fix that.

I'm hosting a potluck dinner for your housewarming on
Saturday morning at ten. As the guest of honor, you need bring only
the luck. And Roger, of course.

No phone or fax. See enclosed map. If you can't figure it out, ask
Sonny.

With Bells On,
The Dowser

My head came up in concert with Roger's.

"What do you have?" I said.

"A wreath."

I could see that. A hell of a wreath, mammoth, fashioned for the funeral of an entire mob family. Artificial fir branches and holly sprigs suggesting Christmas; hazelnuts and tiny ears of maize, Thanksgiving; plastic tulips, Spring. Quartering the circle were crossed candy canes knotted with an orange-and-black ribbon, felt shamrocks woven around the circumference. Surmounting it all was a glass suguaro standing in as a flagpole for a sugar-candy Stars and Stripes. If the wreath wasn't home-made, some local retail store should have been forced out of business by government fiat.

"There's more," Roger said, pulling out a four-foot red-satin banner with WELCOME printed on it in enormous, in seven or eight languages to boot: *Bienvenue – Wilcommen* – well, I'll stop there. The felt-pen markings had run and rendered most of the words indecipherable. "It's from Martin." He lightly shook the wreath and a walnut dropped to the floor. "There's a note that says he made it himself."

No comment was required. I passed him the Dowser's letter.

When he reached the end he said, "Mum knew her, brought her name up a lot."

"Your old mum got around the valley, looks like."

"What do you think?" He waved the letter. "Should we go?"

"I know for a fact we've never met. Four times, she says. I hope we're not playing into the hands of some old maniac desert hermit dame, then again, the diversion would probably do me good."

"Mum never went into too much detail. Pretty typical of her, thinking if she played it down I wouldn't be interested when just the opposite was true. The only thing that sticks in my mind is that once Mum said the Dowser was the kind of woman who made her want to spend a night in a graveyard drinking wine and giving speeches. When I asked her what it meant she didn't answer."

A car roared around the corner and I made it to the slider in time to see the Bonneville skid to a stop on the wrong side of the street.

"Hey," Sonny said. His arm was draped out the window, almost touching the pavement.

"Forget something?" I said.

"Couple things. Note probably says Saturday to drop by but it might not mean tomorrow. Could of been in my pants awhile. Don't matter, any Saturday or any other day is fine with the Dowser. Follow the map and if you get lost don't go walking in the desert with them sandals."

As I looked back inside for help Sonny banged the flat of his hand on the car door.

I tried to look as exasperated as I was. "What's the other thing?"

"Got a date with the Blonde Job." He howled to choking with triumph and floored the Bonny. I could have sworn I saw Boston Charlie bounce into view through the window when Sonny hit the speed bump.

I had to walk. I wasn't at peak fitness but it was time to hit the hills; their proximity a throw-in. Four miles up Highway 74, I pulled the Neon into the Art Smith Trail parking lot. On the march just past the half-mile point, I came to the trail proper and went at it with a will and fierce strides. Switching between views of the desert towns below and canyon isolation, the path led me a merry chase through stark washes and palm oases.

But it wasn't a chase, at least not a blind one, and as I hiked onward and upward, heading roughly northwest along the trail's sixteen-mile length, I reached the go/no-go point where the lure of the destination, the completion, was perfectly balanced by the tug of what was behind me. I stopped dead on the trail and picked the spines of a cholla from my bare calf. Okay. I turned around and went larking down, noticing all the things I had missed on the way up. If the water bottles hadn't been jouncing so much in my pack I might have clicked my heels. Lower down, in a wash strewn with boulders from an old flashflood, I paused to scuff my boot in a scattering of smokethorn blossoms, tiny dry indigo flowers that had somehow retained their color right through the summer and early fall. Then I had to hurry to beat the night as the sun winked behind the peak. Scrabbling through the twists and turns, singing nonsense lyrics to no melody, I arrived at the car just as a dozen berserk motorcyclists howled past on their way up the mountain road. I waved.

Roger was outside as I pulled through the gates. He watched me drive past and turn to enter the garage and I lost sight of him. He was waiting for me in the kitchen, silent and sad and looking as though he'd bloodied many more marys while I was gone. I moved toward him but he spun and went back outside. As he closed the slider behind him the cracked glass let go and smashed on the concrete pad.

CHAPTER 10

I strolled around the compound to give Roger some time, and when I returned the glass was cleaned up and my friend was in bed. I sat on the grass with my back against the partition that partially blocks the air conditioner and watched the lights wink streak twinkle in the sky, then dozed off at some point and was woken by the automatic sprinklers at six.

Roger was digging in the freezer. He'd been woken an hour ago by the phone, and after assuring Sarah that we shared the Board's concern about the sliding glass door and promising to have it repaired posthaste, he went back to bed. After the second call, having convinced Martin the breakage was an accident and around-the-clock guards weren't required, he stayed up.

"You could have woken me," I said.

"I hadn't the heart. Sitting there in the wet grass with the plaster gouging your back and your chin jammed into your chest you looked as peaceful as a baby."

"Anything you want to talk about?"

"I'm fine. . . . Thanks."

As he started peeling frozen croissants from a cardboard tube and laying them on a cookie sheet, I headed for the shower for a thorough scrubbing. On emerging I found Roger sitting on his ass in front of the stove, staring through the tiny window at the rising rolls.

"Are we going to do this housewarming thing?" I said.

"Sonny said the Dowser's fine with any Saturday. I wouldn't quote him as an expert on anything, but the letter sounded sincere enough."

"Okay. Your turn for the shower. I'll watch the oven and mix up a pitcher."

Thirty minutes later, with Roger at the wheel and me in the navigator's seat juggling croissants and pouring bloody marys, we headed for the far side of the valley. Retracing the initial part of my route to Vegas along 62, we cut off onto a side road by the Blue Dog before the highway took the big climb. We wound through the low Indio Hills, highly eroded badlands only a mile or so from the Little San Bernardino Mountains.

Arroyos cut back and twisted out of sight but disappeared quickly, as if the road's presence had smoothed things out along its flanks for the idle traveler. Though invisible, branches of the San Andreas fault system defined the perimeter, an invisible underground threat under the ridges and undulating alluvium. The Santa Rosas and San Jacintos poked up here and there to the south and west, looking a thousand miles away.

The Dowser's map led us past clusters of houses and trailers, isolated parcels of land with only the odd fence or windbreak to indicate habitation. We turned north and pointed straight at the mountains. A ways along, when it looked as if we were about to run out of gravel road, was a gate with a sign that read: *Rest For the Weary and Storage For Trunks—Wells, Fargo—San Francisco*. No fence, just the gate skirted by deep ruts.

Upon cresting a rise a hundred feet up the road we saw the house, set at an angle to the road, with a glimpse behind it of four outbuildings arrayed in a rough circle around what looked to be a low-walled well. Roger passed me his glass. He needed both hands to steer the Neon over the washboard and the chuckholes and around the meandering goats and chickens. He stopped a good distance from the house. Scattered like screwbean seeds were other vehicles, most of which looked permanently anchored but without the scavenged appearance of junkers, each one spruced up with an awning, a flag, a window box.

Admittedly, we felt a little lame showing up to a housewarming party what could have been weeks late and bearing only a pitcher scummed with dried tomato juice, but it was our house we were warming from a distance so banged on the door.

"There you are." The woman was unsurprised, as if we'd taken overlong going out for ice. She took the pitcher from Roger and beckoned, and we trailed her into what looked like an inhabited museum. Before we could even introduce ourselves she told us to look around, that she'd be right back, and went outside.

Roger and I wandered the main room poking and prodding, investigating the shelves of potsherds and native American baskets and fossilized coral and geodes and more—framed newspaper clippings from the Apollo program; brochures from the 1960 Rome and '68 Mexico City Olympics; under glass a London broadsheet celebrating VE Day; a print of Emiliano Zapata astride his horse; a silver Christening chalice; an old double-handled Swede saw; on and on. When the door squeaked we broke off from trying to determine whether the signature on an abstract-impressionist canvas was Pollock's and met the Dowser in the center of the room.

"Sorry," I said. "Easy to get distracted in here."

"Smith," she said. "And you're Roger."

We stood there like two circus bears awaiting their cues. She sailed off toward the kitchen, trailing behind her a scent of patchouli and curiosity.

"Hey! Wait a minute!" It came out stronger than I had intended. "You said in your letter that we had met four times before. I didn't know what you were talking about, but now I realize you're the lady from the Blue Dog."

"And you're the man I thought was a geologist," she said. "Talking my ear off, all worked up over earthquakes and rocks and how many people were killed in Presidente."

"Killed? I said that?"

"Sure." She started scrubbing the pitcher.

"My mum used to talk about you a lot," Roger said.

She shook the water off her hands and stopped in front of Roger right at that transition point between comfortable and intrusive. "You look just the way she described you."

"This may sound stupid," I said, "but even though I remember talking to you I can't remember your real name."

"Dowser is good, it's what I'm called. And if most people like calling you a certain something, why not allow them to? Confucius said that to have a bad name was to dwell in a low-lying situation, where all the evil of the world flows in on one. So I'm lucky to have had my name changed for me." She touched me on the arm then pulled away toward the stove. "I have to start the omelets."

"Morty!" I blurted. "My real name's Morton Cahoot."

Roger turned full side-on to stare at me.

"You told me that name, too," the Dowser said.

"In public? I don't do that."

Raising his eyebrows at me in passing, Roger shuffled up to the stove. "Please let me help. I feel terrible for showing up empty-handed. Are you're planning on other guests?"

"Somebody'll be by," the Dowser said. "Most every day this is Grand Central."

"I noticed the casitas out back," he said.

"Only the tiny one is a guest house," she said. "Pottery shed, reading room and bathroom are the other three. Not a full bathroom, just a john. Welcome to the frontier. I've thought about putting a toilet in the main house but that would mean an addition and I hate construction so much."

"I don't notice a bedroom, either," Roger said.

"Those doors on the wall hide a Murphy bed," she said. "And what I need to know now is whether you want cold leftover Chinese or cold leftover pizza for brunch." She banged the skillet on the ring and shot a semi-congealed raw-egg mass into the sink. "The stove's out again. One of these days I'm going to lead Sonny into the hills and lose him in a canyon."

When it comes to behavior, genes predispose without predetermining, but something on a Y-chromosome shook itself awake and switched on my male fix-it response and I said, "Let's take a look."

By the time I had the rings off and the top up the Dowser was stacking Chinese take-out on the counter. The fridge must have had a secret panel leading to a cold-storage room because the cartons accumulated like circus clowns piling out of a miniature car.

"Couple more guests." Roger was looking through the back picture window.

The Dowser poked her head around the fridge door. "They're just here for water. We're hooked up with the district but the old well still comes in handy. That's how I got my name. I knew there was water here."

"How'd you figure?" I said.

"Almost any place has water under it if you want to dig deep enough. I picked my spot, that's all. The palm oases along this side of the valley are from faults trapping water in underground pockets. So I got some maps from the USGS and had a well dug. Word spread I dowsed for it."

I took in her wild mane of gray hair gathered in a bulging ponytail, her sandals and brightly colored kaftan, her angular, slightly Roman nose, and was little surprised people responded to her with the ancient tendency to ascribe power to the exotic.

"I stopped trying to convince them otherwise long ago," she said. "We believe what we believe. It's a survival mechanism and a comfort. Personally, I think the best practice is to ignore solutions."

The stove top slipped from my fingers and crashed down. I had been completely distracted, pleasantly so. I still didn't recall talking to her at any length at the Blue Dog, though it's probable I did all the talking, being the great dedicated researcher that I am. Given her name and her letter, I had half-expected to encounter a female Mad Mullah with a zig-zagged millenarian turn of mind, and was relieved to be listening to the kind of thing you hear at three in the morning around the kitchen table while you're waiting for someone to volunteer to go to the all-night corner store for cigarettes. All right, more intelligent than that, but you know what I mean.

Roger had the front door open. "Now they're in one of the trucks."

"They live there," the Dowser said.

Not much to say to that, so I went back to fixing the stove by rapping it with my knuckles and trying the knobs for the forty-eleventh time.

Then the ravens came, assaulting en masse on a wing and a caw. The racket drew us out back under an overhang thatched with palm fronds, and we watched them wheel and dart and settle on benches and the out-buildings and the lip of the well, on power lines and the chain-link fence that delineated two sides of the property. The assemblage seemed pur-poseless; there couldn't have been much feed around, no standing water. They perched without a sound. No preening, no disturbance, just dozens on dozens, maybe a hundred black silhouettes against a tawny mountain background. We held our breaths as they seemed to do and suddenly they were off, dashing for the middle of the property and crossing in overlap-ping streaks, a wave interference pattern of shadows, before ascending and raggedly regrouping and soaring north over the hills.

"Every day," the Dowser said after an interval.

"I'm no expert on corvids," I said. "But it seems like odd behavior."

"I mean generally," she said. "Every day out here I see something with the power to wipe out a week of bad news."

Ringing from inside, and Roger and I waited till the Dowser came back, phone to her ear. She didn't say a word, not even a sure or a yeah to indicate she was following the conversation, until a quick, "Okay, Sonny," before pressing the disconnect.

Hearing the name, I braced for a broadside of idiocy.

"Don't go killing yourself racing home," the Dowser said. "But you should leave. Small fire. It's out now. Sonny stopped by your place to fix a window or something but before he could get started the school called. Minor emergency. His son ate a packet of instant bean soup and swelled up, had to have his stomach pumped. He said some defective wiring started a small fire in your attic while he was gone, but he got back in time to put it out."

"Better get moving." Roger set out around the house.

"Anything else?" I said.

"He wants to know if he can have the carpet you nailed over the patio door. You can reach him at the Blonde Job's. Too bad about Sonny—I'm afraid he's a borderline assholic." She accompanied us to the car and hugged us as though our appearance had capped off a perfect holiday. "Soon, very soon."

I climbed in the car and Roger backed us in a half-circle. He shifted to Drive, and as we pulled away I stuck my head out the window and yelled at the Dowser: "Where do you know Sonny from, anyhow?"

"He's my husband!"

The seatbelt snapped tight across my chest as Roger hit the brakes, but the Dowser had already started back toward the house. Once we bypassed the gate and turned onto the main gravel road Roger floored it and off we tore like . . . well, a house afire.

Husband and wife. We didn't talk about it for ten miles. Like a Christmas cactus, the information needed time in the dark before flowering. When finally we ventured into the tangled territory there were no conclusions, all we did was lace the air with speculation diluted by thoughts of flames and smoke and insurance and . . .

As it turned out, the damage was insignificant. Some charring around the fan's base plate, nothing more, though just in case I climbed into the attic with a hand fire extinguisher and sprayed some carbon-dioxide around. When I staggered away from the foot of the ladder covered in dirt, cobwebs and fiberglass, Roger had two e-mail printouts waiting for me. The look on his face made me reluctant to take the pages.

Dear Mr. Smith,

Let me introduce myself without your having to scroll to the bottom of this offensive e-mail box: Charles H. "Chas" Cassidy.

In lieu of a curriculum vitae and a detailed personal biography, I submit that I am a professional journalist, the humble recipient of over seventeen national and local awards, grants and scholarships.

Recently, I chanced upon your website featuring A Quake in

Time — A Memoir. *Without larding you overmuch with praise, let me say it is one of the finer self-examinations I have happened, or intended, upon. Having recently turned my back on the world of increasing tabloidism, and priding myself on same, I have re-retroed, so to speak, and now seek deeper fulfillment. Serendipity has placed you in my path.*

All writers are deeper than their material; I truly believe this.

My next great project—perhaps the grandest of all—is you. I feel this. I eat it, expel it, then roll around in the scat, wash my shirt and repeat same.

I have no interest in the Presidente disaster per se. It is you, you alone. The heart and the soul and the

That's where it ended, that was it. I glanced at Roger. He raised his eyebrows and I proceded to the second page.

Dear Mr. Smith,

I have to accept that you received the last message.

I count my sister as one of my closest friends, but her sense of humor leaves something to be desired. Setting aside her frivolity, I enjoyed your memoir immensely. I have a few minor accomplishments to my name, though nothing like what my sister claimed in the previous e-mail.

Simply put, I'd very much like to interview you. No pressure, no judgment, nothing taken out of context. If you can rise above my sister's idea of a practical joke, a brief meeting at a time and place of your choosing would both help me and put my mind at ease over this unfortunate incident.

Yours,
Charles H. "Chas" Cassidy

"The second one should make me feel better," I said. "It doesn't."

I couldn't avoid the memories, the ones that made my saliva taste like pennies. After my novel's publication I strapped onto the publicity rocket, which I thought I could ride till it ran out of fuel. But the machinery was too experimental—designed for performance above all, with no safety features—and proved impossible to decelerate, so I leapt over the side and crashed to earth. Now this absurd bit of e-mail business about my second book was resurrecting every moribund emotion, making Chas Cassidy and his sister one with the pack of hounds I should have maced those many years ago. The message had wiped out time, the interval was gone, though any kind of supernatural mucking around with time and space was to be expected. After all, Roger and I had just met a witch.

Every neighborhood I lived in as a kid had a witch, who was so designated after meeting simple criteria: Female, elderly, lived alone, kept to herself. It helped if her lawn and shrubbery were untended because only a witch would be so perverse as to not have gardening implements or so diabolical as to not hire one of us kids to cut her grass. Owning a dog ruled out witchdom, while keeping a cat went far toward confirmation. Dark clothing was important, as was garb out of step with the season— a sweater in July, say, or a light coat in January. And hats? A dozen Hasidim couldn't suffuse us with awareness of the mystical as the neighborhood witch could by wearing one of those black pin-down Victorian hats. She stank, of course, of what we weren't certain. Brimstone, probably, not that any of us knew what that smelled like, though we suspected it was worse than the odor of canvas running shoes after you'd been in the river. In any case, she smelled, that was a given, empirical evidence readily available and awaiting only the day one of us had the nerve to go within a hundred feet of her to find out. Curiously, each neighborhood held only one. If witches actually existed, you'd think statistical clumping would have made some areas a hotbed of the evil old bats, leading to some titanic power struggles, but no, one per neighborhood seemed to be the natural distribution, which was easily construed as meaning they were part of a web presided over by a supreme Dark One. The truth of the matter makes me weak with remorse. Years on earth with so many stories, widowed and alone, always poor and often unable to speak the language, they were ostracized for being one thing alone—different.

"I'm putting the kibosh on this," I said. "I'll send an e-mail saying I don't do interviews and I'm getting rid of the website."

"Right now," Roger said. "I mean it, do it right now. At the rate things are accumulating I'm getting scared to answer the—"

DING-DONG!

"Hold that thought." I theatrically rolled up the e-mail printouts. "If that's Sonny, he's going down."

I would have loved to use my paper weapon on the handyman. Quick thrust of the rolled wad into the throat, follow-up kick to the groin, any other technique I had learned from watching fitness infomercials featuring B-grade strippers pantomiming martial arts moves.

But I guess Sonny was still at the Blonde Job's.

It was Juice.

PART TWO

MISCONDUCT

CHAPTER 11

On my sixteenth birthday my father said, "'Let ye who is without sin cast the first stone.'" Later: "What most people ignore is what He said after that to the adultress—'Go and sin no more.'" He swirled his drink and added, "I wonder how forgiving He really was. Seems to me He was saying, 'Clean up your act, Sister, you might not be so lucky next time.'"

Fortunately, a response wasn't expected. Until he hit the rye my father had been planning my future, grilling me while earnestly assigning points on a 1–10 scale to pro and con columns beside a list of thirty professions, simplistic though harmless enough in that I would no more think of using the scorecard as an employment roadmap than consult tea leaves. So I was having some fun, deliberately distorting the exercise by trying for maximum ambiguity.

When we reached *Firefighter*, I blurted, "I love fire!"

My ardor clearly deserved maximum points, but in which column to enter them? My dad's pen wavered over the paper like a perplexed ouija board planchette until he caught me looking too innocent, at which point he crumpled the list. I felt bad and hung around to make it up to him, but my evident lack of interest in what was good for me made him play catch-up with the bottle and soon he was filling the air with eighty-proof wisdom.

His interpretation of the Biblical passage intrigued me, since I'd never heard him question the views of his Church, which believed the Bible was inerrant yet still provided enough latitude to justify their singular dogma. Well, I say that now, though at sixteen my take on it was simpler—they believed the contradictions in the gospels were all true at the same time. Anyhow, despite being intrigued, I still had no response. I waited a polite interval, added a couple of minutes for safety, then just as I was pushing away from the table my dad's eyes welled with tears he savagely fisted away. I stood and looked down at him.

"Time heals all wounds," he said. "But it sure takes its time about it."

Once untwisted, the statement made rough sense. I don't know if time heals, merely disguises or becomes overwhelmed by more contemporary versions of itself, but my dad was right, it sure sets its own pace.

Noon in Vancouver and raining. I hope the weather isn't putting too much of a damper on the Hari Krishna parade. I could throw on a jacket and check out their party in Stanley Park, but that would mean passing at least thirteen places where I could pick up Cassidy's article. The past few hours have dragged, in contrast to the first couple of months in the Coachella Valley, when I might as well have been wearing a calendar instead of a watch on my wrist. When not bolting from our chairs to handle a fresh complication we were mentally bracing for another. I was faithfully recording what I could on the computer as well as jotting impressions on napkins, interrupting what Roger was saying to scribble on a piece of paper, talking out loud as I walked down the street and trying to remember what I said until I could get home.

A junkie—the one who wears high rubber boots and shorts year-round—crossed Hastings Street a few minutes ago, and as I followed his progress I could have sworn the episode took a full day. It's jarring enough to compare the environment of Vancouver with that of the desert without having to deal with a contrasting sense of time. Yet there it is—time and space, temporal and spatial, in the physical universe different only in dimension.

When I left Roger on the patio and opened the front door and saw Juice standing there I knew it was her right off because she slammed into me, threw her arms around my neck and said, "What a beautiful man you are," something that wouldn't have come from any other mouth.

"You didn't make it is everything okay I was worried and thought maybe something happened to you until I got the e-mail and it didn't explain and—"

"—I'm here now."

We were making such a racket Roger poked his head in to investigate. When I disentangled from Juice and called him over, the first thing he did was check out her tits.

"They're real," she said. "I was kidding in the e-mail." She put her hands on his shoulders and kissed him hard on the mouth.

As she stepped back I expected to see Roger rigid with . . . fear? embarrassment? affrontery? . . . he laughed.

"Roger," she said as if discovering a birth parent.

"Juice," he said, and laughed again.

"Look at this place. I love it." She launched into an unguided tour, showing as much appreciation for the bare walls and old-lady furniture as Roger and I had for the Dowser's museum. When she reached the patio door she touched the carpet and said, "Neat idea," which may have been carrying the praise a bit far.

"How was the trip?" Roger said.

"Whoa! Highly recommend taking a bus down the coast."

"Are you hungry? I could fix you something to—"

"—Starving." She beat us both to the fridge, and in something under a minute had a leftover chicken sandwich made and was tearing into it while continuing her tour of the house.

I caught up to Juice as she was opening the folding doors to the laundry alcove. She examined the washer and dryer as if they'd been hand-picked for decorative effect, nodded and left me to close up. When I got to my room she was sitting on the bed. I had barely flicked the door closed when she grabbed me by the hips, pulled my walking shorts to my ankles and took my cock in her mouth. Fortunately or otherwise, I didn't last long. I put my hand on her shoulder to keep from buckling at the knees and continued the pressure until she was on her back and she kissed me and I tasted myself, and then like a phantom she escaped from underneath and before I could get my shorts up was out the door. With the concentration of a lame drunk on a tightrope, I put one foot in front of the other down the hall.

"I just have to check my messages," Juice said, flying past me back into the bedroom and parking at the computer.

I ducked outside to wait with Roger.

He flicked his eyes at my crotch. "Your lipstick's smeared."

We listened to Juice cursing at the computer inside.

"Be honest," I said. "Am I reaping the whirlwind?"

"Maybe it's just fresh air."

"Does she remind you of anyone?"

In a nonspecific way I was reminded of my wife. It wasn't her looks—Juice muscled like an athlete and dark, my wife fair and schoolmarmish—and so far she'd certainly shown none of my wife's inhibitions and seriousness. Really not sure.

"No," Roger said with emphasis. "Well, she does, but not her."

"Then maybe the woman I invented. In the novel. The woman who had no name."

"Her," he said.

"You hated that character."

"Listen, she's not your wife reincarnated and she certainly isn't someone from your novel, so it stands to reason you've created in your mind an image of . . ."

"What? Image of what? What are you grinning at?"

"Take a close look at her."

"Trust me, I've looked." I couldn't resist pushing aside the carpet and looking again.

"There." She almost ran into me before ducking under my arm.

"Any interesting e-mails?" Roger said.

"Nothing," she said. "Perfect."

"Hey!" I said. The jet hair, the dark dark eyes. "Wait a minute—too weird."

Roger laughed. Juice joined in uncertainly while I gaped like a bludgeoned frog.

"What gives?" she said.

"You drive a red Falcon," I said.

"Did."

"The Hari Krishna parade," I said. "You rammed the float. Try telling me you're not the one who rammed the goddamn float."

"Oh that," she said. "The transmission got stuck in martini."

"Roger and I watched the whole thing. You were with a guy who took a cymbal in the head. From the second I opened the door I've been wracking my brains trying to figure out where I'd seen you before."

"I'm glad it's clear to you," she said. "I sure don't remember you from the parade, but you're familiar, too. We must have met somewhere, crossed paths in another life."

"I don't believe in past lives."

"I didn't say past, just another."

"The parade and now here," I said. "What an odd feeling coincidence gives you."

"As long as there's feeling." She kissed me and kept it up till I squirmed.

When she pulled away Roger said, "How did you get here, by the way?"

"Got a ride from some guy at the bus station. I couldn't climb over the gate with my bag."

"I'll go," Roger said.

"We'll all go," she said.

She jumped between us, linked arms, and three abreast we walked down the middle of the road, Juice enthusing over the flowers, trees, houses, comments she gushed and repeated even after we reached the gate and discovered her bag was missing. She could have lost lint from her pocket for all the effect it had.

"Nothing important in there," she said. "Let's keep going."

Alongside the pool enclosure Juice unlinked elbows, scaled the iron fence, stripped off her shorts and checked work shirt and jumped in the water in her underwear. I could almost hear venetian blinds opening, curtains parting, lens covers popping off binoculars. She didn't dawdle, just a quick dip to refresh and back into the shorts, toweling off with the shirt. Her bra was patterned and could have been mistaken for a swimsuit top, albeit one with a hole exposing half a nipple.

"This is great," she said after she'd scrambled back over the fence. Putting her hands in her leather tire-tread sandals, she clapped them together like a kid all the way back to the house.

Once there she declined all proposals to explore, evincing no interest in the valley's attractions—neither geographical nor standard round of boutiques and restaurants—and though Roger tried mightily he eventually ran out of ideas and with a shade of exasperation said, "There's nothing *at all* you want to do?"

"Do?" She looked around as if maybe an item of importance had slipped by her. "Aren't we doing something?"

"We can head up to the drugstore later," I said. "Get you a toothbrush and stuff."

"You have a blender? One of those girlie drinks and some Jimmy Buffet music would be perfect."

I ducked inside, already looking ahead. Sooner rather than later Roger would ask me how long Juice was staying, and I would only push the privilege of friendship so far. Back outside I was hit with hard evidence of the evil of blender drinks—the preparation time multiplies the chances of missing something. Roger was into his portion of the basic introductory conversation, and I didn't want another word to slip by.

". . . known each other for years in Vancouver."

"Here they are," I said loudly, trying to catch Roger's eye.

He didn't so much as glance at me, just picked up his drink, silently toasted Juice and continued: "Anyhow, Smith and I lost touch for a while. We'd run into each other whenever I'd come down here with my mum but we didn't really get close till she died, when she left me the house and … well, with the personal growth Smith did after the earthquake, I mean, he was the perfect guy to help me through the tough times of my own. So, uh, we're just hanging out here now."

Not bad, Roger. Keep it simple.

Juice set her drink on the table and turned to me. "So where you lived, the town, it had an earthquake?"

"Uh … yeah, the one I wrote about."

"Presidente—that's here in California?"

Right there, right at that point is where I should have nipped it in the bud. Okay, it was past budding stage, but the roots would have come up easily by hand. What was I up to in the first place? Of the thousands of books I've read in my life not one has come close to impregnating me with the need to re-type the fucking thing. Early in his massive study of civilization Will Durant stuck his tongue in his cheek and suggested there might have been a class of professional artists among paleolithic men, Bohemians starving in the less respectable caves, denouncing the commercial bourgeoisie, plotting the death of academies and forging antiques. That's me, I suppose, still part of the human bush but out on one of the rattier branches.

Then the phone rang and I answered it and told Sonny he couldn't have the carpet till he'd fixed the door and called him a liar for saying his wife lived in New Mexico when we'd just met her the day before and gave him a right royal ration of shit for setting the house on fire and hung up.

When I got back outside Roger and Juice were halfway up the green-belt, laughing away, Roger with the post-performance relief of a bad actor. I leaned back with a drink, wondering how long to wait before kicking over the basilisk of baloney I'd created and start trusting, well, anyone. Juice for starters.

CHAPTER 12

Christmas music was polluting the air far ahead of the season as I hurried down the drugstore aisle, running a gantlet of wrapping paper, ribbons, red-and-green geegaws, and just as I was launching into my annual inner rant on the evils of commercialism, it dawned on me it was the middle of December, only a couple of weeks from the big birthday bash itself.

Two months had been stolen from under my nose, a loss explained by the attention it took to keep up to Juice. When in motion she set a driving pace, and even in repose her potential energy simmered at the surface, galvanizing those around her. The world ticked along at its usual rate—unseen hands continually inverting the hourglass—but it was happening out There, while our little household relied on clocks set to Juicetime.

And then it tapered off. As the days lost their blaze and the nights grew longer and cooler, gaining a hard desert crystalline edge, Juice finally slowed to a human's pace, and I went her one better, responding with near-hibernation. I stopped reading the paper, couldn't tell you whether the TV was working, in fact the only worldly entertainment came a couple of hours a day when Roger and Juice tuned in National Public Radio for the afternoon mélange of exotic music, the two of them huddled around the stereo like resistance fighters awaiting a call to rise on Radio Free Europe. Roger and Juice had become fast friends, and I admit to a pang of jealousy, as I was undergoing the initial flush of love that requires the undivided attention of the beloved. Overjoyed that this new woman and my best friend were fitting together? You bet. Juvenile resentment over not being the center of attention? That, too.

Juice and me? Thrilling to be with and I loved her and she made me laugh and she was kind and had enviable core values and we were wonderful together in bed but damnit why couldn't I quit trying so hard?

My wife felt I never approved of anything she did except for her writing. Funny-strange, because it was precisely the reverse. I liked her writing, though the jottings and musings and observances were second rank compared to the overall brilliance of her actual self. However, the charge of disapproval had harried me since her death and I wouldn't have it leveled again by Juice. "That's got my approval," I said many times. "I really approve of your take on life," too often was my comment. For variety: "I've always approved of that approach." Once, I got up in the middle of the night to look out the window and Juice reached around my waist with lotion on her hand and started masturbating me. "Now that's something I approve of," was out of my mouth before I could shut down my brain's speech center. She didn't stop, though I detected a hint of violent re-invigoration in her stroking.

By the way, there was a simple explanation for why Juice knew nothing about Presidente and never asked me about the earthquake—she'd read hardly any of the book. "Sort of skimmed it except for the sad parts," is how she put it. "Enough to make me fall in love with you, that's for sure."

It came out on a day I returned from the mailbox and found her lying on the bed flipping through *And the Sea Shook the Rock*. I didn't bother asking where she'd found Nuttall's book because I knew—beneath my socks and underwear, right where I'd hidden it on the day Juice showed up. I snuggled beside her on the bed and she dropped G.H. Nuttall and when we were done making love I casually mentioned my book and all I got was "Sort of skimmed it except for the sad parts."

Few things are more difficult than telling the truth when it's not required. I again missed an opportunity to own up, and went back to approving Juice to a pulp.

After that, time vaporized. Our days were filled with plain living, and other than Roger's steady progress on his clients' tax accounts nothing practical was accomplished, a difficult state to maintain given that my background had infected me on some level with the grim Protestant work ethic.

Sonny's infection was of the type usually in remission, though something must have happened for the virus to flare up, because one day he hauled himself over, re-wired the ceiling fan, repaired the drywall, painted over the scorch marks, untacked the carpet and installed a new pane of glass in the patio door, excellent work. However, he did it all with hardly a word. When someone that garrulous clams up it gives me the same creepy feeling as when a dog growls at nothing, though I didn't want to call attention to anything except Sonny's job at hand so stood back and let him have at it.

Then I saw Juice coming back from the pool and braced myself for their first meeting. Here we go, I thought, Sonny's going to speak on impulse and Juice'll respond with her usual openness and Sonny'll come back with a piggish retort and Juice'll fling it back in his face and Sonny'll climb down the ladder to got a better look at her bra's tit-hole and Juice'll laugh and Sonny'll take it as condescension and Juice won't bother to explain otherwise and there I'll be, in the middle and up the creek at the same time, forced into defending Juice while avoiding a punch-up with Sonny in the kitchen. Happy-go-lucky, Sonny yet had a rough tavern air about him. My guess was he would say he hated fighting, would never start a fight, had never started a fight, philosophically didn't believe in fighting, yet frequently ended up fighting—that kind of guy.

And here she was. Black hair wet and hanging, dark dark eyes shining, in her swimsuit bottoms and the bra with the hole at the nipple, she came through the door and the handyman looked down from the ladder and said, "Hey," and Juice said, "Yeah," and kept going to the bedroom.

Oh. All that adrenaline and nowhere for it to go. Sonny was still up the ladder with his back to me when I asserted the minimum masculinity required by giving him the hairy eyeball, squinting my eyes like an action star—*That's right, buddy, deal with this look if you're man enough. Go ahead and pull that gun, skin that cat, fuck the bystanders and let's get it on*—before quickly averting my eyes when he glanced down.

Roger paid him in cash, which almost got him talking again, but after, "The best, Rog, the best," he was gone, bottoming out on the speed bump on the way to the gate.

My journal-keeping had become as unreliable as my track of time, so I can only estimate Sonny's visit was five or six days before Martin showed up with Juice's bag. I held the door for him and he entered with that look of barely suppressed pride universal in bearers of good news.

"I found it on my rounds," he said. "Well, not on my rounds because I was off shift, but I was still rounding, or going around, I mean. Someone had dumped it in the maintenance area by the pool."

"Martin, right?" Juice said. "Roger pointed you out the other day. Thank you, Martin. You're my new hero."

She brushed off the cobwebs and unzipped and upended the bag, dumping out a man's shaving kit, a change of underwear and a pair of jeans.

"I guess they took everything of value," Martin said, as if he were responsible.

"Nothing missing," Juice said. "Now what can I do to thank you? Honestly, let me treat you to dinner or something, or is that like a kickback to the police?"

Martin chuckled and wiped a pint of liquid uncertainty from his head.

"You eat, right?" she added. "Then it's a date."

"I almost forgot," Martin said to Roger and me. "As of today, Christmas lights and other decorations are allowed on your house. I should have waited for the meeting, except I guess I can trust you guys to keep it under your hats until the official announcement."

"What meeting?" Roger said.

"Gosh, the agendas were mailed two weeks ago. You should have received yours way before now. Anyhow, it's tomorrow. I hope that gives you enough time to prepare."

"We'll stay up all night if necessary."

"It's at the pool. Sarah thinks we'll get a better turnout if we keep it casual instead of using the community center boardroom. Seven a.m. It's early, but even this time of year the sun gets too strong for some of our seniors." He returned his attention to Juice. "Even though you're just visiting, you're more than welcome to sit in with us."

"Thanks," Juice said lightly, "but I hate that kind of shit."

Martin ran his hands down the seams of his Honey Badger Security uniform pants.

"Nothing personal," she added.

After we had waved ourselves silly seeing Martin on his way around the corner, Juice said, "That'll do it. I have enough left to buy Martin a burrito at a cheap Mexican place then it's either back to Vancouver or find a job."

"Oh, for God's sake," Roger said. "If you don't know by now that you're welcome to share, you're not very good at picking up vibes. We love you, girl, so don't insult us."

"Still," she said on the way in, "I'm starting to feel like a slug. It's neat hanging with you guys but I have to do something."

Despite my promise to Martin we went to bed early without cramming for the meeting, leaving till the morning a resolution on how to deal with the shame. When the newspaper arrived, for the first time since Juice's arrival I spread it out on the patio table and read it front to back. While Roger took his turn at the paper I took a turn at Juice, and after we all showered and finished off the coffee, it was shindig time. Juice bid us bye and started bashing ants with the rolled-up paper.

On the way to the pool Roger told me I looked eager, and if I truly was, the only thing I could put it down to was the need to re-engage with the world after two months. If that was the case, it was a short engagement.

On our arrival there were eight people inside the fence, four of them in the hot tub. Roger and I dragged a couple of patio chairs to where we could see the mountains. We sat.

Five minutes before the scheduled start a low babble announced the arrival of the main group, twenty citizens good and true carrying hard-backed chairs and a small lectern, Sarah Kolachuk chivvying the few laggards like an impatient schoolteacher. We stood.

The set-up looked well rehearsed, and once they were arranged on the deck at the shallow end of the pool, standing with their hands behind their backs, Sarah took her position behind the lectern. Apparently, these were our representatives, and the six of us remaining after the hot-tubbers bolted positioned our chairs to face them. We sat.

At a gesture from Sarah, we stood.

Our reps led us in the Anthem. At its conclusion everyone remained standing, as though offering a moment of silence for past Board members who given their lives, the ultimate sacrifice, so the rest of us could live without leaves on our driveways and cars parked in the cul-de-sacs. We sat.

A pile of handouts—*THIS QUARTER'S BUSINESS*—was passed around and returned to the front. The first page held the lineup:

Board: 3 persons, elected annually

Committees:
Architectural (exterior alterations) 1 person, elected annually
(Subcommittee – appearance) 1 person, elected annually

Landscaping (trees, shrubs, lawns) 1 person, elected annually
(Subcommittee – flowers) 1 person, elected annually

Secretarial (computer) 1 person, elected annually
(Subcommittee – printing) 1 person, elected annually

Financial (accounting) 1 person, elected annually
(Subcommittee – fines) 1 person, elected annually

Events (national holidays) 1 person, elected annually
(Subcommittee – garage sales) 1 person, elected annually

Motor Vehicles (registration) 1 person, elected annually
(Subcommittee – parking) 1 person, elected annually

Environmental (wild animals) 1 person, elected annually
(Subcommittee – pets) 1 person, elected annually

General: 3 persons, appointed

No names were included, making it impossible to sort out who was which or whom was in charge of what or whatever. The second page looked to have motions and proposals, and the third through sixth held the list of compound rules in a dwarfish font. On the last page was a poem about duty and honor and love and peace and war and family and tradition in perfectly rhyming couplets I could have sworn I'd read somewhere on a shithouse wall. The whole stapled piece of business was poorly printed on cheap paper, so Secretarial (Subcommittee – printing) was likely under Financial (accounting) in overall authority.

Something important was afoot. Sarah had the sides of the lectern in a death grip, and the committee heads were staring at us like political officers attached to Red Army units. It was my first such meeting and I was determined to remain neutral, so whatever neurochemical event in my brain made my hand go up must have been involuntary.

Sarah stared at my hand as if it had appeared out of nowhere and was floating unattached in the air. Long seconds passed. "Well, okay," she said. "Mr. Smith?"

"Smith."

"Smith, then."

"This is my first meeting, so please forgive my ignorance."

"Your ignorance is noted."

Ooooo . . . very good. I had to give her points for that one. This wasn't the smarmy Sarah who intermittently appeared with oblique criticism at the front door.

"I was wondering about the appointees," I said. "Why they're the only ones not elected, and what their duties consist of."

In a blur, Sarah was two paces to the side and an elderly man was at the podium. I'd seen him around the neighborhood, always pressed and polished and wearing a straw hat he lifted to ladies on their powerwalks.

"You're the Canadian," he said.

"Me and Roger," I said, liberal with the blame.

"To put it in terms you're familiar with from your parliamentary system, they are Ministers Without Portfolio."

Damn. They had a ringer.

He sat and Sarah returned. "Now to proceed with this quarter's new business. . . ."

My evil hand went up again. It must have been a transplant my body was rejecting. "Point of order."

"Smith."

"Isn't it customary to begin by reading the minutes? I think I speak for all of us when I say a recap of the last meeting would provide an important transition."

The other five couldn't have made it clearer I didn't speak for them if their chairs had been on casters and they'd pushed off to the fence.

The old man was half out of his seat, but Sarah fielded this one. "The same point has been raised in the past. Experience shows that when old business is discussed before the new, many of the past issues have been solved by new proposals, and we're trying to eliminate redundancy by forging ahead. Our community is 'forward-moving' and 'progressively conservative,' and it's plain the term 'old business' is exactly that, interfering in our drive to increase property values in the face of competition from new developments and home-building starts throughout the valley."

"Sounds good to me," I said.

I was getting ferocious stares from the Politburo. Aside from Sarah and the other two members of the Board, and possibly the appointees, Roger and I were already in trouble with Architectural (Subcommittee – appearance) and had drawn the attention of Financial (Subcommittee – fines) now that the carpet was off the patio door and back to its spot leaning against the outside of the house.

"This quarter's business," Sarah said.

Roger leaped to his feet. "Oh! Oh, dear—I left a pot of water on the stove! If a fire started with the homes this close together . . . !"

Roger, of all people, Roger, the little prick, was going to abandon me. I shot my chair across the deck in straightening my legs and grabbed a fistful of his shirt. "Not the big pot?" I said. "The big steel cauldron that takes two people to lift?"

I beat him out the gate and he didn't catch up to me till I was two houses from our place. As he fell in beside me I said, "I must have been out of my mind letting you drag me there."

Right then I experienced déjà vu. My mind may have only partially encoded something I had experienced and become confused by similar triggers, but then many times I had watched an hour of a movie until realizing I had already seen it before, and furthermore had bought books before it dawned on me I had them in my collection, and those cases never gave me the tingly hair-rising-on-the-nape sensation, so it wasn't just incomplete coding or faulty memory. One thing I know for certain is that I fall victim to déjà vu only when my mind is on full boil. Things wouldn't stay placid much longer.

Close to home we waved at Tina—one of the few neighbors whose name I remembered—as she drove past. We hopped over the curb and cut to the house and Tina stopped and reversed, pulling alongside the patio and sticking her head out the window.

"I've been meaning to ask you guys over to dinner. Anytime now, just waiting for my remodel to be done."

I couldn't help it: "Your contractor isn't a guy called Sonny, is he?"

"One and the same."

"Tina," I said, "I don't quite know how to ask you this. . . ."

She grinned but didn't help.

"You wouldn't by any chance be . . . I don't know, this is stupid, never mind."

"Yeah," she said. "I'm the Blonde Job."

I took a moment to compose what I said next: "I suppose it's occurred to Sonny that you're black."

"Don't know if it has or not." She drove off.

With the strenuous meeting out of the way, we whipped up a massive breakfast and dug in. Since finding a hatchling lizard on the back wall a month ago, Roger had acquired an interest in reptiles, and as we layered salsa and sauces and syrups onto our pancakes and eggs and french toast, Roger leafed through a book on southwest fauna, occasionally muttering "chuckwalla," and other names that sounded like the noises coming from my stomach.

He'd taken to spending up to an hour each evening watching the western toad as it emerged from under the patio and set off foraging, so his newfound fascination for reptiles had already spread to include amphibians. For the first time, he was gaining appreciation for the beauty in scientific detail as opposed to general observation. My love of nature started when I was young, and I used to spend countless hours poring over textbooks and magazines, though always to the tune of my old man drumming his fingers on the table from both sheer irritation and the evidence I was getting too chummy with this Darwin fellow.

It was a different sort of hobby that had me worried about Roger, and after cleaning up the breakfast mess we had some time together while Juice went to the pool to see if the meeting was over so she could have a swim. Cautiously, I raised the issue of Roger's storytelling. On many occasions I'd heard him shoveling a load of foolishness onto Juice. Nothing serious, just tales of and references to his past that I knew weren't true. Being more than a novice in the area, I cautioned him on lying's spiral effect, salting my sermon with examples of his inventions, only to have him reply that they were nothing of the sort, sincerely enough to be convincing. I was stuck on a shelf. I'd been acting on the assumption I knew pretty much everything there was to know about my friend, so to hear fresh revelations after all this time and furthermore as a third party . . . anyhow, I feigned unconcern and told him I had to send an e-mail and lurched to my feet, suddenly feeling lonely.

"Hey," Roger said, "that was a strong one."

I stopped in the doorway.

"Déjà vu," he said.

I kept going through the house to the desk, not at all happy with the coincidence.

Once the computer was up and humming my e-mail fell upon Charles H. "Chas" Cassidy from an immense height at great speed. I began nicely enough. After accepting his apology for his sister's sending the first ridiculous message, I offered words of praise for his reputation and the sensitivity shown in his follow-up e-mail. I politely declined his request for an interview, explaining how busy I was, how out of touch with the world I'd become while working on my notes for a new project, but it wasn't long till I was pounding the keyboard, trying to scare him off with language Colombian drug lords reserve for photographers. I ended abruptly, punched SEND and swore at the monitor.

There. I shut it down. One solid step toward taking control. If I was right, if events chose once again to accelerate, at least it wouldn't be me providing the impetus.

CHAPTER 13

Looked as though Martin's job description included errand-running. Still in uniform, he dropped by the next morning at eleven, well past his bedtime after night shift, to drop off a summary of the homeowners meeting. Presumably to flesh out the attendance roll, Roger and I and the four hot-tubbers had been included on the list, though with asterisks affixed to our names—again, presumably—to highlight our lack of stamina for the full proceedings.

The day after that Martin was kind enough to bring over a length of picture wire and an assortment of screws, which meant we were expected to shake the black widows out of the wreath he'd given us and hang it on the front door. It was a job too painful to defer, so I did it immediately, after which Martin and I stood back and agreed the multi-language WELCOME sash needed something to bring it in step with the Christmas season.

The next day Martin dutifully did so, glueing on a sprig of holly, in the process knocking off the glass suguaro flagpole. I poured us a small egg nog apiece and we toasted his malignant bush.

The next day he came by empty-handed and apologized for interrupting whatever I was doing, after which he proceeded to interrupt whatever I was doing, for forty minutes jawing about terrorists as though they were a distinct ethnic group that should be banned from country club membership.

And when I went to answer the door the next day—starting to wish there would never again be a next day and wondering what in hell we hadn't covered—instead of Martin there was Sonny in all his glory, the Bonneville afterfiring in the driveway.

"Can't you shut that thing off?" I said.

He left it to die in its own blood and oil and flicked the back of his hand to send me into the house. "Just what I thought," he said, stopping hands on hips just inside the door. "Bigger, Smitty, bigger. Need a makeover, like a wall of mirrors to make it bigger-looking. Carpet's old, tile or wood or something'd be way better. Paint job. Mirrors are the most important, everybody in the valley's got them. Not saying it's a dump, not saying that, just fix it up like the rich gay guys do."

"The rich gay guys."

"Always got money those guys. No expert, just done a bunch of remodels for the gay guys over the years. Most people don't like what they do but the more time you spend with people the more you understand. Example is most people don't know the gay guys golf."

"Now you're stretching it."

"Serious. Golfing crazies, lots of them. Money and time on their hands and none got kids, okay a few, but you get me."

"I want to be sure I'm following the logic," I said. "Major premise—mirrors make a house look bigger. Minor premise—many homosexuals golf. Conclusion—Roger and I should hire you to remodel our house."

"Premises, huh? See? Education, that's what I tell my kids all the time. Sure you're not gay? Lots of them are educated. No big deal if you are. And even though you got the girl here it don't prove nothing, nothing new there, most of the NFL got wives don't change the ass-grabbing in the locker room. Nothing against it but hey, you got money on a playoff game that comes down to a field goal who do you want kicking—straight or unstraight?"

By then he was in the middle of the living room, assessing his future job site.

"Is there anything I can do for you?" I said. "I get the feeling you're not here just trying to drum up business."

He poked the wall with his finger as though expecting it to crumble at any moment. "Close to Christmas, just dropping in. I hear you met the Blonde Job."

"Another ex-wife to be?"

"Got no ex's," Sonny said. "Still married to the first one in New Mexico."

"What about the Dowser?"

"Different kind of thing," Sonny said. "Legal or not don't know, just a promise sort of business, Dowser's bizarro religion. The kids love her like their real mom. Saxon and Delilah hardly don't see the real one anymore. Other kid either."

"It must be tough on them."

"Tougher the old way. No good the kids grow up like me, an old lady like mine. Never met my daddy, killed to bits in a gas explosion in a

Pennsylvania mine. Mom all pregnant with me visiting the boyfriend in Deetroyit. Then after it was pretty rough, a lady like that trying to be a mommy and a daddy at the same time, all she knew about dadding was beatings from her own and that."

I looked at the wall and poked it where Sonny had. For all my father's nonsense and lack of accomplishment, his little world was at least his own, and he did a remarkable job of not exporting what evils it held to mine. I never once felt his hand in anger. My reverie was broken by a startled shriek from out front.

"Got him a robber," Sonny said.

Juice was standing with her back to a fan palm twenty feet from the Bonneville. Jammed halfway through the car window was Sonny's dog, Boston Charlie, slobbering and emitting an eerie growl-whine and waving his front legs like hirsute insect antennae as he tried to gain purchase on thin air. Roger, laden with several bags and a spray of cut flowers, was on the street in front of the Neon. Of the four of us, it was Juice who recovered first. She set her grocery bag down and reached inside.

The first egg was high and outside and arced over the car, splattering on the trunk of the neighbor's honey mesquite. The second just missed the dog's head, whistling past his ear into the car and spreading like a dumdum on contact with a bag of tile grout. Juice looked deadly serious, pushing off with her rear foot and coming hard over the top with each throw. The third egg hit the passenger door and the metallic Boom! caught the beast's attention enough for him to stop his rebel growl. By the time Sonny reached the car Boston Charlie was licking the mess from the second egg off the interior, ingesting great swaths of stucco mix and powder and dirt from the metal and vinyl.

Wacky as the situation was, it held no humor. Roger and I chuckled anyhow to ease the tension and converged on Juice, who was rising with a large can of jalapeños from the grocery bag. I altered my route and positioned myself on a line between her and the car and held up my hands as if surrendering. Without a word and with her eyes focused beyond me, she left the bag where it lay and with white knuckles carried the can into the house.

Sonny should have said his goodbyes and driven off, but no— showing wisdom equivalent to his pet's, he followed us inside and stood scratching his ass at the kitchen entrance. He backed up a step when Juice came charging down the hall from our bedroom.

"All right," she said. "All right, I had a bad experience with dogs when I was a kid, all right? All right?"

"Dog thought you was robbing," Sonny said.

Roger was flush and flustered and busied himself by sorting the groceries on the table. He had already hidden the jalapeños.

Juice reached around him, plucked a package of Marlboros from the bag and lit up. "First one in a year." She sucked and blew and spat in the sink. "Sickening."

Sonny's mouth opened as he watched the smoke rise and spread. He couldn't have been more fixated if the tendrils were rising from a sacred fire.

Juice held out the pack. "Peace pipe?"

"Nope." His hand went to his shoulder.

"On the patch?" Juice said.

"Used to. Got too high with the patch and the nicotine gum and the cigarettes all at the same time. How'd you quit a whole year? Tried everything, me. The hypnotizing, the acupuncture . . . did the cold turkey thing but found I was going through a loaf of bread every day, burning it in the toaster then hanging around the kitchen sucking the smoke."

Juice dragged.

"Substitution plan now," he said. "Experts say the urge for a butt don't last long, should replace it with something else till it goes away."

"Carrying around a bag of carrot sticks or something to nibble on?" Juice said.

Sonny shook his head. "Mostly I want a cig too bad and have a beer instead. Works so far. Used to go through a pack a day or more sometimes, so get twenty-thirty beers in you, you can't smoke. Burned my face a couple times trying, set my shirt all on fire and that."

The vibes of impatience from Roger were growing too heavy to ignore, and as I mentally scrolled down my list of ways to politely give someone the bum's rush, Sonny started to wrap it up himself.

"Anyhoo," he said to Juice. "Like to make it up to you, the attacking thing, my dog."

"Make it up to me? Sure, buy Martin dinner. I owe him and I'm broke."

"Not a guy you really go out with somewhere, Martin."

"I'm kidding. You don't have to do anything. It's a thing between me and dogs."

"Broke though, kidding too?"

"No such luck."

"Always need helpers. Good with power tools or electricals and plumbing and drywalling and that? Tile a floor put up a chandelier fix a fence? White guys mostly run off right when they get paid Friday and don't show up the next week till Tuesday. Too much steady social drinking. Mexicans're hard workers and always there for day hire, but can't blame them they can't usually speak English. Could teach you the technicals about everything while starting you off holding stuff up and passing me nails and that."

"What's the pay?" Juice said.

"Wait a minute," I said.

Roger stopped rearranging the tins and packages on the table and planted himself in front of Juice. "I'm not having you down on your knees and up a ladder all day. You're a guest. If you fell off a roof into a cactus bed or something, I'd never forgive myself."

Sonny snorted. "No problems with the cactus, Rog. Charge extra for outside work near cactuses then before the ladder goes up cut everything down. Tell the owner I pruned the rot, no charge." He turned to Juice. "Going rate for day guys is about six."

"I've been checking around," Juice said. "It's more like ten."

"Man, that's something. Can't believe I'm paying a guy eight, but take it or leave it."

"I need an advance," Juice said.

It was the first time I'd seen Sonny laugh without restraint. He wheezed to a stop and rubbed his face vigorously with both hands. "Tomorrow."

"I need work clothes."

"Yeah, probably not so good nailing baseboard at some billionaire's house in the bra with the titty-hole. Only a couple of working days till Christmas. Job tomorrow, if the owner advances me I advance you."

Like an expert host with socially inept guests, Roger had managed to steer the circle of us to the front door.

"Seven in the morning," Sonny said to Juice. "Pick you up, not every day."

The second the door closed Roger was on Juice like an aunt on an orphaned niece. "You have no health coverage down here. If you're determined to chip in you could at least pick a job that won't leave you maimed."

109

"I know what I'm doing," she said, and before Roger could respond she added, "I'm going to have a cold beer, like a working girl," and headed for the kitchen.

Something out back caught her attention, and Roger and I joined her at the sliders. Careering down the street, the Bonneville ran into the curb and blew the left front tire. Boston Charlie was scrabbling on Sonny's lap, one leg thrust through the steering wheel, another pawing the air out the driver's window, expelling otherworldly dialog from a John Carpenter film, unaffected by Sonny's frantic punches. Juice jumped when I put my hand on her hip then went to the fridge while Roger and I stayed tuned at the door. With a lurch back to its lane, the Bonny shed the remaining rubber from the wheel and roared out through the gates, sparks from the rim jetting eight feet into the clear desert air.

Doorbell.

"God damn it!" Roger said. "I hate this. Can't we have one moment of peace? I mean . . . damn it!"

Juice and I leaned against the kitchen counter and shared her beer. "I think it's a great idea," I lied.

Roger came around the corner and spread his hands palms-up to Juice. She gave me some Christmas cheer by squeezing my package before going to the door. I didn't peek around the corner for over eight seconds.

". . . a full member of our community. A friend of an HOA member is a friend of ours. Of course, in a society like ours there are responsibilities that go along with the benefits."

The Boardhead waved at me over Juice's shoulder, and Roger and I stepped out into plain view. Not that Sarah cared either way.

"Now, if you take a moment to read the rules and regulations, you'll find under the section 'Pool and Spa' the subsection 'Attire.' This is not to be confused with a dress code. If you bypass the 'Footwear' sub-subsection and check the entry for 'Body: upper/lower,' you'll see that Item 4 proscribes undergarments for pool and spa use."

"No underwear in the pool," Juice said.

"You have such a positive attitude," Sarah said.

"What about thongs? I haven't worn mine yet. The boys have been showing me so many things in your beautiful valley I haven't had a minute to myself to shave my bush."

Attagirl, Juice. I bent my wrist and Roger gave me a surreptitious low-five.

"I understand," Sarah said. "And of course the embarrassment increases the more often you spread your legs."

Ooooo . . . Sarah Kolachuk scores with the goalie pulled, sending the game into overtime.

A long pause ensued, and I imagined Juice wishing she still held the can of jalapeños. But she surprised me by raising her Tecate can.

"Want a beer?" she said. "I'll meet you out back. You can take me to see your house."

Sarah beamed and powerwalked out of sight.

Juice went to the bedroom and returned with my backpack. She loaded it with cans. "Be back in a while, guys."

We could find nothing to say so stepped aside and watched her leave through the sliders and tightrope along the curb beside Sarah, who was on safer ground striding the tarmac, until they reached Sonny's skidmark. Retrieving a two-foot length of radial tire that had ripped off the Bonny, Juice tried it on her head at various angles until settling on the traditional front-to-back look and continuing along with her new friend.

"And that's that," Roger said.

"That it is."

What "that" was neither of us knew, though we suspected it was the same as what had sprouted between Juice and Sonny, whatever that "that" was. The nature of it was ultimately unimportant—it was grounded in the woman herself, her identity, as honest as the naked rocks, and it illustrated how monstrous it would be of me to continue even the slightest charade. The fear of getting caught in a lie, any lie, was something I had lived with for so long, experienced so continuously, it had lost its effectiveness, so no, far from dread of disclosure I just had to tell Juice the truth because she deserved it. I'd tell her, that's all there was to it, I'd tell her everything.

As much as was prudent.

CHAPTER 14

How refreshing to tell the truth. Mind you, I hadn't told any of it yet, but just knowing it was on the horizon put a spring in my step.

Respect for my wife was the base of our relationship. The peaks of emotion were susceptible to erosion, the jagged edges succumbing with time to irresistible outside elements that softened the profile—a leveling effect, fascination changing to appreciation, euphoria to friendship, our lovemaking from poetry to punctuation. There was acceptance of the natural process and a new type of love from the metamorphosis. Through it all, the disappointments and annoyances and grievances were buried, and while we no longer looked down on the world from a great height, neither did we have far to look up. My only lies to her were incomplete truths. She wanted to know everything about me, but I was reluctant to share snippets and false conclusions and dead ends. To cede all of me, I had to know what was inside, or it would be no better than leaving a lottery ticket in her Christmas stocking—*Here ya go, babe, good luck.*

The upshot was that I lost the ability to respond to two important questions from my wife: "What are you thinking?" and "How are you feeling?" I took them seriously, and each time would pause, consider, look at her from across the playing field and say, "Fucked if I know."

I woke when Juice returned from Sarah's just before midnight, a hellish time to be up and about in the compound. Other than the rare aquanut determined to enjoy every minute of pool time right to the swimming curfew and hosts forced to keep an eye on merrymaking guests from up north, the only person consistently up late was some crazy on the perimeter of the compound whose lights could be seen shining through the blinds well past the witching hour of nine-thirty. He was a renter, which went far to explaining—not forgiving—his eccentric behavior. He was sighted every few days wheeling through the gates in a gargantuan sport utility vehicle with glass so tinted it could have held anyone from the Pope to a rock star, with wagering about equal between those possibilities. The only unanimity was for the obvious—he was a recluse. He was a recluse and up to no good. No good, probably surfing child pornography websites into the wee hours. A child pornographer suffering post-traumatic stress disorder from the Gulf War and likely operating a hydroponic marijuana farm in his garage. At any rate, far too secretive, and sure as God made little green apples he didn't have a job or even a business card as a normal person would, a normal person with nothing to hide.

Juice was quiet as she slipped under the covers, chilly and smelling of beer and cigarettes and herself. I was instantly hard and physically avoided her while I tried to explain.

"Good time?"

"Martin does stained glass. It's not very good but it's . . . you know."

"What did you guys do?"

"Sarah talked about their daughter a lot."

"Didn't know they had one."

"She doesn't come around. Lives on the coast somewhere, I get all confused about the counties down here, and Sarah talks about her like . . . for a while I thought she was dead, you know? The way people talk about someone who'll never show up? All about the pageants she won as a kid and the cheerleading scholarship and the modeling career, like the old men in my home town who bragged about the local kid who went off to play in the NHL, how they taught him to skate backwards and stick-handle and everything."

"There's something I want to tell you," I said.

"Stupid to drink so much before my first day at work."

"Call in sick," I said. "For the rest of your life."

She giggled softly and snuggled up to me.

"I love you," I said.

"Ohhh, thanks. I needed to hear that."

"Why? Aren't you happy?"

"I'm happy wherever you are."

It wasn't something I wanted to rush but she sounded drowsy—I launched off my telling her my real name. All she did was laugh and tell me that she'd like to keep calling me Smith because that was the last name she used on official documents. It had been her mother's maiden name, and Juice liked the fact that there were so many Smiths around, made her feel close to people she never had and probably never would meet. Good. One thing off the list. Next:

"I didn't really live in Presidente."

"The town in your book," she said. "I figured you didn't."

"You figured?"

"Well, you know . . . I didn't read too much of it but the parts I did . . . I didn't think everything really happened."

"It's supposed to be nonfiction," I said.

"Nothing is."

"I lied to you."

"Everyone lies a little bit when they're falling in love until they're sure the love's there. I don't mind that. Just promise you won't lie to me when you're falling out of love."

"Easy promise to keep," I said. "I'll love you forever."

"Me, too," she said. "Though we can't really tell. You have to say it, same with me, same with everybody. Even if you've said it a hundred times before and been wrong every time you have to say you'll love the next person forever or it won't work. You can't go around saying 'I love you so much it hurts, it really aches when I think of you or when I'm alone, and I'll probably feel the same way later on today, but let's wait and see, check with me again when you get home from work.'"

I rolled on my side toward her.

"I love this," she said. "It's hot, like it's not even part of your body."

"The whole thing," I said. "I made up the whole thing. Not just the part about losing an eye but the earthquake, the deaths, even the town. There's no such place."

"People make things up all the time," Juice said. "It's not always bad. Sometimes they do it to not hurt somebody else or just to feel good for a minute."

"But I did it for . . . there is no reason. It's one of those lies that defies explanation because there's nothing to gain, like when someone asks you if you've ever been to the zoo and you say yes when you've never been within ten miles of the place. It's crazy."

"I didn't think a writer had to explain making up stories."

"This is no good." I got up and paraded back and forth at the end of the bed.

"Come back under the covers," Juice said. "You're going to knock over a lamp with that thing."

My erection was refusing to go away. There's something about an erect penis when it's not being productively employed that reflects poorly on a man. Dissonant, its owner reaps the same baffled stares as a boxer would climbing into the ring carrying a sextant. I resisted the urge to swat it and jumped back in bed.

Juice gave me a boozy kiss. "I bet he'd be flattered."

"Who?" I was breathing heavily.

"That man you got the idea from, that Nuttall guy."

Back to the end of the bed, pacing, still rampant. "Imitation is not the sincerest form of flattery," I said. "That's a line lounge comics use to keep from being sued."

"I didn't read much, though it's pretty obvious you copied some of it. If you're that worried maybe you should ask him."

"Ask him what?"

"His blessing, his forgiveness . . . I don't know, lover, whatever makes you feel better about it."

"Are you deranged?"

Juice went silent, pale in the moonlight filtering through the oleanders outside the window, looking offended. I crept to her side of the bed.

"Juice? Baby?"

She was passed out. I parted her hair on the side to sweep it away from her face and kissed her lightly on the soft spot at her temple. I had never met anyone so full of acceptance. On the rare occasion I hadn't come fully clean with my wife it took endless hours of explanation to get back on an even keel. Juice? This is me, this is you, let's move along, totally assured of her survival.

About two in the morning she stirred. I wasn't sleeping and responded with relief—thank all that's wonderful I didn't have to think by myself anymore. Juice must have been similarly motivated because we clung to each other scary-hard. We made love for over an hour and it was unsettling throughout. There was a dreaminess about Juice that bespoke distance rather than intimacy, a cut and thrust as if she had a goal in mind other than fulfillment. She was atop me the entire time, either bent in close and staring right through me or arched back with her face to the ceiling. We'd been together long enough that I didn't confuse her moans and guttural noises for passion; there was a stridency to them that twice made me push up and brace with my hands and ask her if everything was okay. I was sore and a little sad by the time she rolled off me and spread prone, unmoving, on the bed.

When I returned from the bathroom, having washed up and stared in the mirror awhile, she was tracing a finger along the wall while circumnavigating the room—climbing over the head of the bed so as not to break contact with the surface—and talking lowly to herself. I pulled her to face me and she emerged from where she'd been.

"There's too many," she said.

"Are you awake?"

"Yeah." A couple of blinks and a glance around her and she laughed quietly. "I am now."

"You were sleepwalking."

"I do that sometimes. Probably talking my head off, too. I haven't done it for a long time, I don't think. Once when I was in high school I left the house in the middle of the night and the police found me in front of the little theater talking to the people on the movie posters."

"I love you."

As we rocked together I started to get hard again.

"Ohhh, that'd be nice," Juice said. She drew me down on top of her and judiciously held me with just the right amount of firmness and stroked the outside of my thighs with the inside of hers and fastened her eyes on mine. Once I was inside her we barely moved, all subtle movements and leanings and depth and hooded pressures. We maneuvered secretly and under control and came together, aspirating without moans or mewls. We stayed that way until the flush and the heartbeats waned and lay a long time awake beside each other without speaking. I was trying to match her mood and stayed quiet till I thought I heard her mumble.

"What's that, honey?" I said.

"Nothing. Just stuff." She squeezed my hand.

"Too many what? When you woke up you said something about there being too many."

"Can't remember."

"Okay. 'Night."

"'Night."

I admired her. Tucked away inside me like an antisocial twin was the desire to be the kind of person who can glide through life above the fray, independent to the point of absolute surety, requiring neither approbation nor consent, behavior Juice had down pat. That isn't to imply I thought she was perfect. For example, I had serious reservations about her new friendship with Sarah. I'd rather we all kept our distance from that one, an unsympathetic sort who was likely waiting till the moment we vile foreigners overstayed our welcome to call the INS then fabricate a punishment myth for the neighborhood kids—*Eat your beans, children, or the Canadians will come back from the glacier with a polar bear that'll eat your eyes while you sleep.* If another example of my true love's imperfection was needed, I could take comfort in the thought I had never so much as entertained the notion to pelt a barking dog with eggs, to say nothing of canned goods.

Our love could be forever, felt that way, though duration is no measure of excellence. At any given moment there are thousands of toasts being offered at thousands of banquet halls to couples who have been married ten, twenty, fifty years and who couldn't tell you why in thumbscrews. And if not? Well, maybe Sonny with his cottage industry of wives and partners had it right—keep on loving and quit counting. Hold it. . . . Sonny, I was complimenting Sonny, a snapping Jack Russell terrier too lucky to get hit by a car. Jesus.

At any rate, it was the time of year I shouldn't be criticized for postponing a deeper analysis. It could wait till after the Christmas season.

CHAPTER 15

At seven-thirty the next morning Juice came clomping in my hiking boots back from the gate. She had risen with no sign of a hangover, eaten a hard-boiled egg, picked up the lunch Roger had made for her and gone to meet Sonny at the entrance for her first day of work. Roger had seen her off with the concern of a twelfth-century king for a peace envoy, and her lonely return had him calling his ministers and rattling his saber before she hit the patio. He was hardly mollified when Sonny showed up two hours later and leaned on his horn in the driveway. Juice roused herself from slumber on the couch and left again, carrying the lunch Roger had doubled in the interval. When the ambassador returned at nine-thirty that night, eye-poppingly filthy with drywall mud, paint, sawdust, fiber-glass insulation, it took much persuasion to keep the king from calling in favors from the knights and getting them to launch a crusade. Never has a warrior been so pampered and feted—joints of meat and great flagons of ale were her compensation, and had the monarch not been quartered at an estate so far from his capital, he surely would have secured a troupe of acrobats and singers for her diversion.

With a good day's work under her baldric and a few bucks to her name, Juice was up the next morning before the menservants and ready to go shopping.

"You're not," Roger said. "You worked like a slave yesterday, and I'll not have you wasting your money on us."

We'd talked about it every year, Roger and I, vowing never to repeat the headlong charge into the valley of death, the gluttony and the drunk-enness, the purchasing of Christmas trinkets for people who would use them as interior garage decorations, as we did theirs. Then the next year doing it all again, like gorillas, which have come down from the trees yet are still compelled to build an unnecessary sleeping nest on the ground every night and are the only primates known to foul their own beds. Maybe that's what tradition is—replicating behavior without consider-ing its validity under altered circumstances.

Juice had no intention of trying to buy us presents with only the one-day's pay, but she had to go to Home Depot. She knew the importance of good tools, something Sonny lacked despite his car full of iron, blades and wood.

"If we get out of here by ten we'll be back by noon," she said. "The whole rest of the day we can sit by the pool."

"Okay," Roger said, "okay okay okay—you guys go shopping and I'll stay here and decorate till you get back."

"Decorate what?" I said.

He inflated with righteousness. "I'm not ready to give up every single tradition."

Christmas Eve day, and the hardware stored was jammed. Juice seemed as comfortable with the surroundings as any of the herd of professionals, striding up and down the aisles and plucking items off shelves. Mind wandering, I trailed until running the oversize cart into the back of her legs when she stopped abruptly abreast the fasteners.

She looked down at the basket of supplies. "Were you going to get me anything?"

"Of course."

"I'm not big on presents." Eyes down again.

"Hammer, screwdriver set, work gloves, dust masks," I said. "This is so romantic."

"You really understand me," she said. "I love you."

As I wheeled to the checkout I was reminded of the woman I had created for my novel, a carpenter who built a small house for her sister. Small wonder Juice made me think of her—I've always been attracted to tomboys, however outmoded the term. Had every woman I ever met been afraid of insects, appearing without makeup in public and climbing onto a roof, I probably would have opted for farm animals right at puberty.

The mob in its serried ranks before the twelve checkout stations held an unruliness barely controlled, holiday impatience and ad-company-manufactured urgency causing carts to jiggle, dollies to tremble, and with the mass of levels, squares, drills and hammers available as good stout weapons, all the elements for a riot were in place. But peace on earth, if not exactly good will to men, prevailed.

Back home it looked as though Roger had been enjoying the time to himself. As we approached the house we could see him through the patio doors dashing and dancing and prancing and vixening to and fro. We packed the supplies inside and appropriately ooohed and aaahed at

Roger's display. In our absence he'd managed to deck the halls with an array of boughs and bows, ornaments and peppermints, and had found the time to string miniature lights around and through the agaves and aloes in the front flower bed. I wouldn't have been surprised at the aroma of figgy pudding—not that I know what it is—but I guess Roger had been too busy spraying artificial snowdrifts into the corners of the window-panes, an embellishment I considered on par with using a flag as curtains.

He wasn't the only one in the compound unable to resist transporting northern traditions down to the desert, and when faced with so many things standing geography on its head, I could understand the need. Many a brave Canadian or Michigander who had long ago grown accustomed to erecting defenses against the winter underwent the shock of discontinuity when forced by the desert to invert his seasonal behavior. It worked in reverse, as well—desert natives exercised the same bragging rights as northerners when returning from a vacation, but instead of showing off a February Hawaiian tan, they'd proudly flash a fishbelly pallor on arriving home from an August jaunt to the woods, disembarking at the airport pale and still damp, the lucky ones with trench foot and a touch of bronchitis.

When we had praised Roger for his efforts, including the fake snow, the doorbell heralded our first visitors of the holiday season.

Martin was got up in full Honey Badger Security uniform, and good thing there was security on the scene—Sarah was up to her eyes in holiday cheer.

"Smith," she said. "Smith a Merry Christmas to you and your kin we wish you a Merry Christmas Smith and a Happy New Year."

"Thanks," I said.

"And many more."

"And to you."

"I mean really merry. Really."

I glanced behind me. "We, uh . . . weren't expecting guests so we don't have much to offer—"

"—We do." Roger, humping a new-colony-starting-kit of bags, was returning from the garage. "All the salt and glucose and saturated fat and fortified spirits we need to run us into January."

Sarah plunged past me on a charge toward Juice. "Gir'friend!" she screamed, momentum from a missed high-five attempt carrying her into the kitchen.

"Come in," I said to Martin.

"We can only stay for a few minutes," Martin said. "It's a bad time, but . . . well, Sarah wanted to discuss a little business."

"A little," Sarah said. "A teeny weeny little." She squinted through the aperture between thumb and forefinger. "This is Christmas." She burped and looked at Martin for help.

"The lawns," he said.

"Right," Sarah said. "The cutting."

"The gardeners do that," Roger said.

"No!" She shook her head so hard that she lost her balance and staggered into the table. "The cutting across! People and kids and everyone cutting across the grass and leaving those trails!"

"There aren't any sidewalks," I said. "And only two concrete paths in the whole compound. Where's everyone supposed to walk?"

"Trails." She was on the verge of tears. "The muddy, muddy trails."

Martin's sweat was rancid, all-permeating, corporeal, the kind we northerners ferment after wearing a parka from the first freak snowall till Messiah-eve. "This might be better after. Later, I mean, after the holidays."

"Gir'friend!" Sarah yelled. Juice returned the latest proffered high-five with such enthusiasm that Sarah banged into the wall switch, revving up the ceiling fan. The Boardhead swiveled her head, trying to match its rotation, making her words emerge with a strobe effect: "That's—beautiful—I—love—Christmas."

"Well," Martin said, "we have a lot more stops, dear."

"God bless us everyone!" Sarah said. "And God damn the trails!"

"You've been very kind," Martin said. "Have a truly nice holiday."

Out front, with Sarah weaving toward the road, Martin beckoned me aside and dropped his voice. Scuggins had died. I nodded politely, looking respectfully grave out of ignorance, and he explained that Scuggins was the old gent who had put me in my place at the poolside HOA meeting. He'd been gone twelve days. The Seniors Center sent someone around after he missed their BINGO and silent auction night. He'd been in his bathroom for twelve days, dead in his bathroom. Martin thought I should know, just wanted to let me know, twelve days. He swallowed hard, shook my hand and hurried to catch up to his wife.

A death so close to the end of the year is insulting, as though we've been found wanting, incapable of reflecting on the concept of end and new beginning without the shock of example. The good news was the old man had died while still in the flower of opinion and disputation, and when my time comes that'll be good enough for me. Death should be an interruption.

And as for life, here it was rounding the corner. The Dowser made me happy. Not in an airy new-age fortune-cookie way, she just made me smile, standing there with her mass of gray hair in disarray, layers of clothing and scarves looking blasted on by an air hose, bare feet thrust into woven sandals. A ruin of an old El Camino honked as it pulled away. She passed me a burlap sack—dusty and decorated with purple Hindi script—that at one time held what must have been a hundred pounds of basmati rice.

"You can show up unannounced any time you want," I said. "But not bearing gifts."

"A little something for being welcome in your home," she said. "I am welcome?"

"Ha. Yes, yes of course. Come in."

"Dowser!" Roger hurried over and they embraced. "This is the best Christmas Eve surprise I can think of."

"Wow," she said over Roger's shoulder. "You must be Juice."

"Why wow?" She kept her place by the entrance to the kitchen. "And how do you know my name?"

Roger stepped awkwardly away and the women regarded each other from a distance.

"Wow." The Dowser seemed uncertain herself. "I don't know, just wow. You're a beautiful woman."

"Wow to you too," Juice said.

The Dowser grinned. "Are you so grown up you can't give me a hug?"

Juice laughed reluctantly and they met in the middle of the floor, foregoing the hug, settling for a firm handyman-like handshake.

"The guys told me about you," Juice said. "They want to change this place into a copy of your museum."

"This stuff was my mum's," Roger said. "I'd like to keep it for a while."

The Dowser flicked her eyes around the space. "This is just right. I've come across twelve places made out of bottles around America. Houses, a castle . . . most weren't built as roadside attractions. Homes, just how they wanted. What fits, fits."

"I'm going to put on a big pot of mulled wine," Roger said on the way to the kitchen.

I put the sack by the fireplace, wishing we had gotten a tree, and poured small sherries to start off. Roger emptied six bottles of wine into an industrial-size cauldron and began heaving and crumbling and shaking in spices as if he'd just hijacked a string of camels on the silk road. Juice fiddled with the old radio till she found a dedicated carol station, and we harked, heralded and felice navidaded for an hour or so. When the Dowser swapped her sherry glass for a Mason jar of mulled wine I took the opportunity to change directions. I probably shouldn't have broached the subject, but with the wine and all and Christmas and all and the fact that the Dowser seemed impervious to insult and all, I said to hell with it all and asked her about Sonny.

"Sonny," she said. "Sonny is what Sonny is, and he happens to be my husband in a way. We were handfasted."

"I know about that," Juice said. She left off rooting around in the cupboards and cutting up cheese and pickles and joined us at the kitchen table. Whatever had passed through her mind at first meeting the Dowser, it was plain she was now under the same spell we were. "I used to be into Wicca and everything."

"This was just our own ceremony," the Dowser said. "I adapted it from a basic neopagan ritual. Nobody really knows its start anyway. One belief is the ancient Celts used it as a sort of trial marriage that expired after a year and a day and after that it could be made permanent if both partners agreed. A conflicting belief is it was a betrothal, a ceremony where the couple promised to marry a year and a day in the future. Either way, Sonny and I didn't last the year and a day."

"He's still married to his first wife?" I said. "He claims he is, though that doesn't make me want to mortgage my life."

"Yes," she said, "sadly. He still operates in a bit of a fantasy world when it comes to her. Such as his insistence that she loves kids."

"Then what's she doing in the daycare business?" I said. "Or racket, as Sonny calls it."

"What are millionaire fund-raisers doing in the charity racket? Sonny and I . . . I love him without being in love. He knows people, he can reach them. I guess a cynic would say he knows what buttons to push, but actually he cares a great deal. We had a good short time together, exciting then comfortable, interesting. Completely ridiculous relationship, of course, but that's Sonny. And I guess that's me."

Roger was balancing three snack platters and I snagged the one heading floorward.

"So you're not a witch or anything?" Juice said. "Some of the Wiccans I knew thought they were good witches. I just liked the attachment to nature and all that."

"Good, bad, witch, whatever," the Dowser said. "I have a big catalog of beliefs but I don't worship anything, and without that commitment there's not much chance of being accepted by any group. No, it's just a little of this, little of that—"

"—Eye of newt, wing of bat, pelt of beaver," I said.

"I believe in all sorts of things," Juice said. "But I can't fit them into slots."

"Imagine how strange Christmas must seem to non-Christians," the Dowser said.

"Yeah," Juice said. "Jesus might be about love and everything, but he sure has a mean dad."

That got us laughing.

I set down the platter within easy reach of everyone. "We still get to keep the gifts, right?"

"Any part of any tradition you like," the Dowser said. "We're in a society that's on top of the world economically and militarily and calls itself Christian, so we're not used to thinking other belief systems have much good to offer. But I'll tell you, with all my reading over the years, I've never come across a reference to something like a Buddhist or a Taoist Inquisition."

"This is only Christmas Eve," Roger said. "Can't we stay secular until midnight?"

"Yay!" Juice hopped up and raced out the sliders.

Roger poked his head out briefly then theatrically sniffed his mulled wine. "She's in the flower bed," he said, "making a sand angel."

The Dowser chuckled. "On that note, it's time for me to leave."

Great protestations as Roger and I shuffled and scuffed and light-footed in place with displeasure, like little boys being robbed of a last ride before the carnival shuts down.

She refused both a ride and a cab three times each. On her way to the door she stopped and turned to Roger, approached and tenderly took his head in her hands. "This is the biggest one," she said. "The first one without her. And good or bad, whether you're a Christian or not, it beats all other dates for emotion. Your mother loved you."

Roger stood silent so long I grew afraid the containment would cause a rupture. "I'm doing okay. It's hard, but . . . I know she loved me, of course I know. If she was here, you know what she'd tell me? She'd tell me my color was good. She'd tell me she knew I was healthy and doing all right because my color was good. That's how Mum judged my health and my mental state and everything. 'Your color's off,' she used to say. Or, 'Your color's good.' Only those two things. Funny, I could have had a goiter the size of a football on my neck, but if it was the right hue . . . Mum would be happy, that's all. Good color, so I could go out to play."

The Dowser kissed him quickly on the lips and was gone in a burst of excellent color.

Out back was my girl, flat on her back between an oleander and a hibiscus, energetically waving her arms and legs in the sand. Lots of Christmas Eve to go yet and a bilge full of over-spiced wine to work through. And songs to sing and thanks to be given and nothing much to think about except to select a patch of community lawn on which to start marching back and forth after Christmas in order to carve a fresh trail. We needed a few trails, I figured. Paths to somewhere.

CHAPTER 16

Had we expected chestnuts roasted on an open fire, the patter of little feet around the house and a table gaudily adorned and groaning with platters of provisions, we would have been disappointed. As it was, nothing on that list had a hope of materializing so the three of us were happy to spend Christmas like pigs, loafing and eating nuts and shortbread cookies and tipping a little Bushmills into our coffees and occasionally singing backup to the choirs pelting us with Yule songs over the airwaves—the choruses, at least, breaking off grumpily when presented with some obscure third or fourth verse of a carol that we never should have attempted without a songsheet. It was a silly day. Comfortable and nearly pointless and perfect.

I guess the physical exertion of carving the angel glyph into the sand the night before charged Juice up, because as soon as Roger and I broke her focus she popped erect, said, "Christmas Eve," and dragged me into the bedroom. I should have given her a good whisking, because by the time we were done making the beast with two sandy backs I was scraped raw and had to spend twenty minutes shaking out the sheets and vacuuming the room.

Christmas morning Juice and I were already having a breakfast of salami, pepper-jack cheese and stale water biscuits when Roger shuffled into the kitchen. His body language was uncoded, though I sensed his Christmas sorrow, and before I could think of something nonsappy to say Juice kissed him hard and smacked him on the ass like a coach sending a defenseman onto the ice. Roger immediately came around, returning Juice's ass-pat and loudly demanding a bloody mary.

Roger and I had sworn not to exchange presents. He loved the Guatemalan carryall I'd found for him at the street fair in Palm Springs; in return the fountain pen that had been his mother's would have a place of honor on my desk. Roger gave Juice a beautiful sweater she accepted with much enthusiasm. And I gave Juice a ring—a toe ring. Juice gave us promises of gifts to come and that was just fine.

The Dowser's rice sack contained a gift each wrapped in cleverly twisted and layered desert willow leaves. For Roger, the cracked shell of a desert tortoise accompanied by a note that read: SHOT FOR TARGET PRACTICE—JOSHUA TREE NATIONAL PARK. He got the thrust of the sermon, but was discomfited at why he'd been singled out to receive it. After experimentally poking his finger through one of the six holes he propped it half-covered by the bottom of the drapes against the wall. Juice smiled at her copy of *The Total Home Improvement Guide* and tossed it on top of her sweater.

And I got a rock. A piece of schist, dark with biotite mica, the size of two fists, covered with a patina of rock varnish. "Now that's a goddamn Christmas present!" I raised it overhead like *Homo erectus* with a hand-ax. It went directly onto the mantle.

With the ritual done for another year we reverted to lounging and scrounging. There'd be no turkey going into the oven that day. Oh, we had one—big twenty-pound lunk that wouldn't make the most skeptical scientist question the theory of birds being descended from dinosaurs, enough meat to put us to sleep for a week—but at my suggestion we decided to leave it frozen till the day we had enough people over to go to the bother of cooking it. Later, I jokingly suggested running up to the sandwich shop and picking up turkey subs, a suggestion taken so seriously I felt bad for having nixed the big plucked fowl feast.

I should have known better, because I remembered how important Christmas dinners used to be at the Jeffcoate house. Come to think of it, they were the only meals Roger's mum ever served that appeared on the plate in their advertised form. Bless her ingenuity, but Willa was nearly obsessed with serving perfectly good food in disguise, as though the point of culinary art was to trick people. Her specialty was Ritz Cracker apple pie—recipe on the box—the selling point of which was its indistinguishability from pie made with real apples, leading one to conclude the fruit of the apple tree was rare or prohibitively expensive and thus crying out for substitution. She did the same with all manner of food, and if that wasn't enough, the subsequent guessing games were sure to put you off your feed. Once, when Willa served up liver and onions and exhorted Roger and I to guess what it "really" was, all I could of think to say was: "Jeez, Mrs. Jeffcoate, if you found something that tastes like liver but isn't, I don't want to know what it is." About a week for me on the shit list that time.

We still dined; in lieu of turkey and stuffing and cranberry sauce and spuds and yams and Yorkshire pudding were nacho chips and salsa and giant chocolate Santas and almonds, and by the time we had glutted our-selves and gone to bed the only sugarplums our dreams had room for were coated in Maalox.

Was I prepared? Was the love and camaraderie and fond retrospection that is part and gift-wrapped parcel of Christmas serving me well, giving me the strength I needed to keep motoring? You'd think so. I did, at least till ten-thirty the next morning, when on answering the phone I came mouth-to-ear with a nasty concern by the name of Chas Cassidy.

Water has the well-known property of seeking its own level, as does trouble. A related truism is that shit rolls downhill, yet it still frequently manages to work its way up high enough to hit the fan. So with the trou-bled water sloshing around my ankles and the fan doing its work up top, I did my best to deal with the reporter.

Roger was at the store and Juice was already at work with Sonny, who was allowing his Yankee side to dominate his Canuck by ignoring the tra-dition of Boxing Day. Juice had told us that on her first day of work Sonny dredged up some interview technique obviously learned from someone who'd learned it from someone else who'd heard it from a friend, and asked, "So after your break-in period, in what capacity do you wish to work for the company?" to which Juice responded: "Diminished." Sonny hadn't appreciated the humor, and was waiting out front at seven Boxing Day morning, extracting from Juice a kind of labor penance for her bad attitude.

But the phone call. I politely rejected Cassidy's request for an interview, claiming a hectic schedule and the absence of free time and recurring headaches and what I thought was a touch of ebola, though I knew as I was speaking it wouldn't end there. Mr. Cassidy took pains to assure me his proposed article would be both honest and discreet, twice claiming to be an "old-school journalist," as though the title's merits were obvious. That depended on which way I thought of it—he might be a dedicated, ink-stained, undercompensated slave to accuracy and the truth who doubly confirmed every item that came over the wire and had never ratted out a source, or he could be a drunk with a bad tie who bet on dog fights. Old school or not, he hadn't traveled that far at that time of year to be dissuaded over the phone.

With a heave and a sigh, I called up the messages still lurking in my e-mail trash can, printed them both and set off for his hotel. Not a gleam of interest in my surroundings beyond that needed for object-avoidance as I pored over the letters, trying to memorize as much as a could, searching for an advantage. At the end of a serpentine road flanked by palms was the Marriott. Safely past a scrum of valet parkers and service personnel, I entered the lobby, a grand effort that soared to the clouds and hummed with the presence of those whose version of the Yuletide ritual was a few laps in the pool and a massage.

I'd forgotten the room number so approached the concierge for help. Before the young man could respond I heard "Mr. Cassidy?" behind me, and turned to behold a woman, sort of. She appeared to have recently undergone a makeover honchoed by a cartoon illustrator; I was surprised not to detect Mel Blanc's voice jetting between her collagenic lips.

"I left him still sleeping just an hour ago," the lady said. Her helpful comment was accompanied by a you-know-and-I-know look beneath air-brushed eyebrows on a botoxed forehead. If she had managed to thus transform herself and get down to the lobby inside an hour, her clothing, skin and hair must have been elements of a one-piece body suit.

"You know him?" I said.

As she looked me over I experienced the self-conscious disquiet attached to being evaluated even by women to whom I'm not remotely attracted. I rolled my shoulders and relaxed, letting her have the moment, but when her examination exceeded the socially acceptable time limit I barked, "Oh, come on, lady—what room's he in?" and shook the e-mails in her face as if she were fully aware of my mission and deliberately erecting roadblocks.

She recoiled, wobbling on three-inch Lucite heels with lights in them, recovered nicely and inclined her upper body toward me. "If it's that big a deal—" jabbed a finger over my shoulder "—ask this little fucker."

As I watched her storm off across the lobby, heels clicking and flickering, I felt awful, and not just out of seasonal goodwill. As far as I knew, the woman was a divorcée who had spent her last nickel on dolling herself up and flying to a real desert resort for a big holiday and had gotten lucky with a journalist—a journalist no less, a man of letters, smart and everything—her first erotic experience these seven years since the time her husband returned drunk from a bow-hunting trip to the Yukon and serviced her without showering before calling her a fat bitch and a bad mother and punching her down the stairs. It was impatience and hostility I should have reserved for Cassidy. I could sense through my feet the batholith cracking and the molten rock intruding, forcing up the overburden, creating trouble, and I was little comforted by the knowledge that the fractures were of my own making.

The concierge gave me a shrug and I politely said, "Well, I guess you'll have to connect me through the house phone, you little fucker."

I laid a finger aside my nose and was up the elevator shaft.

Cassidy was wearing a cane-sugar linen suit. Leather loafers poked out from under his cuffs, a gold watch from his sleeve. Although he was dandified too much for the occasion, nothing seemed forced. Overall, an impressive effect.

"Smith," he said.

"Mr. Cassidy."

"The only person who calls me that is my sister," he said. "Chas will do nicely." He loosed a smile, and right there I should have stopped being charmed by the man. He had the teeth of a televangelist, slightly over-large, perfect for cutting Scotch tape. "Drink?"

"Surprise me."

"Schnapps and root beer it is."

I laughed. "Whatever you're having."

As he opened the mini-bar I scanned the room. Perfect order. No clothes lying around, no briefcase open or papers scattered, and I imagined the bedroom down the hall was similarly shipshape, assuming the woman from the lobby hadn't left behind yesterday's castoff body suit. Cassidy returned with two airline bottles of rye and handed me one. I liked the casual touch. We clicked the things and drank by the neck. Without his urging or guiding, I found myself sitting opposite him at a small coffee table.

"Eager as I am to interview you," he said, "I confess I'm combining work with work. I have a speaking engagement tomorrow evening here in one of the banquet rooms."

"Journalism thing?"

"No, this is for the American Self-Image Awareness Movement."

"Ahh, the old ASIAM—I think I still have one of their club ties."

He chuckled politely then dropped his eyes to the papers in my hand.

"E-mails," I said. "I wanted to refresh my memory."

I wasn't about to base my trust on first impressions. His sister could very well have been joking, but seldom does a sibling lie right across the board. As the reporter went to the mini-bar to capture us another couple of ounces, I read her letter out loud.

"You're being cautious." He handed me my drink and sat. "I can understand that, but it's unfair to judge me by something my sister wrote. I riddled her nonsense in my follow-up e-mail. You have it there in your hand. Why would you possibly adopt her position when it positively screams silliness?"

"It says here—and this is something an interviewer would write to suck up to his subject—that 'All writers are deeper than their material; I truly believe this.'"

"Of course I believe it," Cassidy said. "I believe it also of steelworkers, dental assistants and pearl divers. As well, it's such a juvenile observation that I would never use it out loud or in print. Now, we can carry on if you like and I'll refute every line she sent, though it should be obvious my sister is trying to embarrass me. You must be able to tell that you're reading a parody."

I flicked my eyes between the two messages. "Looks like you interrupted her."

"Exactly. I heard her typing and laughing, having a grand old time, and entered the room to investigate. She quickly sent it off. Good thing the silly girl saved a copy. I read it straightaway and immediately e-mailed a correction."

I finished my tiny rye. "Does she do this type of thing often?"

"She does whatever she wants whenever she wants."

"Sounds like someone I know," I said. "Though mine isn't . . ."

"Isn't what?"

"Destructive."

"I'm sure my sister feels it's justified." His voiced lowered. "I've done her harm along the way."

We sat still awhile, and when Cassidy gestured at my empty bottle I shook me head and rose. I drifted the pages onto the coffee table, where they encountered ground effect and sailed onto the carpet. The reporter retrieved them and I flicked my hand to send them to the boneyard.

"I've enjoyed meeting you," I said.

"Come, now, I'll cancel the speaking engagement if you haven't the time."

"Nothing to do with time. I don't have the inclination."

"Why write the book if you fear the consequences?"

"Another thing I don't feel obliged to explain." I quickly gathered the empties and dumped them in the wastebasket.

"Wait!" he said as I neared the door.

I slowly turned. "That was harsh."

"It would be in your best interest to cooperate."

I gave him one of his own shiny-white kitchen-appliance grins and left.

Not even vaguely secure about having scared him off, I was anxious about his next move. It would probably come in the form of surreptitious scuttling around, subtle probing, grilling of acquaintances—he didn't seem the type to pound away with repeated calls and letters hoping I'd finally give in. Whatever his approach, it would have to be done without reference to my website. Although it had attracted one beautiful creature, it was too sticky to be left hanging out there. All sorts of knaves and varmints were liable to get caught in it, critters big and strong enough to kick their way free while destroying the structure. I'd attend to it the minute I got home, wipe it clean. Bloody mess, all of it. For someone who maintains he wants life simple, I sure manage to spend a lot of it neck-deep in uproar.

On the way to the doors I waved at the concierge, who on recognizing me cast down his eyes. I wondered what had happened to quash his holiday cheer. I'd been told by three neighbors over the past week that Jesus loved me, and though I had yet to see a ring from Him, unquestionably there was a lot of nonspecific love in the air. I diverted to his desk and learned the young guy had been called in to meet the manager at shift's end. He dumped on me a sorry tale of badgering and bullying, concluding with the firm conviction he was about to lose his job. I could have lingered to commiserate with him but "Hang in there," was all I came up with.

Halfway home, strolling the sidewalk, I found myself longing for somewhere else. It caught me unawares, and for that matter it might not have been an active longing for somewhere as much as it was a tugging away, a shadowy sense of dislocation. Around me, the geometric bushes and showy shrubs seemed uncomfortably foreign, the jumping cholla and prickly pear positively alien.

I couldn't shake the image of the sad young concierge. I should have stayed, that's what I should have done. Waited till the end of the kid's shift and when he came out of the manager's office taken him on a hike and sat with him on a mountain and asked how it had come to be that he was scared shitless of a pipsqueak hotel manager, why he wasn't painting pictures or swamping out horse stalls or deckhanding on a sailboat or anything that fed him a meal of more than one course, told him shaving his head was okay, if that's what he wanted, and playing a guitar in some damn bar some damn place wasn't the dumbest damn thing his father had ever heard of and if it was his damn old man hadn't heard of much then walked him back to the hotel and stood guard in the hallway while he short-sheeted a dozen beds and stolen a couple of hams from the kitchen then gotten him drunk at a Mexican bar and pissed with him off a bridge, howling like coyotes into the desert night, told him he had to steel himself for the years ahead with errors of spirit and exultation, nothing to hide, nothing to fear from a silly-assed little manager or even a spiffy reporter.

I jumped.

"You were talking to yourself," Roger said through the Neon's passenger window.

"Eh? Where'd you come from?"

"Screaming, actually."

"You going to offer me a lift before you're rear-ended by a Winnebago?"

I jumped in, and Roger drove along the bicycle lane until he could merge. Half a block later he said, "Not that it's important, but what were you yelling about back there?"

"Wasting my breath," I said. "The little fucker probably just wants to be a golf pro."

CHAPTER 17

New Year's Day, brand shiny spanking new year. As G.H. Nuttall appreciated, the need to start over is usually shoved down our throats. But now and again we need to create our own new beginning, even if just to show we have a hand in the matter. Pick a date, any date, take a step back, regroup and reassess, forge ahead, lose weight, stop smoking, a new lease on life. January 1st is handy.

For Roger and me the new year was nothing like a rallying cry. We'd had one fresh start August past, and until we wore that one out it seemed piggish to claim another. Besides, when had I ever used a new beginning to good advantage? Riding around questing and jousting and challenging just brought me more trouble—*Hi honey, nice to be home, the dragon was too big and I couldn't find the gold or rescue anyone now keep the kids quiet while I sew my arm back on and catch up on my sleep.*

When first faced with a future without my wife the expectation of renewal seemed hopelessly extravagant. Surrounding me was a world that to my surprise had been merrily attending to its own affairs, and I wanted no part of its concerns and priorities. I felt much the same every holiday season, yet something must have shifted in me since August— here it was January 1st and I hadn't thought of her. Not Christmas Eve, Christmas itself, Boxing Day, or that interminable chunk of dead time that has to be endured until the rosy new year makes us jettison the leftovers and clip coupons for a gym membership. It wasn't until the drive to the restaurant that a pleasant guilty sorrowful relieved recollection of her came upon me and I looked out the window at the blowing sand and cried just a little and Roger asked if I was okay and I said yeah. I can't swear it was indicative of healing, though it was movement along an axis in some direction.

Blowing sand was pockmarking the Neon's paint job as Roger steered around the tiny sand dunes jutting out from the shoulder, trying to take our wheels hostage.

Juice wasn't with us. My love was working that first day of the new year. Every morning since Boxing Day she'd been rising at the first sparrow fart to pull on her shorts and grab her tool bag and go smoking in the Bonneville through the gates. All three of them smoking, that is—Juice was up to a pack a day in Marlboros, Sonny to something less than that in cheap knockoff brands, and the car double it in cans of oil. Sonny was trying, had to give him that, back on the nicotine gum and stop-smoking patches. He kept the stickers on so long they'd accumulate dirt and sheetrock powder under their edges, and when finally they fell off he was left with a treasury of blurred circles on his upper arms and torso as though an office party had been using him for a coffee table. Hanging in.

So it was just the two of us who pulled up and parked among the SUVs and trucks outside the restaurant. I wished I'd been sharing my thoughts so I could apologize to Roger for not addressing his concerns, for forgetting August had been a new start for him, too. Assuming he had his house in working order was as grossly demeaning as writing him off as a hopeless case. But no sense explaining and apologizing to him at that point; he'd shrug it off as dross and wonder why I was going to the bother. Roger was far too understanding for my own good.

Then we were inside the restaurant, and before I could spot our party through the sea of tourists that had surged to the checkout stand and was foaming around and crashing against it—each wave shuddering the structure and drawing gasps from the young women trapped inside the delicate breastwork—Roger looked up at the thirty-foot ceiling and around at the expanse and said, "Oh, George, what have you done?"

The pilings of Sameshima's seafood joint had been cut and the whole mess recycled as shipworm tapas. Eminent domain, or some such vicious tripe, had enabled the city to level the restaurant, along with a used-clothing store and an ice-cream parlor. Excited gasps had been issuing from the citizenry for weeks in anticipation of the new parking garage slated to rise from the rubble. Artist renderings of the development—accompanied by text extolling its virtues as a can't-miss-cash-generator and downtown-core-revitalizer—had been dominating the front page of the newspaper, relegating to deeper sections picayune battles about water shortages and power outages and child abductions and gang shootings and messy squabbles about the exact definition of an endangered species and silly body counts in the Middle East and ass-over-tit developments from Russia.

What's a fella supposed to do except open a new place? The Big Happy Fun Chinese and Western Buffet Palace was a converted warehouse. George had gotten a good deal on the lease so couldn't be blamed for the structure, though he could be for the conversion. The list of offenses was long. Suffice to say the simulated nautical gimcracks and buccaneer collectibles from his defunct seafood place had been replaced by ersatz Asian furnishings and knockoff Chinese ornaments. Given the time span of Chinese history compared to that of the Spanish Main and the corresponding wealth of eras to plunder, the effect generated was that of a Sino-Disney theme park.

Then again, why cavil when the whole point of going to a buffet is to eat to a state of wretchedness? I saw the Dowser's hayrick of gray hair bobbing over her drink. She had called the day before with an invitation to join her in launching the new year. We'd been planning to stay in New Year's Eve, and as I switched the phone to my other hand to give me time to invent a polite plausible excuse she said, "Tomorrow, of course, the First," and went on to explain she observed nothing until after it arrived and had time to settle in.

Roger and I stepped around a winding partition—a chest-high version of the Great Wall—to the main part of the room. Across from the Dowser was Martin, wedged between his wife and the owner. He waved madly when he spied us approaching, and after we joined the table he spent the better part of the next hour flabbergasted by the coincidence of our all knowing one another, at every break in the conversation injecting expressions of disbelief, stupefied explosions of air, head shakes, and in general acting so electrified I was tempted to claim I was his long-lost brother to add fuel to the fire. He finally came to accept the nonmiraculous nature of the event, though maybe he just wound down out of fatigue; Martin wasn't used to much more than hemming and hawing. Anyway, it gave his wife time to wipe her chopsticks after stabbing him for the jeezly-third time to get him to shut up.

Wiping things was about all Sarah was doing. I hadn't seen that side of her before, though I should have guessed it, and I soon had my hands full fingering everything on the table just to see her whip out her napkin. Every couple of minutes I'd shift the Chinese tea pot a few inches or move someone's cutlery out of the way and giggle to myself as she attacked with her rag, and I congratulated myself on starting the new year off with good solid adult behavior. Sarah's main donation to the conversation was wondering aloud where Juice was and how long it would be till she joined us. My musings on industrial accidents in which Juice could have been involved were ill-received at large, and eventually I let Sarah have both her semi-obsessions. They didn't seem to be bother-ing anyone else.

George Sameshima looked wearier than I remembered, though at least in his new place he had foregone the theme-costume idea. Dressed in jeans and a golf shirt, he looked much like any other male diner, or would have if he'd cut his queue and donned a ballcap. Far from taking umbrage at Sarah's cleaning bee, George grunted with appreciation and shot repeated glances at the busboy.

Until the others showed up we ate just enough to stay alive—spoon of soup, fork of egg roll, glass of tea—resisting the urge to plunge our arms to the elbows in the steam table trays. The Dowser was limiting herself to the tea, sipping from a porcelain cup and listening more than talking. She looked at ease, though I'd never seen her so intently observant—not so much looking at the rest of us as examining, an artist addressing sub-ject matter. Her reserve was unusual but she wasn't the type to make you worry, and our table was free of those helpful souls whose mission is to make all in attendance part of a happy family by coercing participation. All right, Sarah was there, but she was too busy cleaning to organize an intervention.

Then after an hour or so the Dowser's face relaxed, she broke from her scrutiny and smiled. I smiled back until realizing it wasn't for me.

"Sorry the wait," Sonny said. "Sorry, sorry, big emergency job some Bighorn development billionaire guy's got vee-eye-pees coming, had to fix one of his toilets." He looked as if he'd been diving for pearls in one.

"You must be Tina," the Dowser said.

She was, and looking beautiful in a silk blouse and short indigo skirt. "Hi, everybody."

Sonny helped her to a seat beside me, but wasn't inclined to take one himself, hovering directly behind and half-over my head. After thirty sec-onds I wished Sarah would take up a cloth, reach across the table and swab his spit from my skull.

"What do you think?" George Sameshima, energized by Sonny's arrival, swept his arm in an arc.

Sonny pivoted. "Thought I was in China when I walked in. Said when we come through the doors, must be in China, must have taken a wrong turn off the freeway and ended up in China. Of course I did most of the work myself, not bragging."

"Sonny helped remodel the place," Sameshima said to the rest of us.

"Should we be wearing safety helmets?" the Dowser said.

"Dowser," Sonny said.

"Where's Juice?" Sarah said.

"Like that table, Smitty?" Sonny said.

I pinched the edge. "Good one, very table-like."

"All of them. Brought them in off the delivery truck and spread them around, that kind of thing. Got a decorator's eye, me." Heading for the Great Wall, Sonny elbowed past an elderly man standing in place looking lost, an empty plate in his hand, and appraised the barrier, shielding his eyes as though assessing its ability to repel invaders. He gave it a hefty boot and the thing resounded like a kettle drum. Satisfied, he returned to the table.

"Where's Juice?" Sarah said again.

"Long time since I ate at a Chinese restaurant, usually I just get the take-out kind, love that dinner-for-one. Daughter Delilah can't eat it, the em-ess-gee and her heart and everything, and the other kids hate it but I tell them hey, a hundred Chinese guys can't be wrong."

There wasn't much action at the buffet. A glance around revealed most of the patrons on the mop-up, leaning back from their tables while prodding the remains on their plates, legs straight but ankles uncrossed to delay the onset of gout. Aficionados were loudly comparing George's offering with famous buffets of the past—the Holiday Inn after the Santa Ana softball tournament; the ship's smorgasbord on the two-day cruise to Ensenada; the pig and corn roast after the demolition derby that year in Barstow, which technically wasn't a buffet but gosh darn did they eat! The odd braveheart who advanced on the steam trays yet again was cheered by admirers of the human spirit—applause and shrieks, a quickening of pulses. The tables around us were debating the merits of various antacids and herbal purgatives and estimating the break required before driving to Del Taco for the Mega-Macho-Bigass Burrito.

Sonny had hit the far end of the first row and was on his way back along the inside flank of the second when George stopped him and snatched his plate of meatballs. The owner went a half-block up the table, slid the greasy spheres back into their steam tray and loaded Sonny's plate with Chinese fare.

Sonny tssked. "Nothing wrong with meatballs, even Canada guys eat meatballs right Smittybaby?"

George was approaching with a mound of food layered like an archaeological site.

"Sonny," I said. "How long will Juice be working?"

"Done. Knocked off early after the toilet job. Dropped her at your place, we had a drink and she got a phone call some guy looking for you. Give her a ride to the hotel." He looked at a wrist that held no watch. "Grab a cab, be by here sometime after, she said."

Roger had overheard, and swung around up the line. "The Marriott?"

"What other one?" Sonny said.

"There's dozens of hotels in the valley."

"Sure, but why would I drop her at a hotel she doesn't want to go to?"

Roger paused. "There's another side to that I can't quite put my finger on."

By then Tina and the Dowser were back at the table. George had loaded his own plate while he was preparing Sonny's, so Roger and I picked up the pace and hustled along the range of trays and displays, accumulating chunks and scoops and tongfuls of food without prejudice. We might as well have stuffed a little of everything in a blender.

"Good thing Juice is Juice," Roger said on our way to join the others.

"Even so," I said. "I don't want Cassidy anywhere near anything dear. With his speaking engagement done he should be gone already, not that I expected him to be."

"Maybe you should do the interview," Roger said. "Neutral, boring, hard-working-scribe nonsense. There was a time you were pretty good at that."

"He's going to write what he wants in any case so why volunteer anything? Besides, I'm hardly a good subject for an unauthorized biography."

"You will be if he finds out who you are. Throw him off, give him plain oatmeal."

"Not one word," I said.

Roger stopped ten paces from our table and looked down at his food. "I'm not hungry."

My stomach took the comment to heart and let it go to my head. "Me either."

Apparently Juice was. She had entered unnoticed, pillaged the tables and now startled us from behind with: "Keep moving, guys, working girl coming through."

She kissed me when I turned, accidentally transferring a slippery stratum of chop suey onto my plate. She'd had more time than Sonny to change—or he hadn't bothered—and looked great in a denim shirt and khaki shorts, skin aglow from exertion and a good hard scrub from a loofah. The tan she was acquiring, along with her black hair and dark dark eyes, amplified her exoticism, and she was reaping stares from the men in the room, men who would need a couple of hours' digestion time before having the potency even to fantasize about her. She forked the chop suey from my plate back onto hers.

"Ha!" she said. "Look at this! I've never taken a pile of food this big in my life." She started eating with her fingers, selecting dry garlic ribs and dipping them into the watery parts of the plate.

"Glad you finally made it, dear," Roger said. "I had visions of your talking shop at the Marriott bar and getting passed around a power-tool convention."

I should have laughed with them but I was in too much of a rush. "So what did the reporter have to—"

"—Gir'friend!"

With a clashing of cutlery, Sarah shoved away from the table and power-walked over. She gave Juice a European double-kiss and stepped back wearing a Rorschach of plum sauce on her blouse. She reached out and touched a cut on her gir'friend's forearm. "That Sonny has to stop working you so hard. You're much too artistic to be doing this kind of thing."

"I'm not artistic at all."

"You are. I can tell. The next HOA meeting I'm putting you up for Artistic Director."

"There's no such title," I said.

"Democracy evolves," Sarah said. "I read an article about it in *Redbook*."

"Let's sit down."

"Look at your eyes," Sarah said while Juice starving-carnivored a piece of rib gristle. "If you shaved your eyebrows and moved them up a bit, you'd look just like an Egyptian. The old ones, I mean, the ones who built the pyramids, not those new ones who just want to blow themselves up and never win any medals in the Olympics."

"I need a beer," Juice said. "Something about this kind of work makes me want to finish off the day with a couple of cold ones at a strip club."

Sarah did her best to stick tight but Juice plunked herself down beside Tina.

"You're Sonny's friend, right? The Blonde Job."

"That's me," Tina said. "And you're his new handyman."

"The Hand Job."

As the girls laughed Sameshima said, "Hey—family restaurant!"

"You must be George," Juice said. "Really nice place. I love it, really."

He instantly softened. "Oh. Thank you." Another convert to Juicism.

Grease-rimmed smiles and much chewing and gumming until the Dowser crumpled her napkin and gave Juice a one-arm hug. "I do wish we could have had more of a chance to talk, but I have to get going."

A monsoon of protests.

George Sameshima rose with the Dowser. "You can't go. You organized the whole thing."

"Yes, and I'm so sorry, but I have commitments I can't ignore. New Year's Day and everything, things to do." She handed Juice an envelope. "This is for you, open it when you get home." She beamed at the table. "Thank you, George, as always. Everyone here—I love you all and wish you a wonderful year. Please excuse my hasty departure, must fly."

"How did you get here?" Roger got to his feet, and the rest of us shoved our chairs back and bumped our knees on the table and wiped our mouths and our hands on our napkins or our pants in case a kiss or a hug or a handshake was required. But none was.

"Bye." And she was gone, leaving all sails out of wind.

We weren't so rude as to check our watches, though everyone started eating more quickly and the talk died and the banquet felt more and more artificial and forced until with no forewarning Juice got up, whipped a quick thanks at George and made for the door. Roger and I allowed an indecent interval before following her out.

We heard a pair of shoes snapping along the concrete behind us and Sarah calling to Martin to hurry up, followed by a plea for Juice to wait, wait a minute wait up wait for me and then we were in the Neon and Roger was racing us out the parking lot and weaving through traffic until Juice pointed out the obvious, that Sarah knew where we lived, so there was no sense trying to lose her in a car chase, and Roger could slow down any time before he killed us all, not that Juice was afraid of speed but Roger wasn't the most expert driver in the world, no offense. We arrived at the neighborhood and Roger clicked and braked to a stop on the far side of the entrance, blocking the opening till the gate slid closed behind us. Like pre-pubescents, we hung our heads out the windows and watched as Sarah—Martin slumped down and barely visible—pounded the brakes, chirping the tires as she brought the car to a rocking stop.

"She'll be okay," Juice said as we continued to the house. "I'll take a bottle of Bailey's over tomorrow and we'll have a girl talk."

"Wear a condom," Roger said.

The garage door motored up and we were home. So much for the new start.

CHAPTER 18

I had four dogs while I was growing up, all strays, all trouble, one after the other with barely enough break between them for me to clean the mudroom, where each of them pissed and shat as if it were one of the house rules passed on in the changeover.

They were loved, of course they were, but each moved on to a better life, a canine heaven of unleashed romping and table scraps and free hippie-like humping without the threat of a garden hose. That's what I believed it was like on the Farm, where my father told me they were sent. Unburdened by eschatology, the dogs were free to accept or reject whatever came along, and if at the end of it all was farmland bliss, an existence of running room and rabbit chasing, that too was fine.

The Farm. Not a specific plot of land—not *The* Farm—just a kind of metaphysical Nirvana, a severing of all attachments. According to my father, it was where all dogs went either on reaching old age or after the third attack on a human, whichever came first. The assertion clashed with my dad's strict separation of reward and punishment, but a religion that recognizes no continuum among living things and claims the greatest possible gap between those with a soul and the benighted Others allows much latitude for a general shitcanning of the rules.

The concrete nature of it was another thing. As we knew no one who owned a farm or who had lived on one or who would be able to recognize one that didn't have the word lettered on the side of the barn, it was odd that I accepted my father's explanation each time I came home from school and found another mutt gone. Long after I was old enough to appreciate the falsehood I clung to it rather than accept that they had gone the way of the neighbors' animals and been aced at the pound. I guess it was wishful thinking, but it made me feel good to ponder the fictional Farm, the Elysian fields of the crotch-sniffers.

The equation between the Farm and the Dowser's retreat impressed itself on me as we entered her property, as the three of us jounced past the Wells, Fargo sign promising Rest For the Weary and Storage For Trunks, and caught sight of the Dowser's house and saw the vehicular dwellings and got a few waves and curious stares from the occupants out taking the air on their dirt plots.

Home from the restaurant the day before, Roger and I had come so close to begging that Juice gave in with a laugh and read us the letter: "'Visit. Soon. Tomorrow's perfect. Bring the boys and sleeping bags— Dowser.'"

It was an invitation gladly accepted. Juice didn't know when she'd be working again, as Sonny had to take a break to fly his daughter to a specialist clinic in Houston for her heart. When Roger and I voiced our acceptance, Juice jumped up and kissed me.

"Thank you for trusting me. The biggest kind of trust is letting someone do what they want. My whole life everybody's tried to tell me what's good for me and make me stop doing everything I like and do stuff I hate instead. You're just perfect."

"No need for an insult."

"It's true. Perfect and I love you for it. I love you to bits."

"It's only a sleepover," I said.

"I mean the reporter."

I tried not to stiffen in her arms, and considering she had already let me go and was pacing, I think I pulled it off.

"You're not like most men," she said. "Most guys would ask why I went to see him and what we talked about and all that . . . yah-yah-blah-blah . . . you really trust me."

"I was going to wait till we were alone," I said. "And, uh . . . tell you whatever you feel like sharing, how little or how much, is good enough for me."

Roger stretched the web of his hand across his forehead, likely to keep his eyebrows from raising at what he'd just heard.

"I'll tell you about it on the drive," Juice said. "Where's the sleeping bags?"

I hadn't stumbled on any in my house travels, but Roger assured me they existed. He dug through the set of storage cabinets in the garage and surfaced with four bags old enough to be prototypes—cobwebbed, drowned-man-gray sacks with the stuffing torn loose and bunched at the bottom. A swing by the sporting goods store on Highway 111 had us set up with new ones at ten dollars apiece that were insulated with whatever you get for ten bucks, rated to keep you warm and toasty even if you encountered a freak storm that stranded you on the side of a mountain in weather around room temperature.

The valley was rimmed with clouds. Not the monochrome felt stratum of home or the dramatic thunderbumpers of the prairies, but a playful collection amassed around the mountain peaks, sneaking a look over the ridges as if aware of their incongruity in the desert and too shy to show anything that would reveal their intent.

Decreased rainfall over the past few years had turned into a full-scale drought. Less than a half-inch of precipitation in the preceding eighteen months was causing all sorts of consternation in the natural community. The natural survival strategies of succulence, drought tolerance and drought avoidance were enabling the plant life to hang on, much of it appearing dead but in fact no more so than a hard-working uncle taking a nap. Except that with no rain, no flowers; no flowers, no insect pollinators; no pollinators, no seeds; none of the above, no rodents; and all of a sudden lock up the pets and watch the kids! because the snakes and coyotes are down from the hills looking for a buffet.

Like bastions the world over, the gated communities in the upper valley were finding fortifications no security from anything hungry and determined. As for our compound, Sarah had planned a special meeting of the HOA to address the problem. Not three days went by without someone on their way to the pool or the mailboxes discovering a patch of striped fur or a gnawed tabby head at the end of a desegmented bone trail and claiming the shadow they had seen on their walk the night before was that of a coyote, definitely a coyote, that or maybe one of those wolves the tree-huggers had re-introduced into Montana that made its way down to where the living was easy. A coyote or a wolf for sure, or else that beagle the people on the corner owned, the one that was probably rabid, either rabid or just crazy, one of those vicious cocksu . . . one of those gosh-darned untrained wild things like the one the guy who lives by the gate almost hit, maybe it wasn't him but his cousin, his cousin or somebody almost hit this wild animal on his motocross bike that came this close to killing him and would have if his reflexes weren't honed from the Iron John course he took.

The drought was turning the valley folk squirrely, and they were giving vent to their frustration in the media and on the streets. Backyard water features—decorative falls and rapids and such—were costing more and more as the water petered out, and if you can't have fancy water features in the desert, what's next? It's normal and natural to improve a harsh environment, right? It's all about quality of life, and what quality is there in something that just sits around looking like it was born that way when you can clean it up a little or add some decorative trim or excavate it to make room for a spa and an outdoor kitchen with a Jennair? All you had to do was look around to see how cockeyed the desert world was—sand blowing all over the place, lizards and bushes and crap like that keeping us from getting another eight ten hotels, and now coyotes killing cats. Coyotes killing cats—come on, where's the fun in that? Not even something you can get a bet down on at the new casino.

Itching for rain, I commented on the clouds, and Juice jumped in with: "I hope it pours. I want to smell something. It's too dry here to smell anything."

"Hard to know what's behind the ridges," I said. "Might be some nimbus coming to give us a good soak."

"Nimbus," she said. "I don't like names. As soon as I know what things are called I feel like I'm back in school."

"I like the details," I said. "The more I know about something the more it amazes me."

As much as I pumped her on the drive, Juice couldn't remember much of the meeting with Cassidy—"Why would I tell him anything about you when you weren't even there?" was her comment—other than the fact he'd spent as much time hitting on her as he did asking about me. The relief was minor, the reporter's snooping worrisome, and Juice had made it worse out of innocence or plain impetuousness. Why couldn't she have just stayed put?

"There's the gate," Roger said. "Chez Dowser."

Other than the squatters, the dominant species was the common raven. We stood by the car a few minutes watching squadrons of them in loose formation pass over the house. It was different from the last time—I'd never seen ravens or crows travel with anything approaching this much symmetry, and couldn't help thinking we were observing tiny black geese looking for water or a grain field. They swooped low on strafing runs over the cars in the yard and dogs barked and leaped and children ducked and laughed and adults looked up in wonderment, as if seeing snow for the first time. Perhaps it was as simple an explanation as the brain registering patterns that weren't there, though if that was the case it was a hell of a meeting of minds, for we all felt the queerness the ravens dropped on us as they carpet-bombed the Dowser's patch of land with enchantment.

Our hostess came out front and stood in the sand and raised an arm over her head. I thought she was hailing us and waved, but she was shielding her eyes from the sun and watching the birds as they peeled off and vanished over the roof toward the Little San Bernardinos.

"What would make them do that?" Roger said.

"Got me," I said.

"You're right about details, about digging deeper. You're gradually winning me over after all this time. Funny, but I still think about the desert lupine you told me about."

Rainfall isn't just low in the desert, it's unpredictable. If all the annuals grew and flowered after the rains and something happened to wipe out that generation, the species would be screwed. So not all the seeds sprout. Part of each desert lupine seed crop won't germinate for ten years even if all the conditions are perfect, money in the bank for a rainy day. Survivors is what they were, along with every little thing around us still pulling its weight. Those plants among the ancestral lupine population that had the genetic variation preventing total germination managed to survive and reproduce through the tough times that wiped out the rest— with a change of environment a flaw became a life-saver. Sometimes it doesn't matter how you start out.

I was about to tell Juice the story but she was greeting the Dowser.

"I'm teaching these big resort-livers how to shop cheap. We just got these sleeping bags for ten bucks each."

"Excellent, you won't miss them. Price of admission. I've given away hundreds over the years."

"Neat," Juice said.

Roger and I grabbed the overnight kits and followed the girls toward the house, fanning out to avoid tearing the new bags on the staghorn cholla bordering the path.

"By the way," Roger said. "What's with the ravens?"

"They've been around since your visit," the Dowser said. "Fairly regularly, not every day."

"Acting that way?" I said.

"Every way imaginable."

As the others entered the house I stopped and turned to scan the sky for moving motes of black, hoping to see even one lone fledgling, a young fighter pilot that had broken from the flight through sheer joy of solo undertaking to beat up the enemy airfield. No black but plenty of encroaching darkness. The clouds had abandoned all stealth and were whooping and hollering their way toward us from the west side of the valley. A quick look at the mountains rising from the edge of the Dowser's acreage revealed no action on the eastern front, though that didn't mean there wasn't water vapor condensing out of sight, waiting for the pivotal point in the battle to join the main host. It felt like rain, smelled of it ahead of its time, and visible along the Santa Rosas was an oblique sheet of streaked draperies.

I was elated and not alone in the emotion. The others reappeared and quietly joined me. The barometer was dropping, and the advance edge of the system was sending forth dust devils and tendrils of wind to snake through the cuts and canyons, cracks and fissures, hitting the Dowser's place at unpredictable angles. There were more people on the property than I would have guessed. A sand-blasted Volkswagen Westphalia gouted three adults and two kids, other vehicles added a nuclear two-and-two, triples, a solitary old man. The front of the house became the hub, gathering those who were drawn hypnotically from out back and a couple from inside and roping in stragglers who had been on the perimeter or near the road. An old El Camino raced in around the gate as if late for an event never to be repeated.

Eyes to the west in anticipation. The clouds were tearing with unseemly haste across the valley, kilts of rain brushing along the floor. The excitement built, and when Juice ripped off her top in preparation for the approaching downpour it started a wave of imitation, at least among the men and children. Juice gloried in the freedom, threw her head back and opened her hands and Roger and I and the men and kids rubbed our bare chests and swung our arms. Then the leading edge of the clouds broke off into a line of scud, angling away down the valley, and the remainder picked up its skirts and started to dissipate. By the time the whole fractured mass reached us it had lost all potential for rain and glided with increasing incoherence over the mountains.

We blinked a couple of times and looked around the yard.

"Aww," Juice said. "That kind of teasing could get to you."

She was still staring after the clouds. Around us the others, variously interested and indignant, were staring at her.

"You might want to pack those away," I said.

She idly drew on her shirt, never taking her eyes from the ridgeline. "I think if God made everything, deserts are Her favorite spots. The rest can take care of itself. Elves and fairies and trolls and all that, they look after the forests and lakes and caves. Out here is just what you see, and you can see everything. I think She needed a place to look at and see what She made." So there we were at the Dowser's . . . sanctuary, I guess is the word. A place of asylum for people who knew for certain the sky was falling and could produce hard evidence. For all the wealth in the valley there were many such individuals, severed, misplaced, miscast.

Many days since Roger and I arrived a wander through the paper's classified ads turned up trifles for sale: *Used ironing board, good shape—$3*. Another: *Playing cards, red and blue, bridge-size—2 decks, $4*. Asking less than the cost of an ad is a mistake no one makes. Wallets on strings in the middle of the road is what they were, lures, bait for chat or the smallest interaction. We were tempted to call once or twice, didn't, feeling sorry but unwilling to get mired in conversation—*Many a good game of bridge played with these cards, afternoons of sandwiches and coffee and on special occasions a little white wine as long as the girls aren't driving, but none of them drives anymore, and there's just the three of us, and we don't get together much, not like the old days, and if four dollars is too high, well, why don't you drop by and have a coffee and a sandwich and we'll play a few hands so you know you're buying value and you can make me an offer, the weekend would be fine, any day, really, any time. . . .*

Many plants have extrafloral nectaries that feed ants and other defending insects, trading nourishment for protection, working together. Not a bad plan if you don't want to end up selling your cards.

CHAPTER 19

I woke early. The Murphy bed in the great room was only a single, and after an hour of inadvertent prodding from Juice's elbows and knees and a couple mouthfuls of her hair I rolled off onto the floor and shivered for another hour until remembering my sleeping bag in the corner. The Dowser had insisted we take the bed and was kipping with Roger and some others aligned under the window, feet toasty in kapok lining, illuminated by moonlight lancing into the room.

It had taken a while for our visit to gather momentum yesterday after the raindance was foiled. Juice in particular felt let down, as though she'd bared her tits on a New Orleans balcony before discovering Mardi Gras was the week after. Inside, shaded from the victorious sun, she appeared disinterested, even uninterested, in the house, blandly nodding as Roger led her on an inspection and turning down the Dowser's offer of food or drink. She took pleasure only in rolling the sleeping bags out on the floor and trying each one on for size and comfort. There was delight in the simple act, and before anyone could ask we learned that she'd spent most of her childhood sleeping on the floor with threadbare blankets that slid out from underneath her when she rolled over. Never anything to tuck into, to wrap around her, to hold her tight, old and musty and safe. The playtime revived her, and as Roger and I waited around the corner in the kitchen while the Dowser changed clothes Juice started revving up to the higher energy state I'd come to accept as part of the package.

Until she was cut off with: "Right out there."

We men took it as our cue to enter the main room. The Dowser was pointing out the window. "The mountains are farther than they look so take plenty of water. There are empty bottles in the pantry. By the time you get there and scramble around I'll be back, just going to the market for supper."

Horn.

"My ride." On her way to the door she added, "Take that referee's whistle by the sink in case you get in trouble, twist an ankle or anything. It can be heard from the yard. And some trash bags under the sink for what you find out there that doesn't belong."

We followed her to the door and watched her climb into the bed of the El Camino, where she kneeled and laid her chin on her forearms atop the cab and wiggled her fingers at us. The driver reversed all the way to the gate, the wind parting the Dowser's mane in back, wrapping it around her face where it writhed, sending out suckers.

We ignored the advice, left the whistle, substituted a case of beer for water, walked the property to the foot of the mountains, picked a level spot, drank the beer, humped back the empties as it was growing dark and waited a further two hours until the Dowser returned with neither food nor explanation and had a very nice time sitting with her around the kitchen table eating leftovers from the fridge and talking about almost nothing.

In the morning I was a little stiff from the floor, a tad groggy, though not too bad and any lingering fatigue vanished once I stuck my head under the tap. At the sound of the faucet the house came alive. An assortment of men and women and kids trooped out the doors as others entered and helped themselves to bottled water and crackers from the pantry and dropped off blankets and pillows. Roberto—I think his name was Roberto, or Raoul—took charge of the sleeping bags, and after extracting a hybrid puppy that had tunneled to the bottom of an old canvas-covered mummy sack had them shaken and secured within two minutes.

Chunk-chunk-bwaaa! The tap heaved and shook, desperate for air.

"The shower kicking in," the Dowser said. "Outside."

I craned my neck over the sink and saw a stucco wall jutting ninety-degrees from the house. Already there was a string of people waiting in line like Cold War Muscovites for onions. It seemed odd, until I thought of half-mile lineups for concert tickets and other examples of the human ability to piss away time staring at the back of someone else's head for reasons far less worthy than a morning shower or something to eat.

"Little chilly this time of year," the Dowser said. "No one seems to mind." Holding back her hair with one hand, she plugged in a huge electric skillet. "I'll need some elbow room unless you're volunteering to chop." She pointed at a bag of bell peppers on the end of the counter and handed me a knife. "Plastic plates on the shelf to your left. As soon as the breakfast is done I'll be passing you the fixings for sandwiches and tortillas. Stuff everything into these bags." She dropped a fistful of squeeze-locks beside the sink.

Coming or going, everyone picked up or dropped off something—breakfast on a plastic plate, small bit of food in hand, large amount of food in bowl, empty plate to be washed, bag to be recycled, empty beer can, found shoes, extra laces, bleeding child, bandaid, light bulb—a swift communal exchange while out the window the line for the shower gradually shuffled itself out. An orange school bus honked from the road and the place cleared out. Kids toting book bags and lunch bags and bottles of water loped toward the bus, parents hollering last-minute encouragement. On the bus and off up the road toward the real world, here we go, honk! honk!

Amid the clatter and clutter the adults with jobs peeled off from the oasis, those with serviceable vehicles giving the others a lift, housepooling to work. Given the logistics of getting everyone fed and watered and scrubbed and dressed and transported, the operation went off without a hitch and ended abruptly in a smokeless flash.

The remaining void was enormous. With no morning paper around and our group attending to wakeup ablutions, I killed time by starting on the dishes.

The Dowser came in from the shower, twisting her hair into a hawser to squeeze out the last drops. "Hot water's almost done. I can hear Roger screaming."

"You haven't had much chance to ease into the day. I can't remember all the hubbub last time."

"You weren't here in the morning," she said.

"I didn't expect to see that many people going off to work."

"Most of the people here have some kind of job. The unemployed ones don't stay that way long. Not many idlers, though when you see what Mexicans get paid, you wonder why not. It's not always this crazy. They come and go, not a soul around for days then suddenly it's like a convention. There were two families out front last night I still haven't met, some familiar faces go weeks between stays, then there's Roberto and a couple of others who've been here most of a year."

"Tough for the kids."

"I'm not so sure. The experts stress the importance of stability, though that was the least important thing to me growing up. I didn't care where we moved or how many times I had to pack my toys in a box or make new friends at school."

"Any kids of your own?"

"Two stillbirths," she said. "Long time ago."

I fiddled nervously at the counter, rearranging bowls to no good purpose. "Now I understand your comment about not going out on New
Year's Eve. You said on the phone you don't celebrate anything until it's
had time to settle in."

"Not what I meant. Trust me, you're going to hurt your brain drawing connections like that."

I stood back and watched her slam away the dry dishes with such
celerity I couldn't help wondering whether the Dowser had just lied to
me for the first time. Had Juice been in the kitchen she would have
cleared the air with one comment, whereas I let the matter grow and
grow before filing it with every other loose inference in the back of my
mind.

"*Hola.*"

I hadn't seen Roberto since his taking command of the sleeping bag
detail, and assumed he had left with the other workers. My height,
Zapata mustache, actress-skinny in the arms and shoulders with a round,
perfectly proportioned pot belly that looked grafted on for humorous
effect. He was moving fast toward the door and stopped dead when he
got no reaction.

I cursed under my breath, then cleared my throat and carefully said,
"*Buenos días.*" Another clearing of the air passage before: "*¿Como está?*"

He gave the query counterfeit consideration. "*Muy bien. ¿Y usted?*"

"*Muy bien. ¿Y usted?*"

"*Muy bien. . . . ¿Y usted?*"

"*Muy bien,*" I said. "All things considered, pretty *bien. . . . ¿Y usted?*"

"*Bien,*" he said. "*Muy, muy bien. Todo está bien. ¿Y usted?*"

"*Avez-vous la plume de ma tante?*"

"*¿Qué?*"

"Well," I said. "Guess it's time to hit a few fungoes."

"Whatever," he said. "See you after work."

As he plunged out the door I turned to the Dowser. "That fucker
speaks English!"

"Good thing."

"He put me on the spot a dozen times yesterday, tried to make me
speak a language I don't even . . . no, that sounds stupid even to myself."

"Imagine how most of them feel."

"I don't have to imagine," I said. "My wife and I won a cruise once, a contest run by the developer of the first mall in our town. Mediterranean nights of dining and dancing, that kind of thing, ports of call. On the second morning we hit Barcelona and when the gangplank went down I almost sprinted ashore to escape. Wandered around the city all day, my wife hating it but me right at home. You know the feeling you get for certain places—only partly the architecture and the culture, mostly just a sense of being perfectly positioned. Around suppertime we went into a bar for a sandwich or something, anything other than eat on the ship, and there was a group of locals having the time of their lives. Not a party, just laughter and drink and food and I guess because my wife and I hadn't been talking or getting along very well I could have signed divorce papers at the table and called a cab to take her back to the boat and stayed right where I was for the rest of my life. Only thing stopping me was the isolation. I was already feeling alone, and to belly up to the bar with those people, to join them and not join in, to kill the conversation by babbling along in English and have them laugh at the three phrases I knew in Catalan—fuck it, you know? I was lonely enough."

"There are many ways to be misunderstood, that rob you of your sense of place."

"My wife," I said. "I didn't mean to . . . I haven't talked about her for a long time. I'd rather not."

"Do you hear me asking?"

At the sound of the back door she passed me a dish towel and I wiped my eyes.

"This is like an adventure tour," Roger said. "Feels good, but I'm glad I brought a sweatshirt." He looked at me leaning against the counter. "You okay?"

"Just sad that I don't know Spanish."

"Sure you are," he said. "If you want to get over it, you can always use the program I installed in the computer, the one I told you about three months ago. I'm going on record as saying I'll practice dialogue with you any time you like."

"Nothing good comes out of that machine."

"Juice came out of it," he said.

"What did I come out of?" Juice barreled in from the shower soaking wet, and not just her skin—the water had wicked into her shorts and T-shirt, making her look like an extra in a beer ad.

Roger ran a finger between Juice and me. "They met on the Internet."

"I was sort of a stalker," Juice said. "As soon as I read his book I knew I had to meet him, so I started e-mailing and everything just happened."

"It's on the Internet?" The Dowser dipped her chin and looked at me from under her eyebrows. "When we met at the Blue Dog, I figured you were researching some kind of writing project, otherwise you wouldn't have been talking about a town I know perfectly well doesn't exist."

"It's gone," I said. "Some computer virus. Can you believe it? How vicious would you have to be for that kind of mindless destruction? Millions of people affected every day, business matters, intellectual property . . ."

"I'd love to read it," she said. "Next time bring a hard copy."

"Don't have one."

"I do," Juice said.

"What?" I said. "How the hell did you—"

"—When I set up the site I made it impossible," Roger said. "You shouldn't have been able to—"

"—The whole point," I said, "was to . . . well, I was experimenting with a new medium. I didn't want it to appear in print." Roger started to dig the hole deeper but I cut him off.

"Good thing Juice has a copy," the Dowser said. "I'd say that's a godsend."

I forced a smile at Juice, squeezing my eyes. "You came through again, sweetheart."

"I'll send up to Canada for it," Juice said.

I mentally praised our compound's row of communal mailboxes and Roger's mum for leaving just one key, then quickly changed the subject to Sonny's daughter. The Dowser told us Sonny was close to bankruptcy trying to pay for those treatments not covered by his insurance, and expressed relief that Sonny himself was healthy, as was his son, Saxon. I asked about the other one and finally got a name: Quinn. The Dowser had never met him. Close to thirty, but she was guessing, as Sonny didn't talk about him much. Behavioral problems, violence, and she changed the subject as abruptly as I had minutes before.

After that we played good guests by entertaining ourselves while the Dowser took care of her daily chores. Roger and I poked around the well and the outbuildings and Juice made house calls, leading a loose parade of toddlers from vehicle to vehicle, an exotic Pied Piper stopping to say hello, introducing herself to the caregivers left behind after the others went off to work, being Juice. Her lack of Spanish posed no difficulty, no trouble making her point, laughing and yakking and chopping the air with her hands and once or twice bending to draw in the sand. Even the women who had been most offended by her peep show the day before came around and let their kids join the merry troupe.

She was in no hurry to go anywhere, and though Roger and I felt perfectly content, I found myself checking the time every few minutes. Roger went inside to browse the Dowser's book collection and I joined our hostess out back, where she was taking cactus cuttings. She caught me looking at my watch and asked if my pass had expired and I said not at all, I just didn't want to overstay our welcome, and she snorted and I took off my watch and put it in my pocket. So I don't know the precise time when it all broke loose, around four I guess.

I'd gone for a quick walk, taking the road to the first highway sign, where I waved to the kids in the bus returning from school on its drop-off rounds. On the way back it passed me again, empty, and the driver tooted. Skirting the gate, I saw Juice sitting on the roof of a housecar, a Marlboro jerking up and down in her mouth as she talked to a woman down on the hood of the split-level. The Dowser came around the side of the house just as Roger opened the front door.

The wind had been freshening, escorting in a new batch of clouds, and so quickly had we grown callous from yesterday's anticlimax, we missed the buildup. It wasn't a storm you stand out in, face upturned, mouth agape, arms extended, hollering for joy after a long drought; not one that prompts you to tear off your shirt; not even the variety that makes you ooh and aah with terror-pleasure. This evil bastard meant business.

Juice and the woman jumped off the car and into it as I slipped and fell on my ass for the second time. I struggled upright and caught the Dowser's eye and we split around the house to sweep for children, but they'd all taken or been dragged under shelter. Roger held the back door open and we burst in with a rip and a roar and a blast of water.

So much for worrying about the time.

CHAPTER 20

I didn't wake at all the next morning because I hadn't slept. The house was packed with wet and worried people peering anxiously out the windows through the feeble morning light, awaiting the return of friends, lovers, wives, husbands.

About four in the afternoon it had started, and by four-fifteen a pitted Chrysler was seen sliding toward the gate, an old man behind the wheel steering madly as though fleeing the DEA in offshore waters. A teenager beat Roger and I to the vehicle, pulled the captain from the boat and let it crash against a granite promontory aswirl in waves, after which the vessel backed and mired on a sandbar. Roger got the old salt inside while I latched onto the teen's belt to keep him from being swept to the Sea of Cortez. That's when Juice and her new friend abandoned the Potemkin safety of their car and splashed along behind us to the house.

It rained, that's what it did, it rained so overwhelmingly there was nothing to do except check out the windows for stragglers and walk around the house on padded feet, afraid of further disturbing what was already out of control. It rained cats and dogs and vinegaroons, horror stories and bad memories, aching knees and migraines and lost loves and yeast infections.

All TV reports came from news desks. Daily highs and lows and colored areas on the map and funny shots of folks in Chicago losing their umbrellas in windstorms could be left to TV Weatherpersons, but an event of this magnitude could only be entrusted to people much better looking.

There had never been such rain in the valley. Years back the Whitewater River—a dry channel sporting scruffy bushes and a few grocery store carts—was partly straightened and portions of its banks were paved, alterations that greatly aided runoff through the resort areas but now had the deleterious effect of increasing the downstream flow to fire-hose speeds, carving new bends, re-routing, undercutting trailers, toppling date palms.

Initially it was reported that a cold front had shoved down from Alaska and collided with an unseasonable monsoon bringing a cyclonic flow of saturated air up from the Gulf of Mexico. The warmer air was driven aloft, decreasing its ability to hold vapor, which condensed and commenced to terrifying insurance adjusters. As it was January, there was some acrimonious on-air debate between two meteorologists over the Gulf-air part of the explanation until the anchorprimate cut them off to go LIVE!! to Palm Canyon Drive, where a fully loaded two-ton landscaper's truck had hydroplaned into Sonny Bono's statue, littering the area with branches and grass clippings and a Toro ride-a-mower, which on impact had vaulted from the back of the truck and performed a crash landing on a restaurant's balcony, crushing the railing and a patio set and promising much free publicity for the eatery's owner once the rain stopped.

Neither thunder nor lightning till ten o'clock, then a frenzied bass and strobe concert. By that time the phone was dead and the power was out and candles were guttering and people were muttering enough already, enough with the rain!

In my novel, I described at some length spring prairie floods, which, while costly and destructive, for us kids served as epic adventure—a sense of awe in the face of the natural world combined with the adult responsibility of helping sandbag, and the even more instructive experience of watching grownups cry. But this was of a different order and the children were rightfully scared shitless. No disobeying orders to sneak down to the river and check on how much it had risen overnight, as we had done, hoping school would be canceled for another day. No, this was a direct assault, and the only thing for the kids to do was to take peeks out the window at the deluge while staying close to their parents under the Dowser's groaning roof.

Rock and sun-fired earth. No trees no grass no roots. When the rain hit the mountains it might as well have been falling on tempered glass. At four in the morning a churning torrent of desert batter—water, silt, rocks, deadwood—blasted down from the hills and hit the back yard, obliterating the outbuildings. No more guest house or potting shed, gone the reading room and bathroom. The newborn river rampaged on into the darkness. Fortunately it was of such power it scoured its own trench, yet its outreach managed to smack against the house and in minutes the place was swamped shin-high. A berserk salvage party broke out, everyone scrambling to find a spot above the high-water mark for baskets, books, pottery, linens, anything we could save from the inundation. Many prayed, more cursed, and we waited out the night in a state of high alert.

At first light the spectacle, partially obscured by the continuing rainfall, was exactly what we had expected—it looked as if it had been pouring rain for fifteen hours and everything had washed away; no surprise there. Okay, not everything. The cars and trucks and vans out front had been spared the river running through the backyard, and though they were standing on noses and rears and sides they were fairly secure, half buried and anchored with wet sand. We could barely see the Neon through the downpour though it looked upright, shielded from the runoff as it was by a slight rise and the trunk of a fallen palo verde. The new river was coursing within its banks; high up and far away the storm must have ceased, pinching the flow and reducing the watershed.

Grooves and channels intersecting and coalescing were carrying off excess all around, and by eight in the morning we could open the doors and start shoveling out water with our hands and pieces of wood and begin bailing with pots.

I was taking a break out front under the overhang, watching Juice pull on her cigarette, when she flicked the butt into a small ocean and jerked her chin toward the road.

There he was himself, Sonny Lemmatina, motoring blithely up to the house in his Bonneville, conceding nothing to the conditions other than carrying a high rate of knots to avoid sinking into any of the larger depressions. He plowed to a stop halfway up the drive. Boston Charlie stuck his head out the passenger window, scoped the yard for activity and wisely pulled back under cover. Sonny rounded the front of the car and fed the dog something from his pocket. He straightened and waved at us just as the sky lightened, which drew a hey! from me and a whoa! from Juice. By the time Sonny had slogged to within hailing distance a hole had opened in the clouds and every patch of sodden ground and shredded creosote bush and scoured automobile was coruscating in the light and drawing heys! and yays! and similar sirens of excitement from inside. Sonny kicked his way toward the house, booting at the puddles as if they would realize it was him, come to their senses and vamoose.

"So here you are," he said to Juice, stopping short of being smart enough to come in out of the rain. "Missed three days of work counting today, people supposed to fix stuff theirselves, do the remodels theirselves and everything?"

"The Dowser invited us," Juice said.

"I can see that, she does that always the time." He was more interested in trying to light his smoke in the rain than he was in taking his helper to task, and he must have known by then that Juice couldn't be intimidated, so by the time a procession of bodies began streaming out the door, ignoring the rain, embracing the rays targeting the yard through the clouds, he'd turned his attention to me. "Smitty."

It was hard to tell whether the folks were more excited by the patch of sun or the sight of Sonny. The old man we'd pulled from the floating car stretched out his hand to the light while the other adults clustered around the handyman, nattering away and grinning and acting generally like serfs welcoming a liberator promising free land. The kids shimmied and jimmied their way to the front, yelling Sonny Sonny *Señor* Sonny and holding out their hands for little slaps of howdy. The kept their mitts out while he pretended to study the sky, then resumed their singsong of Sonny Sonny *por favor Señor* Sonny until he rooted through his pockets and distributed a round of cookies. Much squealing as they danced around under the overhang, gnawing on their rations. To give Sonny the benefit of the doubt, he might have stopped by Trader Joe's or some other specialty food store and found kiddy treats shaped like dog bones, though the parents didn't think so, and spent the next few minutes confiscating the biscuits from their children and throwing them in the yard.

The rain stopped.

The sudden silence quashed all movement, catching people in midstride and freezing them in unnatural postures. The wind died down where we were but was moving briskly up top, threshing the clouds, carrying away the chaff. Blue and more blue until all that was left in the sky were streaks of cirrus and a few puffballs.

The Dowser appeared in the doorway, squinting and blinking along with the rest of us at the assault of light. She looked between Sonny and the Bonneville a couple of times.

"Figured you could use supplies out here and that," Sonny said. "You been stranded since yesterday."

"Good man," the Dowser said. "We could use a hand with the cleanup more than anything."

"Good, got no supplies. Not so much tread on them tires. Every time I went and tried to turn into Ralphs or Von's to get some food I shot right by. Big mess in town, got six calls already from people worried about getting the barbecue lit when the rain stops." He transferred his gaze to the front yard. "Best I call a guy that owes me a favor, get his backhoe up here, dig out them cars if people don't want to be sleeping in the ditches. How's all your inside stuff?"

"Wet," the Dowser said.

"Wet, yeah. Better take a look at the property, the casitas and that."

We walked the land through veils of condensation fog. If Sonny actually had a friend with a backhoe, and the friend actually owed him a favor, and was more dependable than Sonny, things would go quickly. Otherwise, a communal shoveling bee would be high on the to-do list. The well was full of sediment and the pump was clogged. The concrete pads for the outbuildings were invisible under silt, the one for the bathroom sprouting angled pipes that looked not unlike a lot of the vegetation around.

"That's the first thing," Sonny said. "Bring a spare toilet from home, bang up some walls, don't know if I got a sink or not."

"Thanks, Sonny," the Dowser said. "We really could do with that as soon as possible."

He turned to Juice. "You working or playing?"

"Working," she said.

"The best. Get you dropped off at the lumber yard when I pick up the throne. You need a truck, sure would help. Tell the boys here, your partners, get rid of that bumblebee car and get a decent truck."

As we took in the effects of the hydrodynamics Sonny stood there with his fists on his bony hips rambling on about a downstream expedition to salvage the wood from the outbuildings. Then he stopped and spat and approached the Dowser and put his arms around her and said, "Well ain't this just the drizzling shits, darling," and they hugged each other.

"All this about my problems," she said. "How's Delilah?"

"Not so good. Keeping her there in Texas awhile."

"What exactly did the doctors say?"

"Didn't exactly say nothing. Talked to the wife, she might be going to see her, sure loves kids that one."

"Uh-huh."

"She's making tons of money now. Baby-namer, her new job. People having a kid get her to think up a name that fits its aura or something, energy and that. That's the kind of job I need. Go through the paper, there's dozens of names in there. Seen this word in the paper last week— glottal. Let me put my hand here on your fat belly, ma'am, get the energy of your kid . . . yup, you got a Glottal in there, couple months you'll have a bouncing baby named Glottal. Twins, come on back and I'll pick another name for you no extra charge."

We chuckled and the Dowser said, "You've never had any shortage of ideas."

"I just pull them out my head."

"That's not where you pull them out of."

Abruptly, Juice took my face in her hands and kissed me. It made me feel good, and she knew it and kept kissing until Sonny told us to get a room and the Dowser told him to shut up.

"Anyways," Sonny said, "should get going, fix the toilet before everybody gets back. Might just squeeze in some handymanning stuff, make a couple bucks before dark."

We finished up the tour, dodging trickles and skipping over rivulets.

And then Sonny told us about his land. Ten-minute drive and a spit away, a place for his kids. Delilah loved art, and Sonny planned to set up a studio for her replete with skylights and a wall of windows to give her natural light. His son Saxon was a born handyman, could fix anything even from a wee age, and his dad was going to set up a workshop and an auto garage with a hoist just as soon as he got his hands on the land. Five acres, but there was—no shock—a small problem.

"Developer guy wants to build a town with my five acres right in the middle. Eight nine thousand houses going up, luxury hotels and golf courses, twelve golf courses. Twelve. National park on one side of her and preserve land the other, do a bangup job of snuffing out what's left of the animals and real desert. This guy, this development guy's going to make it okay, he told this reporter on the TV last week, explained that scientists got a tough time figuring out how bad development is for the wildlife so he's got a big idea—proposal, that's what it is, a proposal—his big idea is to let the scientists come and go in the community right from the startup, give them all the hard facts they need so next time they know how much stuff gets killed by development. Makes you laugh in your whole head, don't it? Says it'll help more than it hurts, even says he's putting in green spots and walkways and that for the animals. Like a rapist bringing an air mattress to keep the woman from getting all scratched up. Space, he says, need space, growth in the valley's good for everybody."

There was another small problem—Sonny didn't own the land. He did, however, have a solid plan. He'd been working for the owner for nothing over the last few years, as well as tendering loans to the man, an inveterate gambler. The way Sonny had it calculated, the amount he was owed would cover the down payment on the property. I recognized the robotic stare that surfaces when Roger's been conquered by numbers, a glazed severing of the outside world that looks like a prelude to drooling, but our resident accountant recovered nicely from his minor heart attack and pointed out the obvious flaws in the scheme. Hard to tell whether Sonny heard a word.

At some point Juice had opted out of the tour, and we left the banks of the once-mighty river and started toward the house.

"You promise about the toilet?" the Dowser said.

"Almost done already," Sonny said.

Juice was out front watching the mass arrival. A small Ryder moving truck had dropped everyone off on the road and they were making their way up the drive in two columns along Sonny's tire tracks. They looked tired but not otherwise put out, and though they were greeted with enthusiasm there was none of the home-the-survivor festivity in the air I had expected. Normal rhythms had returned closely on the heels of the sun, and while there was some serious discussion amid the overturned and upended vehicles it was adulterated with much laughter. A storm's thrashing of their sleeping quarters ranked low on the big list of concerns.

To my surprise, George Sameshima climbed from the truck's driver seat. He reached back in and pulled out a rolled sleeping bag, then looked up the track to the house as though wondering whether he should have stayed at base camp. Finally, he tucked the roll under his arm, put his head down and began the slog.

Juice was ready but we had forgotten about Boston Charlie, who lunged half out the window the second she came within insult range. Sonny offered to leave the dog with the Dowser, who wouldn't hear of such generosity, suggesting instead that Roger and I take Juice home to get her tools while Sonny traded the mutant mammal for a toilet then swung by our place on the way back. We protested, but the Dowser gripped the sand with her bare toes and insisted there was plenty of help at hand and that Roger and I would be better off getting home to check on the damage there. True enough, so with effusive thanks for the hospitality and promises to help with the rebuilding, we wrung out and packed our things while Juice said goodbye to the others.

After excavating the Neon we jammed two water-ruined area rugs behind the rear wheels for traction and Sonny linked it with a chain to the Bonny. Roger jumped in to drive, and Juice sat on the trunk to increase the grab of the rear wheels, shielding her eyes and squinting into the distance. I picked a pushing spot in the middle of the hood between two volunteers. With all the preparation, we broke the inertia with one heave and Sonny pulled the Neon straight back along his own tracks all the way to the road. We pushers exchanged back slaps, mutual congratulations for being the key element in the big rescue. Just for fun, I guess, Sonny kept going a quarter-mile up the gravel—Juice yee-hawing and Roger swearing—until the chain ripped free of the Neon and slung back into the Bonny, wiping out the grill.

Before I got to the road the Dowser called. I met her halfway to the house, we shared one last hug and she slipped me a Spanish language book, a brand new volume with *SPANISH NOW!* emblazoned across the cover. I took the title as a direct order. *"Muchas gracias."*

Her parting comment, freighted with significance, bordered on a command: "Be careful. The storm wasn't it."

Cryptic advice, but it had been a strange couple of days. Wild and wooly, not without its rewards, or maybe that was the reward. If nothing else, it was the first time I'd felt safety instead of idiocy in numbers. Before I could think of anything to say, Roger laid on the horn and the Dowser pushed me lightly on the chest.

Across the freeway we entered a world of social insects. With hardly a break after the deluge, thousands of workers were climbing palm trees to skin broken fronds, clearing roads and boulevards, re-burying exposed sprinkler lines, patching stucco torn from walls, replacing clay roof tiles, installing new transformers, stringing wire, tearing up buckled roads. An invader had penetrated the ant colony's perimeter, eventually succumbed to the soldiers, and now had to be hacked to bits with mandibles and carted away from the entrance.

At home, there was no need to punch the clicker-thing—the gate was back on its rails. As we approached the gap the Kolachuks' car rocketed by on the right, cut us off, crunched into and careened off the post in turning the corner and sped off toward their house.

Roger jumped on the binders. "She almost hit us! What's that all about? Don't tell me our dear Sarah is hitting the cocktails before noon these days."

"That was Martin driving," I said.

"Martin? Really?"

"*Sí.*"

PART THREE

RUMBLE AT THE MOHO

CHAPTER 21

On my seventeenth birthday my father asked, "What do you want?"

He hadn't left my present till the last minute. The question had broader implications, and as it was the first time in years he'd asked me anything deeper than surface scum, involuntary blinking set in at the novelty and didn't cease till I joined him in breaking tradition by answering.

"Support," I said. After a few blinks of his own, I added, "Your support," in case he figured he'd get off light by propping me across a couple of sawhorses and bracing me with a timber.

A downcasting of his eyes. "You got it."

So I had it. What the hell was I worried about? Not that I'd really been worrying, just that I thought my old dad had flipped his lid and my answer, or any answer, might force him to start issuing his usual pronouncements before I had to phone the guys with the Houdini jackets to cart him off.

"You got it," he said again, firmly this time. "You got it. All the way. Got it."

That kind of support could soon grow crushing, so I excused myself with some stock piece of bushwa and started to leave the kitchen.

My father almost let me escape before saying, "There's a price to pay for support, you know. Price to pay for everything in this world."

I looked at him sitting with his elbows on the table and couldn't stop myself. "What do I owe you?"

He had the grace to ignore me. Up went his glass and gently down. "There's a natural hierarchy among people. The gifted and blessed rise to the top. I admit I'm not suited for a high position in society, but that doesn't mean you can't be some day. It's what I want for you."

I didn't show his grace. "I know you hate it when I waste my time collecting rocks and reading books, but I gotta do the things I . . . you know, my own things. What do you want—for me to think like you already? Nothing scares me more than the kids at school who already act like their parents. You know what? I think the most dangerous cult in the world is the Junior Chamber of Commerce."

"Those are the sons of the movers and shakers, boy. Future leaders, captains of industry."

I jammed my hands in my pockets. "They sure get beat up a lot at school." My father came exquisitely close to laughing, encouraging me to press the advantage. "You liked Churchill, right, I mean you quote him and everything and you can't say he wasn't a leader."

"Of course. A great leader, a lion."

My hands came out of my pockets. "Well, Churchill was in power a lot and also part of the official opposition a lot, and he said that the duty of the opposition is to oppose. *Duty* to oppose, Dad. Even if it's just to delay things to give people time to look at an idea different ways and not go off half nuts just 'cause it sounds good off the top of their heads."

"He wasn't perfect." He reached for the bottle of C.C. "I have no truck with the school of thought that says all power structures should be opposed."

"What if the power structures make up their own history—and they do—and tell us how we should be living by using that same history as proof—and they do—turning the world on its head by saying everything in the past led up to this point, that all of what we do and what we think is important was bound to happen, that history meant us to end up this way? What then? What they've done is make the world the way they want it, and later make up the history to show that's the way it should be. That's going in circles, just crazy. So I'm going to collect rocks. Rocks and books and figure out whatever I can, then one day when someone asks me to join the leaders I'm going to chuck one of my rocks right at his fucking head." That time I made it out the door.

Of course, what I believed had nothing to do with the real world, at least not my father's apprehension of reality. "Well, time to get back to the real world," he'd say after a couple of days at the lake, or even just one of the nights when the whiskey perked him up instead of beat him down. I'd return from a school field trip, excited by the tactile and emotional experience of learning outside the pale green walls of our classroom, and my dad would welcome me back to the real world, as if through artifice people had crafted the actual and had to resign themselves to the existence of nature's illusion, a bad piece of work, sloppy and haphazard, that eventually would go out of style.

Even back then it obvious the possibilities racing through my mind were no more fantasies than were the rock-solid-tried-and-true preach-ings of my father. My world was as real—his was just more common. Not that I was any brand of rebel. As much as I cherished doubt about con-cepts as howlingly empty as historical inevitability, my skepticism was mostly internalized. Good grades, no trouble at school and one argu-ment with my father in seventeen years hardly qualifies as sedition. I had read *On the Road* by then, but had also had come across an article on Kerouac claiming he did most of the actual writing at his mother's kitchen table in Lowell, Massachusetts, which took some of the edge off his rebellion thing. Maybe young Jack was a little like me, young Morty Cahoot, and had a bunch of unfulfilled desire mixed in with the anarchy. Or maybe he was a whole lot like me, and just had a shitty car trip that he mostly lied about when he got home.

And now sitting here in Vancouver, I'm at the point in my notes when Roger and Juice and I got home from the Dowser's after the storm. It was then that the baleful shifted to the baneful, the start of the real trouble, and how a man with even average perception couldn't have arrested events or at minimum mollify the consequences is beyond me.

The three of us pulled into the garage, dry and sound, unharmed by the storm. Hardly any destruction around us. A eucalyptus and two olive trees were on their sides in the greenbelt amid clay roof tiles, but a slight advantage in elevation had spared the compound from flashfloods and most runoff-related problems. While Juice got her tools together, Roger and I went through the house resetting the time on all the electronic gear till there wasn't a blinking red 12:00 in the place. Sonny called to say he was having trouble locating the spare toilet, but for Juice to be ready to go at a moment's notice because it had to be somewhere. I envisioned him patting his pockets and checking under tables, asking the kids whether they'd seen it while they were playing.

Inspection tour complete, I felt disappointed at the normality. I missed the Dowser's place already, and no question we were home—Sarah was at the door.

She looked less athletic without her power dumbbells but more impressive overall with a postman's bag and a straw boater featuring an ER MARSHAL hatband. She tilted her topper, said, "Emergency Response Marshal," fished a booklet from the mail bag, shoved it into my hand and followed up with: "Complete emergency instructions.

Evacuation procedures, mustering points, basic first aid, all in the book."
She recorded our house number on a palm pilot; when she looked up she
was crying.

I tried to soothe her by explaining that the storm had hit some areas
much harder than ours, and that we'd work together to recover . . . that
wasn't it.

"Martin's hard at work on the case," she said. "Funny, usually I'm the
one who's good in a crisis. The police said it was random but Martin's
sure we were targeted. Anyhow, it's not your responsibility." She clipped
the palm pilot back onto her belt. The tears had dried on her cheeks.

"We've been away," I said. "If something's happened, you'll have to fill
us in."

"Our house was broken into," she said. "Horrible, evil attack. I'm so
glad it turns out that you weren't here. I knew it, I knew Juice would've
come by if she'd heard. All we have is each other in times like this."

I promised the three of us would come right over to do what we
could. Sarah had six more emergency instruction booklets to deliver and
would meet us there. She advised us to approach with caution—Martin
was looking for clues the police might have missed and had taken to
drawing his weapon at the slightest noise. As well, so saturated was the
air with bad vibes that Sarah couldn't muster the willpower to cook, and
it would be appreciated if we brought along anything we had in the
fridge. She looked sadly and unfocussed into the air for so long I cleared
my throat, drawing a final sharp glance before the ER MARSHAL, devo-
tion to duty unimpaired by her inability to prepare food, labored off to
complete her rounds.

Roger thought we should beat Sarah to her place to give us a chance
to get the straight goods from Martin, so I hollered over the shower at
Juice to meet us there.

The destruction was awesome. Smashed furniture and savaged personal possessions littered the house; hideous wallpaper had been made
worse with knife cuts and smeared fluids; lights and sconces dangled on
their wires where they'd been ripped from ceilings and walls; the bathrooms were a rubble field of pulverized porcelain and tile; pervading the
place was a dank heaviness from the soaked carpeting; most upsetting
was the Kolachuks' clothing, which amid the shambles had been artfully
arranged in poses—shirts buttoned and tucked into pants, blouses

paired with skirts, all of them taped upright onto chairs and lying on the couch and even nailed to the walls in disturbing mimicry of real people.

"They broke all my stained glass," Martin said. "Even the soldering gun." Not a whit of self-pity. He was at the kitchen table methodically numbering plastic Ziploc bags with a felt pen and recording their contents in a ledger. "The police think it was kids because nothing was taken. They're wrong. Even kids would grab a watch or something on the way out. This is a hate crime. They wrote 'Partners of Scum,' across the vanity mirror in the bedroom. They wrote it in human feces. It's the only piece of evidence I got rid of. The rest of it, well, the police went all through the place, but when they wrote it off as kids, troublemakers one of them said, like it was nothing, I decided to conduct my own investigation."

"Smells like it's been wet awhile," Roger said.

"Since New Year's Day, we found it like this when we got back from George's restaurant."

"Anything we can do?"

"Sarah called on her cell and said you'd be bringing something to eat. I sure can't ask for more than that."

"Uhh, cupboard's bare right now," Roger said.

"That's okay." Martin squished across the carpet to the kitchen and took a Polaroid of the broken pipes under the sink. As he waved the print dry he told us about their daughter. "We were hoping she'd come for a visit, the first time in . . . and you know, we thought she'd be sick of hotels. She's been staying in them ever since she was seven and started entering pageants. Now the modeling career takes her all over, living out of a suitcase, this would have been a real home visit. We went to see her four years ago to surprise her. She was doing a fashion show in Spokane, her picture on the poster and everything, except when we got there her manager said she'd been throwing up all night before and the show was in two hours so we couldn't go backstage. He said he'd get us complimentary tickets, but when we went to the booth right after they were sold out. It was a big lie, of course, though I didn't mail the letter Sarah wrote to Alliyah complaining about the manager. That's our daughter—Alliyah Essence. Maybe you came across her in a magazine. She's in all the big ones." He put the Polaroid on a stack of others beside the phone. "Now this."

"She'll just have to visit when the house is back to normal," I said.

"Her real name is Monica. Sarah changed it when one of the pageant judges said Monica was too plain for someone who was bound to be famous one day. It was my mother's name, but Alliyah sounds better, more modely."

The doors and windows were open to the scouring air, and we heard Juice calling back to Sonny as she came up the walk. She entered in a rush and almost literally dug her heels into the carpet. When Martin saw the look on her face, his newfound strength fractured; Juice crushed him in a hug to hold the pieces together. None of her insouciance here, no blithe acceptance of circumstance and situation. As Martin pulled away and roughly tugged his Honey Badger tunic straight, Sarah came through the door and was wrapped in Juice's arms before she could shuck off her mailbag.

"Sonny told me," Juice said. "But this . . . I didn't expect this."

"Sonny knew about it?" I said.

Horn.

"Okay," Juice said. "We have to get to the Dowser's. I'm bringing a sleeping bag back and moving into your garage until your house is more beautiful than it was before. I mean it, no arguing, you guys. Beautiful. Architecture magazine stuff."

I started to protest, explaining we lived just around the corner, but she whacked me out with a smile and I came close to telling her to pick up two sleeping bags while I moved a table and a hotplate into the Kolachuks' garage.

Juice took a last look around. I thought for a second she was going to break down, but she willed herself out of it and in a tiny voice said, "Animals. Worse. Worse than animals."

We accompanied her to the driveway. Sonny was hanging half out the car window.

"Colombo them," he called. "Save up all your clues and act real nice, then at the end Colombo them, Martybaby."

The Dowser's salvation was strapped to the roof. Inverted, the toilet was lashed down with about twenty meters of duct tape stretched over the bowl and through the open windows, the mass off-center to allow the tank to hook over the side. After Juice lost a hank of hair to the gummy gray tape maneuvering her way into the passenger seat, the relief expedition roared off.

We lingered on the driveway till Martin suddenly banged his hands together and said he'd taken too much of a break and had to get back at it. The house was ugly and raw, yet despite his mission's wretched genesis I was happy for Martin, glad he'd shouldered the task even if his determination was mostly gumshoe bravado. Whatever the upshot of the investigation—and surely the police had it right; it was, after all, just a property crime—maybe one day Martin and Sarah would be backstage at a fashion show or behind the lights at a photo shoot and be fobbed off by a personal manager and would shove past the toady and barge into their daughter's dressing room and say hello darling we just drove a thousand miles to tell you we love you. And even if it all went to hell, it'd feel good while it lasted.

When Oliver Cromwell said, "None rises so high as he who knows not whither he is going," nobody could claim the old Puritan was quoting scripture. That one came from his guts. Sure, in 1660 he was hanged as a traitor and had his head stuck on a pole over Westminster Hall, but by that time he'd already been dead for two years and his enemies had to dig him up to gain their revenge.

I could live with that.

CHAPTER 22

The handout entitled *EMERGENCY BUSINESS OF THE HOA* had been drafted in an emergency, therefore held no business, just a number to call for additional emergency-response brochures and a small advertisement for Bunny's Bail Bonds and Pawn Shop.

The pool area was full. The attack on the Kolachuks was an attack on us all, and every homeowner and renter had turned out in response to the clarion call for solidarity. The folding chairs ran out early, so those people who lived close to the pool kindly supplied seats, including a reclining lounge and two picnic benches. A gigantic 3500-series Ford pickup jacked six feet in the air on extended springs and jumbo shocks and flying twin Stars and Stripes from poles attached to the cab arrived with dozens of kitchen chairs jumbled in the back, but by then the meeting was about to start, so no one took advantage of the largesse.

Compared with the previous meeting, the stage area was almost bare. Sarah, Martin and three others—tight compact council, ready for business.

The ER MARSHAL approached the bunting-draped lectern and the crowd went silent. Sarah milked the moment almost dry then said, "I have a job to do."

Roger and I were hemmed against the fence at the back, too squashed to join in the applause.

"They attack like cowards, in secret, in the dark. They attack at night, uh . . . which is the same thing as the dark." She recovered with: "Although in this case we think it was day."

It was a crisis. The crowd was forgiving.

"It's plain as the noses on our faces that this is tied in with last year's spray-painting of the intercom at the gates. Along with the illegal pruning of the oleanders along the north wall and the dish detergent in the spa, it's obvious that this latest act of vandalism is part of a pattern."

"Ow!" Someone beside me had pinched his hand in the fence. Once we rearranged ourselves in the peanut gallery and determined there was no medical attention required, Sarah continued:

"Our best response is to go about our daily lives as normal. But in times like these, it is essential to cut to the chase of the bottom line. Many of us have concerns about the functioning of our neighborhood, a neighborhood I for one am proud to call the 'neat-as-a-pinniest' in this part of the valley."

A second applause break.

"Now they seem trivial. Ask yourselves, ask yourselves in your heart of hearts, whether you should be worried about the little things when our safety is threatened. Our forefathers gave their lives for the freedoms we have. They fought at Bunker Hill, the Alamo, the Dominican Republic, Granada, and now that way of life is under attack."

No applause, except from the guy with the monster truck, yet Sarah still had their attention and drove on:

"So we have to tighten our belts. Guard the gates. Focus on the important issues twenty-four-seven. Twenty-four-seven, people!"

That got the clapping going again and the monster-truck guy—one up on the rest in the applause department—craned his neck, proud to be the leader in following.

"By now you'll have noticed the changes to the committee list," Sarah said.

A mass rustling of paper suggested the contrary.

"For the sake of streamlining, to make your representatives more efficient and more responsive to the new situation, Architectural, Landscaping, Events, Motor Vehicles and Environmental have been combined and now fall under the direct authority of the Board. Secretarial and Financial have been meshed and assigned to another Board member, who is proud to take on the extra work. The General Committee has been reduced from three to one, yet still keeps all the responsibilities, plus the additional role of Assistant Emergency Response Marshal. Lastly, a new position has been created, that of Public Safety Officer. You all know Martin . . . " She gestured to the new appointee.

For a second I thought she'd left her husband for an old Soviet Chief of Staff. Apparently, the vandals had spared a footlocker full medals and decorations, and Martin was wearing the whole kit and a double portion of caboodle. He started to speak but the Boardhead wasn't finished:

"The reorganization will minimize red tape and increase efficiency. The five of us will work twenty-four-seven to serve and protect. Of course, the added burden on the Board will result in a few delays here and there, so to give us all time to settle in and get used to the new circumstances, the annual HOA elections will be postponed. The new measures are for all of us. Our safety. Our future. Our children's future. Together we can make this work."

The truck guy raised a fist in the air and hollered, "God Bless America, motherfuckers!"

The crowd roared out an edited version.

"One last thing," Sarah said when the cheering subsided. "Bunny's Bail Bonds and Pawn Shop has agreed to be our official sponsor. Other businesses in the area are being solicited, and the additional revenue will enable us to tighten security without putting an extra burden on you, the homeowners. As you can see, the new Board is already hard at work."

Someone started a chant, but after a few Buuuny . . . Buuuny . . . Buuunys, it died of accelerated old age.

"Our safety, our fate, is in our own hands," Sarah said. "White, black, beige." Pause to stare. "Large, small, medium." Pause to glare. "Catholic, Protestant, Other." Pause to inhale then blare, "We're in this together!"

She stepped back from the lectern.

I expected a Super-Bowl-kickoff response—Sarah's face showed she did, as well—but the crowd was busy processing the message and standard clapping was all she got. The scraping and folding of chairs did much to tone down the excitement, and there were more comments on the smashed beer bottle the truck guy dropped than on Sarah's closing remarks. As room opened for the SRO section to expand and Roger and I stretched the knots out of our limbs, several people—Tina among them—huddled on the far side of the enclosure, soberly assessing the surviving Board members.

Tina's group of skeptics was outnumbered by an order of magnitude by the mob around the Ford. The monster-truck guy was in back, passing out beers and leading a singalong of patriotic tunes.

As Roger and I surveyed a route around the action we heard "You two," and turned.

"Where's Juice?" I said. "You leave her at the Dowser's? She said she was coming back to help Martin and Sarah."

"Don't know about that," Sonny said. "Just that she's going like a hellcat out there, mopping and cleaning and getting ready to paint when I left. Sleeping another night with Roberto or somebody in some car, don't worry, not sleeping like that, Smitty."

"What are you doing here?" Roger said.

Tina darted out to join us, and as we all walked toward the house, Sonny filled us in: His wife in New Mexico was suing for custody of the kids. To date he had talked only with her lawyer, who claimed possession of solid evidence regarding Sonny's mistreatment of the two youngest. Specific instances—though Sonny couldn't remember the lawyer listing any—backed up by an eyewitness eager to testify. Bad father, the lawyer had said for his client, too much drinking and a dangerous car and an even more deadly dog and a house unfit for habitation.

So Sonny needed money for an attorney of his own, and as usual he had an airtight plan, this one involving an advance. If we coughed up for his lawyer's fee, he'd work a startling transformation on the house, customize it to our exact specs while boosting its market value out of sight. Financially, I was out of the equation. This was Roger's deal.

"Let me crunch numbers," he said. "Give me some time."

"Time," Sonny said. "Lend me bus money then. I'll jump the Greyhound go visit the kids in New Mexico." He leaned in, put his fists on the table and fairly screamed at Roger: "New Mexico, Rog! I get the galloping shits just visiting the *old* one!"

"Sonny . . . let me think."

"While you're thinking I better take every job I can." He was already walking and we followed in a small vee like Canada Geese. Roger and I held back and let Tina catch up to him, and when she put an arm around his waist he visibly relaxed.

At the Kolachuks' Sonny pulled away from Tina and started talking to Martin, who was down to an undershirt, dragging a splintered chest of drawers to join a pile of smashed homegoods at the curb. He looked our way and smiled wearily and we stood in the front yard like farmers discussing a hailstoned crop. Other than a few yeehaws and some rebel music from the house where the monster-truck was parked, normality prevailed, and I took comfort in the formation of gardeners promenading past in close-order, leafblowers strapped to their backs, scouring the tarmac with a punishing wind. Sarah joined us, and it didn't take much to convince us her skit at the meeting had been overreaction to the break-in. She had dropped all trace of fearless-leaderism, reverting to the Sarah we knew, an average middle-class pain in the ass.

As yet Martin had uncovered no evidence, though he'd been successful in bringing the police around, convincing them there was more to the matter than juvenile vandalism. He made much of his new contacts on the force. A Sgt. Coy Brickman and his partner Paco had been assigned to the case, and were taking keen interest in Martin's theories which, though incomplete, they both agreed were based on sound principles of deduction. Coy and Paco—Martin brandished their first names as though the three of them had spent thirty years together policing the New York docks—his buddies Coy and Paco, were keeping him up to date, and even passing on information they should have been keeping under their hats.

Passing drivers either laid on the horn and shouted support or motored past silently with their eyes fixed straight ahead. The HOA meeting had sundered the neighborhood's much-vaunted unity, and I began to feel like a policeman myself, one caught in the middle of a domestic disturbance, trying to arbitrate a dispute while catching grief from both sides. Eventually, after a round of goodbyes and thank-yous and take-cares and a keep-your-chin-up, we left Sonny with Martin curbside and headed home.

When we reached the house, I said, "I need a nap. I'm tired, really tired."

"Sleep the whole afternoon if you want," Roger said. "I'll put the slow cooker on and we'll have some comfort food when you wake up."

I awoke at two in the morning. Not a dream I could recall, not a break for a piss, unadorned oblivion. I reeled down the hall, groping my way toward the light. Roger jerked upright on the couch, pawing his eyes. The slow cooker had run out its time and a pinprick of red on the dial showed it was on warming mode. Roger reached in with the tongs through a mound of rice and green peppers and pulled out a chicken bone that had been stripped clean. I was ladling what had become soup when Roger came back from the bathroom and keyed in the phone code for messages.

"Three new ones . . . hangup . . . hangup . . . it's Juice . . . be home in the morning . . . getting a ride . . . oh, hey—" He shoved the receiver at me and shook his hand as if he'd been burnt.

—really mean it. Maybe it's all the stuff happening, but I need your cock and your tongue inside me and have you look into my eyes the way you do. I'm not pulling away from you or anything. I guess there's just people who need me now and that makes me need them, you know? I love you so much and you love me, I really get that, but a lot of bad things are happening and we're paying attention to that instead of each other. That doesn't mean we should run away and ignore everything just to be together. It'd be neat but other stuff would happen and I guess what I'm saying is we have to do something. Almost all my life horrible things have happened to me and I just let them go and tried not to worry about them and now with you I don't want to do that anymore. We're so perfect together and I feel safe and I'm really in love. You probably think I'm nuts or drunk or something to leave a message like this in the middle of the night, but the Dowser just went to bed and everybody else is in bed and I feel lonely. Maybe a little bit scared too, and wondering what to do, and then I feel guilty worrying about me all the time, and us, when everybody else is hurting, I mean, what's George going to do now? All his work and everything. I don't know what I'm saying. Anyhow, sorry for leaving all this on the message and I'll be home tomorrow morning, maybe even before you get this and I'll erase it and say everything again right to you and let you kiss me until everything's okay. Love you tons and tons and I love Roger too. Goodnight, you're my prince.

beep.

Roger gave me a second after I hung up and let me stare out the window.

"Have I been ignoring Juice?" I said. "Taking her for granted?"

"If I answered with something like, 'No more than you do anyone else,' would you be offended?"

"Something happened to George Sameshima. She didn't leave details."

The moon was casting so much light through the window I could barely make out Roger's reflection in the glass.

"She's not the same," he said. "She's not someone you dreamed up for a novel because no one in your book ever learned a thing. You deliberately stunted their growth, cut it off at a certain point. It's not always like that, Morty. Some people do something with their pasts other than keep re-living them. They redefine them, redraw the picture."

"What if she is? What if she's my wife and the woman from the novel and everyone else? What if they're all the same, every woman in my life?"

"You haven't known a woman yet with the insight and caring to leave a message like the one you just got from Juice. That's what makes her different."

I turned from the window and looked at him as though we'd just met.

"Shit," Roger said. "I apologize, I really do. I checked the messages an hour ago. Something in her voice worried me and I listened to the end in case there was an emergency."

"You could have put it on a speaker phone," I said. "The insult is you tried to hide it."

"You two are all I have right now," Roger said. "I can't even feel Mum."

"It's okay," I said.

He looked at the counter. "Chicken soup."

CHAPTER 23

I wanted Juice. I wanted her after so many years of solo undertakings; of pots abandoned in cupboards as submarine sandwich bags piled up; of waiting to critique a matinee until I saw Roger; of Triple-A baseball games at Nat Bailey Stadium, watching a bang-up play and nodding appreciatively to a total stranger next to me; of learning, or wanting to learn, with time for introspection yet mostly staring out the window and reading unchallenging books for the second or third time and pouring back the booze for lack of alternatives. I wanted her there all the time, wanted to be her center, though I knew I couldn't be and that was that. I'd known it from the start. Juice held to no orbit, and I wasn't much of a candidate for orbital focus in the first place. Still, if I couldn't exert the centripetal force needed to keep her on a continuous arc around me, at minimum I could serve as a reference point and that, going by the evidence, would have to do.

Eating the night before was a silly thing to do, breakfast of chicken soup in the wee hours then an unhealthy stretch of waiting for my digestive system to shut up so I could fall asleep again. My brain matched my belly and didn't call it quits till sometime after five. I woke at eight in the morning feeling grumpy and not at all eager for what was next.

Roger was approaching the house, weaving tiredly with a towel around his neck along the road from the pool. He rarely went for a dip in suitable weather, and this was nothing like it—a keen wind fetching from the San Gorgonio pass was bringing winter from points north and west. Roger pulled his robe tight as a gust feathered his hair, and he had to lean on the slider to close it. He was still dry, having discovered a sign on the gate declaring reduced pool hours to cut down on disturbances.

He set down the mail, a cord's worth of softwood product promoting meat and veggies, lawnmowers and loafers, equity loans and pearled teeth and mammoth fake mammaries. He retained a single sheet of paper, and after a grimace and a grunt passed it to me. He went down the hall and I heard the furnace kick in. I glanced at the paper, a desktop publication with the artless title *Sunday or Die!* When Roger returned and held his hands up to the hot-air vent, he saw the page lying on the table.

"I already looked at it," I said. "Observe the Sabbath or perish—the usual house of horrors."

"A few lines from the bottom, between the Bible predicting September eleventh and the beast enacting the death decree."

"'. . . will come the rains, and after the rains the houses of the people. And the children and infants will not be spared and a plague shall dwell on the land and the desert will deliver the sign of the beast.'"

"It didn't come in the mail. I found it tucked under the ashtray on the patio table. Same with the houses backing onto the pool, looks like they all got a copy. Maybe everyone did."

"So there's a nutter running around. Big deal, this is just a home-grown ripoff of Revelations or some other part of the Bible meant to scare the living shit out of people."

Over his shoulder, I saw George Sameshima's car enter, deposit Juice roadside and turn toward the Kolachuks'. Roger and I met her on the greenbelt.

She looked great—dirt-smudged and sweaty, hair winning the fight against two elastic bands trying to hold it off her face. She leaned her pack against a palo verde, grabbed our hands and towed us along back the way she'd come.

". . . we even got some planting in. The Dowser's collected all these seeds from desert wildflowers, little paper bags full, and we went out this morning and scattered them all over the backyard. Everybody really got into it, and just for fun we scratched out a space for a vegetable garden between some cars out front and planted some beans. The crows or whatever ate them, but so what. Sonny was the greatest. We got the toilet hooked up and it was sitting there all by itself on the concrete pad with everyone staring at it and thinking they'd rather keep pissing behind boulders and everything, and Sonny had a couple of beers and went out and sat down on it to take a dump. All the kids ran around squealing and a couple of old ladies tried to grab them, but pretty soon everyone was laughing, and two guys pulled out guitars, and the rest helped Sonny drag hunks of salvaged wood—you should have seen how far the water took everything—drag these hunks of wood back and we nailed up walls about this high. It's still open on one side, the part that faces the moun-tains."

"Sounds like you're back from a Peace Corps posting," Roger said.

Opposite the pool, Juice released us and in two shakes was over the gate and down to her underwear and into the water. I got hung up on the fence, bracing myself with both hands to keep from crushing my nuts. Roger had stayed on the path, senses on high alert for the arrival of a Black Maria full of thugs looking for our papers. As Juice climbed out and started pulling on her dirty clothes I made it over the fence, landing like some spastic Olga Korbut in the flower bed, and by the time I had splashed off the dirt with pool water, Juice and Roger were halfway to the road. By then I had climbing experience and made it to the summit of the fence and back down without supplemental oxygen. I jogged to catch up.

Other than the kitchen table, which had two-by-fours lashed to the broken legs for support, the Kolachuks' house looked like any other waiting to be remodeled. They'd cleared out most everything, and the mess could as easily have been from a demolition crew as a vandal. The table was overloaded with books and notepads, Martin's investigation in progress. A collection of cushions and pillows—some slashed—were aligned along one wall, providing seating for Sarah, Martin and George.

Juice was still dripping and Sarah, curfew-conscious, almost tore her eyeballs loose trying to look down at her watch without moving her head. George acknowledged us with a press-lipped nod. I'd come to suspect George's problems were perpetual and interwoven and impervious to diagnosis. True cause and effect, victimization, happenstance—hard to say. Did it piss rain on his head every time he went outside, or did he arrange things so that he had to go out every time it rained? I wondered what it was this time.

Martin uncrossed his ankles and rose from the cushions, a look on his face of crushing duty courageously borne. Summing available media information, his own educated hypotheses and inside information from his police buds Coy and Paco, his good buds Coy and Paco, he rattled off the situation as it stood:

"Fact—a woman became violently ill at the Big Happy Fun Chinese and Western Buffet Palace. Fact—she fled said restaurant in a panic and presented herself to the emergency room staff at the Millard Fillmore Center. Fact—she telephoned said restaurant, informing the hostess of her condition. Fact—at this particular point in time we know nothing further, though an unidentified doctor at the Fillmore assured us that in all probability as far as he can tell with the information at his disposal and not ruling out other possibilities, it is VATS—Very Aggressive Tracheal Syndrome—the same virus that has killed four to twenty-seven people in mainland Chad."

"All of Chad is mainland," I said.

"What?"

"The information seems . . . sketchy. Has anyone verified it?"

"These are facts," Martin said. "You don't verify facts, you verify other things. Speaking as an investigator, we'd never get anywhere if we spent all our time verifying things we already know."

George took over to clarify the situation, and we learned that the woman hadn't stayed long enough at the hospital to leave her name, so no one knew her identity. I pointed out the unlikelihood of a twenty-minute strain of a killer virus, but by then George was explaining that it had been a busy night at the restaurant and the hostess couldn't remember whether anyone had actually called about getting sick. And of course they didn't know who the doctor was. The only certainty was that there were a lot of facts, which taken together had caused the authorities to shut down the Big Happy Fun Chinese and Western Buffet Palace. The media, with nothing to go on, was reduced to covering the spread of the virus in Africa, though Martin assured us that investigators always held something back from reporters, privy information as he called it.

"I don't think anybody knows anything," I said. "Privy or not."

"You have to admit things have been spooky lately," Juice said.

"Yes," Martin said. "The evidence points that way."

"What way?" I said. "To spooky? Ladies and gentlemen of the jury, you've heard all the testimony and examined the evidence, and I'm confident you'll do your duty by returning a verdict of spooky."

"You're so negative," Juice said. "You know that? Negative."

Trying to be positive, I asked about the Kolachuks' repair plans. I could have screamed when Juice offered to stick around to help and Sarah beamed her acceptance.

I ran my fingers through Juice's hair and wearily said, "I'll take your pack in. Anything that needs washing?"

She shook off my hand and said, "You sit right there, George. Tonight I'm making supper."

Farewells and out the door and down the street and around the corner once again. At home, Roger let me puff out my cheeks and blow air and piss and moan until I spun on him and said, "How much did your mum talk about what went on around here?"

"Mum rolled along," he said. "After my dad died she started to disengage. Not one of those people whose life is tied so closely to her partner that she has no life without him, just someone who adjusts by avoiding new things."

"I know that much about her," I said. "It's not like we never talked. But right to the end she struck me as being a pretty aware old gal, and she had a lot of time by herself down here after your dad went. Didn't this place drive her crazy?"

"She said nothing ever happened. Even when I was here visiting it all was a little boring."

I was tight, knotty, and while stretching my hamstrings and shoulders out back I heard Roger on the phone. No call was innocuous these days, so I immediately went inside.

Down went the phone.

"Cassidy," Roger said. "He knows you plagiarized the book—"

"—How did he—"

"—or faked it, anyhow. Probably faked, because he didn't bring up Nuttall's name. No threats, he just wants the interview. Don't worry, if we present a solid front he won't have a way in. We should do our best to keep him away from Juice, though. She's too compulsively honest."

"I don't like him around at all. Sarah, Martin, Sonny, even George—too many cracks for him to squeeze through."

"I guess we'll have to out-wait him."

"At least the website's gone," I said. "He can go shit in his hard drive."

"Who are you yelling at?" Juice popped in from the patio. "I decided to come home. I miss you."

Her beauty doubled in my eyes. Had she parachuted into Hollywood at that moment, she'd be cast in eighty-five chewing gum commercials by the time she released the harness. Roger coughed and politely left.

"Quick," Juice said to me.

In the realm of things impossible, near the top of the list is criticizing the behavior of someone with whom you are joined at the genitals. As I drove and shifted inside her, I wanted to scream warnings. There was too much deviltry in the air for Juice's openness, sightless unpredictable mischief looking to stab at a soft underbelly exposed by open arms and a wide smile and offers of her time and self. I feared for her, and yes, I'm aware of how ridiculous that sounds—events of the past few days had showed Juice was much better equipped than I was to cope with the world when it bared its canines. Still.

We came together, and as we squeezed everything we could reach I wanted to tell her right then, to warn her, to help her find a way to hold on tight to her beautiful guileless self while having the sense to draw on some armor. Be well, that's all—be well and stay with me and stay alive. Then she grinned and laughed and I snapped out of it, feeling a total idiot, wondering how I had drifted like that, how so quickly I had managed to lose myself in clouds of foreboding, as though we'd been transported from making love in a southern California bungalow to the stone floor of a Bram Stoker castle.

Juice laughed again and licked a finger and stuck it in my ass, which was scary enough on its own.

CHAPTER 24

I opted out. Bad news fallout was clogging my lungs, and I withdrew, sur-viving on the least amount of interaction. By way of contrast, Juice was up to her elbows. She couldn't have been more helpful to all around her, and while I admit to a ration of discomfort at playing consort to a queen concerned with more weighty matters than her love life, it was good to see her happy. Roger too stayed involved—on a lower level of saintli-ness—and most of my journal entries for the month came second-hand from the two of them. Being hearsay, none of it would hold up in a court of law, even though it was undoubtedly more accurate than if I'd been present and recorded it myself. Here's the roundup:

Sonny couldn't catch a break. He was dying to start work on Sarah and Martin's, but the insurance company was out to set a new standard in unhelpfulness. Not only had they refused to pony up, their activity on the case had slowed to the point of paralysis and a simple returned phone call was cause for a minor celebration. Every day or two the Bonneville could be seen bullying aside more well-behaved vehicles on its way to the Kolachuk house. Sonny would get out and lean against it and smoke a cigarette while he stared at the project-in-waiting, a prize tantalizingly out of reach. On top of that, while still being hammered at by his wife's lawyer, he had to contend with an additional legal matter. A couple had hired him for a bathroom makeover, and on completion the plumbing let go, flooding the master bedroom, destroying the carpet and ruining the legs of an antique bureau. In the grand tradition of North American litigation, the couple was suing our handyman for costs, repairs, inconvenience, mental anguish, personal suffering, potential toxic-mold development, lost work time and the price of sixty-seven invitations and eleven pounds of spoiled crab legs after their Tribute to Gerald Ford party had to be postponed till at least Flag Day, if their ther-apist could work miracles and have them back in the land of the living in time to hit the target date.

Instructive as I found the developing legal soap opera, Sonny was up the creek. And to add insult to inglory, it was an inside job—Sonny fig-ured Quinn, the other kid, had sabotaged the job site.

Sonny claimed his son was the ultimate bad seed. Arrested at thirteen for driving a stolen welding truck the wrong way on I-10 outside Banning, Quinn was let off light by a sympathetic judge, and celebrated by staying drunk into his late twenties. Over the years succeeding judges were more inclined to treat him with boxing, rather than kid, gloves, and he bounced between juvenile detention centers and home, then jail and home, then jail and the street, then the street and home, and was now off in the desert doing something with somebody for some reason. Recently, Quinn had been dropping by Sonny's at odd hours to borrow what money was offered and stealing what wasn't. Boston Charlie had a visceral dislike for him—understandable, considering at fifteen Quinn trapped the dog under an overturned chair and stripped eight inches of skin from its tail—and last visit had gotten loose from the back room and captured a piece of calf muscle as Quinn raced for his car.

Our handyman was on a bit of a rampage, blaming his son for every dram of recent trouble, all of it, from initiating the custody battle by phoning his mother right on down the line. Big goddamn plan, the whole works. Probably wrecked the Kolachuks' house, somehow got the Dowser's place to flood, cut off Sonny's work, responsible for the law suit, all that stuff, bad kid, every kind of horrible, twelve kinds of trouble. All for revenge, plain spiteful revenge. When Juice asked what Quinn had to be so angry about, Sonny told her the kid had been threatening vengeance since he left the house at sixteen. When she probed further, looking for any kind of insight into Quinn's motivation, Sonny said he and his son just never had seen eye to eye on anything and, as if to temper the harshness of his judgment by giving Quinn a break, added, "And of course I did shoot him that one time."

As Roger hadn't yet agreed to the land deal, Sonny was scrambling for money. Time was short. A report in the paper said the project encircling Sonny's five acres had been revised upward, an increase in homes demanding an additional golf course and spa-hotel, bringing the numbers to ten-thousand houses, thirteen sets of links and four hotels. Much was being made of the wildlife corridor strategy, a system of trails and greenbelts expected to buffer the impact on the fragile ecosystem. Assuming the success of a proper training plan to teach the local fauna to follow the clearly marked paths and not venture into the encompassing world of pets, golf carts, Hummers, mowers, clippers, blowers, skimmers, bubblers, aerators, misters, hyper-fertilized runoff and country-clubbers, it would probably work. If it didn't, well, they say zoo animals have very easy lives.

On other fronts, good news and bad could easily be confused.

All Home Owners Association meetings had been suspended due to the outbreak of VATS. Gatherings of any kind were being discouraged by the public health authorities, so for the time being our neighborhood would be governed by Board fiat. Thriving on the crisis, Sarah began cannonading the compound's citizenry with Emergency Health-Watch Bulletins, collections of hortatory statements urging us to "pull together" and "form a united front" and dire warnings against failing to pick up our pets' "business." Within two weeks, the list of newly proscribed behavior included, among others, spitting, sending a parcel containing anything in powder form, swimming without having a current vaccination certificate and leaving trash by the curb for more than one hour before the garbage truck came, this last causing no end of ruined sleep for people who found it difficult in the first place as they punched off their alarms and humped their bags, boxes, cartons and bins to the curb at five-thirty each Monday morning before staggering like gut-shot wildebeest back to their dreams of scratch handicaps and a world in which you could chuck shit out front of your house for it to be whisked away by faceless civic employees who asked for nothing more than a sawbuck in a card at Christmas.

The coyotes were upgraded from cat-assassins to possible mammalian bearers of VATS, and it was now illegal to feed wild animals, pet wild animals, harbor wild animals, or take pictures of wild animals in the event it "encouraged" them.

As for the virus itself, our lives were sufficiently soaked with idiocy that the epidemic scare was just another spray from the hose. Hot on the heels of the SARS outbreak, VATS was able to piggyback on the publicity and cause a shitfit all its own. The World Health Organization had yet to comment, though that didn't stop the experts from analyzing, the pundits from pontificating, the seers from prophesying and the Movie-of-the-Week scriptwriters from stealing scenes from past MOWs starring various ex-*Charlie's Angels*. Airwaves, websites, newspapers, talk shows were crammed with information; medical authorities, politicians, tourism officials, restaurateurs weighed in on the subject. The Coachella Valley was abuzz.

No deaths had been reported, though dozens of people were under medical supervision for symptoms ranging from pulmonary edema to shingles. Sales of surgical masks were brisk, and a Palm Desert boutique began stocking a line in designer colors, including desert camouflage to show support for the troops. The virus carrier was still at large, small wonder with not so much as a description available. Anxious for solid information, I did what any eight-year-old could have suggested in the first place—went Googling. All praise! to the World Wide Web for raising us out of ignorance and delivering us. This is what I learned:

– VATS was the result of all those African guys fucking monkeys again.
– Saddam Hussein developed it.
– the Russian Mafia was spreading it.
– if not the Russian Mafia then a rogue element within the CIA.
– or the French.
– it was transmitted by physical contact, just like Alzheimer's.
– a woman in Vermont went crazy from it and murdered her husband.
– her husband deserved it, the shiteater, for breaking all those promises.
– chanting prevented it.
– so did Vitamin C.
– and shark cartilage.

Armed with the straight goods, who could remain afraid?

Finally, I came across a newspaper article that had at least a nodding acquaintance with plain sense. A Norwegian physician, Dr. Narfi, practicing out of the Millard Fillmore Center, boldly stated that VATS was not present in the valley. The mystery woman, in his opinion, could not possibly be running around spreading the contagion, since she did not exist. Every patient exhibiting signs of the disease was suffering either sympathetic or hysterical symptoms. No woman, no man, not one case. Moreover, he went on to assert, there was not a shred of scientific evidence supporting the actuality of VATS in the first place. Claims and reports from Chad resisted corroboration, and were so vague they could not even be investigated properly, never mind proven. In politic terms he basically told everyone to shut up until they knew what they were talking about.

At noon Roger called for me to come check out the TV. A CNN interviewer was chairing a panel discussion from Palm Springs with Dr. Narfi as the featured guest. The format was familiar. The host, nicknamed "The Virus Stud" for his bravery in traveling the world to report first-hand on epidemics, pandemics and epizootics, gravely posed each question before ceding the floor to Dr. Narfi, whose opinions were then savaged by a panel of experts consisting of a homeopath, a science-fiction writer and an actor who had had a bit part in *The China Syndrome* so knew more than your average layperson about syndromes in general. To frequent interruptions for commercials and vase-rattling martial music that played each time *The WAR on VATS—CRISIS in the DESERT* flashed on the screen, Dr. Narfi acquitted himself well. He was almost out of a visibly uncomfortable experience when a member of the studio audience leaped to his feet, denounced the doctor's stance as a coverup and accused him of being an al-Qaeda sleeper. Understandably annoyed, Narfi responded, "The Norse haven't had any terrorists since Eric the Red," just as CNN was cutting to a story on anthrax, presumably to be hosted by a Bacteria Stud.

At six o'clock came an evening news report that Dr. Narfi was in stable condition in his own hospital after being struck by a car in a hit-and-run following the CNN broadcast. A group calling itself Knights of the White Satin was claiming responsibility, vowing never to rest until the country was cleared of not only Arab terrorists, but Red ones, starting with Eric, as soon as they could get their hands on the filthy Viking Communist fanatic.

The eleven o'clock news roundup led off with the announcement that a wire-service reporter in sub-Saharan Africa had faked the VATS story. The whole thing, deaths and agonized suffering and whatnot, was bogus. No disease, no victims.

A hasty poll showed 40 percent of the population believed the crisis over. The majority thought otherwise. When a local reporter did a series of streeters, most of the passersby were reluctant to let go of their trauma, responding with versions and offshoots of "There has to be something to it" and "There's no sense taking chances" and "I'm not eating in a restaurant again until they catch that Eric guy." But the novelty had worn off, and sometime in the night the percentages switched and by the next morning most everyone had consigned their surgical masks to the dustbins and concealed their odd facial tan lines with self-bronzer.

George Sameshima's Big Happy Fun Chinese and Western Buffet Palace stayed closed. George stayed at the Kolachuks', a bankrupt-in-residence.

Sonny blamed the whole episode on Quinn. I was just glad it was over. And good thing it was—the wickedness was about to mushroom.

CHAPTER 25

I didn't awake from a long slumber revitalized and ready to three-stooge the world by tweaking its nose and snapping its suspenders. No, the time adrift served me poorly, doing nothing more than turn my hiking tan sallow, and transform me into a hermit imagining skullduggery and railing at scumbaggery. I assumed Juice was at the Dowser's again. She and the water witch were probably out on the property doing good for someone, and I couldn't help begrudging the recipient the attention. For a month I'd kept to myself, and now I was a baby who wanted my parents to stop with the going to work and the indecipherable blabbing and the cooking and the washing already! and pick him up.

I felt unglued, and Roger must have read my delamination through the walls, because when he came through the door from the garage and saw me sitting on the carpet with my back against the liquor hutch, he presented me with the car keys as though I'd just won the Neon in a draw.

"Go," he said.

Twice I swerved off the road, launching roostertails of sand into the air, but with luck I made it to the Dowser's in under an hour, missing a driveway collision with the exiting El Camino by the width of a rearview mirror. Not much looked different. The elements had softened the broken features from the storm's punchout, that's about it, and the place hadn't been a spa to begin with. Inside, I realized how truly out of glue I was.

"You look awful," the Dowser said.

"Tired, that's all. Juice here?"

"No, but come on, there's a huge vat of mulled wine waiting to chase away the February blahs."

I sniffed. "You put work socks in there?"

She laughed, and by the time we were sitting out back looking out and up at the Little San Bernardinos I felt better. I ran the cinnamon stick under my nose, its tropical aroma holding the chill at bay.

"Coldest winter since the seventies," the Dowser said.

"Long way from snow."

"Long way from home. You've been here almost six months. Part of your problem—starting to wonder whether the desert has accepted or rejected you."

"It's weirder than that."

"Weird how?"

"Bad weird," I said. "Nothing new to the world. I don't have to file for a patent. I have no thoughts on whether the desert accepts me or rejects me because I've barely seen it. I've even cut out my walks. Outside of going to the mailbox or the bathroom, I haven't been on foot for ages. No walking, just looking, looking around and all I see are foul things and people acting bad. And me, inside my head, a shift going on inside, a ratcheting up of . . . I don't know. I'm not right. I'm acting wrong. Okay, not acting wrong, though I sure haven't helped anything. Thinking, thinking weird. I guess I mean violent. There—violent. I find myself wanting revenge on people who haven't done anything to me other than offend my sense of what it takes to get along with everyone else. And if that doesn't overload my irony circuitry—I want to hurt people who hurt people. And I'm not even sure what I mean by the second part of that. They're just doing what they do, what people like that do, surely I can understand that. Undirected anger, that's what it is, or frustration or helplessness or whatever the fuck, undefinable urges, like the feeling you get on the edge of a roof or a balcony that you want to jump, even when your life is okay and nothing of the kind would cross your mind if you were down on the ground."

The Dowser put her hand on my knee, a mother's touch, and I almost cried.

"Give yourself the same break you give everyone else."

"I don't give everyone a break. It's a great concept and I try it on for size a lot, but every time I jump on a grenade to save the others in the foxhole I end up rolling off and throwing it into the crowd."

"You don't have to do anything. You don't have to fix things, even yourself till you're ready."

I rose to get more hot wine. "You fix things."

"I just have spare parking spaces and running water."

"You love people, you're connected. I can tell, everyone can."

"No one can tell anything. Rough suspicion is the best we can do. As far as you know, I was behind the VATS scare, and maybe I got Sonny up to his ass in trouble, and what if I vandalized Martin and Sarah's. . . . Maybe I need so badly to be loved and admired that I set up this little desert drop-in place to make me feel complete."

"That sounded way too dramatic to be anything other than an attempt at therapy. Don't try cutting yourself down just to build me up."

We sat quietly together until the drawn-out sound of a car horn spiked the peace.

Dust and dander and jetsam and cast-off thoughts and old cranky opinions and hunks of cardboard blown off sleeping street people and a junk shop full of every other bloody thing you could think of were adorning the sky behind the vehicle. It had to be Sonny driving so recklessly, and I dreaded the first glimpse of the Bonny once it came over the rise. But it was a car I'd never seen. Nevertheless, it cranked into a ninety, turned up the driveway and slid to a stop in the sand.

It was Juice, and the look on her face as she broke from the door made me shiver.

"Help me get her into the house." She scrambled to the passenger side.

The Dowser beat me to the vehicle and ducked to see in the window. "Tina."

"Yeah." Juice yanked open the door. "You take one arm. . . ."

"I'm okay, you guys." Tina got out and shrugged and struggled her way through the gantlet of helping hands. Her face looked a mess, though on closer scrutiny it was mostly sand adhering to a small amount of blood and sweat.

"What happened?" I said. "Should I call the police?"

"No." Tina sounded unsure enough to send the Dowser inside for the phone.

"Your leg looks hurt. You go off the road?"

"Let me," Juice said. She took an arm and steadied Tina with a hand to her back.

I took the other arm and we shuffled our way to the house. By the time we hit the overhang I was supporting almost all Tina's weight.

"Oh, this is stupid." Gently I carried her inside and waited till the Dowser pulled down the Murphy bed. Once under a blanket, Tina thanked us through ill-suppressed tears.

"The police and an ambulance are on the way," the Dowser said.

"It'd be faster to drive her myself," I said.

"We've moved her too much already," Juice said. "Just wait for once."

"For once?" I said. "I'm not the one who's been running around the goddamn valley—okay, sorry for that everybody."

"Some water?" the Dowser said.

Tina shook her head.

"What the hell happened?" I said.

Tina and a girlfriend ran a small cactus-and-pottery store near the highway. Juice had been on her way to see about helping out at the shop, but by the time she got there it was closed. Being so close, she set out for the Dowser's, and just a half-mile before the turnoff came across Tina crawling through the sand and creosote bushes toward the road.

"They were gone already," Juice said. "The fucking pigs."

"Start at the beginning," the Dowser said to Tina, dropping her voice and adding, "You should take some water. And I apologize, you don't have to say a word, dear."

"I was closing up," Tina said. "My partner was sick and I called to see if there was anything I could pick up for her on the way home. Annie, I called her at home to ask, she told me she'd forgotten to phone her boss. She has a second job at a bar, Annie works a second job at the bar, that one down the road, she forgot to call her boss and book off. I go right by there on the way home so I went in to tell him. He was okay about it and everything, even though I hate the place and him too, I told her that, I told Annie that a lot, that she shouldn't be working there. Anyway, he bought me a beer, the owner, the owner of the bar, and I drank it to keep the peace, you know? I got back in my car, and then just before cutting down towards town I had to pee. I was behind some creosote bushes, all scrunched down, and I heard footsteps. I started singing some stupid song to let whoever it was know there was somebody there, one of those songs, it doesn't mean anything, it just pops into your head, and I started singing it so they'd know somebody was there. Next thing I knew I was on my face in the gravel and I stopped singing, I think."

"Just rest," Juice said.

"I don't think I was . . . I mean, I'm sore but . . . I don't think he could, you know, reach. He wasn't on top of me or anything."

"It's just all so sickening," Juice said. "I feel sick to my stomach, really, like I could puke."

"Somebody who followed you from the bar?" I said to Tina.

"I didn't see him," she said. "After, I must have passed out for a while.

I can't remember anything except waking up and then after that, after I woke up, I pulled my jeans back up and crawled to the road, I crawled all the way to the road, and when I got there I saw that my car was gone. And then Juice came by. If I had passed out again or something, there by the bushes beside the road, it was almost dark already, if I'd passed out by the road behind the bushes or something in the dark, if Juice hadn't seen me . . ."

"I wouldn't have seen you on my own," Juice said. "All I saw was your car pull out up ahead and swerve like crazy booting it out of there. When I got to the spot I slowed down, and you were almost at the road by then. I didn't do anything. You'd done so good by yourself that somebody would have noticed. You did it all."

"So you couldn't have been unconscious long," I said. "Juice was pretty close if she saw the car."

"I don't know," Tina said.

"There must have been a second man with another vehicle," I said.

"Leave it to the police," the Dowser said.

"I was only wondering—"

"—Let her rest!" Juice said.

I went out front, ostensibly to watch for the cops. The sky was dark. No moon, no stars, and with no light pollution from the bead-chain of cities across the valley, it must have been a film of clouds that was rendering the inverted bowl opaque. When Juice joined me we stepped into the sand.

"How's she doing?" I said.

"She didn't explain everything," Juice said. "When I picked her up she was scared and mixed up. Even if she wasn't raped . . . she thinks whoever it was stuck something in her, up her."

"Aww, fuck. Fuck, honey." I turned my face to the mountains.

"I'm glad we're all here, that we were so close when it happened. The Dowser and you and me."

I glanced back at the house. "It feels odd with all the cars empty and nobody around."

"They come and go, like the Dowser said."

"The place looks wiped clean. I saw that old El Camino on the way in, that's it."

"It still feels good, safe," Juice said.

"We can leave." I drew her close to me and she rubbed her ear against mine. "The whole valley. I don't want to be anywhere that makes you afraid."

"Don't worry about that," she said. "I don't think I get scared."

She pulled away and I followed her toward the road.

As we passed the car I noticed the Avis license plate holder. "You didn't have to rent a car, baby. You could have taken the Neon, or I could have given you a lift if you wanted to talk to Tina about a job. And if you wanted to come here after, you could have done that, too. Stayed here, anything. I want you to do what you want to do."

"I have to get it back first thing in the morning," she said. "I borrowed it from Chas. He called yesterday, and I know you don't want him around, so I went to the hotel again to try and get rid of him. Don't look at me like that—he's harmless. He talked a lot about being really well-respected in his field, that kind of thing, even has a certificate on his wall, framed and everything, a newspaper award. Can you believe it? A guy carries around an award and sticks it on a hotel-room wall. It's not even real, one of those things you get at a carnival like those fake newspaper headlines, World's Greatest Salesman kind of things, or get your picture on the cover of *Time* magazine. I went on the Internet to check him out. If he's a reporter he hasn't done very good 'cause there's nothing about him at all."

"You borrowed his car," I said. "You said you were going to get rid of him and you borrowed his car?"

"I talked to him for an hour about my job as Sonny's helper, drywalling and the best caulk to use around the outside of a window instead of the inside, and how to change the transformer for a doorbell, and you should have seen the look on his face. You can tell he doesn't know anything about the real world. If we just act like we're normal people and nothing's going on, pretty soon he'll lose interest and go away. People quit things 'cause they're bored."

"You borrowed his car."

"Why are you stuck on that?" she said. "A normal thing to do."

"This is southern California," I said. "It's like borrowing someone's pacemaker."

"Don't worry, we've got more stuff on him than the other way around."

"You can't threaten a writer with exposing his lack of success," I said. "If no one's heard of him, there's the proof right there."

"I bet he's making up all kinds of garbage. Remember you told me about that goofy e-mail from his sister? Well, he doesn't even have one. I asked him right out if he had any brothers and sisters and he said no. He got real emotional about being an only child, except I could tell he was only looking for sympathy. What is it with guys they think every woman falls for the sad kind? And there's more going on with him, I can tell about people like that. I'm pretty sure he's the one who's been sending those pamphlets, those watch-out-or-you're-going-to-hell things we keep getting. He's got a big picture of Christ on the Cross beside his award, all in black and red and there's lightning in the background, scary. And he talks that way sometimes. You know, the day's coming when we'll be judged for our sins, and God sees everything so you'll be fried if you're evil. And another thing is he told me we live in a real nice neighborhood, and how would he know that? So really, I think he's got other problems, and if we just keep going on from day to day then he'll lose interest."

As I was about to point out that Cassidy was still around after weeks of no contact, having somehow mastered his boredom, the ambulance— preceded by two wailing police cars, trailed by another and flanked by a pair of outriders with two wheels apiece kicking up rocks on the shoulders—came over the rise. They swept into the turn toward the house, blinding us with their fourteen headlights and circus of flashers.

What seemed like the whole mob knew the Dowser. As the medics trundled in a gurney and gave Tina a quick examination before rolling her to the door, the cops variously looked out the windows and checked in the fridge and sat on the kitchen counters as if they'd only recently been occupying the squatters' cars outside. A serious-looking older officer followed beside the gurney, interviewing Tina until realizing her sedatives were precluding substantive answers. At the ambulance, he peeled off and shooed me ahead of him back into the house. He looked around at the other cops without a word until the battalion reluctantly detached itself from the furnishings and left.

After the Dowser handled the introductions the detective, John Legree, turned my way. "You the one who brought her here?"

"She did."

"Yes," Juice said. "And I can show you exactly where I found her."

"We have officers there," Legree said. "Witness called it in anonymously. We had no idea where the woman got to till the Dowser phoned. What time did you find her?"

"No watch. Just about dark, though."

"She did say she passed out, but we don't know for how long." He turned back to me. "Where were you?"

"Me?" I said. "I was here."

The Dowser confirmed it with a nod.

"Around four-thirty, five?"

"About that," I said.

"You don't sound too sure."

"I'm not."

"Where were you coming from?"

"Listen, I drove right past there, okay?"

"Easy, not accusing you of anything," he said. "Just trying to establish a rough timeline."

"Sorry, I meant . . . I feel bad. It's the thought of driving right by without seeing anything. If Juice hadn't come along Tina could have died."

"We got the tip. We would have found her."

We finally sat down and Juice told the detective everything she could remember. The Dowser and I had little to add, and overall Legree seemed satisfied.

"What about the bar she mentioned?" I said. "You have trouble there in the past?"

"The Blue Dog?" the detective said. "Ongoing trouble, in spite of the fact half the force drinks there."

"So what's next, John?" the Dowser said.

"We'll know a lot more once we get the reports from the scene and the medical examiner. I'm going to follow up on both right now."

"Don't waste any more time here. I'll see you to the car. You still have the number?"

Legree smiled like an old lover and they went out front.

When I returned from the bathroom the house was empty. In the front yard, the Dowser was standing right where the rental car had been.

My sigh was so heavy I almost ruptured heaving it. "Hospital?"

"She wants to see Tina alone," the Dowser said.

I let the caterwauling in my head scream itself out and followed her back inside, and we took our drinks into the main living area. Without a second thought, I stretched out on the bed I had laid Tina on and went through a fire-alarm of awful thoughts when it registered where I was.

There was a vision, a revolting image of Tina in the sand behind a creosote bush with her jeans down and her ass up and a man with a bottle—jerked upright, sweating. I got up off the bed of bad dreams and went to the kitchen. I had to move, to be active, physical movement as a salve.

The Dowser let me be, allowing the momentum to dissipate, and chose precisely the right moment to lead me by the hand outside and swing the subject around. She talked of the desert and the mountains and the people of the valley and my anger and unrest percolated away. I asked her about herself and learned that she'd just told me, that in a way she was defined by the entwining of earth and folk around her. I wondered aloud how she supported her tiny desert empire and found out she dowsed. Unable to keep a perfectly straight face—half amused, half embarrassed—she told me that's how she made a living. Aware herself that there was no such thing as actual provable dowsing, still she played the game, answering the call from corporations to whole towns to show up with a forked stick and look for underground water. She'd mumble to herself and tell everyone to stand back so they didn't interfere with the Hartmann Lines or block the E-rays, and bring out her desert willow fork and find them water. If she didn't find it, well, there was bad energy in the town or interference of some sort.

"So you're a scam artist." I raised my glass.

She matched my hoist and we drank, and after a strong embrace she walked me to the car.

As I fumbled with the keys she said, "I'm looking forward to reading your book."

"Maybe some day. Too bad Juice left it in Vancouver."

"Don't be silly," she said. "She already gave me a copy."

It was so dark the headlights created their own tunnel. One more stop.

CHAPTER 26

I ran out of road. I must have driven right past the Blue Dog on the first go, and despite slowing down did so again on the return. Third time lucky, if you want to call it that.

I spent a lot of time in taverns of that stripe after my wife died, tap rooms with cauliflower ears, raw places from which you could get barred for being drunk and refusing to fight. Despite the desert's lack of scent-carrying humidity, the saloon smelled of nineteenth-century steamer trunks and piss. I hadn't been there since my research days, and as that was an admittedly hazy time, I avoided the few patrons as if it were my first day in prison. The table at farthest remove from the bar placed me less than a pool-cue length from two men with ponytails already giving me the hairy eyeball, so I entrusted my safety to Stan at the bar, hoping he remembered me, and sat on a stool with my feelers up. I like to think I know how to behave under duress, despite much evidence to the contrary. Sometime after my wife's death I got talking in the local Legion to a vet who had served in both WWII and Korea, and he told me that everyone runs. "In war, the heroes are the ones who run toward the enemy," he said. "The cowards are the ones who run away. And when the shit hits and the stress gets awful, so awful you can't stand still, you're going to run all right, you just don't know which direction till the time comes." Made sense to me. All reactions are understandable at such an elevated level of stress, courage and cowardice being two sides of the same groin.

I don't know what I'd expected from stopping in—a besotted stranger with a loose tongue bragging about taking some black chick down? A cop sniffing around for clues? I guess I just had to see the place again in its new light. I left a generous tip in case I ever found myself in there again and needed Stan's backing, and nodded goodnight to the old guy beside me. He cackled at something on the TV over the bar.

I hoped Roger was still up, but no such luck. I stretched out on the couch and jacked the remote and flicked a few channels until turning off the TV and falling asleep. Sometime later I awoke to Juice's silhouette.

"How long have you been standing there?" I tried to stand but she was in close, looming over me. I put the side of my head against her stomach and wrapped my arms around her hips. "How's Tina?"

"What were you doing in the Blue Dog?" she said. "I went by on the way home from the hospital to check, wanted to . . . just see it, to make it real or something. I saw you pull out."

I eased her away till I had room to stand. "I promise never to try to run your life or tell you what to do, but please, you're doing enough for everyone already. Don't get too deep into this one. Whoever attacked Tina . . . I can't stand the thought of you by yourself running around the desert, hey—you weren't there all this time?"

"Didn't even go in," she said. "I drove, went driving all over. I ran out of gas a few blocks from the Marriott, and left Cassidy's car there and walked home."

I ran my hands up the back of her legs and under her shorts.

"Tina's in and out of being awake," Juice said. "Really fuzzy on the details. I didn't like the way that detective was going after her, like it was her fault or something. He won't tell me what they found at the scene. I went there from the Dowser's, and when I pulled over he almost screamed at me to get out of there. Leave the area, he told me, get the fuck out of here. They didn't even have that yellow tape up, just a bunch of lights and some men hanging around like after a high-school football game. Two of them had beer on their breath. I hate cops, you know? I fucking hate them."

By then I had worked her panties aside and was gently massaging her with two fingers. I might as well have been shaking her hand; she pulled away and went to the kitchen, snapping on lights, and I followed.

"You guys okay?" Roger was peeking around the corner. "I heard. Sonny's number was on a piece of paper in Tina's wallet and the police informed him. He phoned here looking for . . . I think he just wanted to talk to someone."

"She has no family here in the valley," Juice said. "I should stay with her when she gets out. This guy, this stalker or whatever, might come after her again."

"What's happening?" I said. "What are we doing here? We were coming down to soak up some sun and get away from, I don't know, whatever we needed to get away from, and here we are up to our asses in shit and nonsense and everywhere we turn. I'm sick of it, sick of waking up to bad news and people making it worse, sick of trying to stay out of it and getting dragged right back in. Sick of everybody."

"Thanks," Juice said.

I whirled. "Not you. Although you're not helping anything running around like Joan of Arc."

"Who?"

"What? I don't know—Helen Keller, then. One of them. The Lady with the Lamp, Mother Teresa, any of those fuckers."

"Do you want to go?" Roger said softly. "We can leave whenever you want, you know that. It's not the first time I've offered."

"Offered," I said. "See? Offered. I have to wait for your offer, as if I'm incapable of cutting my own path through the disorder. Even with you—" I rounded on Juice "—you sent me an e-mail and I boiled over like I just had my first wet dream."

"Say the word and I'm off."

"Oh, I don't want you to go anywhere. But you're acting strange lately. There—if we're talking plain then I'd like to say you've been acting strange."

"You mean by not spending every second with you? Paying attention to people who need my help? Besides, I'm not the one who disappears every day without saying anything to write notes for hours on end."

"How about tonight?" I said. "I woke up all sleepy on the couch and so happy to see you and you acted like I wasn't even there."

"Right," she said. "Our friend's attacked, and I come home from the hospital and don't turn to jelly when you grab my cunt."

"That's not what I—"

"—Maybe Roger's right. Maybe we should all go home."

Where to go, what to think, what to do. "I'm seeing shadows that aren't there and reading plots into everything and making things worse. Tina. It's nauseating, driving home, just heading home from work one minute and the next there she is in the hospital brutalized and scared out of her mind."

"She needs us so we help," Juice said. "Right? Right, lover?"

"Of course of course of course."

"She's getting good help at the hospital. The doctor's really nice, didn't worry about me being just a friend instead of family, she told me everything she could."

"Ahh," Roger said. "One of those Florence Nightingale fuckers."

I would have been a barbarian not to laugh.

I'm not sure my bout of foot-stomping and breath-holding qualified as clearing the air. It felt more as if I'd changed the state of the garbage, burning it to clear the land only to transform it into noxious aerosols, but I'd said my piece, and good thing I squeezed it in when I did—The Handyman Cameth.

So adroit was Sonny at dealing with life's sticks and stones, it was easy to forget his bones were breakable. It was four in the morning when the Bonneville loosed a muffled afterfire and settled down in the driveway. Sonny entered without knocking, and nothing seemed more natural. He got a hug from Juice and heys from me and Roger. He pulled a plastic container of leftover pasta salad from the fridge, leaned against the counter and dug in with a dirty spoon he found atop the coffee can.

"The Blonde Job doing in that bar the first place? She could've phoned, they got phones these days."

"Who could have known?" Juice said.

"Not about knowing, not that at all. Just if she didn't have that beer she wouldn't have to piss at the side of the road. What's that? Pissing at the side of the road out in the desert when it's almost half dark? Anyhow, safe and sound now, home sleeping."

"They released her?" Roger said, or maybe the three of us said it at once. "This time of night?"

"Yeah, released her just like that."

"Think about it, Sonny," I said. "What are they going to do when they find her gone?"

"They don't like it they can lump it," he said. "Lump the shit out of it."

"What if there's internal damage?" Juice said. "You listen to me, you better be sure she's well enough to be at home."

"Not all stupid, me. They were going to let her go tomorrow anyhow."

Sonny had gotten no more information from Detective Legree than we had, which for now was fine with him. It would give him time to get to Quinn on his own.

"You can't possibly think your son did this," Roger said.

"I'd take a drink," Sonny said. "Anything high-octane'd be okay. Be back in five."

On his return he assured us Tina was still sleeping soundly. We threw on jackets and arranged ourselves around the patio table, half-lit from inside. Sonny was in charge.

"I went to school."

Not enough details to call him a liar.

"Same with Saxon and Delilah," he said. "Probably it would've been good for Quinn. Home schooled him, my wife. Taught him all right, always been trouble him and me. But I don't know, doesn't matter sometimes who does the teaching, things still get all sticky. Take Martin for an example. Enough school to do him some good, had a business and a house and a wife and a kid and everything and now what? Never sees his kid and here's his house wrecked and the insurance company stonewalling 'cause of the fraud."

That was the first we'd heard of it. The insurance company thought it was an inside job, and according to Sonny the Kolachuks certainly needed the cash. Martin had sold his interest in the golf car business years back, and was being kept on just to clean up around the place and to talk to customers from the old days. The profit from the sale had been plowed—almost literally—into George Sameshima's string of restaurant disasters, which besides his defunct Mexican and shut-down Chinese ventures included an initial Greek and subsequent Ethiopian.

"Not that George screwed them out of the money, he's just sort of Georgish with business. You all can read him a mile away. I mean Rog, your mom must've told you about him from away back, she knew all us guys."

"How—"

"—Dowser and her were old buddies. All that thing they had going on. But enough about that, it's not what we're talking about."

Clearly it wasn't and shouldn't have been enough for Roger. This was mother-son stuff, astronomically more important than the spiral of personal misadventure afoot, of blame and justification and finger-pointing and backward-glancing in which we'd become enmired. Roger tried to draw him out, but Sonny was flying solo at an altitude out of earshot, staring at the sun as it rose under the branches of the big eucalyptus in the green belt.

"Funny thing," Sonny said. "All them stars up there, how big everything is, goes on forever some of the scientist guys say, and just a hundred-thirty-mile away from here is Los Angeles. People and their yachts and sports cars and bars and restaurants and theaters and that, and a few hours from now they'll send out a baseball team with guys making millions who'll lose afuckingain."

Whatever his point, we raised our glasses to it.

But Sonny still wasn't done. He leaned his elbows on the patio table and looked at me gravely. He held my eyes and in measured tones said, "Smitty, you saying you drove right by there on the way to the Dowser's and didn't see nothing? Can you tell me how that could happen?"

CHAPTER 27

Not a shot fired in anger—a quiet palace coup, and just like that Sarah was deposed and the HOA cleansed of her cronies. There was much neighborhood breath-holding in anticipation of trouble at the changeover, but nothing of the kind materialized, no random slaughter, no streets aswarm with prisoners pardoned from dungeons, not even Sarah's head on a pike.

But with no new leader, the golden age couldn't last long, and it didn't. As the ranks of the revolutionaries swelled with opportunists, potential putschists multiplied, and within a week infighting had us on the verge of anarchy. Rules changed daily, or at least rumors of them did, since the HOA meetings were still suspended and not a soul wanted to propose legislation for fear of being caught on the wrong side of the factional spasm once things settled down. All this, however, was in the upper echelons. For the disenfranchised renters—the great unwashed—the period of doubt with its possibility of a new social order brought pure glee, and they threw themselves into the false spring, swanning and jackknifing into the pool beside the NO DIVING placard; planting unapproved annuals in their flower beds; encouraging their children to play in the green belts, where the young nihilists pounded the grass with soccer balls and unshod feet.

That era too was short-lived, and by the beginning of Week 2 of the New Society the masses were growing wary of such unchecked libertarianism. People reverted to honking their horns in greeting rather than flashing the upraised fist that had been so in vogue during the heady first days of liberty; the shrubberies gradually resumed their geometric profiles after a week of botanical madness; parents confiscated soccer balls and bought their kids new footwear.

By then the command structure was crystallizing. Not all was positive—scuttlebutt had it the leadership favorite was the monster-truck guy, even though he hadn't been seen in the compound for weeks—but we were living in a free land, and gave thanks for our leaders' benevolence in not taking the flats of their swords to our shoulders for lack of revolutionary zeal.

As for more serious matters, Tina was getting constant care and attention from Juice, who had moved into the house with her until such time as . . . well, there was no time limit. I checked on them the first few days, toting groceries and offers of help, but Tina was withdrawn and Juice was committed and I had no idea how to change the situation or whether it even should be attempted. Sonny was in the same boat. Whenever he showed up the two of us followed the girls from room to room around the house like orphaned hatchlings imprinting on surrogate parents. I never feel more of a man than when faced with its limitations.

Detective Legree called most days with an update. Tina's car had been found across the Arizona border in Yuma. Wiped clean, no evidence. We'd surmised correctly—the attacker had arrived by vehicle with an accomplice, though both the second car and the criminals had vanished, leaving not so much as a skid mark. The anonymous phone call was all they had to go on, and whatever Legree had gleaned from that he was keeping to himself. He didn't trust me, that was certain. He had me go over my route to the Dowser's—where I'd turned and what I saw and at exactly what time—so often and with such intensity I lost track of whether we were still talking about California, and if so, what year. I actually began to doubt my own story, and several times wondered how many suspects in how many places how many times had confessed to crimes of which they were innocent just to shut everyone the fuck up.

Sonny couldn't shut up. "Quinn!" he shouted over Tina's shoulder into the phone every time Legree called. "It's Quinn! Find him! Do your job!"

Quinn? Roger and I didn't believe it. Try as we might, we couldn't summon the necessary mindset. No matter the abuse, real or perceived, visited on a child by a parent, to gain revenge in such a circuitous way was impossibly alien to us, notwithstanding it happened all the time. Tina allowed for it, but a good part of that was to placate Sonny. Her voice had shrunken since the attack, and she responded to his tirades about Quinn with a string of maybes and couldbes, which were easily translated into whateveryousays. She was scared and cowed and no, I'm not blaming it on Sonny. Juice was close to being convinced. She'd been unintentionally leaving a trail of clues, emotional responses out of scale with the conversation alluding to an upbringing even more awful than her earlier references indicated. She had trouble with the hypothetical scope of Quinn's activities, but identified with the mental disposition required for an individual to strike out in any way possible, violent assault on a third party included.

Violent and sexual, definitely sexual. When Sonny wised up the morning after talking to us and took Tina back to the hospital, the doctor confirmed it. Tina had been violated with a length of glass, most likely a soda or a beer bottle. Her face ground in the sand, ass in the air, raped at arm's-length.

Martin's beefy shoulders had much to bear. As a sop to continuity he had been retained by the HOA leadership as Public Safety Officer, and felt Tina's case fell within his bailiwick. His anguish was real, but not to worry, he was on the job 24/7 and all evidence was being passed on to Coy and Paco, who assured him another detective from the station, one Maynard Rivas, had been assigned full time to the case. Legree, though . . . Detective Legree, John Legree . . . nope, didn't sound familiar, maybe a new guy transferred in. Martin told me he'd check into the matter, and quickly, as Coy and Paco would be some steamed if some outside cop was horning in on their case. No telling where this Legree, was it? came from. Fed maybe, maybe with the Feds. When I told him the detective seemed to know the Dowser from away back, so probably wasn't a newcomer, Martin got embarrassed and chided me for providing unnecessary information, the kind that stopped investigators from getting to the bottom of important cases like vandalism and rape and suchforth. Suchforth, our Public Safety Officer said.

I had only one good talk with the Dowser about it. My simple-minded conspiracy theories—most involving Sarah—were muddying my brain, and I needed help. Waiting till Roger and Juice were on their way with a casserole for Tina, I phoned without really expecting an answer. But I guess the Dowser was as needful of contact during that period as any of us.

The first thing she told me was to stop linking every single event.

"A pattern exists," I said. "I just can't decipher it."

"We perceive closely spaced things as having been caused. We see patterns because we look for them, it's too hard to accept an absence of plan. Besides, you're not seeing patterns, just clumping. Blindfold someone and tell her to jab a piece of chalk onto a blackboard a thousand times and the dots will never be evenly spaced. That would be a pattern, which would never happen unless she could see through her blindfold. What actually emerges are clumps of dots in various places. Our eyes are drawn to them, and we take the clumps to be a pattern and extend it by tying the clumps together. It isn't long till we start making something out of the connections. A face or a bear or a swan or a hunter, a pattern with influence, power . . . a purpose. A reason for the lack of symmetry."

"This isn't news to me," I said. "I just want to know why I can't resist it."

"Because you're feeling guilty and sad. All these things are happening right around you so you think somehow you're responsible. That's an egocentric way of looking at things, if you don't mind my saying so. The concept that you occupy the central position is so childish I should offer to wipe the spit from your chin."

"Don't talk to me about guilt," I said, and confessed. Right then I told her flat out that A *Quake in Time* was a diddle-job, how its creation had me spooked, but before I could get into details she told me she already knew. What? Besides the obvious fact that I was passing off a fictional event in an invented town as a memoir, she said the story felt stitched together. Early clues were my sloppiness in peppering maritime metaphors throughout a desert tale, and that twice I called the earthquake a storm. But the telling point was that all the emotional drama simply didn't sound like me. My voice was recognizable in passages about the catastrophe—all well written, she assured me—but it was another's that narrated the familial tragedy, everything of importance.

And then she delivered the KO punch: "Your novel was more consistent, and much better."

"What the hell are you doing to me?" I yelled. "You saw through me at the get-go and ever since you've been killing me in increments, very lightly kicking me to death."

"You were using a false name and I assumed there was a reason. When you volunteered your real one it showed you were reaching out. It's what we all do. That's what a society is, interaction and sharing. My job wasn't to break you down. Not only that, you operate as if Roger's the only person in the world in on the big dark secret. Maybe you even believe it, but if you do you're undoubtedly wrong, and the secret isn't very big and not very dark in the first place."

"The whole world may as well know."

"Maybe it does but it doesn't care. It's much too big to worry about singling you out. I knew because your novel touched me, still affects me after all these years. It was a wonderful piece of work, wonderful in the true sense of the word. I read that book and I read it again with four fingers—each one acting as a bookmark so I could refer to the passage again or tie it in with the page I was on—and the fingers helped. There are more nerve endings in the ends of our fingers than anywhere else on our bodies, unless, well, the cock and the pussy have to have more, but maybe not, maybe not as many as the tips of our fingers, the tips that can touch the ends of our thumbs and grasp things, make a circle, make us human."

"Uh, this may sound odd, but you haven't been contacted by a reporter lately, have you?"

"Cassidy?" she said.

"Fuck."

"He came out here by cab looking for his car the day after Tina was attacked. He's not the kind of man you warm to right away, at least I didn't. Put your mind at ease, I told him nothing."

My neck was getting sore from shaking my head. Good thing there was only one more thing to clear up. "What was the warning about?" I said. "'Be careful. The storm wasn't it.' You said that to me when we were leaving after the big flood."

"Don't assign insight to me," she said. "Illusions, that's all I create. My answers are the same as yours. I'm flattered someone who could write what you did looks upon me as a font of wisdom, but I'm fresh out, if I ever had any. Pick and piece together is all I do."

"I used to have insight," I said. "Pretty good handle on things."

"But after, Morty. After your wife died and your novel was finished, maybe you didn't use the recovery time very well. You lost your certainty. After the grieving came the groping."

"Good line," I said. "I'll have to steal it for a book."

"I have no good way to wrap this up, but I have to. Just heard the truck that's bringing in a new batch of immigrants. One last thing—I really truly no kidding loved your novel. Horrible as it was about the family and all the tragedy, I got the message."

I hung up and had only started to replay the dialogue in my mind when Roger poked his head around the corner from the hallway, startling the hell out of me. On his heels were Sonny and Boston Charlie.

"Smitty," Sonny said. "I need some chicken."

I laughed. Really laughed, I mean, a good bloody roaring that made me put my forehead on the table. The two of them waited. "Sorry guys, don't know what got into me, just chicken, you know? I just got off the phone with the Dowser and now chicken."

Sonny took the Bonneville on a bird run and came back with a barrel from the Colonel's and we ripped through it at the kitchen table till deciding it was time to play cards and Sonny cheated and took Roger and me for eighty bucks apiece and we laughed some more because that's what you do when tension becomes personified and the man dealing the cards has just had his loved one raped with a bottle and he thinks his son did it. And by the time we called it quits and Sonny and Boston Charlie passed out together on my bed and Roger gave me a hug and I returned it, things seemed a little better.

Chicken. I fell asleep on the couch with the TV on and grease all down my front and that pasty gravy the Colonel makes staining my shorts.

CHAPTER 28

Sonny left with B.C. sometime in the night. A week went by with neither sunburned hide nor cropped hair of him, and surprise of surprises it bothered me. Can't say I actually missed him, though I was looking forward to the visit, if that's the term for bailing a man out of jail.

Juice brought Sonny's car over from Tina's, but after all this time I was still alarmed at the thought of her behind the wheel, unable to purge the image of her black hair flying and her dark dark eyes boring as she propelled her Falcon over grass, flower beds and asphalt at the Hari Krishna parade, so I commandeered the keys to the Bonny and insisted she ride with Roger in the Neon. As well, there was an itch I had to scratch alone.

I wouldn't be going anywhere till I found the seat latch. I had to be six inches taller than Sonny, but couldn't have reached the gas pedal with a garden rake. I groped under and between my legs, pulled the only thing I could lay my hand on and slammed into the steering wheel, rammed back to full extension, forward and beeped the horn with my chest, shot rearward and finally released the handle before I accidentally blew the dragchute or something, settling on a position that left me reclined like a SoCal gangbanger in his low-rider. Easy after that—a turn of the key and thunder-rumble-lurch I was off toward the gates, chin up to see over the dashboard.

The Blue Dog's dirt parking area was almost full. As I pulled the desert schooner beside a wreck that wouldn't have looked out of place in the Dowser's front yard, two men in crumpled cowboy hats dropped their cigarettes and bolted inside. I got the Bonny's door closed on the third slam and looked up to see Stan on the plank verandah, a shotgun cradled in the crook of his elbow. He raised the barrel an inch or two and moved toward me.

I said the first thing that came to mind: "When does the band start?"

At least it arrested his progress. The shotgun dipped, he said, "Bands," spat, and finished with: "About when I die."

I considered the shotgun, and let him have a moment to reconsider whatever he was considering. Fortunately, Detective Legree stepped outside and took the gun, which looked more natural in his care than in the owner's, or at any rate more benign.

"The fuck you doing here?" Legree said.

"And with that?" Stan waved at the Bonny.

"Thought I'd look around," I said.

"Sonny done enough already."

"I'll keep my hands in my pockets."

I expected to see a few loose hinges, dings and dents, at most a cracked bar mirror, but Sonny had done a bang-up job of banging up the place. Six or eight workers were measuring and sawing and hammering and wiring alongside a squad of women painting and telling them to hurry up, get a move on, and commenting on how much nicer their houses would look if only the men would approach home repair with a fraction of the commitment they were investing in the bar. Anyone too old or injured or drunk to help with the labor sat watching with a barroom squint, the rheumy-eyed stare that comes from habitual reassessment of the past.

On the bar was a field of beer. Two bartenders were dropping fresh glasses in sync with the disappearance of the old as each worker peeled off from his task, grabbed a drink, downed it on the way back and slapped up another board or stripped another wire before rejoining the counterclockwise gyre to the bar. It reminded me of old Klondike Gold Rush photos, prospectors and speculators in endless lines snaking up and over the White and Chilkoot passes, sandwiched tight, since to fall out meant hours of waiting to rejoin the procession.

"What made you stop by the night of Tina's attack?" Detective Legree said. "You didn't tell me about that."

"Aw, he didn't do nothing," Stan said. "Sat awhile, tipped good."

"What's with Sonny's car?" the detective said.

I told him about meeting the others to bail Sonny out of jail, sending the wind up the owner's shorts. "Told you I weren't pressing charges," he said to Legree. "Just wanted him cleared out of here."

"He didn't stop at wrecking the room, Stan. Four cases of assault."

"These old boys do worse to themselves every Friday night. Assault my ass, Johnny."

"Not my decision," Legree said.

"Well, he better get out soon," the owner said. "Lots of enthusiasm when the beer's free, but somebody's going to screw up something in here and I wouldn't mind a professional checking her out before she goes up in flames from a bad wire, or comes crashing down on my head the middle of the day."

I was somewhat surprised Sonny was allowed back in the place, and employed to boot, but if Stan considered Sonny a professional, maybe he'd taken a lick in the head during the fracas and couldn't be held liable for his actions.

"I should get going," I said. "They'll be waiting at the jail."

Out on the verandah Legree said, "Heard you been calling yourself Smith. Names are important, you learn that in this business. All lying starts with the alias."

The glare outside was too much after the gloom of the bar, and I'd left my sunglasses in the car. I shielded my eyes, stepped into the gravel and asked Legree how the investigation was going, dropping Coy and Paco's names in passing. He'd never heard of them.

"Martin Kolachuk says he's working with them on the case," I said.

"The guy around the corner from Tina? I wouldn't put my life on the line over what he says."

We reached the car and I put my hand on the roof. "Am I free to go?"

"Eyes and ears open," he said. "Keep me informed of anything that seems out of place."

"Not with the way you put it."

"You could find yourself in a lot of trouble."

"Only if I was involved," I said. "I'm not, and this isn't 1950s Alabama, so I don't expect to be hassled by some cop who turns out to be the son-in-law of the governor or something. Not that I'm averse to helping, but from a request, not a demand."

"Getting real close to making me suspect you again."

"You don't suspect me at all. You've known all along I have nothing to do with this—you've been on my ass for reasons of your own. Now if you don't mind."

"Hey!" Stan shouted from the verandah.

Before the owner could reach us Legree quickly said, "I don't like what's going on in that neighborhood of yours. Keep your head up, be careful."

"Damn it all." Stan pulled up in the dirt and spat. "One of the old boys cut through his own cord with the power saw. Wouldn't happen to have one in the back?"

We ducked our heads to check out the entanglement of construction supplies behind the front seat. Considering the fact Stan wasn't pressing charges, I figured he should get some kind of recompense, and I told him to take whatever he needed. The owner and the detective agreed, pillaging the Bonny of an assortment of tools and supplies and piling them in the dirt.

Thirty minutes later I pulled up to the police station. Sonny was lighting a cigarette from Juice's coal while Roger paced the sidewalk. I told Sonny about the tradeoff as I gave him his keys, and he stuck his head through the passenger window, assessing the interior like a prospective buyer.

"Fair's fair," he said. "She looks good all cleaned out, like a new car."

"I can't believe you went there," Roger said.

Sonny slung back the keys, claiming he didn't want to do any work on his first day of freedom.

"No trouble with the bail?" I said to Roger.

"He was already out and waiting for us."

"Appreciate the offer," Sonny said. "Good friend stuff and all that, but usually I use Bunny for the bailing."

"Let's do this at Tina's," Juice said. "We'll meet you there. I'm supposed to pick up a cake to celebrate."

"Bit much, isn't it?" I said. "Sonny, you've been in there less than forty-eight hours, right?"

"Grinds a man down, Smitty." He couldn't keep a completely straight face. "Makes him hard."

"Get in the car," I said. "And this is the last time I'm driving this thing."

"Keep giving my tools away, last time for a lot of things."

On the trip to the compound, Sonny craned his neck around as though expecting to see dramatic alterations—extraterrestrials mingling with the populace, maybe, or at least flying cars inside a climate-controlled dome over the city.

"Joint gives you time to think about things, Smitty. Thinking a guy should bank community hours, prepare for trouble like this. Have a little time on your hands why not plant a tree in the park or pick up trash and that. Ever get in Dutch with the law again, you got something to fall back on. What's that your honor? A hundred hours community service? Well, you check my account book I think you'll see it's you owes me ten hours or so, and you can start by picking the kids up from school and cleaning all the shit out my garage."

I chuckled and swerved the gunboat over the centerline. "How do you do it? Seriously, how?"

"Seriously is the problem. Seriously made me freak out my head and wreck the bar and a few guys. With Tina and everything, that's sort of all the serious you can handle you know? Daughter Delilah, not so much of a heart thing if you know what I mean. It's more of an ugly type of business. The worst. Doctors or nobody can say how she got it, just got it. Funny, right? Start finding out about kids and women, makes you wonder about when we first heard, everybody saying it was just the gay guys and them. Not like it's any different than the way people look at most bad stuff, I mean you find out a bunch of people got something bad that you don't and it makes you think you're doing something right for not getting it."

"Full-blown?" I said with a dry mouth.

"Still just the HIV part."

"Whatever we can do."

"I know it. Thanks."

We drove and thought unthinkable things until our time alone was up. When Tina greeted Sonny with forced lightness he took it in stride and tried to make her laugh, but there wasn't much to joke about. I went outside to give them time. Juice and Roger would be along shortly, and until then I could sit and wait, daydream about hiking the streets or the hills or the forest or the beach, isolated observation without the constant chatter.

I'd told Sonny to call on me for help, but was certain he wouldn't take me up on the offer. Our tiny world was lousy with bad news, and I'd begun to wonder whether a leg up or a helping hand or a shoulder to cry on or a safe place or a sounding board or any other crutch, consideration or bit of cold comfort should be relied on. Maybe the ultimate way is unavoidable—lock the violence in a cell with just enough food to keep it pissed off until one day it breaks out and goes hunting.

My mood didn't change once the party started. I held myself apart, consciously choosing not to live the moment. I offered little response to Juice's announcement of a new job, so she actually turned her back on me and addressed the others with the details. The attack on Tina had given her partner a case of the yips and she'd bailed. Unable to manage the enterprise single-handed, particularly now, Tina offered to groom Juice as a replacement, teaching her the ropes at the shop with the idea of gradually incorporating her into a partnership role. Sounded good to me, though again I'd been left out of the loop—Juice had been to the shop three days the past week and neglected to tell the love of her life.

There was more: Tina had been picked to be one of the leaders of the new HOA council, but with going back to work without a qualified partner and still recovering from the assault, well, wouldn't you know she'd suggested Juice as her temporary replacement.

"I need this," Juice said.

"And I need you," Tina said. "I need help and the council needs help and Juice is here. Sonny, I know I have your support, but beating people up and wrecking a bar isn't going to accomplish a thing. More of the same, causing damage to undo damage, it's no good. We have to find a gentler way, strong but gentle. Kind."

Wham! Unable under the circumstances to even conceive of a graduated response, Sonny had leapt from his chair and jumped in place, bringing his boot heels down hard on the tile. "You crazy? You two crazy?"

Juice stepped in front of Tina, and Sonny jerked and flashed her a jittery jumped-up look that made me glad I hadn't been in the Blue Dog the night he cut loose.

"Crazy!" Sonny said. "Go ahead, turn the homeowner thing upside down and make things the way you want, nothing bad about that, somebody on the council will make enough money to buy a bigger place somewhere and new people'll move in here and turn things around again anyhow. Far as that goes, good idea Juice works for you. Got a good shop going there, cactus and pots, I mean who can't use cactuses and pots? And it's . . . gentle, that's plenty gentle you ask me, put a cactus in a pot and stick it on the porch. But kind and turning the other cheek and everything only works till you're out of cheeks. And going up there la-dee-da to the middle of nowhere right after you been hurt is too much. What, you think that guy don't know where you work? Figure he just seen you in the bar and decided to follow you with a snap of the fingers? Even the cops don't figure it that way. Why you think they been giving us the runaround? Drove your car to Yuma, left it in a parking lot and took off somewhere never to be seen again—sure fuckin-A-right that's how it happened. Lying cocksuckers."

"It wasn't your son," Juice said. "I'm saying that in plain English. It wasn't your son!"

"You don't know," he said. "Not when it turns bad you don't. Coming down here a big friendly Canook all in love, and next thing you're helping everybody and making yourself feel warm and fuzzy and you think the whole world's like that."

"Don't you ever try to tell me what I've seen," Juice said. "Don't you fucking dare. Enough? You're right, I haven't seen enough, not nearly enough, and I'm not stopping until I have."

The sound of heavy breathing was all we were left with until Juice quietly added, "Quinn's getting his HSED, his high-school equivalency diploma. He's learning, trying to learn. He has a tutor in Desert Hot Springs." She turned to Tina. "That's how I've been getting to work from the Dowser's."

The Dowser's? Hadn't Juice been here at Tina's every night?

Tina then did something that appeared extraordinary under the circumstances—she picked up a sandwich and took a bite. I wished I had something so normal with which to occupy myself. Sonny interlaced his fingers at his belt buckle and squeezed them white.

"He's given me a lift lots of times," Juice said. "I'm not saying he isn't messed up and scared, just that he's trying. He's not a monster, for sure not a rapist. He couldn't attack anyone. Adult education, Sonny, your kid's going to school."

Finally I was on my feet and moving to where I could see her face. "Lots of times?" I said. "What, he's your personal chauffeur?"

"Of course not." Just the thinnest scalpel of her anger remained. "He stays at the Dowser's mostly, and whenever somebody needs to go somewhere he drives them. It's like his way of paying room and board."

"Sonny!" Tina said.

I hadn't caught his advance and reflexively stepped back.

"Just need the keys," Sonny said from nose distance. "Give, Smitty. Keys."

"Stay here," Tina said. "Don't go, not now. Please, we . . . we have a cake."

She was shaking and pale and raised her hand and looked at the sandwich as if it were of great importance. And she was right. At that point, a sandwich, simple sustenance, was very important. Somehow Sonny got it, tangled as it was with his fury and his ache, and he took the wedge of food from her hand and kissed the tears from her cheeks and whispered in her ear. Then he pulled away and looked at me like a normal man who wanted his car keys. There was nothing to do but let him go. Tina put her forehead against the kitchen door frame and Juice put her arms around her and Roger coughed and mumbled something about getting the cake.

As I watched Sonny peel away from the curb, I had my answer. Just like that I knew how he did it, how through nonsense and humor and love of life he was able to break the stranglehold of demons and personal tragedy: He didn't.

CHAPTER 29

After the stretch of cold weather it was disappointing to relegate the long pants and the sweaters to the bottom drawers. I'd grown used to feeling something hugging my lower legs, shirts with collars, those funny shoe-liners Northerners call socks. Now it was back to shorts and T-shirts and flip-flops. It was hot, let me tell you. March had come in like a lamb and was going out like a lion, in a kiln.

The traffic was light now that the girls were opening early. I had been driving Tina and Juice to the shop and picking them up at closing time, and would be doing so until Tina's attacker was apprehended. A reasonable compromise that any philosopher king or wise parliament could have drafted, the only drawback being the alienation of all parties concerned. Tina and Juice felt infantilized, Roger on those times he joined me wasn't equipped defensively for their grumbling ingratitude, and I had to do all the driving. Ten business days, it had been, and while open protest had transformed to dull resentment, a new arrangement was screaming from the wings for attention.

But it was prudent and safe and what Sonny wanted. He'd phoned us at Tina's from the Dowser's while we were halfway through his Get-Out-of-Jail cake to tell us Quinn wasn't there, or the Dowser, or anybody except Roberto, with whom he proceeded to get drunk enough to phone again three hours later with the great idea of my playing secret service agent, haranguing me about safety and security and keeping on my toes and how my driving the women to work wasn't enough, I should get a gun, he'd get right on that as soon as he got home and could find one, he had a bunch of them in his storage shed with the tools waiting to be fixed, clean them up, a little WD-40, got to be some place has a special on bullets with all the terrorists around lately, there you are set, Smittybaby—couple honest girls can get a ride to work to make an honest living.

And that was it from him, gone these two weeks, Sonny up in smoke. He wasn't at his house, car not to be found, no dog, hadn't shown up at the Dowser's again. As for the rest of the family, Saxon was missing from school, Juice hadn't seen Quinn, and our sleuthing garnered no information from the hospital in Houston beyond the fact they had finished Delilah's recent round of treatment and released her in her father's care. The whole damn family had been spirited off by a dust devil.

But we stuck to the program. Usually we went in Tina's courtesy car, a loaner from the dealer while they paid her the courtesy of taking over-long to fix the minor damage to her vehicle and charging her for umpteen items not covered by her insurance. Each morning we'd jump through the ridiculous hoops of having her and Juice bring it over from around the corner, then switch seats so I could drive in case, I guess, we encountered a roadblock manned by rebels gunning specifically for the wheelman.

That morning Tina had a meeting with the Washington Mutual loans officer, so it was just Juice and me. It felt good, the two of us starting off the morning with a drive, windows down, coffees in hand, Juice with a smoke, oldies on the radio. We could easily have been going to the beach for the day, Stanley Park back in Vancouver for a picnic. Juice felt it. I could tell by the way she held herself in the seat, how she blew the smoke out the window, worry lines ironed out of her brow. I loved her so much and came close to the thrill I felt that day I opened the door, expecting Sonny, only to find this beautiful strange woman.

The pan pipes playing in my head must have reached her, because she leaned over and kissed my ear. "I wish I had known you all my life," she said. "We could be sitting here talking about when you used to walk me to school."

"I thought you hated this."

"Not hate. I just don't like people doing things for me. Tina is, but I picked her as much as she picked me. She's so great. I sure hope everything goes okay at the bank, because if there's no more credit what'll she be left with? This is more important to her now than ever. She's still scared, and with Sonny pulling out . . ."

"I wouldn't call it that, not pulling out."

"Partly my fault," she said. "I want to tell him that."

Juice had been trying to help, to be more than a sluggo helping him haul trash and fix roof tiles. It was her who had gone back into the house and tightened the pipes too hard on the remodel Sonny was being sued for. Ashamed more for her coverup than the mistake, she wanted finally to take it like a handywoman, even if it meant funneling all she made at the shop Sonny's way and working after hours for him gratis.

"Too many," she said.

"You've said that before, the night you were sleepwalking."

"Too many everything. Too many people, too many rules, too much. I only want to live. Why can't we just be?"

She'd been prone to screaming off on tangents lately, so I rummaged for anything to keep the pan piper playing. "Look," I said, ducking my head and squinting through the windshield, "a hawk." Not a gem.

She stuck her head out the window but it wasn't to look at any goddamn bird. Black hair streaming, she screamed into the wind. When she pulled back in I laid my hand on her thigh and, thankfully, she covered it with her own. She flared another smoke and we rode the rest of the way in silence. When we reached the shop—a faux Santa Fe box surrounded with clay pots and lawn ornaments and desert flora in easy-to-transplant containers—I told Juice I loved her. As she was ducking out the door I got the same back along with a seeyalater, tarnishing the sentiment, though I was pulling onto the highway before I thought of it and was too caught up trying to merge to feel its impact.

Two honks and a curse and I was in traffic traffic traffic. The valley was bulging these days with tourists and ex-coast dwellers on the hunt for affordable housing. Slow slow slow and I was glad for the extra rehearsal time, but after parking by the Marriott's spa and walking back to the lobby and waving to the concierge and making it up the elevator and down the hall to Chas Cassidy's room, I had forgotten my opening line.

Fortunately, he took the lead: "This early and my day's already made. Please come in."

I helped myself to a can of Heineken from his mini-bar.

"You have me at a disadvantage." He belted his terry robe tighter.

"I'm drinking at seven-thirty in the morning," I said. "Who's disadvantaged?"

"To what do I owe—"

"—Stop it," I said, draining and crumpling the can. "Just stop all of it. Take this as a threat or whatever you like. Go home or go away, I don't care. Last time—stay away from Juice, stay away from the Dowser, don't talk to Roger, keep out of my life and my business. And one more thing." I reached into my back pocket and came up empty. "I forgot it at home, but you know what I'm talking about. *Sunday or Die!* No more of it, no more warped propaganda, no more plagues on the land and signs of the beast from the desert. I'm perilously close to having nothing to lose, so walk lightly."

He didn't know what I was talking about. I could tell by his face; no one could fake the subtleties involved in that level of incomprehension.

Then again, I could have been wrong—it's not as if I were on a roll of astute perception—and I couldn't give up so soon. Now, what was it Juice had told me? Right. I quickly scanned the walls. Skirting the coffee table and planting my feet, I pointed over the couch at a picture of a long-haired bearded fellow with his arms outstretched, feet together, head lolling. "That's Jesus. What's that all about?"

"Well, roughly two-thousand years ago in the town of Bethlehem there was born—"

"—What's it doing here?"

"It's a picture. On my hotel-room wall."

Having a beer at that time of the morning was one of my poorer decisions of late. I muffled a burp with my fist. "I don't take kindly to veiled threats."

"I'm a Buddhist," he said. "Does that convince you of my innocence?"

"A Buddhist?" I said. "What's that all about?"

"Well, around twenty-five hundred years ago—"

"—Shut the fuck up. You know what I mean."

He claimed it was his sister's. Not much of a Christian, still she found Cassidy's Buddhism hilarious so brought along the picture to irritate him. Likewise the fake journalism award beside it. According to Cassidy, she regularly e-mailed him pictures of animals fornicating and obituaries of people with his first name and of course all articles on journalists who had been caught faking their sources and inventing stories. I'd had enough of his overused excuse and told him I meant to check into this supposed sister.

"As I said, she brought those with her. At the moment she's in the bathroom."

It takes commendable composure for a woman not to react in any way to a stranger's barging in on her while she's reading a magazine on the toilet. I respectfully eased the bathroom door closed.

As I tried to make my escape Cassidy said, "With all my reading, your novel has stayed with me longer than any of it. I won't say it's the best book of all time, rough and rambling, but perhaps therein lies its charm.

It was a long time ago, I should have looked you up sooner, but I thank you for that piece of work, Mr. Cahoot."

Might as well custom order a jacket with my real name stitched in crimson across the back. Oh well, with luck I'd put the fear of the Lord into him, or whoever scares Buddhists.

When I told Roger he was impressed. In his estimation my behavior was watertight—alternative ways of handling the situation should not be entertained given that I'd entered the situation without the slightest amount of forethought. As well, I'd been drinking on an empty head, so all hypothetical scenarios were equally valid. Furthermore, I was a profoundly silly man and my actions should be evaluated with that in mind. He finished his observations with two direct questions:

1. "Why do you believe Chas over Juice?"
2. "Did the woman on the toilet confirm she was Cassidy's sister?"

My responses were equally insightful:

1. "Never thought of it that way. Fuck me."
2. "Fuck me. Never thought of it that way."

Roger smiled and set a plate of sandwiches—triangles, crustless—on the table. Nothing turns my stomach while I'm eating, neither subject matter nor graphic violence on TV, sour smell nor rotten food, but I came close to spitting out what was in my mouth when I saw Juice come through the front door.

Her beautiful black hair was mostly gone. Face a charcoal mask. Bandaged from wrists to elbows. "Don't freak out or anything," she said. "I'm okay."

We freaked out, a good portion of blather until she shoved between us and sat down. Once Juice assured us she'd seen a doctor she told us about the fire.

"I had this thing set up, this big piece of paper set up on Tina's desk to sketch out some ideas—you saw the place, baby, the outside looks pathetic—and I wanted to try designing a courtyard or anything that makes it look like it isn't on the edge of the road leading to the dump, so—" She put her elbows on the table and raised them in pain. "—anyhow, I went out front for a cigarette and it just went up. The whole back part of the building where Tina keeps her paint and varnish and everything for decorating the pots, it just caught fire. I heard it right away, or I smelled it right away, the fan blew it through the whole place, and then I heard it and I ran back and it sort of exploded, I mean, not exploded but a huge jet of flames and hot air and everything just hit me and my hair was on fire. I slapped it out with a cloth then I didn't know what to do, it was scary and I stopped in the middle of everything and cut off the burnt part with a pair of scissors. Then I sort of realized where I was and what was going on and it was too hot and I ran outside. I looked down and my arms were burnt, not very bad but it was sickening at first, I could smell my own skin burning. And then the weirdest thing was that I was standing out front in the dirt and I started to think about how I had managed to cut my own hair off. Why would I stop to do that when I should have just run? Isn't that far out?"

She left a gap for Roger and I to answer. We started to but she was off again:

"And this guy drove by. Real slow. I could tell he was looking and that made sense, I mean, there was smoke and flames coming out of a building so who wouldn't stop and look? Except he didn't look at the building like one of those people who slows down on the highway to check out an accident then zooms off again when he's past. He slowed down and stopped and his window was open and he was looking at me. So I ran out to the road and I didn't get very close, I could see he was a little guy and that's about all, and then he drove away."

The firetrucks hadn't yet arrived on the scene when Juice left for the clinic, but Tina went by after the bank meeting and confirmed that everything was under control. Hadn't been much of a fire to begin with, just the one burst that caught Juice rushing back in. She sat there with her knee bobbing as if she were working an old sewing machine, until confessing she hadn't gone to the clinic.

"A man and his wife were driving by and I got a ride to the Dowser's. She had bandages and everything—good thing she's so close. Sorry for lying, but all I could think about was being out of work again and I couldn't have you guys pay for a doctor."

"There's such a thing as being too concerned for someone else," I said. "That's just dumb, honey."

"Get off your high horse," Roger said. "She was almost killed in a fire."

"So how did you get home?" I said. "And don't say Quinn or I'll jump in a fire myself."

"Quinn. Yeah, that's what I said. If you hate him, that's your hate, it's what you have to live with."

"I don't hate him," I said. "I've never so much as laid eyes on him. If I sound surprised it's because I thought he'd poofed into thin air with Sonny and the rest of his fucked-up clan."

"Delilah has HIV and you call her fucked-up."

"That's not what I—"

"—Let's calm down," Roger said.

"This is shitty," Juice said. "I had great news and was hoping to come home and have a big celebration and now everything's shitty."

It took so long for me to ask Juice what there was to celebrate that the unofficial time limit ran out. She winced extending her hand for a triangle of tuna-on-white. A year off my life at least, that's what it cost me to follow her lead instead of locking her in the closet for her own protection. But I suppose the Board would have stormed the place and freed her now that she'd been elected as one of the "trio" ruling the HOA. Uncomfortable enough with the thought of Juice temporarily replacing Tina, now I had to deal with her as one of the leaders. I remarked that "trio" sounded like a folk group, that "triumvirate," a good old Roman Empire term, was more appropriate, and Juice took it for the sarcasm it was.

"I can't help it," I said. "Look what's happened in the space of three hours—you were in a fire and got a ride back here with some guy suspected of spreading terror through the land and shoving a bottle up your best friend. I'm supposed to feel happy about waiting to hear all these things when you feel you want to tell me? Naturally I'm worried, naturally."

"That's why I told you about the new committee," she said. "We have to focus on the good things. Good isn't just stronger than bad, it's more important. I'm over the fire, so if you want to help . . . anyway, aren't you happy for me? Aren't you glad?"

Then she caught sight of Tina through the sliders, and Roger and I were left staring at the sandwiches. Before we could speak Juice burst in the front door as quickly as she had fled out the back.

"Just to keep you up to date," she said, "there's a charity softball game Saturday at the park. We want to raise funds for a headquarters building without upping the homeowner dues. How's that for a good idea?" She started to swing the door shut behind her.

"Who are the other two?" Roger called. "On the Board?"

"Martin and Deep Tread."

I almost snapped my spine pivoting in my chair. "Who on earth is—"

"—Before you go off your rocker, he's calling himself Deep Tread for the sake of the movement. All great leaders have nicknames."

"You're right," I said. "The Terrible, The Unready, The Butcher . . ."

"You're nuts but that's why I love you," she said. "And I really do."

When I was reasonably sure she wasn't going to barge back in, I picked up my sandwich. "Deep Tread. My money says it's that swine with the monster truck. Deep Tread, Martin and the lovely and talented Juice, the Kingston fucking Trio."

Roger laughed without mirth and rubbed an eye hard with the heel of his hand.

"You all right?" I said.

"I don't think so."

I felt like an ambassador receiving directives from home to negotiate matters on which I hadn't been briefed.

CHAPTER 30

First Saturday in April, already hot at eight in the morning. Big day, big softball game, big fun, and I wanted no part of it. My entertainment glands were drawing themselves in like terrified testes now that Juice had been exposed directly to the plague of malignity. If the firebug proved to be Tina's attacker back for another round, Juice was too close to the action. Other than Roger and me, there wasn't a person in our circle who hadn't been dosed with misfortune. And concerned as I was for Roger, I couldn't help worrying more about myself. Who would want to harm a man like Roger? Who was next in line if not me? So I was doing what I could to keep the two of them safe while dropping a load in my pants at loud noises.

And now in the middle of everything we had to play softball. A softball game against a team from the other end of the compound to help pay for a new and improved HOA headquarters building. A charity match against ourselves to raise money for ourselves. I'd like to repeat that to underscore the irony, but it's too painful.

Roger had been out buying equipment. In the corner was a red aluminum bat, on the table two Authentic Professional Major League baseball gloves made from the hide of a vinyl cow. Stiff as they were, there was no need to go through the boyhood ritual of oiling and wrapping to break them in, since the tag guaranteed: READY TO PLAY! Roger had never played, and I didn't want to, but we figured it wasn't the best time to tell that to Juice.

Before we knew it the game was on. That's a rather abrupt way of introducing the event, though it jibes with my notes. There were many things leading up to the opening pitch I could have elaborated on, not the least of which was the absence of the event's organizer. Although Juice had talked to the fire department investigators as soon as she recovered from the trauma, it wasn't till three days after the burnout that Detective Legree got around to calling her in. So while we neighborhoodians cavorted on rented space at the Palm Desert softball park, Juice was at the cop shop.

My observations are choppy and disjointed. The larger event effaced the smaller, and by the time I sat down at my desk there was nothing much to say about a Saturday game of softball that lasted less than one inning. This pretty much covers it:

– four diamonds arranged around a central snack bar. Bathrooms, water fountains. Sights, sounds, colors, nice, pretty cool. Grass level, newly mowed. Golfers past the fence on the driving range too far away to hear their curses.

– a band, if you can believe it, a mariachi band in white outfits, playing to beat the . . . well, the band. It feels a little like Oktoberfest; the overlap of oopmpahpahness between Mexican and German music is strong.

– keen edge to Mt. San Jacinto where it meets the sky.

– Roger goes to the food kiosk, brings back hot dogs.

– where's Juice? Expecting her to pop up at any moment because that's what she does.

– Martin, in shorts and Honey Badger Security shirt sans shoulder patches, HOA sash worn like a Sam Browne, rubber softball spikes. Jesus Murphy.

– turn my head to the next diamond over, game just ended between two teams of kids so tiny their batting helmets look like salon hairdryers. One kid says to his dad, "Did we win?" Dad says, "I think so." Love it.

– believe this one? Chas Cassidy shows up. Roger goes over, Cassidy tells him he's a reporter, that's all, a reporter reporting, nothing to say he can't report on what he wants. Softball game, sure. Roger comes back and sits down, scowling, and not just in anticipation of going 0-for-4.

– Sarah on the other bench, looking pumped for the competition. House wrecked, no more leadership role, her negative worldview needs an enemy, opposing softball team good enough in a pinch.

– beside Sarah, George Sameshima, wearing a Dodgers cap with his queue sticking out the adjustment hole in the back, looking sad, dumped on, probably getting plenty of support from Sarah to stay that way.

– Sonny shows up. Yeah, Sonny, haven't heard from him in how long and now he appears at the softball game. Cruises over from the parking lot. No, not cruising, strutting. As my English granny used to say, "Cock of the bloody walk." No word to anyone, just goes to Tina, hug and kiss then back to parading. Big cats, lions and such, are retromingent, they piss backward so the urine hits their legs and they spread their scent just by walking around. Sonny, little guy weighing about one-forty, bowed legs, cowboy boots and walking shorts, tops of one and bottoms of the other almost meet—nice look.

– Sonny promenading in front of the other team's bench, other team made up of the folks who live backing onto the main road. Our team is the backing-onto-the-land-for-sale types from the opposite end of the compound. Big rush to the umpire, every-body arguing about whether Sonny can play till Tina pipes up: "He lives with me," clearing up his residency status.

– Deep Tread has to match Sonny. Deep Tread, sure enough the monster-truck guy, one of three in charge of the new HOA. Deep Tread, captain of the main-roaders, big guy, big truck, Popeye forearms, got to keep up to Sonny's strutting. Five bats, big mag-nesium championship fast-pitch sticks, Deep Tread's swinging them all in a bunch in front of the dugout.

– Sonny, mini-ass shoved out like inviting a bird to peck it, veers toward him. They circle, two guys eyeing and profiling and fuck you too.

– warmups. Away from the diamond Sonny's pitching like he's played some good ball in his time. Windup, windmill delivery, ZIPSMACK! into the catcher's glove. Hard, fast.

– big argument again, everybody saying it's supposed to be a lob-pitch game, but Deep Tread eats up the challenge and declares every batter gets to choose. Adds a bat, now swinging six.

– women getting antsy, which is what women do when men decide to act like men and the women are smart enough to know it won't end till war's declared to protect our way of life, or even a one-run lead.

– game's on.

– first inning, Sonny pitching, hitters elect slo-pitch, Sonny throwing little spongy lobs, walks the first three batters.

– our team furious. We're not looking good, getting too hot, flies coming after the babies in strollers. Fund-raising fun, but already our team's kicking the fence and slamming down bats. Crazy, want to quit and head for a pub but stay. Heavy vibes, everybody gotta win, win or lose, baby. This is Backing-Onto-The-Main-Road versus Backing-Onto-The-Land-For-Sale. Ever seen such a matchup? No wonder it's tense.

– Deep Tread's buddies cheering from the deck of his monster truck, chucking empties at the batting cage past third base. Mr. Tread drops five bats and stands in with the sixth, crowding the plate. Look in his eyes says a pissant pitcher with paint on his shorts and plaster on his knockoff Tony Lamas can't strike me out.

– everybody on their feet, kill Sonny if he walks in a run.

– First Pitch: high and outside. Deep Tread takes. Ball one.

– Second Pitch: high and outside. DT takes. Ball two.

– Third Pitch: low and inside. DT takes. Ball three.

– DT laughs, switches bats, yells, "C'mon, bring it, bring it on!"

– everyone standing, screaming, first inning and survival is in the balance.

– Fourth Pitch: way outside. DT takes. Ball four.

– DT drops his bat, shoots Sonny the finger and heads for first base. Runner on third trots home, game's first run. We're down 1–0.

– Fifth Pitch: Yeah, that's right, Fifth Pitch. Sonny takes the throw from the catcher after the walk, turns, short windup, rips a fastball halfway up the first-base line, hitting Deep Tread square in the side of the head, dropping him in the dirt.

– Oh shit!

– Oh shit again! DT's not hurt. Gets up and charges the mound. Sonny doesn't even fake the hero stuff, turns and sprints over second base into center field.

– Deep Tread runs after him. Buddies jump from his truck, all yelling at once, "That fucking guy! Can you believe that fucking guy? Let's get that fucking guy!" and such.

– Sonny slows down in center field. High chain-link fence.

– DT's buddies have stopped already, one pissing in the first-base coach's box and the others on the way back to the truck and the beer chest.

– chasing Sonny, between the mound and second base Deep Tread staggers. By the time he hits the outfield he's fallen, gotten up, fallen, gotten up. Falls again, hard this time. Stays on his hands and knees.

–the rest of us too are slipping and weaving and falling, reaching hands out for people to latch onto. I grab Roger and he grabs me.

–look around for Juice, forgetting she's not there. First thing on my mind, Juice, and what the hell I fall against the dugout's corner post and don't even feel it cut me from hairline to cheek.

And then it all slowed down. Rather than compressing events, the earthquake drew them out for appraisement.

As best I could while trying to stay upright, I regarded the ballpark through the blood dripping into my eye. Exquisitely tended Bermuda grass littered with gloves and hats, chain-link outfield fence rippling like muscle, soft drink syrup shooting from broken lines at the snack bar, people shrieking and racing for their children and the elderly, incomprehension, loss of control, blind attempts to do something, anything. Topsy-turvy earth beneath our feet, plastic nature of the foundation all too evident, life on the edge, coin toss.

Our species evolved in step with and partly because of shifting climate, changing geography, which goes a long way to explaining our need to constantly pound our environment into a shape that robs it of its power. Beat it down, make it behave, strip mall safer than sand and scrub, view from the deck more important than trees leveled to achieve it. We cavort through a fantasy world in which we've achieved mastery over our environment yet the underlying truth of the matter still smolders, and when a demonstration of it is so dramatic we can't rationalize it away we respond the same way we always have—by feeling small.

Rock talk: We stand on the crust, which overlays and differs chemically from the mantle. But who cares about chemistry, you say. Chemistry made me go to summer school my senior year, ruined the mucous membranes in my nose, defoliated Southeast Asia. You're right, so let's do what the rock-jocks do and think about it mechanically, call it the lithosphere, which ropes together the crust and the upper part of the mantle, a relatively rigid shell over a viscous fluid. When you're not keeping your eyes and your instruments peeled the bugger slowly moves on you, spreading from rifts, colliding with other sections.

O! what fun it is to ride. And why should we prefer a ride to stasis? Come on, do we really want to be stuck with just erosion? Water barely flowing across level land, fun only for the odd arthritic canoeist glad for the absence of white water; wind blowing the topsoil around. Where's the drama in that? We're nothing if not a species that craves drama. Without subduction—one plate riding under the other at the meeting point, melting and forcing its mafic goo to the surface—volcanoes wouldn't exist along coastlines. Without the earth's interior heat and the collision of land masses—bubbling down below and grinding and uplifting and slipping and faulting above—there would be no mountains. Nix on the Alps, the Rockies, the Andes, the Himalayas. Hell, Edmund Hillary wouldn't have scored a knighthood for climbing Everest. "Well," he would have said in the club in 1953 while an interviewer across from him scrambled to sharpen his pencil, "Tenzing Norgay and I pulled on our boots at eight in the morning and summited at 8:05. Are we done, here?" It would be Nature in all its circumscribed glory.

In California, as the Pacific Plate meets the North American Plate and rides northwest relative to it, great stresses build up till the ground bends and eventually snaps, creating or enlarging a fault, of which there are many intertwined, bent and braided for over eight-hundred miles along the San Andreas system. All because the ground we stand on is not to be trusted, all because of the Moho. Where the crust meets the mantle, where the chemistry alters and the mechanics start to change, is the Mohorovicic discontinuity. The Moho, where it all starts to change, deep beneath bedrock and batholiths.

By then the initial panic had retreated. Two softball teams and a few spectators were clumped in the middle of a grass field—a scene repeated on the other three diamonds—and unless a fissure opened beneath our very feet, unzipping the park and tumbling us into the netherworld like a bunch of ballcapped sinners in a medieval painting, we were safe.

But just in case, Martin was there to save the day. He stepped out front and held his hands in the air, urging us to silence. He fished in his tunic, brought forth a pamphlet and slowly passed it left and right as though building up to a magic trick. "You've all seen this."

EARTHQUAKE!
Are you READY?

Guidelines for Preparation
and
Recovery

"As Public Safety Officer," Martin said, "I'd like to go over this material before the crisis gets worse."

Despite talk of getting home to check for damage, we listened, pawing the ground as if to uncover latent cracks.

"'Preparation,'" Martin said, reading from the left flap of the foldout. "'One—Prepare an emergency kit of food, water and supplies including a flashlight, battery-operated radio, medicine, first-aid kit and clothing. Two—Know the safe spots in each room. Under sturdy tables, desks or against interior walls. Three—'"

"—It's already happened!" someone called from the back. "The earthquake's already happened, you idiot!"

The roar of a motor was our cue to turn our backs on Martin and join the throng trying to leave the grounds. Manning the monster attack truck, Deep Tread and his entourage commanded the heights, though their observation post was isolated in the sea of people coursing through the service area. DT was revving his engine and adding to the confusion with continual blasts of his air horn, while the boys in the back threw trash at the crowd and lashed out with fists and boots, clearing space for the captain. The second DT had maneuvering room he gunned behind the rear ranks and took off overland. In seconds he had traversed the diamond, mashed flat the outfield fence and was racing across the adjacent driving range, ripping up turf, oversize tires spurting out golf balls like grape seeds. His soldiers were pounding on the sides, loosing rebel yells and curses into the wind and waving the flags they had ripped from the cab. Once across, Deep Tread became entangled like bycatch in the thirty-foot-high netting erected to keep errant golf balls from slicing onto the main road. He reversed, he charged, the engine screamed, the lugged tires dug in and finally, with rebel yells turning into cries of outrage as the cording swept around the cab and lashed the troops, Deep Tread broke free, after which he immediately plunged into the runoff ditch alongside the street.

We waited. *Nada*—they weren't coming out.

Upon clearing the grounds, we pulled over opposite where the truck had disappeared and jogged across the road. The ditch was now a crevasse, torn a half-kilometer in either direction. Wedged in the earth's crooked smile, roofline ten feet below the surface, still upright, engine dead but radio playing, was the monster truck, half-crushed but with not one of its thickheaded riders sporting more than a torn shirt or a scratch.

"Hey," Deep Tread called up to us, sounding deeply offended at fate's fickleness. "You motherfuckers got a rope?"

We crept closer to the edge and looked down at the flushed faces. For once, Roger instead of I did what was in the back of my mind—he kicked the lip, sending a shelf of dirt over the edge, and as the rebels yelled and spat we recrossed the road to the Neon.

We didn't have to fumble with the clicker-thing. Everyone had arrived at roughly the same time, so we got in line and followed the procession through the gates. As we turned toward home someone beat on the roof, and I looked out the passenger window at Juice's armpit. She appeared calm, but as soon as Roger pulled over and I got out she ran her hands over my face like a blind woman getting to know me. With her chopped hair and bandaged arms and the tears on her cheeks . . . I waved Roger on and walked with her, my thumb thrust down the back of her denim shorts, fingers gripping the waistband to keep her close.

Her first thought was of Tina, who'd pulled out ahead of Roger and I and should have been home by then. We went straight there.

"I waited at his car," Tina said after greetings of relief. "I remember seeing him by the fence when the quake hit, but when he didn't show up after I waited at his car. His stupid car, and stupid me I went back looking for him and you and Roger and I couldn't find you and by the time I went back to the parking lot again the car was gone. I don't get it. He came back just to throw a baseball at somebody's head? I haven't seen him in . . . he came back for that? So I got a ride home and he wasn't here and . . . since he left the last time he hasn't even called me, then he shows up at a baseball game and throws a baseball at someone's head and disappears?"

"Maybe he saw you were okay and went to check on his kids," I said.

She looked at me blankly. "Good thing I'm not a mother."

Juice got a set of channel-locks from the garage and went outside to turn off the gas while I inspected the interior. Not much damage, a few hairline wall cracks, broken glassware, fallen pictures. I told Tina to reset her phone message in case Sonny called, and to join us at our place. The fear in Juice's eyes was gone now that she had a good strong tool in her hands and was reefing at the painted-over gas valve. I gave her a kiss and went up the greenbelt.

Our house was fine, nothing a more dedicated handyman than Sonny couldn't repair. Roger had the windows open and the fan on to clear out the dust—eventually we learned the quake had split the ductwork in the attic, allowing the air conditioner to fling sand and dirt throughout the house—and was assessing a crack in the wall that started in the laundry area and bifurcated into rifts running across the ceiling and around the corner into the hall bathroom.

"Gas?" I hadn't been able to help so far and was going to stick with what I'd learned from Juice.

Roger had already attended to it; apparently I was the only one in the household who hadn't read the earthquake pamphlet. We hadn't seen much of the neighborhood, but it didn't look bad. No fires or major collapses. Roof tiles missing everywhere you looked and a bunch of trees down, perimeter wall bust in a few places, pretty lucky, and we'd yet to hear a police or ambulance siren. Juice and Tina arrived and we ate. We ate and drank and talked the earthquake up and down, eventually into where-were-you-when? status. I called the Dowser but of course got no answer. They may not have been affected much out there, then again they could be under a hundred feet of fallen mountainside.

There was to be no Sonny, though no shortage of other visitors. The neighborhood was full of people roaming the streets and the greenbelts, maintaining contact. I'd never seen so many folks afoot at one time around there, pokeying along, waving and greeting and checking in, many of them still wearing shirts emblazoned with BOMR and BOLS, softball teams that mere hours ago were enemies. From the adjoining compounds came residents walking freely through the open gates, apprehension over aftershocks conquering their fear of mingling with denizens of an alien ghetto. Offers of food and water and showers, confusing and overly hospitable until word got around that many nearby compounds had suffered much worse damage than the shattered Franklin Mint collectibles and overflowing toilets we'd heard about from our neighbors.

As the light faded, we stood with a couple dozen people watching fireworks jet from the vicinity of the pool, arcing and exploding over the roofs of the houses across the greenbelt. Someone must have dipped into their Fourth-of-July cache, obviously having loaded up out of state because there were more illegal bombs bursting in air and proscribed rockets' red glare giving proof through the night that the flag was still there than Riverside County ever would have permitted. With a little noise and a bunch of food and good cheer, the ruptured crust could kiss their American asses. Good for them.

Tomorrow would likely bring another notice informing Roger to get a new garage door to match the others in the neighborhood so property values wouldn't suffer, and the morning paper would feature a slew of letters-to-the-editor claiming the quake was a sign of God's wrath for letting Palm Springs host another gay festival, but in the meantime I'd watch the fireworks and just hope everyone didn't link elbows and start singing "Kumbaya." They didn't. Obeying the desert imperative of early to bed, they wandered off each to his or her own. Tina was the last to go, laden with a basket of demands to call if she needed anything, to call right away any time don't hesitate don't be silly.

The three of us by ourselves, quiet, pensive.

While stroking the back of my neck, Juice pointed along the wall and snickered. "At least there's one thing we can fix."

We followed her to the side of the house, where the rolled carpet had fallen down, protruding between two oleanders. Juice squatted and I put my beer can on the grass and helped her hoist the rug. It seemed years ago that Roger and I started putting out the carpet, taking it inside, putting it out, inside, out, and somewhere along the line we'd stopped playing the silly game. The rug had been there so long it was saturated with water from the sprinklers and impregnated with sand, and it took all of us to get it upright. Before we could lean it back against the wall Juice slipped and fell laughing into the flower bed, and Roger and I dropped it.

When we dropped it a body rolled out.

I mean it—the carpet unfurled and a body rolled out like Elizabeth Taylor in *Cleopatra*. Well, not like the scene in *Cleopatra*, because this body was dead. An actual body rolled out of a rug beside our cute bungalow in the middle of a walled and gated compound in the golf and casino capital of Southern California. A woman, naked, misshapen, an unnatural hue to her skin, hands clutching empty air beside her bare swollen hips, dead.

Juice stared for no more than two seconds from where she was sitting in the sand. Then she leaped up and sprinted wildly across the greenbelt.

PART FOUR

ROCK VARNISH

CHAPTER 31

On my eighteenth birthday my father said, "I miss your mum." When I didn't answer he repeated it with exactly the same intonation, as if he'd been rehearsing by rote without exploring for nuances: "I miss your mum."

I needed the repetition to convince me he hadn't brought up the subject for its novelty. I'm not denying his sadness over the years, merely saying that since she died on my fourteenth birthday my mother resided in an inaccessible region of my dad's mind. I hadn't mentioned her myself for a long time, and felt supremely uneasy as I leaned against the stove and waited for my father to elaborate.

Aside from the sorrow it evoked, we avoided the subject because we remembered two different people. Separate remembrances, one apiece, a wife for my father, a mother for me. His skew I couldn't fathom, an assessment of someone far too boisterous—blabby storyteller at parties, writer of letters to editors, opinionated for fear of being caught without one. Conversely, I remembered her consideration, which in a strange way mirrored my father's, though where his issued from self-consciousness hers flowed from an abiding respect for alternative ways of viewing the world.

The constraints of society chafed her raw—government too custodial, church too peremptory and authoritative—and admittedly, she was a nettle in the neighborhood. Felled trees had to be answered for, barking dogs defended, social outcasts protected. Once when I was twelve, Mum even brought home the street's witch, one who met all the criteria—female, elderly, lived alone, kept to herself, cat, hat—and treated her to lunch. My mother had often lectured me on the deadliness of prejudice and, snatching at the chance to spoon out a little applied social science, pulled me out of school for the afternoon to join them. My mum had called it right. The old lunch guest was no different than the other neighborhood mothers, particularly after she got half a skinful of gin in her by three-thirty in the afternoon and on leaving stood out front of our house loudly denouncing my mum as an interfering twat, all within earshot of the kids coming home from class, gaining me much status at school for having survived a close encounter with the stinky old sorceress.

Dumb, that's what my dad thought of his wife. He hadn't the nerve to say it aloud until she was dead, and even then only when thoroughly rye-and-watered, but she had to be dumb, dumb as a bunny. After all, she painted pictures and made ceramic cookie jars and wore mismatched clothing and never got her hair styled and smoked cigarettes and broke things reaching for them in the cupboards instead of using a good practical step stool and went swimming in the lake when it was freezing and played ball hockey on the street with the kids and brought home witches. Oh, right—and she was bad with money. Had to be dumb to have no respect for money.

There was one more thing I didn't grasp till I was older, incontrovertible proof of her stupidity, something my father thought but would never say—she'd married someone like him, hadn't she? Yes, she had. And she loved him, loved him right to the end with all his faults and his perfectly matched clothing and smart haircuts and church-going and . . . well, it doesn't really matter, does it? She loved him through the seasons. She thought he was handsome and as dashing as a prince and she championed him to the world.

Immeasurably sad was that my father never forgave her for it. He couldn't understand, at least till the day of my eighteenth birthday when he said, "I miss your mum."

Then he gave me a high chair. I shit you not, he went down to the basement and brought up a high chair. He must have been planning for it, because I heard no rooting around or moving of boxes, he just went downstairs and came back and stood a baby's high chair on the kitchen floor and pushed it up to the table as if inviting me to hop in and start spitting mashed peas. He'd made it by hand two months before I was born. I looked at it a while and touched it and worked the pivoting tray up and down. Before I was born. I should have said something, but what? To discover my father hand-crafted a high chair for me and didn't let it see the light of day for eighteen years . . . what was there to say? I ached for him, a scared repressed man who wanted the right things, to do the right things. I could have said that, I guess, that I ached for him. And I could have said I too missed my mum.

She fit in no category while alive so shouldn't be branded with clichés in death, but she died far too young. Too young for everything. She had looked forward to the day when she was out of the loop, old enough to be ignored, wise and experienced, the time when she could stop answering to anyone and everyone and start, in her words, getting away with shit. At such an age, no one would have any right looking over her shoulder and taking her to task on her behavior, highlighting her faults and foibles. It would be inaccurate to say she "aimed" for any particular age, for she appreciated the capriciousness of life, that it can snuff you out whenever it so chooses, that to mark time in an unchallenging existence in hope of reaching a magic number that may never occur is a life misused. She said many times she didn't want to spend ten years getting used to tofu wieners and shoes with good support then get hit by a fucking truck. So she'd aim for nothing, wait for it to come, while enjoying the chase and playing ball hockey on the street with the kids.

Anyhow, that's what happened—hit by a fucking truck. Me, turning fourteen that day. Mum, hit at forty by a truck going sixty. Dead far short of getting away with shit.

If she'd lived, she would have had her own house and could do whatever she wanted in it, because I was going to build it for her as soon as I made a bunch of money and was old enough to know which end of the hammer did the cutting. A palace, that's what. I might even have gone overboard and put two whole bathrooms in it so Mum wouldn't have to wait for anyone. I don't know why I picked that particular hopeful promise to advertise my love, though I suspect it had something to do with acknowledging her generation. My mum was from a time and a place when you built your own house with help from the neighbors and hoped like hell the winter wasn't too harsh to bag a deer or two and a rabbit or six and prayed the easterners who sold you the land would get their act together enough to extend the railway if for no other reason than you'd need seed in the spring after the killer frost and killer runoff. A house, everyone needed a house, a place to come back to or to remember in case you stayed away forever, pencil marks on the door frame to keep track of the kids' growth, and a faded spot on the wallpaper where the mirror hung until it was smashed that Thanksgiving the police came to haul off one of the uncles.

Then came the truck and that was it for Mum and me and the house. It gave me my first tentative taste of adulthood, a preliminary test I failed, unless being a grownup meant blinkered selfishness and nonspecific aggression.

Did Roger ever save my ass. Just fourteen years old and he saw me going under, saw me sink, grabbed me by the hair, pulled me to the surface, and while he hadn't the strength to get me into the boat, he gave me time to breath free and clear till I recovered enough to do so myself. He was beaten up for taking my side and was ostracized as fully as I was and even got kicked out of school with me. If there's a level of hell for liars, Roger will join me there as my sergeant, having earned his stripes and a pension for the work he did lying to friends, enemies, teachers, school officials, store owners, car owners, his mother, his father, my father and the police. He saved me, raising uncertainty about what was left of himself, what substance remained after shredding and riddling his integrity to help his friend. At the time I didn't see it, knew he was there in a vague way, but he could kiss my ass along with everyone else and that went for my dad too, the stupid bastard, for thinking my mum was the dumb one.

"I miss your mum," my father said on my eighteenth birthday.

I'm not about to claim everything above raced clattering through my head before I responded. Right then all I could do was fall back on the way I had always dealt with my dad, a lame sad way of plugging in.

"I miss your mum," my father said for the second time.

"Yeah," I finally said. "But she's in a better place, Dad—there on the farm with all those dead dogs you sent."

He didn't laugh. Worse, he didn't get angry. "Last."

"Sure, last." No idea, just talking to advance the clock.

"That's where you're going to finish, son. You don't take anything seriously."

"I've tried that."

"Competition," he said. "Serious competition is what separates the wheat—"

"—from the chaff," I said. "The men from the boys, the wolves from the lambs. I've heard it all before, at school and from you and from all the neighborhood dads who haven't done anything anyway but who treat even talking about competing as a kind of competition. You don't have to compete at everything! Come on, Dad, do men really have to compete to see how many oysters or pancakes they can eat? Or who can grow a beard the fastest?"

"You're doing it again," he said. "Horsing around, always making fun of important issues. You have to learn to apply yourself. Hard work never hurt anyone."

ROCK VARNISH

"Try telling that to an asbestos miner," I said.

"I'm serious."

"And you're wrong. If hard work doesn't hurt, why is it used as punishment? You don't see criminals getting sentenced to TV-watching gangs, just chain gangs. Hard work isn't good or bad and easy work isn't either. If you're not doing something that fills you up then it's all just work. I don't mean getting enough to eat and putting a roof over your head, I'm talking about the crazy slaving and driving to beat people, beat them down and beat them up just so you can finish ahead of them. Whatever that means in the first place—ahead—what the fuck does that mean?"

"There's a nobility in bettering yourself that—"

"—When Mum died," I said. "After Mum died . . . I don't ever want to be that serious again."

Why couldn't I leave him alone, let him have the day, nod at his grim wisdom and let my hand rest on the high chair as if it were the finest thing I'd ever received? His need to have me battle and win sprang from his having done neither, the soil of his upbringing sown with salt from the day of his birth. More shame on me, because I was aware of it. My mother had told me not a month before she was killed, told me of my father's childhood and many other things, as if she were hearing voices from the God of Vehicular Manslaughter and wanted to clear the air, fill the void in my knowledge of the family before being side-swiped to heaven.

The Manitoba farm on which my dad was reared was no kind of farm, certainly not the type dogs, my mum or any other mammals would enjoy. Beyond constantly telling his son he would never amount to anything, my father's father, my grandfather—the term and its genetic implications pain me even to put them on paper—kept a poplar switch inside the back door off the mudroom. At least once a day on coming through the door the son would take a cut of the switch across the back of the legs, and if he ventured through tears to ask what it was he'd done wrong was told by his old man: "Nothing. And that's to make sure you don't."

Year after year he was told he'd never amount to anything, that he was a sorry excuse for a son who was unable to learn and who should have died at six years old instead of his twin, Stuart. The dead kid, Stuart, was better. Better dead than my dad was alive, my dad, whose own dad called him a stupid horse's ass every time he drew a breath.

Still, should an explanation become an excuse? I've never been comfortable with the notion of permanent contagion. Why my father thought my mother dumb when he knew intimately what it was like to be on the receiving end of that kind of disdain is a mystery unsolved by saying he was merely passing on learned behavior or was trying to even the overall score. He never said it to her face, just to me and only after she was dead, and maybe that was it, that the dumbest thing she'd ever done was not to fall in love with someone like him, but to fall in love with him and then die too young at forty. I felt a dose of it myself, exasperation at the stupidity of someone who dies and leaves you alone, and though helplessness is a more accurate word, stupidity freights more blame, and someone had to be blamed.

But why didn't I recover? Hominids evolved in the teeth of the storm, thoroughly mauled by geology and climate. The paleolithic members of our lineage couldn't paint pictures in a cave without an ice-age blocking traffic and wrecking the opening, but they worked around it. Fashioned by the imperative of being flexible, they rebounded and adapted. We germinated in change, sprouted from variety and catastrophe, grew by leaving one-track answers and specialization to stick insects and tribute bands.

In the meantime, I don't much care if it keeps raining the whole way through to the age when I can start getting away with shit. I took a break from my notes and my apartment again, this time to buy cigarettes and beer. I quit drinking when I started my walkabout in the Santa Rosas and I stopped smoking many years ago, but right now both vices can do me no harm. I can't find Roger, which means he's not trying to find me; I can't find Juice, which is disingenuous because I'm not actively looking for her—I need to see her though the prospect gives me fits—so I've decided to fall back on past habits and do whatever the hell I want, whether I get away with it or not.

My dad was dominated by outside forces to the extent that he abdicated authority until inheriting it from my mum. To my mother, external control was a disgraceful concept indicating lack of trust in her personal judgment. Around the time she revealed my father's past to me Mum gave me a glimmer of insight into her own by mailing me a ten-page letter. Yeah, she mailed it, young as I was, addressing and stamping the envelope to acknowledge my stature as an individual. It was a brief summation of her childhood growing up in a large family called, appropriately, *One of Nine*. While I'm having my fifth cigarette and sixth beer, indulge me while I quote from it:

> The Red River, only three blocks from home, had a strong current and was the receptacle for raw sewage. In addition, when trains crossed the bridge they dumped their sewage into the river. We were repeatedly warned that swimming in the river was not even to be considered. Well, that meant we had to put our suits on under our clothes, have our swim and dry off before dressing and returning home. Into the house, past my mum, down the hall and a "Get back here right now." Back to the kitchen. "You've been swimming in the river." "No, I haven't, honest." "Yes, you have, now get to your room and stay there." How did she know? No one would snitch because we were all involved. Years later when I asked, she said, "Ha, it was easy, I could smell you as soon as you came in the house."

My nanny could smell my mum. And my mum could smell me, had always been able to sniff out the rotten pheasants hanging from my eaves, but both the old broads laughed at the scent. I could smell Juice that day through the e-mail and when I had my tongue inside her and crawled up her belly to look into her dark dark eyes and let her taste herself in my mouth, smelled her when she was beside me or miles away.

When the carpet unfurled and a body rolled out, when an actual body rolled out of a rug beside our cute little bungalow in the middle of a walled and gated compound in the golf and casino capital of Southern California—a woman, naked, a little misshapen, an unnatural hue to her skin, hands clutching empty air beside her bare swollen hips, dead—and Juice leaped up from where she was sitting in the sand and sprinted wildly across the greenbelt, I could smell something rotten.

But I let her run off on her own.

CHAPTER 32

Roger looked again at the body, over to me, and I waved him after Juice. Someone had to stay, and it was me. After calling the police, I went back to the site.

Between the houses was a ten-foot moat of sand planted with olean-der bushes, the shrubbery's monotone green broken by slashes of color visible in the light from our spare bedroom window. I avoided the naked corpse and tried to compose myself while regarding a sheer mauve blouse and a red satin skirt arranged on a bush as on a mannequin. Hooked over a branch was a small silver purse. Forefront in my mind was the need to not touch anything at the crime scene, yet I fingered the gar-ments nonetheless.

Detective Legree came attended by the same society of eager beavers that had shown up at the Dowser's the night of Tina's attack, precious pups and Keystone Kops and amateur bodybuilders flaunting their badges as if they'd been deputized for the emergency and were aware of their authority's transience. By the time they had the yellow tape up and Legree had done a quick walk-through, the young cops were fanning out to canvass neighbors and search for witnesses, and they didn't have far to fan. Late though it was, the sirens had brought the masses forth, solici-tous concern after the earthquake having morphed to voyeurism—the greenbelt was polluted with rubbernecking swine.

Juice had run off in the direction of the Kolachuks' house, and maybe because of the clothes on the bushes, I had the awful feeling I was look-ing at . . . I shoved through the crowd. On the edge of the road, I blinked at a beam of light from a home video camera and blundered into the cameraman, clumsily knocking his gear to the pavement and inadver-tently descending on it with both heels two or three times.

"Hey!" Legree yelled through the mob, which turned in my direction at the new development. "Where you going?"

Apparently nowhere without him. Legree joined me at the curb, and after listening to the filmmaker's complaints about my maltreatment of the camera the detective accidentally booted it twenty feet up the street.

I filled him in, though by the time we reached the Kolachuks' my concerns were fading. If that's where Juice had run to, surely by now Sarah and Martin would be on their way to confirm the news. With luck I was wrong.

I wasn't. The front door was ajar, allowing access to a space suffused with tension. And more—Sarah and Martin were painting. With a pole roller Martin was coating the ceiling as Sarah brushed paint in the corners. The living room was crisscrossed with shafts of light from desk lamps along the baseboards. Juice was looking out the window, crying. To an unfamiliar eye, Roger would look contained enough, but I knew he was close to unraveling.

"Alliyah," Sarah said without pausing in her task. "Alliyah Essence. That's the name we want on the report, or certificate, the paperwork. Alliyah Essence, not Monica. Monica's a dead name, it's not hers."

Martin was the first to leave off the busyness. He literally opened his hands and dropped the roller on the floor, where it splotched a design on the tiles. "Yes, that would be all right," he said. "Monica was my mother's name, but—"

"—This is our daughter we're talking about," Sarah said. "Our daughter, Martin, not your mother."

The detective false-coughed and said, "Mr. Kolachuk—"

"—Martin, okay? Please. Professional courtesy."

His wife hadn't the mind to grant Legree any kind of courtesy. "You haven't done a thing about this," Sarah said, waving her brush, lightly spattering the detective and me. "Now all of a sudden you're interested."

"We're getting ahead of ourselves," the detective said. "We don't even know if it's your daughter."

Sarah started trembling and Juice firmed up, wrapping her arms around her. "It's Alliyah. I can identify her."

"How can you have any idea?" I said.

Legree silenced me with a look and concentrated on Juice. "You know the woman?"

"Leave her alone." Sarah shrugged free of the hug. "Juice did the most beautiful thing anyone could do."

Juice had set it up. She knew how much it would mean to the parents so met with Alliyah, explaining about the house, how sad her mum and dad were that she couldn't stay with them, how much they missed and loved her.

"She was staying at the Marriott," Legree said. Sympathetic as he was, there was no chance of him forgetting about Juice. "That right? I found a hotel receipt in her purse."

"We met there to plan . . . the big reunion, I guess you could call it."

"Mr. Kolachuk," the detective said, "your daughter hasn't been over since she arrived in town? Nothing?"

"We haven't seen her," Sarah said. "We didn't even know Juice had done such a wonderful thing. We're starting to fix the house because the insurance company has pictures. They got hold of photos of the feces on the mirror and they didn't know about that because Martin cleaned it up. Now they think we faked the whole thing. They said they're not going to pay for the repairs unless we take them to court. And Sonny, nobody can find him, and we want our house to be beautiful again for our beautiful daughter. What are you doing here anyhow, our house was destroyed and someone went by Martin's work and slashed all the tires and smashed the golf cars and you're wasting time asking us the same thing when we already told you we don't know anything. Go find him! Go find who killed Alliyah and leave us alone, let us fix our house for our daughter!" She went back at the wall. No paint left on the brush, but the up and down and back and forth motions seemed to be settling her into a soothing gate.

No soothing Juice. There wasn't much she could relate, having met Alliyah only a couple of weeks before, after deciding the vandalism shouldn't stop the Kolachuks' daughter from visiting, and the little she did have to say was bitten off and spewed out at the detective near top volume.

"I'm doing no good here," I said. "Our place is probably full of people looking for souvenirs." I tried to offer my condolences but Martin and Sarah were madly painting.

The fresh air felt good and I almost ran to the street. "I couldn't breathe in there," I said to the detective, hustling to catch up. "What kind of response is that to the death of your only child?"

"There is no standard way," Legree said. "Seen all kinds. One time a father hung cardboard cutouts of his kid's face all over the outside of the house. Never can tell."

Strung out in a straggly line, people were leaving the crime scene. As we passed, those who hesitated now that two of the key players were returning to the main stage were treated to Detective Legree's glare and a fierce "Move along." In other circumstances it might have prompted protestations of trampled freedom and violation of civil rights or plain old bitching about the cops shoving people around, but with a dead body in a carpet on top of an earthquake, sensory overload was ruling the moment and they did what they were told, stepping briskly off into the night.

Legree directed the police photographer to take several additional shots then beckoned me inside. I haven't described the detective yet, and there's no real reason to do so, since you couldn't determine his profession from appearances or even tender a thumbnail sketch of his personality. He looked like a guy. I didn't offer him a seat and he made no move himself.

"The clothes," I said. "On the bush. Same thing as at the Kolachuks'. Whoever broke in arranged their clothing around the house as if Sarah and Martin had simply melted out of them. A couple of sets were even nailed to the walls like people standing around."

"The blouse and skirt on the bush aren't the girl's," he said. "Wrong size. You saw her, one of those big-headers, those models and actresses so starved their heads look stuck onto the wrong bodies. I'm no expert on women's clothing, but that blouse and skirt were bought for someone else, and recently. They've never been worn."

"Copycat?" I said.

"Don't get tabloid on me."

"I'm just saying there's far too much overlap around here. You don't know the half of it."

"Then give me the half you got."

Thankful for an attentive ear, I filled him in best I could. I went into some detail about Chas Cassidy's pursuit of an interview, but Legree was uninterested in the reporter, a few religious nutbar tracts and a possibly faked sister not doing much to convince him of Cassidy's homicidal nature. My wild-ass descriptions of the neighborhood goings-on he dismissed as "your own personal crap to handle." Despite his urging to repeat the details over and over in hopes of striking something of importance, it was a waste of time—I was just pissed off and jumped up from being caught in the middle of bad times and a revolution involving Juice, that's all.

I thought we were nearing the end till he brought up Coy and Paco.

The detective had asked at the station and discovered they were characters from *The Secrets of Harry Bright*, a Joseph Wambaugh novel.

"That Martin's an odd one," Legree said. "Been in a little trouble over the years overstepping his authority with that security firm. Like most of the guys who couldn't get accepted for the regular force, he likes to think he's on a SWAT team or something. Nice enough, so you tell me, but . . . sometimes the quietest guys . . ."

"Oh, come on," I said.

He stuck his hands in his pockets and looked at me with cop eyes. "Tell me about your girl."

"You're prying."

"The fuck you think I do for a living?"

"You have something specific in mind?"

"Back at the house you were surprised. She never told you about meeting the daughter, did she? And the hotel receipt I found in the dead woman's purse—it was for four months."

"Juice was planning a surprise and was probably afraid I'd let something slip to Martin and Sarah. As for the four months, I don't know why she'd come home and not tell her parents about it for that long, but who knows what goes on in families? Martin told me . . . well, it's pretty obvious they've written themselves a fantasy when it comes to their daughter. Sounds to me as though she didn't want anything to do with them."

"Then why show up at all?" he said.

"Why ask me?" I said. "The fuck you think you do for a living?"

He snorted and wandered to the slider and looked out into the dark. When I got back with a beer from the spare fridge in the garage, Legree was gone. I popped the top and the can foamed and before I could get my mouth over the opening I glanced up and saw the detective at the edge of the road under a street light, talking to Juice and Roger.

Put the beer down and quickly now, quickly . . .

". . . nothing on there that has anything to do with her murder." Juice was livid, her color visible despite the feeble light. She was clutching a videotape with both hands. "It's from when Alliyah was a kid. It's just for me, Sarah made me promise. I can't let you have it."

Not unkindly, the detective took the video and said, "Let's compromise. I'll see if the boys are ready to wrap it up."

"She's gone, right?" Juice angled toward the corner of the house.

"Sweetheart," I said, "don't . . ."

She stopped. "Nothing left except a bunch of footprints. They've taken her already. She came back and now she's gone. They took her, she's been taken."

Legree told us to wait for him inside and to set up the TV and VCR ready to go. As he passed Juice, I thought she was going to make a grab for the tape, but she merely followed him with her eyes.

Juice and Roger were together on the couch. The detective stood to one side and I matched his position on the other side of the room. Roger asked if any of us was hungry, the first thing out of his mouth in two hours. I shook my head to let him know someone was listening, and then it was show time. The tape was reproduced from old footage. No sound, adding to the surreality of watching a dead woman preen and prance from childhood through puberty, grainy flickerings of accomplishment:

FADE IN

INT. BEDROOM – DAY

A small bedroom in perfect order, bed freshly made, music box on a yellow bureau. Along one wall is an ornate vanity with a large oval mirror over a kneehole for a chair. MONICA, a young girl of about six, cute and pudgy, is being made up by her mother, SARAH, twenties. They are chattering and laughing as the mother assesses a collection of lipsticks and makeup.

Camera unsteadily ZOOMS to C.U. of Monica, lids heavy with bright-blue shadow, eyes deeply outlined with mascara that give them an exotic, almond shape. A light dusting of glitter sparkles from her cheeks.

PULL BACK to reveal Sarah taking a great swatch of hair from the back of her daughter's head and pinning it on top. She rakes a hank over Monica's eye, à la Veronica Lake. Tugs too hard and Monica flinches. A small amount of mascara begins running from a tear in the girl's eye.

Just as her mother makes a horrified face and reaches for a tissue a MAN, her father, twenties, comes into view in the mirror, an old Super 8 Camera to his eye.

CUT TO:

EXT. SCHOOL PARKING LOT – EVENING

The sun is setting as Sarah escorts Monica toward a school. They pass other mothers and daughters, all carrying garment bags, hat boxes, etc. Small nods here and there of acknowledgment but no fraternizing.

Camera PANS to the school, which is festooned with bunting and a large banner: *Tiny Miss Pageant – Regional Finals.*

INT. SCHOOL – EVENING

We follow the mother and daughter to a registration table, and after an elderly MATRON checks her list, continue along a hallway until a SECURITY GUARD, large, fortyish, menacing-looking, looms in the Camera.

CUT TO:

INT. SCHOOL GYM – LATER

The gym is packed with adults on metal folding chairs. On stage is a WOMAN, wearing an evening gown, speaking into a microphone.

MONTAGE:

Brief segments of individual young girls tap dancing, twirling batons and speaking seriously into the mike held by the Woman. They are too far away to clearly make out.

CUT TO:

INT. STAGE WINGS – LATER

From stage left we see Monica on stage, dressed as an Egyptian Queen, chubby chest forced into a semblance of cleavage, giving a dramatic speech in recline on a fainting couch. The Security Guard appears at the edge of frame, Camera is violently wrenched sideways and for ten seconds we see dizzying shots of the floor, curtains and young contestants jumping out of the way.

CUT TO:

EXT. SCHOOL PARKING LOT – NIGHT

In barely enough light to see, Sarah emerges from the front doors. In her fist is a trophy, and she raises it above her head, shouting silently in triumph at Camera. When she is halfway to the car Camera PANS back to the school as Monica, toting a large garment bag, emerges. She trips over the edge of the bag, falls and skins her knee on the pavement.

CUT TO:

EXT. STADIUM – DAY

A small football stadium, seating a few hundred, on a bright autumn day. The teams on the field can barely be seen through a forest of heads and hats. In the background is a one-story building on the side of which is painted, John Paul Getty A&M University.

Camera rises as the teams depart the playing field. A squad of cheerleaders runs to the center of the field. They assemble in ranks and wait. To one side, a marching band fiddles with their instruments.

Camera swiftly searches the sidelines until finding Monica, eighteen, as she's embracing one of the uniformed players. After the hug she lights a cigarette and leaves the bench area, slowly jogging to join her squadmates. As she nears the group she takes a last drag on her smoke and flicks it on the turf.

Camera jerks and refocuses, and we see Sarah running down the aisle toward field level.

On the next CUT, which led to a close-up of a plaque engraved with *Betsy Ross Modeling and Talent Agency*, I was out of there. Fortunately, I was at the side of the theater and didn't have to excuse-me-excuse-me-sorry my way through the punters to make my way to an aisle. At the concession stand I took a beer from the fridge. I've always thought bursting through a door and into fresh air was a hokey way of leaving an untenable situation behind, yet I did so for the second time in an hour.

The others stayed till the end of the credits. When they emerged and Roger handed the tape to Legree, who passed it immediately to Juice, she held it loosely like an old scrapbook of newspaper clippings in a dead language impervious to translation.

The detective turned to me, dug into an inside pocket of his sportcoat and said, "The pictures sent to the insurance company—these the ones?"

I fanned the sheaf. "No idea, but these are of the house, all right. You've seen the place yourself, other than the fresh paint it looks about the same." I passed them back.

"These were in the dead woman's purse," he said.

Juice moaned, a strangled sound. "I don't want to know that. . . . Please, she didn't have anything to do with it, she couldn't have."

I gently held her shoulders. "The receipt was for four months. She's been here four months, baby."

"No, it couldn't be, it doesn't work that way. Nobody, especially some fucking cop, is going to tell me Sarah's own daughter did something like that to her parents' house. We only met once but we talked. She was real polite and everything at first but we really talked, like we were friends already. We had lunch and drank wine and laughed about the same things. She's normal, you have to believe me she's normal, just a normal woman. She has her own life, one that takes her all over the country, and you can't expect someone in that line of work to live stuck out here in the middle of the desert just so she can be near her parents. She's working toward something, she has a goal. As soon as she gets too old for the business, even for TV commercials and everything, she's going to—oh, fuck! she's not going to do anything."

She loosed an anguished squeal and I stepped toward her but stopped when she started in again with: "It wasn't her, not to her own parents. I couldn't stand it if—" She thrust her face at Legree. "It's not right even thinking that way. How can you live with yourself being a cop and having that kind of shit in your head every day? She's gone like she was never here, and her mum and dad are over there painting. Fucking painting."

"We don't really know anything about her," I said. "I'm not saying anything about . . . with the pictures the officer found, all I'm saying is give him a chance to look into it more."

"You ran out of her movie. She was just a kid. Not everybody can be a writer or a cop or an accountant or anything. Most people do stuff, any kind of stuff that they're told to, some of us don't have a choice and that's it, our life that we have to finish."

Legree passed a look around the semicircle, giving each of us a good taste of attitude. "I feel for you all, but keep one thing clear—I'm not your friend. I'm not your enemy either, but it's important that you know I've been a cop for twenty-seven years and I'm not bad at what I do. Tell me the truth, all of it, and we'll be fine, maybe we'll have a coffee if we ever run into each other at IHOP some Sunday morning, but if you keep anything from me I'll shove the coffee cup up your ass. Think, remember, tell me, and make it the truth."

As we digested his little speech, he spun off toward his car.

CHAPTER 33

Juice came in from Tina's at nine in the morning. Roger was still in bed and I'd been up only ten minutes myself. I waited for the sound of the shower. It was always the first thing Juice did on arrival because the Blonde Job's bathroom plumbing was on the fritz. We'd invited Tina over time and again to use ours, but that was a nonstarter, she was satisfied to stand under a barely dripping shower head and be gurgled clean till the day Sonny reappeared and repaired it.

There was no sound from the bathroom, and when I checked there was no Juice. I had the feeling she was outside at the corner of the house and allowed her time. As the coffee maker dripped she burst in the back, right past me and set up a rustle and clatter in the bedroom. When I heard her coming up the hall, I stepped out of the kitchen in barely enough time to catch her leaving.

Her ratty tool pack was slung over a shoulder. She opened the front door and when it hit the stop she leaned against it, letting her bag slowly slip to the ground on the far side of the transom, two fingers still hooked to a strap. "Just for a while. Maybe longer. I don't know. How long's awhile?"

Not the Kolachuks' or Tina's or even the Dowser's. Just going.

"I can't blame you for being afraid."

"Afraid?" she said. "If you think I'm afraid why don't you tell me how you'll protect me and make me safe and be there for me? You will, as much as you can, but you know I'm not scared, not that way. I've done it again, that's all. I touch it, I touch something and it starts to change. I can feel it shake, I really mean that, I interfere with the vibes or something and it all starts coming apart. It makes me laugh to think about working for Sonny, trying to fix things when all I've ever done is wreck them. That big construction project I told you I worked on? It was a house, I built a house. And it was terrible. I spent all my time hoping it wouldn't burn down or fall down or blow up, and when it didn't I spent the rest of my time hoping it would."

"That was a hundred years ago," I said, "a thousand. And who cares about a house? It's just a thing."

"There was this boy in school," she said. "We were little, eight or nine, and I liked him. Silly, trying to get him to notice me by calling him names and teasing him, that kind of stuff. I forgot all about him over the summer holidays and the next year when we went back to school I started getting caught for everything. I was always in trouble, but now I was getting blamed for stuff I hadn't done, and even when I worked hard I got worse and worse marks and in more and more trouble. Then one day we were on a field trip, only half an hour out of town at a Hutterite farm. They showed us the animals and everything, funny because all us kids knew about farms, and they told us how in the Hutterite community they all work together, for one another, you know? And when we were getting back on the bus one of the men, a Hutterite man, they're scary to a little kid, was outside talking to the teacher and I knew they were talking about me. That sounds freaky but I knew and I was right. This boy, somebody but it had to be this boy, had gone into a couple of chicken coops and smashed all the eggs and told the Hutterite man he saw me do it. So the teacher called me off the bus in front of everybody and then rest of the kids got off too. I had to stand in front of the whole class and the teacher and a bunch more of the Hutterites 'cause they all gathered around, and I had to tell them I did it and ask the farmers' forgiveness and God's forgiveness and the teacher's. So I did. I didn't even try to explain. I told everybody how sorry I was and started crying and I even got down on my knees and prayed with my hands together in front of me. And the teacher was still mad but the Hutterite man put his hand on my head real soft and said something about repenting. And I don't know why, but I pushed it away and said, 'Get off me, you fag.' Don't laugh—I didn't know what it meant, it's just something my dad called everybody."

"Sorry, it took me by surprise, that's all." She didn't say anything so I added, "What about the kid, the one you liked?"

"Nothing," she said. "Nothing happened to him 'cause I never told who it was. They called my mum and dad into school the next day and my dad hit the teacher. She wasn't very big, one of those skinny ladies you see in old pictures from the Depression my mum used to show me, and he punched her right in the face and broke some of her teeth and her jaw, she was all wired up for a long time."

I looked down at the bag.

"He got put in jail, my dad went to jail. Nothing happened to me, only later, a long time later, my dad had been out of the prison a long time, he didn't hit me or anything but when he found out I was pregnant—I know I never mentioned that before but it's like I never had had a baby—and doesn't that sound funny? My dad wouldn't let me come home till he was dead."

I reached for her but it was the wrong thing to do.

"Let me finish—the baby, right? He made me give it away and all I wanted to do was take care of her. He made me give it away and then after I did he wouldn't let me come home. Now look at this, all this fuckup I'm making."

"It was out of your hands. She was your daughter but you were just a kid. Maybe she . . . probably she had a good home and a good life. Same with now—you can't be blamed."

"The pictures," she said. "I sent them to the insurance company. With a letter telling them to pay up. I had to do something, right? They were going to make Sarah and Martin fix the place themselves. And it's not just the fixing, the fixing's nothing, me and Sonny could have done that in a few days and it wouldn't have cost hardly anything. Except they needed help, those guys. When something that . . . wrong, happens, that wrong, it's like an invasion, right, like they've been violated in their own home, somebody has to do something."

"Even if you didn't mean to make it worse, the insurance company thought it was fraud in the first place. You had nothing to lose trying it your way. "

"Don't talk to me about losing," she said. "And don't baby me. I made a bad decision, let's face facts, I make them all the time. I made copies of the pictures and gave them to Alliyah to get her to come home and how stupid is that?"

"I thought she'd been here four months."

"Yes, four months. She was working in Palm Springs, modeling, but until I showed her the pictures she didn't even think her parents wanted her to be with them. I explained they were embarrassed about asking her to stay there when the house was wrecked. You saw it—some crazy person went nuts and anyone who's crazy lets off a stink you don't want your own daughter to smell. Now she's dead. It's all sorted out."

Death sorts out nothing. As for Juice, death couldn't touch her. Wouldn't die, couldn't, too unpredictable, too much of a moving target, and for all her guilt, or because of it, she was strong. Even slumped against the door she exuded force—cut black hair mostly grown in, arms remarkably unscarred from the burns, dark dark eyes refracting and flashing through the tears a million, two, five million years of instinctive survival.

She'd already seen Legree about the pictures, and felt she didn't have it in her to tell Sarah and Martin. This time when I tried to hold her she thrust herself off the door and gripped me around the neck till it hurt.

"I don't like being told anything," she said. "But tell me. Right now I need to be told."

"Stay," I said. "See this through with me. It'll pass."

She dissolved and melded with me and we held each other until Roger, unshaven and disheveled, came around the corner.

"Stay," he said. "Both of you. We'll be okay if we stay together."

Juice wiped her face on my shirt. "I'm hungry."

How could I not be in love with a woman like that? Roger, the old Roger, beamed. We had a quick bite to eat while avoiding the subject of the murder, talking of hummingbirds and the swarm of desert crickets in the garage and the fascinating mountain color schemes that changed by the minute as the sun sailed over the naked fissures and canyons. It felt like a fresh start. With renewed buoyancy, Juice set out for the Kolachuks'. I told Roger he could eavesdrop any time he liked if he was going to turn things around the way he had, and his eyes filled and I held out my arms and he squeezed me every bit as hard as Juice had. Our whiskers scraped as we parted and I couldn't possibly have refused him anything. Although I came close when he asked me to go with him to Ralphs.

Manufactured as the fresh start was, once we entered the store the slant had me capering down the aisles like a mad jester, and I didn't stop till Roger was thoroughly embarrassed. Shopping for food, that's all, yet I felt immense freedom, juvenile asininity on the heels of hellish revelation, just as the world turned according to my mother. Roger picked through packages of spaghetti as I counted to six the varieties of aerosol cheese sprays, and in the next lane he waited while I inspected the hot-sauce section—Mild, Tame, Dash, Slash, Medium, Pepper, Mexican, Jalapeño, Habañero, Scotch Bonnet, Scorch, Blazing, Fire In The Hole, Mule Kick, Mother Of Mercy, Peckerwood, Call Yo' Mama, Call The Doctor, Screamin' An' Killin', Dress The Wound, F*** You Up, Buy A New A**hole.

"Can we get going?" Roger said. "Before Juice changes her mind and ends up in another state?"

"Exactly how hot do you think 'Peckerwood' is? That one has me confused."

"You're a confused man."

I grabbed a bottle of Mule Kick, and followed him past the shelf of garlic-and-rosemary potato chips before pulling up short when he stopped for tomato paste. I admonished him for taking so long to price-compare over the matter of four cents, and without preamble was informed we were broke. That sudden—Broke, said with the lack of emphasis that Roger has always used to underscore things that require it.

I forced my mouth into a vertical cartoon oval and slapped the Mule Kick back on a shelf.

"I'm serious," he said.

Our supply wagon took a direct hit from a cart containing two kids tearing open packages of red licorice with their teeth. Roger reversed and moved to the shoulder as a woman who'd had so many facelifts she could have nursed a tot at her temples shot past, yelling at her children to stop whipping each other with the liberated Twizzlers.

"How broke is broke?" I said.

"I got too fancy last year after September 11th," he said. "I anticipated a quicker rebound in the market. When it didn't happen I started gambling on currencies and futures and . . . I turned into a gambler. Me, a gambler, if you can believe it. The house will be okay, but you know the way I've set up my business. This is April, so after tax season things will be lean. As for cash flow, I'll have to go up to B.C. to find some work. I've already talked to a couple of community colleges in Burnaby and North Vancouver about teaching introductory accounting."

His financial acumen might have been impaired, but his shopping instincts were still intact. Spotting an open checkout aisle with a burnt-out number on its pylon, he veered left, crossed behind two lineups and pulled in behind a lone man whose groceries were already bagged. Unfortunately, it was an elderly fellow who was having more trouble with the automatic debit machine than he'd probably had fighting his way to the Yalu River in Korea.

"Why didn't you say anything till now?" I said.

"You have your hands full," Roger said. "The last thing you need is to be worrying about money."

"Which way does the stripe go?" the old gaffer asked the checkout girl, a cute Mexican with a Ralphs/*Bonita* nametag.

"Down and on the right side," she said.

"Do you take checks?" the old man asked.

"Not out-of-state without identification, sir. Swipe it again. No, on the *right* side. No, your *other* right."

"Clean me out," I said to Roger. "Whatever's in my pot." When he didn't look at me I added, "So you took out a loan, big deal. We can live on almost nothing, you and me. Put a hold on my allowance, divert the royalties from the novel into a common slush fund and we'll ride it out till you make your big comeback."

The old man was almost in tears. Frenetically, he ran his card again and again and again through the debit machine. The checkout girl backed off at the display of geriatric rage. By then shoppers in the other aisles had formed up behind us in a line stretching past the golf shirts, the tiki torches and halfway into the display of electric stainless-steel wiener smokers. As Roger was putting the last couple of items on the conveyor belt, I was violently propelled forward and fetched up staring at a magazine called *Entertainment or Nothing*, the cover of which advertised "Weekly Quiz: Match Wits With Mariah Carey." I pushed away from the rack.

It was Deep Tread. He positioned himself between our cart and the old guy, rested a paw on the scanning register and exhaled raggedly through his nose, letting the clerk have a good taste of his impatience. "What's the holdup?" he said. "What's the problem here, Ralph?"

"Bonita," the checkout clerk said.

Deep Tread noticed Roger and me. "Hey, motherfuckers," he said pleasantly, apparently forgetting we had abandoned him and his buddies in a crevasse the day before. "How they hanging?"

About at my eye-level was script on his T-shirt: Don't Mess With Oklahoma!

"Isn't that supposed to be, 'Don't Mess With Texas'?" I said.

"Fuck Texas," he said. "What, they think they're the only ones you can't mess with?"

"She won't tell me which way," the old man said to the desert giant.

"Tell him which way," DT said to the girl. "C'mon, Ralph, there's people waiting."

"Down and to the right," Bonita said. "I told him."

"Tell him again."

"Down and to the right," she said.

"I tried that," the old bugger said. "I tried it a hundred times."

"He tried it a hundred times," Deep Tread said. "This is an emergency, maybe you didn't hear about the earthquake. I'm a HOA leader, can't be waiting around in a emergency. Macho Man Savage don't wait, he climbs in the ring and gets the job done."

Roger cleared his throat and said, "Miss? Maybe you could do it for him."

The principals looked dumbstruck at the sublimity of the suggestion. Appreciative murmurs from the people behind us.

Deep Tread pointed a sausage of a finger at Roger and said, "Number One, motherfucker, Number One, my man."

Bonita worked her magic. "There you are, sir. Now just enter your code."

"My what?"

"Here." DT pulled out his wallet and threw some bills on the counter. "Only six bucks, the whole world held up by six bucks." Before the geezer could catch up to events Tread snatched the plastic bag off the counter and thrust it at him. "Git, Colonel."

The old gent toddled off.

"Would you like to go ahead?" Roger said.

Deep Tread stared at him until determining, I suppose, there was no ulterior motive behind the offer. "Naw, rules is rules, right? Where'd we be if everybody went and did what they want?" He elbowed past us to resume his place in line.

Three minutes later Roger and I were outside, waiting on the sidewalk to let a woman pass with a miniature hairless dog Dr. Seuss couldn't have invented.

"There's another way to handle it," I said. "I could stop acting like your dependent. Give the royalty checks straight to me and let me start keeping track of my own money. Even some of the household expenses—set up a list or a table on the computer and I'll start taking care of as many bills as I can manage. It'll take some of the pressure off so you can devote yourself to rebuilding your portfolio. We'll be back on our feet in no time."

Roger was only half listening. A few feet away, bag at his feet, face pressed against the window, the old man was peering into the store. Roger and I joined him, visoring out the glare with our hands. Deep Tread had made it back to the checkout counter. Clearly it was one of those days Bonita was having trouble communicating—Mr. Tread had ripped the debit machine from its cord and was bashing it on the rack of batteries and phone cards. The old guy stepped away from the glass and danced in place, hooting with joy and pumping his bony fist as though he'd just kicked a winning field goal.

On the way to the car Roger pointed out a problem with my plan—the royalties had run out. Again, that sudden—Run out, but this time with the emphasis required. Looked at my feet, squeezed my nose with thought, but oh well, bad time for it to happen, though I could hardly complain given that I'd been garnering a paycheck for work so long ago completed.

"That's a pisser," I said. "But it was a good run while it lasted."

Roger tucked the groceries away and shut the trunk. "There never were any royalties."

I figured I'd walk home. Not nearly long enough to cleanse, it would still afford me time to sift through my shame and decide which parts to live with and what to throw in Roger's face. I wasn't going to bear all the disgrace on this one—some of it had to go his way, if for no other reason than punishment for patronizing me. So far as I know, freeloading isn't even recognized as a social faux pas when it's unintentional, and though it must have amounted to thousands, maybe hundreds of thousands of dollars over the years, rough ass. I'm surprised he hadn't been telling me how to spend it. I'd tell him that, too, straight to his face, the minute I got home.

So my star was burnt out. With not enough mass to go supernova, my little novel had blazed brightly enough to light a few lives and to drive me underground then collapsed in on itself until winking out and being left in the sky as a cinder. Gone, and to the greatest extent forgotten. Roger had fictionalized the fiction, propped me up. It meant also that I'd been hiding for nothing all these years, though it's difficult to blame something like that on a wad of bound pages and some noisome publicity. No, part of my wiring, I guess. Name please? Morton Haig Cahoot. Occupation? Hider.

No natural catastrophe had befallen me, no rocks on my head or overturned boat sending my family to the seabed, and if the troubles around me were human then they were vulnerable, susceptible to being taken up in my own good hands and shaken. I'd start with Roger the minute I got home. I knew why he'd done it and I'd probably end up thanking him and telling him that I loved him but either way it was time to start straightening the furniture. I wasn't about to sneak in through the back sliders, either. Nope, right through the front door I'd go, fling it wide like a man with a plan and tell him right to his face.

At home, I retrieved Juice's bag from where she'd left it out front and paused. Shook it. Unzipped it and looked in. Ran my hand around and around the inside as if I were in a blizzard searching for my door key.

Empty.

CHAPTER 34

My false bravado disappeared as I came through the door carrying Juice's bag and saw Roger sitting at the kitchen table nursing a scraped knuckle. A broken bottle of Ragu sauce adorned the counter, lasagna noodles crinkled the floor from doorstop to dishwasher. I cleaned up the mess while Roger changed into shorts before heading without a word down to the pool. He returned midafternoon and we didn't talk and the sun lost its lofty vantage point and ran astern and down till it was later later late. Juice still hadn't returned from the Kolachuks', so I put on a pot of instant noodles and Roger and I had soup. However much out of our purview, we speculated on the murder with *Law and Order* expertise while avoiding for now talk about the royalties. Not much to say about the latter anyhow.

My cut from hitting the softball fence broke open in the night, and in the morning I threw the pillow case in the washer and dosed myself with peroxide. Juice awoke from where she'd been sleeping on the couch, and as she helped squeeze aloe on the wound and apply a new butterfly bandage, she doled out a recap, recounting the day before as though dictating a letter—fits, starts, backtracks.

She'd barely had the chance to apologize. When she tried to explain about the pictures Sarah and Martin cut her off, pooh-poohing the issue while expressing so much admiration for her honesty that it stripped all value from her confession. I guess the situation was already bad enough—after twenty-four hours of fasting and prayer it had been revealed to the Kolachuks that their daughter was the vandal. When Juice heard that, she ramped up and laid into them, over and over again stressing how shaken their daughter had been when she saw the photos of the damage. And much more—the deep feelings for them Alliyah had expressed, how sorry for her absence all that time, adrift from the lack of familial ties as she jetted around the country. But Sarah and Martin were fixated on the timeline. Four months Alliyah had been so very close without a word. She'd been on a photo shoot, Juice explained, but nope, they stuck to their guns. Four months, since before the attack, the invasion, the insult, the destruction and the clothing and the message in feces on the mirror.

It made no sense to me. If she'd avenged herself on her parents those months back, why stick around this long? Absurd, the lot of it. Most disturbing was Sarah and Martin's leap to a conclusion on no evidence beyond an unexplained yet explainable overlap in time and place. The three of us worried it with our teeth until essentially giving up. What do we ever know of people we glimpse in a flash of sunlight distorted through a lens of funhouse glass and subject to our own rickety analysis? Lives in the neat-as-a-pinniest community in the upper-central Coachella Valley intersecting with one on a grainy video, go figure.

How to explain the murder? Not enough to go on, though it didn't prevent us from hypothesizing. The clothing on the bushes was likely a calling card of some kind . . . or did we have it wrong? Rather than a calling card maybe it was a turnabout, a mocking bit of revenge. Sarah and Martin had . . . none of us wanted to get close to that fire. Not her parents, they couldn't possibly—everybody shut up about it okay? Not another word.

The local media could only thinly disguise their excitement. Although Morton Downey Jr. was staying in Palm Springs, reporters and paparazzi were stripped from their sniper posts and observation balloons to report on the murder, leaving a lone platoon of mercenaries to man the trench system outside Downey's hotel and direct artillery fire in the event the poor bastard attempted a breakout for supplies. A nonstop fusillade of speculative baloney was offered as if Oliver Stone had taken up the cause, all of which was easily dismissed.

Dismiss them I did, all but one item in the paper. According to the coroner's office, confirmed by a Dr. Narfi from the Millard Fillmore Center, Monica Kolachuk, aka Alliyah Essence, had died from an overdose of Ecstasy. I remembered the doctor as the VATS debunker, and adding to my interest was the byline, a freelancer named Charles H. "Chas" Cassidy.

After two days of fermenting with not a word from Detective Legree, I drove to the hospital. Dr. Narfi had become a kind of hero to me, a desert James Randi popping the mendacious bubbles of fraudulent claims and muddled thinking, though if I'd been expecting a refreshing discussion and hard answers, which I was, the trip was wasted. The doctor was a busy, very serious man. He was unconnected officially with the coroner's office, though he had no reason to mistrust its report on Ecstasy as the cause of death. Other than that, he refused to discuss the matter and disavowed giving an interview to Cassidy, or any reporter for that matter. I was told to call in advance the next time I wanted to talk to him, and that when the next time came, and I called, he would refuse. I was left standing in the hall and was about to go when the doctor returned. Aha! I pulled out an Internet printout on Ecstasy that Roger had given me and enjoined myself to keep the interview brief. Narfi thrust a pamphlet in my hand, executed a nice heel-spin and scooted into an elevator.

I glanced at the brochure:

ECSTASY
MDMA—methylenedioxy-n-methylamphetamine
$C_{11}H_{15}NO_2$

Not the information I'd come for, but a crumb. I hollered a thanks at the elevator door.

On the way to the car I skimmed densely packed script describing the effects of the poisonous, at times deadly, mind-and-mood-altering substance, and figured—in keeping with the theme—I needed some booze to enhance my appreciation of the material. In fifteen minutes I was at the Blue Dog, wiping my hand on my shorts from the cascading head overflowing the beer glass.

"Bad stuff out your way," Stan said.

"Yeah."

"Seen you on TV. Think it was you, big crowd, pretty dark. Been talking to Johnny? Usually drops by after the lunch rush."

Quarter after twelve. Not a roach or barfly in the saloon, though the sound of a dispute was audible from the small patio out the side entrance. Stan filled a tray and headed that direction, and I opened the doctor's foldout. Inside was a chemical analysis of the drug followed by a summarized case study and a list of effects and Bewares! I laid it and Roger's printout beside each other on the bar.

Consummate correlation. All negative effects from the health authority pamphlet were touted as positives by the website, and to evenly distribute the spin, the medicos refused to acknowledge the benefits or even the attractions of the druggies' claims for their chemical of choice. I'll combine the information and pair up the entries:

Effects of Ecstasy (MDMA)

- extreme mood lift
- death

- increased willingness to communicate
- tendency to say things you might feel uncomfortable about later

- increase in energy (stimulation)
- post-event depression and fatigue

- feelings of love and closeness to others
- inappropriate and/or unintended emotional bonding

- increased awareness of senses (eating, drinking)
- nausea and vomiting

- neurotically based fear dissolution
- possible psychological crisis requiring hospitalization

- bright and intense sensations
- mild visual hallucinations

- profound life-changing spiritual experiences
- strong need to repeat the experience

You get my drift so I'll wrap it up—ego diminution visual distortion appetite loss increased awareness and appreciation of music muscle tension restlessness shivering short-term memory loss crash hangover liver toxicity neurotoxicity erectile dysfunction difficulty concentrating increased heart rate and blood pressure hyperthermia dehydration.

And hyponatremia, the one that got Monica, assuming the circle around the item was Dr. Narfi's doing. Hyponatremia—low salt; water intoxication—had done her in. Fluff aside, two big problems after taking Ecstasy: Too little water and too much. Dehydration is understood, a common enough term, and to experience its effects just come on down to the Coachella Valley in July and bend over to tie your shoes. But it works the other way, too. In some Ecstasy users there's a need to drink enormous amounts of water, lowering the relative amount of salt in the body, diluting it beyond a critical level. Monica had suffered a cerebral edema from unbalanced electrolytes. She drank water to death.

"Library closed?"

"Dropping by for your afternoon snort?" I said.

Legree looked around and nodded to Stan as he returned. The owner poured him a coffee and disappeared through a swinging door off the end of the bar. After shrugging off my complaints about not hearing from him, the detective turned sham-cryptic and let me know the murder was tied in somehow with Tina's attack.

"Don't worry," he said. "You're off the hook. Your alibi holds up for the Kolachuk girl. You were smart enough to be with someone every place you went that day."

"Yeah, that was my plan." He was still standing, so I got up and leaned my elbow on the bar. "I wouldn't think you'd worry about any of us. Isn't it unlikely a murderer would leave the body beside his own house?"

"Unless that was the point. All kinds of people do all kinds of things to draw attention to themselves. . . . Or attention to someone else."

"Oooo," I said. "Spooky."

Legree pointed at my empty and I looked for Stan. The detective took my glass, reached over the bar and poured me a fresh draft backhanded. I was grilled at some length about Sonny, whom Legree referred to as "that slippery bastard," but his latest disappearing act was news to me. The whole family was missing again, except for Quinn, and in regard to him, the detective told me to put my mind at ease. Quinn was one screwed-up man, but no killer.

"Then who?" I shoved off the bar. "Who, Legree? Sonny, is that what you're hinting at? We've just had a body dumped on our doorstep, and after interviewing us for about ten minutes each you've been as hard to reach as the cable guy."

The detective merely poured himself a draft and checked his watch.

"Something stinks in here!" A large silhouette in the patio doorway.

Deep Tread broke from the frame of light, advanced, halted on hard boot heels. He glared at Legree, sniffed the air. "Yep, stinks bad in here. Pig or something. Pig."

"Maybe it's you," the detective said.

Tread sniffed an armpit. "Huh, you're right."

I quickly raised my glass to my mouth.

"What you laughing at?" he said. "Hey, you're that motherfucker, Juice's old man. One happy camper in a few days when she takes over as top dog of the HOA."

"What happened to the triumvirate?" I said. "The revolution promised three people on the Board."

"Too much arguments. We're getting rid of Martin, that queer, deporting him back to security. Supporting Juice all the way. I'll be second in command, Two-Eye-fuckin-Cee. Tell you what, you're one lucky guy. There's a chick with balls for you, and a mouth to swallow you whole."

I threw a five on the bar, resisting every natural urge to deal with it right there. I couldn't possibly take him, though I had the feeling Legree would be happy to exercise a little authority on my behalf. When the detective put down his empty glass and started to leave, I folded my pamphlets and followed. In the parking lot I thanked him and he asked me what for. What for? Who the hell knew? If I'd given him an answer, it would probably have been along the lines of appreciation for his friendship. Strange, we weren't friends, he'd done nothing to encourage the feeling that we were, I wasn't sure I liked him all that much, he'd done nothing but dodge everything I asked, and as much as he claimed the contrary I knew I was a suspect. Still, there was an elementary decency about the man that attracted me, or maybe he represented safe ground in our enfiladed hike up Vimy Ridge.

Before he got in his car he scanned the parking lot—histrionically, peering down his nose—and said, "Wonder where the monster truck is?"

Pulling out behind the detective's car, I asked myself the same thing. The vehicle was a symbol of sorts, the cheesy mustache on a villain. Oh well, another useless voyage of discovery at the Blue Dog.

I discovered very little for the rest of the month. Aircraft pilots describe the character of their work as hours of sheer boredom interrupted by moments of stark terror. With the recent acceleration of natural assault and human wickedness, I awoke each morning expecting something beastly, but the moment was gone. Back to straight-and-level boredom.

I wanted Juice to have her surprise so said nothing about her elevation to command of the Board. She and Deep Tread met every day to draft a new constitution, something I learned second-hand because Juice didn't talk about it. She was marked by a live-wire edginess, trying to be all things to all people, shuttling like Kissinger, mapping out her time as though devising a train schedule, actually looking at her watch in mid-conversation and saying things such as: "Thirty seconds—let's wrap it up, people," even when we were alone together.

My chauffeur duties were suspended by proclamation, but I found comfort in being there in other ways for Juice, taking over from Roger the task of making sure she left with a bagged lunch, tucking some folded walkaround in her jeans, generally playing the herd mother, letting her gambol and explore while I kept alert for predators. Shitload of strain, though.

As for Roger—"Anything's possible." That became his pet phrase. I couldn't stop talking about the murder case, Tina's rape, Cassidy, Quinn, the salmagundi of clutter and infection our lives had become. "Anything's possible," is what I got each time from Roger.

I found him one day sitting cross-legged on the living-room floor, surrounded by papers and books, poking his finger in and out of the bullet hole in his tortoise shell. "You're really getting into the reptiles these days," I said.

"Anything's—"

"—If you want to be a swami," I said, "go live on a mountain. Just because anything's possible doesn't mean everything's equally likely." I snapped it out harshly and still didn't get a rise. But he stopped saying it.

A few days later he latched onto another stock term—Society—and his speech was soon clogged with it. "Well," he'd say, "in a society like this . . ." or "That's society for you." or "It's no surprise considering our society." I expected one day to see him stumping around with his arms held in front of him like a patched-together monster in a '50s flick, mechanically repeating "Society . . . society . . . society . . ." until the townsfolk got tired of the collective blame, took up their sickles and carved him a new asshole.

The play had gone out of him. Not an overly joyous man, Roger yet had an appreciation for absurdity, in on the big joke. But these days he was doing a lot of cowboy acting—staring off at the horizon while pretending to chew—and I didn't know what to do about it. I thought many times a change of environment might do him good, but not a chance. We weren't done with the desert, not done by half.

The rhythm of our lives had been corrupted and it wasn't till May 1st, with the Christmas turkey thawed and the innards in the sink and Roger fussing over the stuffing, that we had a chance to sit down, all of us together, and take a look-see. Juice was supposed to pick up Tina and be home by four—promised, *promised*, cross her heart. She'd told us to be ready for a surprise, and I assumed we'd be hearing the official announcement of her promotion. May Day. I couldn't efface the image of Juice atop a thirty-foot platform reviewing a march past of soldiers fronting two miles of main battle tanks and portable missile launchers. The girls were on time to the minute with a bouquet of mixed flowers and two squat oatmealy candles. Roger was as cheery as I'd seen him in weeks, and it was hard to say who was having the most fun, him with his TV-chef excitement or the girls with their secret. I was happy just to be able to walk around without eggshells underfoot, and tried to work myself into a state suitable to the occasion.

Watching her beam and chatter, I was amazed that not so long ago Juice would have chosen death by increments over attending a homeowners meeting, and now she was top-prick porcupine. The politics behind her selection were of course transparent. Tina's group, reasonable people with legitimate complaints, had been involved in the initial action against the *ancien régime*, but had been swept up in the flash flood of revolt and now, tumbling about in the current and being bounced off the bottom, were further from a direct say in matters than ever before. But it was a fractured constituency, and those in charge needed at least the appearance of being representative, so who would be more acceptable than a powerless, possibly illegal immigrant figurehead? Appearance was all, and I was under no illusion Juice was anything other than a front for DT and his bullyboys. One bad lot replaced by one tougher, centrists stuffed. Scary scenario, my friends—Deep Tread, the power behind the throne, a stinky drunken Richelieu with a giant truck.

As Roger basted the bird for the last time, they let us have it in a rush. I don't even remember how they broke the news, just that one minute we were laughing about having turkey dinner in May and the next—

"—so exciting!" Tina said. "This is the break we've been waiting for, a turnaround, we have the chance to do some actual positive good."

"I'm as surprised as you guys," Juice said. "It started off as sort of a volunteer thing by filling in for Tina and now I can do it all! Improvements, progress, especially protection—having a firm set of rules is what keeps us from being animals. Sarah was too easy on everyone. You see what's happened, people running around out of control doing anything they want, and then Tina—" a nod from Juice and a downcasting of her friend's eyes "—and eventually murder. Loose laws plus loose morals equals trouble. It's all about looking inside ourselves and making a commitment, a covenant with the truth."

"I don't think the problem is too much freedom," I said.

"It's time for a war on crime. Deep Tread is starting his own security company and we're going to have triple patrols."

"Law enforcement should be—"

"—Don't start with your goofy arguments," she said. "We have a plan. For starters, once a week everybody will hand in a card reporting violations of the new code, keeping us up to date on neighbors and other suspicious characters. Also, we're keeping the VATS rules that the old board brought in. Just because VATS wasn't real doesn't mean it couldn't be, so if something like that happens in the future we'll already have laws to cover it. We need to be safe. If you haven't done anything wrong there's nothing to be worried about, right?"

"Security isn't a zero-sum game," I said. "Being safe doesn't depend on everyone else feeling insecure."

"I'm glad you brought that up," she said. "You're forgetting about the good people. We're going to keep the good people happy. For example, every weekend we'll have an old-time field day. Wasn't the softball game fun? Okay, I wasn't there, but everyone I talked to said it was great. Anyhow, we won't do anything the people don't want, as soon as we can tell who should have a say."

"Some won't?"

"Which is why everyone will submit an essay about themselves, just a short list of where they've gone wrong in the past. Self-criticism, right, Tina? Then we'll all be starting fresh on the same page and it'll be easy to pick out the good people." She kissed me on the cheek and said, "I choose you. You'll see how great it's going to turn out."

"Will we have to pay the fine for having the carpet against the house?"

"Don't mention that thing! It's vicious, not a joke. And anyhow, the good people aren't going to be treated the same as the troublemakers. That's what the new start is all about, making the bad ones realize their mistakes and do what it takes to be a good one. Eventually, when every-body's good—whoa!"

"Paradise," I said.

"With guardian angels for everyone," she said. "Deep Tread is totally committed to the cause and ready to do whatever it takes."

"I don't doubt it. Any full-grown man with a favorite wrestler can't be expected to think twice."

Roger quietly went to the kitchen and removed the turkey from the oven. Tina initiated the descent from paradise by faking a swoon at the aroma, and we sat at the table. It was good food, though not a good din-ner together, because I had a troublesome sulk on and Roger had revert-ed to his silent mode; we filled our bellies with bread while Juice talked circuses. Tina oscillated between her world and ours, and the metronom-ic pattern of it had me acutely concerned for her stability. She laughed and she cried at Juice's plans for the neighborhood, laughed and cried when she spilled cranberry sauce on the floor, laughed and cried.

After the meal we sat around with labored good will until Juice said Tina needed her rest and the two of them left. I told Roger I'd clean up and he went straight to bed.

Guardian angels. I hoped there was one assigned to Tina. Juice didn't need a guardian, and Roger was his own angel. Me? I could use one. And not one of those High-Renaissance, Pillsbury-Dough-Boy kinds, the farts who flutter around your head dispensing morality and inspiration. No, I needed the Crusader variety, a good strong saint with a sword, itch-ing to do some serious fucking smiting.

CHAPTER 35

Special patrols were in effect. Despite the recent surge of hard-core effluent, there had never been much crime of the petty variety in the neighborhood, partially, I suppose, because it was too hot for burglars to pull pantyhose over their heads. But the world had changed and the solution was more cops, more guns, more *pronunciamentos* and eleven—that we knew of—security cameras mounted in strategic spots around the compound.

Recovering nicely from the demotion, Martin had replaced his Honey Badger Security uniform with garb reflecting his authority as Public Safety Officer, and while I'm not fond of black with silver trim and shirt collars with chrome lightning bolts, I must admit the getup had a slimming effect on him. The rest of the security forces had been dumped on us by cronyism, and I was getting tired of going to fetch the mail or walking to the pool and being saluted with a two-foot stick by some guy who not long ago had looked perfectly positioned in life drinking beer in the bed of Deep Tread's truck. They actually saluted like that, by the way, tip of the stick to the brim of the cap, like nineteenth-century cops in a film. I don't doubt they were meeting in secret once a week or so to drill on the parade square, run obstacle courses, sight in their weapons.

I didn't raise the issue with Juice. Not that I saw her anyhow—in, out, sandwich, piss, love you, kiss, later. I reverted to entering most of my notes on paper, as she'd taken over the computer to log trends, violations, rumors and other nasty stuff that needed tracking.

A few days under the new regulations and I drove out to the Dowser's for a dose of her sanity. Not much doing in the yard other than a sow enduring an assault on its teats from a tribe of mottled shavers. I spied her out back and cut around the side, almost running into a man going the opposite direction, trading sorrys.

"Never seen that guy before," I said to her in the middle of the yard.

"Can I get you anything before you go down the well?"

"Nice segue," I said.

Undercut by the flash flood after New Year's, the wall had finally let go, leaving a quarter-circumference standing, the rest of the bricks and mortar down the hole. The lid was splintered and jammed in the opening.

"You don't really have to go down," she said. "But I could use a hand getting the top out and this load spread to level the ground before the new bricks get here."

The pile of fill looked gouged from the dump. Wire and rebar, plastic and a couple of window frames polluted the sand and topsoil.

"Pretty hot day for physical labor." I kicked a chunk of concrete down the shaft.

"You could have brought help."

"Some help," I said. "Roger's holed up as if he's in the witness protection program and Juice thinks she's Madame Mao."

I felt bad for the slander but worse for the isolation. Three people with three strategies going in three directions. Juice, at least, had a cause, but Roger was sinking into depression. Certain leaf hopper nymphs defend against attack either by running and jumping, or the last-ditch expedient of falling down—the literal jaws of death cause them simply to let go from their perch and plummet to the forest floor. My best friend seemed to have done all the running and jumping he could.

"I did something shitty," I said. "We've run into financial problems and even though he told me . . . well, I'm used to getting the mild version. I'm scared he's going to lose his mum's house, and I'm an anchor around his neck in the money department, and with his reaction to the murder and all of it . . . I went through his papers. I came across a letter, looked like just a draft, addressed to that reporter, Cassidy, the one who came here that day looking for Juice and his car. I have to tell you I've been driving myself round the bend with conspiracy theories, and up till now Roger's been the voice of reason. But this letter's like nothing that's ever come out of him. A personal attack—anger, hate, threats. I'm surprised the page was spotted with blood."

"There's nothing wrong with that," the Dowser said. "It's a form of release, getting it off your chest without actually saying something you'll regret later. You're a writer, common enough therapy in your line of work. Mark Twain wrote outrageous rants knowing ahead of time he wouldn't mail them. Hunter S. Thompson . . . all right, he actually sent his, but the point remains."

"Even if he didn't send it . . . I've never heard him like this, that's all, never. And you don't know Roger the way—"

"—It's plain what he's doing. He feels it slipping away and he's frightened. We'll do anything to protect the person we love."

"That doesn't explain it," I said. "I love him, too."

"If we're going to talk, do me the favor of not being deliberately thick."

Right. I wouldn't talk. One giant step and I was at the well, with a rupturing effort freeing half the lid and dropping it in the sand. The Dowser looked satisfied at the good start and went inside. After breaking the second half of the lid to get it out I dragged the wood clear.

The Dowser, humping a large yellow pack, reappeared and set off toward the hills. "I'll be gone less than an hour!" She flapped her hand at the house. "Help is on the way!"

I watched her plug along then bent my back, eager to complete the job before she returned. By the time George Sameshima and Roberto came out I had the surface of the earth pile rid of garbage and was filling the wheelbarrow. Straightened, rolled to the well, dumped, again. The boys were keeping their distance, as if the mound were carcinogenic tailings they'd been ordered to pack around their reproductive organs.

"You guys going to help?" I said.

"*Buenos días,*" Roberto said.

"*Buenos días,*" I said. "*¿Como está?*"

"*Muy bien. ¿Y usted?*"

"*Muy bien. ¿Y usted?*"

"*Bien,*" he said. "*Muy, muy bien. Todo está bien. ¿Y usted?*"

"Blow me," I said cheerfully.

"Your mother swims out to meet troopships," he responded.

Roberto picked up the rake and started leveling around the well. I manned the lone shovel while George watched, though after another two loads the erstwhile restaurateur took the wheelbarrow for a trip. We settled into a pattern, Roberto spreading the fill while I shoveled and George wheeled. No talking, just work, the temperature rising, grunts and sweat, dirt sticking to skin and clothing. I tried to get George going—asking why with VATS mostly debunked he wasn't re-opening the Big Happy Fun Chinese and Western Buffet Palace, whether he planned to take a run at a new restaurant, what the hell was up in his life— without a sparerib in response. He announced that he had to take a leak, then instantly forgot the fib and instead of heading for the outdoor crapper went inside the house. I returned to double duty, shoveling and wheeling. Fine with me. The work was dirty and grueling and felt good, hot as hell and I loved it and didn't want help. My dad would have been impressed.

I was glad to be there without Roger. I couldn't remember seeing him in such a state, though the warranty on my memory was long expired, if I'd even mailed in the registration card. Memory is individual and encodes to fit how our emotions and personal history interpret what we observe. I remember all things that have truly jarred me, and while they may be distorted they are recognizable; in no way do I seem to display memory repression. Faults and fissures, that's all, and though I can acknowledge the existence of flaws in my recollections, I accept them in inverse proportion to their importance to my survival. I may disagree with other witnesses on details of a traffic accident, but I remember everything I ever said to my wife.

The sweat had coursed into my mouth and I blew a beluga spout into the air. Roberto was working as hard as I was. Mawkish as it sounds, a bond was formed between us as we silently labored, a causeway between backgrounds and ethnicities superseding the need to talk. Each time I dumped a fresh load for him to spread, he grinned and I grunted and we locked in and worked harder. On the second-last trip, I tipped the wheel-barrow and Roberto upped the urgency, digging his rake into the pile and saying, *"Amigo."* I checked over my shoulder and saw the Dowser in the distance. I raced for the last load, we both spread it, frantically erased our footprints and waited—forearms propped on the upright tools—for her arrival. When she was closer, George came outside and stood hang-dog with dirty hands in the sand.

"Look at my crew." The Dowser took off her pack, dumped a collec-tion of cutlery and empty Tupperware on the ground and shook the sack clean. "Now there's just the dishes to do."

Roberto and I fastened our eyes on George till he retrieved the plastic mess kit.

"What were you doing up there?" I said.

"Picnic," the Dowser said.

I glanced at George balancing the pile of dishes on his way to the house. "With a hockey team?"

Once beyond us, she pulled off her T-shirt and vanished bareback into the outdoor shower. Roberto fetched a towel that he hung on a nail beside the stall and I did some superfluous leveling to kill time while waiting. And waiting. Roberto had gone for his own towel, and clearly George was finding dishwashing as arduous as wheelbarrowing, so I went to the shower and knocked on the door. As the hinges squeaked I stepped back and stood looking and not looking at a naked water witch. Crystal balls of water clung to her mane and pubic hair. As she reached for her towel, I felt my neck and lower jaw inflame and my throat engorge.

We moved away from the house at the scrunch of a car on gravel. I was enormously relieved when the Dowser wrapped herself in terry, tightened the knot, took up her clothes and walked barefoot out front. While blindly raking rock, I peeked around the corner of the house and strained to hear. Only a few minutes, and when Detective Legree climbed back in his car I scampered around to the rear door. The Dowser changed in the kitchen—George was caught staring before clueing in and attacking the Tupperware with extra vigor—and came out to the main room wearing raggedy jeans and a cotton blouse damp around the armpits.

"Done," she said. "Now, you have questions."

"Like what?" I said.

She'd grabbed us a couple of beers from the fridge and handed me one while I suppressed the urge to scream: I dug your dirt while you had a picnic before coming back and giving me a hard-on and talking to the only guy who has the answers I'm looking for so quit jerking my chain, stay in one place for one second and stop stringing me along, which is what you're doing and you know it. "Thanks," was all I said, and popped the can.

She called for George and he popped his head around the corner—it was only then it twigged that he'd cut off his queue—and the Dowser asked him to run into town for a couple of flats of water. I had to lend him the car, as his had been repossessed. Now I was in for it—just me and the Dowser together with no transportation. She raised her can and I shook my head. By the time she had a fresh beer I was sitting against the wall.

"Your first question: What did I learn about the rape and the murder while you were eavesdropping? Nothing. John was looking for Quinn."

"Last time I talked to Legree he said he wasn't worried about Quinn."

"Doesn't matter, I didn't tell him anything."

"Why not help the cops?" I said.

"The real question is why I'm helping Quinn. And the plain answer is he deserves it. We all do things that are incomprehensible to others. His way hasn't been normal—wait, that's not the word—it doesn't fit with what's expected, it hasn't been *safe*. Well, when you're young nothing's safe and nothing's risky. There's too much time ahead to be able to predict the right path. Twenty years ago, if a kid was asked what he wanted to do when he grew up, and he said to spend the rest of his life inventing video games, he'd be written off as a kook and a candidate for military school. Now it's a common, almost conservative, goal, because a bunch of kids made a bunch of billions doing it. What I'm trying to say is that whether something is safe or risky can be judged only in context. The answer changes with the frame of reference—and the faster that changes, the less accurate any predictions can be. The best thing, the smartest thing, is to do what you want."

"So do we get more rigid with age? Or are we just better able to cull what's bound to die anyway?"

"Nothing's one or the other."

"You've given it some thought," I said.

"Not really," she said. "That was mostly from Quinn."

Before she could re-gear, I went for another beer. Again against the wall. "Sit down," I said. "This is hurting my neck."

She sat in the middle of the floor and crossed her ankles.

"What's my next question?" I said.

"Why did I intentionally come out of the shower naked knowing you were there?"

"You're worried about showing me that old thing?"

She howled with laughter. "Introduction, or continuity, a starting point and a reference all in one." She cast up her eyes and took a breath. "I used to be a whore."

Too much time passed so I said, "Whore." Another gem from Morty.

"And I managed a whole house of them. That's right, and it must be draining to look so blasé, so you can stop it while you listen to the rest."

"Yes, Madam," I said, putting a smile on her face.

"That's what this place started out as. It's why it became a spot for wayward souls, lost people taking over for horny ones, or maybe it's the same thing. I used to run the valley's only brothel, fun palace, mink ranch—it's been called all those things over the years. Whorehouse, that's what it was, a drink-and-screw motel with lots of dry air to absorb the stink of booze and piss and cum, blood sometimes, puke and runny bowel movements." She leaned forward. "And lots of fun. People getting away from there and coming here and leaving with a smile and a visit-again note in the back of their minds. What's wrong with that? Is there anything wrong with that?"

She was doing the asking.

"Look at Quinn," she said. "Here's a man who's never been married, never had a steady girlfriend, probably never cried in the ear of someone while he was making love to her. He has a father who lives life the way it should be lived, but who won't let his son do the same. Why? That goes for both of them. Willa, Roger's mother? She was my partner. Oh, she wasn't a whore, just in charge of logistics—that's what she called it, logistics, pretty easy to see where her son got his flair for organization. She'd coordinate bus trips from Idaho and Kansas and Manitoba and Europe, yes, Europe a couple of times. She'd come down to the desert to get away from . . . if we're talking plainly, her husband and her son and whatever they had going on up in Canada. Her life. Not a bad life, but constrained by her own past, her own history. Funny, each trip she'd tell me how great her son was doing with his hockey team. Roger—we're talking about the same man. She'd get shy and nervous when I asked about him, and she'd tell me how he was lifting weights to bulk up to make the Canadian national team, how he was such an animal on the ice, a tough player everyone was scared of. I made a joke once—of course, it wasn't really a joke—about what she'd do if it turned out Roger was gay, and you know what she did? Made apple pies. Didn't answer, just went to the store for the ingredients and when she came back I helped her bring in the groceries. Not only that, but she hadn't bought apples. I made another joke—a real one this time—and she said Ritz Crackers had been on sale so that's what she was going to make the pies out of. I'd heard of it, but I didn't think anyone would actually . . ."

"It's really quite good," I said. "Can't tell the difference."

It didn't knock her a millimeter off stride. "But you know what? Here we are."

"To be honest," I said, "I'm still a little confused about the nude thing."

She scrunched her legs under her and hoisted erect and walked across the room and bent and kissed me, probing my mouth with her tongue while mine fought back and grew thicker until she put her palm on my cheek and the other on my shoulder and said, "I love you. I'd fuck you to bits and run away with you, but I'd do that with many, many men until there was no place to run and I'd come back here and make breakfast for whoever decides to come through the door."

I didn't want to wipe her taste off my lips but did, with what I hoped was a casual gesture. "Does Roger know?"

"If he does, he didn't learn it from his mother."

"How about Juice?" I said. "Have you told her? She thinks the world of you, hangs on everything that comes out of your mouth. This is the first place she thought to come after she was burnt in the fire."

"I wasn't here that day."

"Oh. I thought . . ."

"When people need guidance, partial truths and a little soft shoe can be important. No matter how ridiculous, from psychic hotlines to Tarot cards to plain old astrology, it doesn't matter, it gives them what they need—the belief they know what's going to happen."

I wouldn't have minded some of that myself, but now all I wanted was to get home. I needed my people, or maybe I just had to keep moving. Tough luck in either case—the Dowser told me that whenever George got his hands on a vehicle or could hitch a ride he slept outside the restaurant till the sun came up, like some cult follower waiting overnight for tickets to a Charles Manson Quartet concert. Jesus. Screwed by another alien. Forced to stay the night, I figured I'd pull the cork, drink for drinking's sake, roll around in the dirt a little and fall down the well and not try to climb out. The Dowser allowed as how that wasn't too shabby a plan at all, but advised me to call Juice before liftoff.

When I declined she stood up, tarring me with shadow. "I've been wondering how you took her surprise. And I'm disappointed you haven't brought it up. Not calling you to account, but it makes me sad."

"Not that big a deal," I said. "It's mostly my being grumpy. I don't trust her to be in charge, that's true, but I can live with it for the short haul. Besides, I don't trust *anyone* whose main motive force is to be in charge. Of anything. If power corrupts, it only does so to people who lust after power in the first place. And if absolute power corrupts absolutely, having pissant power like being head of a homeowners' association makes you barely powerful and halfass corrupt—you don't win on any scorecard."

She wrinkled her nostrils as though trying to filter a bad smell. "I wonder whether your sense of humor always works for you. I'm talking about her pregnancy."

Really nothing to say. I squeezed and crinkled my beer can until we were thoroughly uneasy.

"Oh," she said. "This is no good. Very bad."

I didn't get drunk after all. To be sure, I felt like it, but not a chance— it would be getting roared and having a high old time for the wrong reason. So the Dowser stepped in as my surrogate and got loaded and silly and made me laugh against my will and kept her clothes on and didn't kiss me again and told me salacious stories about cops and movie stars and plain old guys who used to visit the bawdy oasis until I was glad I wasn't drinking so I didn't have the urge to run away with her.

CHAPTER 36

On the way to the picnic site the next morning, it was already hot enough to make the Dowser rue her hoot of the night before. She bore it well, minor grumbling, though each time we hit the top of a rise she stopped to pull at her water bottle while claiming it was for the view. On the subject of water, if the level kept dropping in the well it wouldn't be long till her old demimonde was as dependent on the piped variety as any golf course clubhouse, and another desert survival technique would revert solely to the flora and fauna of the sadistic ecosystem. There'd better be some hocus-pocus left in her forked stick or she might as well hang it up.

We'd gained enough altitude to glimpse the Salton Sea, the surface bleeding into haze carrying high into the sky. The Dowser capped her bottle and led me up a gentle incline.

As much as it would be good to see the lunatic handyman again, I was impatient to get the climb behind us and for George to bring back the car. At last we rounded a corner and came across his campsite. No sound, little movement, eerie in the way of an Old West hideout; I suppressed the urge to walk in with my hands up.

"Smittybaby." Skinny as ever and fearsomely dirty, Sonny came out of a crouch beside a pile of sticks. "Going to drag a propane bottle next time, used my last match on my last smoke." He looked around and gestured. "Not much to do unless you brought a volleyball set. Not much of a camper, me."

Delilah—who else?—a thin young girl with a face expressionless as can be imagined, was sitting on a sleeping bag picking at her feet. When I said hi she smiled then dug back in between her toes. The Dowser opened her knapsack and took out a pair of large canvas sneakers, and the girl waited till they were on the ground beside her before acknowledging the gift with another smile.

A boy in his midteens, looking not much like Sonny, was standing off on his own.

"You must be Saxon," I said.

"Saxon," he said, as though correcting me.

"Sure. Hi. I'm Smith. I hear you're pretty good at fixing stuff."

"Like what?"

"Uh, cars and all that, I guess."

"No."

Okay, then.

Water was distributed and greedily sucked then Sonny banged his hands together. Saxon and Delilah pitched in by rolling their sleeping bags, all the pitching required. Not a trace of other camping gear or supplies. Sonny led the way, carrying the bags by their strings, one in each hand—he hadn't brought one for himself—and I followed, while farther behind the Dowser wrangled the kids. A gap developed and once on the scree I looked back for the others, but Sonny was forging ahead and waving me up beside him.

"Not a perfect father," he said. "Never claimed it. Dowser tell you the wife's in town?"

Sonny's wife was hoping to win a road game. The baby-namer and her lawyer had set up a litigation HQ at some local hotel, where they were probably secluded in an unused wing comparing intelligence reports on Sonny's whereabouts and moving markers around a map table like field marshals in their bunker.

"We'll see what happens," he said. "Just I had to keep them away a bit longer, do the dad thing out in the wild one last time. Full-on now. Back to Houston with her, into the hospital, see what's what, new kind of therapy they want to try. Time to work with the wife on this one, better go see her and figure out what we're going to do, hope she's got more money than she says."

"Sonny," I said, "I'm—"

"—Could use a lift."

"As soon as George gets back with the car," I said. "Where's the Bonneville?"

"Crapped out. Just like Boston Charlie."

"He died?" I said.

"Not so much died. They don't call it died when a dog eats poisoned hamburger."

The Dowser's place seemed to be getting no closer. Dark spot of paint on a sandy canvas, frame overlarge for the picture.

"Too much patching," Sonny said. "Fixing stuff good enough to give me room to breath till they break again a week later. Rats in the house, I get a cat. Too many cats, I get a dog. Dogs pile up, I get a cougar. Cougar wrecks the place, I invite over a hunter. Hunter drinks all my beer, I get a Democrat. Democrats get too thick, I get some Republicans, and there I am—back to rats."

"Some stuff starts off broken."

"Best is if it's broke a little bit not to let it break more. Check it over, check it out, maintenance like you're going to need it later. Poor old Juicio, she's trying to build a new one from scratch. She could camp out in the Home Depot store and couldn't find enough tools to fix her stuff."

"I'm trying to do what's best for her," I said. "Or I'm not trying, is more like it. I don't want to put on a patch."

"Sometimes that's all it takes," he said. "But you got to know what the hell's wrong before you do anything. Personal, just me? I don't think you did yourself any favor right from the start."

"You don't know what you're talking about."

"Sure, Morty."

I stopped on the trail. Sonny pulled up just in front of me and we turned at the sound of faint laughter. The sun was high and the ground was baked and the air was calm, and picking their way through the rocks and the scrub and the thorns came an uncertain teenager and a young girl and an old magic whore.

Sonny's eyes welled up. "From here, looks like nothing needs fixing."

We waited till they caught up and walked as a group the rest of the way. Roberto was out back beside the well, and he waved at the Dowser as though he hadn't seen her since childhood. Puffpuff—the two sleeping bags hit the dirt. Sonny tore across the dry streambed, dodged the reconstructed crapper and raced around the far side of the house. All I could see was a plume of dust rising over the roof. What now? is all that went through my mind, what now? I picked up the sleeping bags. Roberto ripped off something in Spanish and the kids ran over to him. The Dowser had kept walking and I followed her inside.

Sonny was already there, hands on knees, sucking and blowing. The Dowser immediately set to work fixing tacos, handing me green peppers to wash.

"He drives an El Camino," Sonny said when he could breathe freely. "When he used to come by the house he was always with some criminal driving a truck."

Holding a good sharp knife in her hand, the Dowser stared him down. "Yes, he drives an El Camino. There. Happy?"

"Your car's back," Sonny said to me while holding the Dowser's eyes.

George entered. With a shaved head. The contrast between his alabaster dome and the facial tan he'd gotten from hanging around the Big Happy Fun Chinese and Western Buffet Palace parking lot made him look like a Zulu who'd headbutted a snowman. Dazed, George couldn't remember whether he'd remembered to pick up the water. He pulled up a chair and sat in the middle of the kitchen. "My poor old place," he said.

"Shut up," Sonny said. "You—Sameshima. George. We got business here, get up and fuck off."

George momentarily froze, his glistening cranium pink down to the hairline. Up he shut and up he got and off he fucked.

A couple of glances between the Dowser and me.

"There!" Sonny pointed as Delilah and Saxon streaked past the window and burst into the house. The kids didn't break stride, just ran in and Delilah did a somersault—one of those pitiful ones you do when you're not very athletic and haven't been coached and you don't give a damn except you're so excited you have to get your ass over your head and around again—and Saxon gave her a little boot in the bum when she was upright and she chased him back outside.

"They can't be all that's left," Sonny said. "I got three, not just two, not just one."

The Dowser moved toward him but he turned to me. "So what about the lift you promised? Shouldn't take long there, fill the wife in on Delilah. If it's not messing up any big plans hang around if you can, give us another lift to the Indio bus station, too far to hike all the way to Houston."

He collected the kids, then just before leaving said to the Dowser, "I don't blame Quinn for nothing."

At the Marriott, the parcel of Lemmatinas went up to the room while I waited in the bar. I had no money on me, and wasted much time trying to convince the bartender that just because I had an accent—"I don't know from where, but we're on Orange Alert here at the Marriott and you refuse to give your fingerprints"—I shouldn't be turned down to run a tab.

I pointed across the lobby. "He can vouch for me."

After the concierge confirmed that I was not only a repeat visitor but a sympathetic ear, I got my bottle of beer and five more besides. When

Sonny finally appeared he had the kids halfway to the car by the time I wrote his wife's room number on the check and left it with the bartender. I drove them in silence to Indio. The look on Sonny's face . . . well, I pulled in and dropped them off and knew Sonny would thank me when he got around to it. I drove straight home.

Much better. Peace. Quiet. No music, no TV, no body.

I had a leisurely shower and shave. I wasn't hungry but made a sandwich because I could. I opened the mail and threw it on the table. I stretched out on the bed and got up and looked for something to read and couldn't find anything new. I laid down again. Just the house. Me in the house alone, and right before I could appreciate the solitude I jumped up with my brain afire wondering where everyone was. I turned on the AC. Maybe another sandwich. On this pass through the kitchen I saw Roger's note. He was out for a walk. Isn't that something? Me zorching around the valley in the Neon and Roger afoot. Me alone, by myself. Nothing to do. Just as I was seriously considering heading back to the Indio bus station and jumping on the gray dog to wherever it was loping, I looked out the sliders.

Juice was driving past, alone, in Deep Tread's monster truck.

An hour later, when she walked in all cheerful and clueless of my mood, I was primed. "Crush any cars?"

"We're really getting somewhere." She pulled off her shirt and used it to wipe under her arms. "Although I'm worried about Tina. She was so progressive, so positive, and now it's like she's one of those people who bounce from place to place with no commitment. She's really quite a negative person, I told her so. 'You have to put all that rape thing behind you or it'll affect your whole life,' I said. She started crying, of all things, and I stayed till she was okay even though it made me late for the meeting."

"I'm seriously concerned about this HOA business, and that's just the first of a list. We need a talk, sweetheart, I need to talk to you."

"I feel so free not having to work for Sonny anymore."

"I saw him earlier today," I said.

"He can be such an asshole."

"Go easy," I said. "Delilah's on the way down. It's AIDS now. Little girl, a kid, and she still managed to come running into the Dowser's and—"

The jeans and panties came off and she twirled in place. "I might have found it. My calling, my thing . . . I've never felt so close to being complete."

I went to the table and picked though the mail, flicking the empty envelopes onto the floor till I found what I was looking for. "What's this? Addressed to you, a past-due notice for ninety-two bucks from Office Depot for printing."

She snatched it from my hand. "If it's that big a deal, I'll take care of it. When did you turn into a money freak?"

"Why don't you put some clothes on."

"Want me?"

"Most of all I want to talk to you."

"Good, I'm not in the mood. I want to suck up life, not your dick."

"This is something we have to do. Now."

"Oh, come on, people."

Juice spread-eagled herself against the slider, mashing her breasts against the glass and planting a dewy triangle. I hoped there was nobody walking a dog along the greenbelt or one of the compound's brownshirts out on patio patrol.

"Have you found religion?" I said. "It's hard to share faith, I can appreciate that. I was thinking maybe you'd printed all those *Sunday or Die!* pamphlets. I need to know. And not just about that. I feel like we're strangers lately. After falling in love so fast and . . . you're different, that's all, different from the woman who e-mailed me. You've gone from one thing to another and probably I'm overreacting because I do the same all the time, have actually caught myself doing it and not had the brains to arrest it."

Her feet and the glass door formed a tripod, apex at her ass. It was her midsection I couldn't take my eyes off. No anatomist, I knew roughly where the uterus was—between the vagina and the stomach, right? Was Juice swollen, or was it merely a fold and a bulge due to her jackknife stance? And would it show at this stage? Whatever the stage—counting back in my head, losing track along the grade between constant lovemaking and humping for release—it was a stage, a point of development; a girl who would grow up to be disease-free and wise and happy, even a beauty queen if that's what she wanted; a boy who would write a book or fix a motor. Who could tell, especially since the unborn girl or boy might not be mine.

Oh, don't think that hadn't been sparking my neurons since the

Dowser let it slip that Juice had a pit in the olive. What then, eh? Not my kid. If stepping-out was involved, Juice could give birth to a baby who breached wearing a ballcap and a rebel tattoo. No—frustration and ignorance were painting that picture.

"Come here." I held out my arms. "Come here for a minute."

"What for?" She didn't sound repelled or even wary. Matte, as if she truly didn't know.

"Because I love you." My hands were already in my pockets.

"And I love you," she said. "That doesn't scare you, does it?"

"The bad scares me," I said. "The horror. And that's what it is, horrible. Nothing's getting solved. I've almost forgotten about Sarah and Martin. Not forgotten, just that it seems far away."

"I agree with you, it's horrible. All that talent and a mum and dad who loved her, and she went and did something so stupid."

"Drugs," I said. "Yeah, I guess they're stupid. Like booze is stupid and cigarettes and skydiving and cutting across the street between traffic and quitting a good job and repeating your mistakes and all the rest of it."

"When you make a decision," she said, unsticking herself from the glass door and coming closer, "it stays with you. Eventually you have to pay."

"Sure, love. But in her case it's a price beyond what she owed. She didn't deserve what happened."

"You don't know that. She could have done something sickening in her past that made her deserve exactly what she got. Or someone else could have, and got away with it, and she just caught the shit. You have to pay—that's the way it works. There's no free lunch."

"What do you want from me?" I said. "What do you want me to do? I can love you and support you and stand beside you but I can't just sit in the house while you jerk the world around on a leash." She was so close to me I reacted, getting hard and wanting to thrust into her and pound our way back to the way it had been, but I backed away.

She threaded her fingers up her nape and flared her uneven hair. "It's grown back enough to get it cut, right? Do you like it long or short?"

It happened in a blur. I can honestly say I can't remember what it was she said or did, but we ended up reverting to the human default emotion and laughing together and she pushed me on my back beneath the kitchen table and had to duck her head under the edge to fit my cock inside her and she came while still laughing. It was too awkward for her to back out so she rode off and exited over my head, dampening my nose. It was stupid of me to try to see up her all the way to her womb, though I did. When she was clear I scrambled out to join her. She was already pulling on her jeans.

"Stay in one place for a minute," I said.

"I have to oversee the sign," she said. "Vista de las Pantalones—the new name for the neighborhood. Deep Tread picked it, and I have to admit it sounds beautiful. The workers are putting it up by the entrance."

"Are you sure about the name?" I said. "It's better than what we have, though it's a bit, well, illiterate. I'm no expert on Spanish, but—"

"—If you're no expert then you should shut up about it. Oh, right, you have a book, the Dowser gave you a Spanish book. She really has trouble minding her own business sometimes."

"No reason to get worked up," I said. "All I'm saying is I think *pantalones* is masculine and *de las* is feminine, so they don't go together. I could be wrong."

"It's perfect to the ear," she said. "It's gorgeous and romantic."

"What does it mean anyhow? *Pantalones*, I'm pretty sure that means 'pants.' If I'm ever asked, 'Where do you live?' I can say, 'Well, I live in Pants. Drive east of the Rancho de las Montañas Country Club, turn right at the Palm Presidio Golf Course and take the next left into Pants. Actually, it's Vista de las Pantalones—View of the Pants, I have a little place in View of the Pants. Ever since I was a kid I wanted to own a house within sight of Spanish trousers.'"

"That kind of thing really pisses me off about you."

I swallowed. "Let's head out. I'll walk you to the new sign."

"You must have notes to write," she said. "This'll take too long. Deep said the contractors hired a bunch of illegal immigrants, and you know what they're like."

"Maybe they can't believe what they're reading."

"Being in charge is great, but it sure eats up your time." She started for the door.

"Honey?" I said to her back. "Shouldn't you cover up?"

"Whoa! That's why I love you. Hand me my shirt."

CHAPTER 37

It all came apart right as it all came together.

Sometime deep in the night I sensed Juice in the bedroom. Groggy as I was, I'm sure it wasn't a dream. A body in a dark place exerts gravity apart from its mass, and I felt her presence beyond the foot of the bed, cutting through the gummy resin of sleep. She didn't move, just stood inside the door with it closed behind her. I sat up. We could have been wild animals in the woods assessing our predator-prey relationship through absolute blackness till she whisked off on a gust of sweat. I was chilled and rattled and couldn't say whether I heard the door shut or thought I did, even wondering if it had been closed all along and that Juice passed through it and I had a moment of doubt over . . . just doubt. I fell right back to sleep so I couldn't have been too disquieted, though maybe it was my system fortifying itself for what was to come by knocking me out, desensitizing by way of advance shock. Innards, as my English granny used to say, my innards knew before my head did. It's all innards, and she'd know because my granny was the witch of her neighborhood.

Shortly came an interruption from the outards.

"What's so important at this time of night?" I said, as though crucial events should align with the clock and express themselves at a civilized hour.

The detective crossed the threshold with his nose in the air, perhaps catching Juice's scent. He asked where she was and told me to get dressed.

"You could tell me what's up," I said. "You owe me that much."

"You don't have a bag packed by any chance?"

"I'm going back to bed," I said. "Ransack the place and dust for fingerprints if that's what you have to do. Big movie thing—toss the place till you find a clue in a hollowed-out book."

"You want to find her as badly as me," he said. "Did she stop here?"

"I think so."

"Wake Jeffcoate up. Give him this card and tell him to call my cell the minute Juice makes an attempt to contact either one of you."

"You taking me in?" I said. "All right, I'll get some clothes on." At the entrance to the hall I turned. "How bad?"

"No arrest, I just wanted to question her. She came along willingly, like it was a big game. At the station, I left her alone for two minutes and she bolted. Witness said he saw her run out to the street and get in a jacked-up truck that jumped the curb and rammed my front wheel before heading south. Her boyfriend must have followed us from the Blue Dog. Sorry."

Could be she was on a tear; I wasn't about to jump to the conclusion that she was scared and running. Legree had said he was just going to question her and besides, hooking up with some asshole before thinking it through wasn't anything new for her. The detective told me every cop in the area had been alerted, and with the limited number of roads out of town, Juice and Deep Tread wouldn't get far.

"There's no warning out?" I said. "I mean an armed-and-dangerous kind of thing?"

"It doesn't have to end in violence," Legree said. "Now move it."

Looked as if Juice was barging out the way she had barged in, with a whoop and a holler, a stone skipping across unsuspecting water—man to man to man, from pissy-blond passenger in Vancouver to bullshit artist to all-wheel-radial thug. The most fortitude I'd shown in my slippery life had been playing itself out on stage this past while, the courage to put love for someone above what I needed in return. True, I was harnessed to a woman abetting a possible murderer, so couldn't claim full marks, but that much passion must contribute something to the commonweal. Besides, there are worse things than being in love with a woman who's resisting arrest with a barbarian in a cartoon truck being pursued by a brigade of cops through the Southern California desert in the middle of the night. Right?

For the first part of the drive, the detective was polite enough to listen to my fresh batch of hypotheses, but he soon started making sounds in his throat, and by the time we reached the Marriott he'd twice told me to shut up, the last time threatening to run me in if I didn't.

Cassidy was dressed and waiting for us. I had expected strutting, but though he was dandified enough—white suit at that time of the morning, like Tom Wolfe in a reality-TV show getting up to take a piss—he wore a look of genuine sympathy. He immediately apologized for lying to me about being in town as a motivational speaker. On arrival he had seen posters for the American Self-Image Awareness Movement in the lobby and a few dozen stupefied souls roaming around and staring into the lounge wondering whether a drink would ruin their self-images before the seminar even started, and adopted the convention as his cover. I pointed out he had been after me from day one, and couldn't understand why the hell he needed a cover of any kind.

Before he could answer, his sister entered. She said something to Legree about not expecting him till later, a quick shift of her eyes toward me. It was Cassidy's sister, all right, plain now that I saw them together with her not knock-kneed on the toilet.

"All I've gathered so far is that Juice is in trouble because she's been sleeping with a criminal. Don't think it doesn't hurt, but I'm already fed up to here with being out of the loop, and the numbness is greater than the pain." I twisted my head to the detective. "I'm sure you can show opportunity, but that probably goes for half the people in the valley."

Cassidy was kind enough to get me a beer from the mini-bar.

"And as for opportunities," I continued, shredding my palm trying to twist open a bottle that didn't have threads, "Juice has been using most of them to do good for her friends and the community."

"She's lied," Legree said.

"Really?" I said. "The world stops turning in surprise."

Cassidy offered me a hotel opener, but I shook my head and put the beer down, too wound up to trust its accelerative effects.

"We're trying to get to the bottom of this," the detective said. "With Mr. Cassidy's help, we've established that you're the key."

"What am I, bait? You expect her to come running back by holding my feet to the fire? Besides, so far all she's guilty of is bad judgment and impulsiveness."

"You have to trust us," Cassidy said.

"And you have to be kidding."

"I may not have been entirely open with you," he said, "but I've been in the middle of a touchy situation. True, I put myself there by trying to get a story, but I'm not the kind of scandal monger you think. All you had to do was call up my name on the Internet for ample evidence of my credentials. I'm a reporter, that's all, a reporter who wanted to do a piece on a man named Smith who wrote a very fine memoir full of heart and understanding. That, of course, was before Juice told me about G.H. Nuttall."

He pointed down to the coffee table, atop which, exhibiting my misdeed like a Wanted poster, was a printout of *A Quake in Time* and what looked to be my copy of *And the Sea Shook the Rock*. I picked up the stack of paper. I'd never felt my book, and in a way hadn't really considered it was one because of that. The story was an alien construction, the spoils of a hijacking that had ceased to exist the second I electronically pulped it with the Delete button. I held the printout like an ignorant young boy with a wild bird's egg, cupping and turning, fascinated, until smashing it down on the floor like, well, an ignorant young boy with a wild bird's egg.

"You told me you read my novel," I said. "You knew who I was all along."

"Juice again," he said.

At that, the sister retrieved a book from the desk drawer, and even at that distance and over all these years I recognized it. She handed it to Cassidy and I exhaled harshly.

Old worn soiled dog-eared cloth-covered novel. Cassidy thumbed it down the side like a flip-cinema booklet, loosing people and places and images and more—a flurry of marginalia and underscoring and black ink circles and highlights. He held onto it, probably afraid I'd start tearing out pages and stuffing them down my throat.

As I worked for words, Legree started in on the timeline. It was all about establishing a timeline, timeline this and that, Juice and Deep Tread and the timeline. Yeah yeah sure timeline stick with what you know but what do you expect from me I can't account for all her actions jesusfuckingchristalmighty I'm not her keeper, is roughly what I replied.

"When did she tell you all this?" I said to Cassidy.

"Some time after she let me in on *Sunday or Die!* She claimed the religious pamphlets were part of a practical joke. It sounded reasonable to me, considering what I'm used to dealing with." He got an eye-roll from his sister. "When I finally clued in, I shifted my research to include her, and on discovering she was keeping a room here in the hotel, the story swung even more in her direction. Until your friend was attacked it was merely interesting, another peculiar fork in the trail I was following. Reporter out to interview an author finds an inside source, a mysterious lady with secrets in a hotel room. Quirky but hardly explosive."

"A room?" I said.

Legree jumped back in by warning Cassidy not to file anything with his paper until the detective's say-so; the reporter countered by claiming their agreement covered only the criminal acts, not the story about me. They went at each other about Cassidy's withholding of information, which the detective claimed voided the deal for an exclusive, and it ended only when the reporter threatened to write about Legree's failure to act on available evidence after Tina's attack and before the murder. The other thing ending the argument was the rattle of the door handle. Legree reached behind him and in walked Sonny.

"Smitty," he said. "What's with the look?"

"It's that big sign you carry around that says 'Brace Yourself.'"

"Where's your wife?" Legree said.

"Still in the room," Sonny said. "Don't get me going. Can't make someone do nothing against their nature and her's isn't about letting me off the hook. Wonder if lawyers are worth the cost of admission when anyone can just dig their heels in and keep saying gimme, that's mine, I want more, not enough, I'm right and you're wrong, till you're just plain tired and give in. He's sitting right in there with her. Looks like a lawyer, nice suit and that, talks fast and smooth and probably would've had me fooled right up to handing over the kids now that I got no money for one of my own lawyers. But on our last camping trip Delilah told me when the wife came to visit her in Houston she had the guy with her. They kept asking, but Delilah wouldn't say nothing about how bad of a dad I am. Then they started talking to each other right in front of her like a kid can't understand. Especially a sick one, I noticed before how people think sick people lose their marbles. Anyhow, the guy's not any kind of lawyer. Insurance salesman in New Mexico who hooked up with the wife. He probably can't sell enough policies and I guess the baby-naming business dropped off, so they went after the loot. I came right out and said okay you can have the kids. No picking neither, love them all or leave them all, Quinn, Saxon, Delilah, the whole bunch. Nope, cash is what they want, all lies her wanting the kids, wanted to scare me with the law to make me cough up, now I don't have a nickel they're out of luck. Told them they could have the Bonny if they could get her started. Funny, they didn't even take it bad. Shrugged their shoulders like, oh well, it was worth a shot."

"Atta go, Sonny," I said.

He didn't look all that happy, but on the way past gave me an intimate knuckle on the arm. He took up the beer I'd set on the coffee table and opened it on his belt buckle.

"Tell him," the detective said.

"Better you should arrest me, too," Sonny said. "Wife's okay. Left her stuffed under the big king-size mattress with a chest of drawers on top. Boyfriend might need some attention. Took the open hand to him, more of a insult to a man than a honest punch. Whipped the shirt off him with the lamp cord, too. Should probably get the maid to sponge the blood out the rug before it sets. Little room damage but nothing I can't fix. Work cheap."

Legree gave up and addressed me directly. By then I could have guessed it was Juice who had made the call and filled the woman's head with stories about Sonny's abuse, Juice who suggested getting a lawyer and going after the kids. Alongside everything else it seemed trivial, but I asked about Sameshima's restaurant and sure enough, another item in her inventory of incomprehensible troublemaking. I got around to the dead woman by saying that the Kolachuks suspected her of the vandalism, only to learn that wasn't the case at all—Juice had led them to believe it was me. Legree ruled me out after the Dowser confirmed my alibi, and it was about then he started homing in on Juice, that far back. Neither Legree nor Cassidy could explain the hotel room—a home base? a way to cover her tracks?—but it was Juice's receipt in the purse; the dead girl had been in the hotel only two days.

I had a flash of overview. Not out-of-body, though definitely an appreciation for the tableau, a freezing of all characters allowing time to convene the senses and cut through the abstruse chaos. When motion resumed I felt Sonny's forearm resting atop my shoulder while he drank his beer, and I couldn't see through the shoals till I wiped my eyes with the heels of my hands.

"Let's focus on the murder," I said." Let's talk about something that makes no sense. Was it even a murder? How the hell does someone get murdered by Ecstasy? Giving someone a drug that might—just might, in rare instances—make them drink so much water that they die, is hardly a calculated execution. And the only other possibility I can think of is that the two of them got high together and one died."

It wasn't Ecstasy. Oh, there was a tiny amount present in her system, and the police kept quiet and let the media report what they wanted, but the cause of death was poison, the same poison found in Boston Charlie.

"It has to be Deep Tread," I said. "What about it, Legree? You and Cassidy have been working together, and you wanted to keep me in the dark, and you still only half trust me, completely understandable under the circumstances. But now's the time to bring me up to speed. Say something to help me understand why she hooked up with that murdering fuck. That's the part I don't get—the motive. What and why, otherwise there's no point in this farce in the middle of the night in a hotel room."

"We don't want anyone else hurt," Legree said. "If we have you on board, it increases the chance of bringing her in peacefully."

"She won't contact me," I said. "I know that in the depth of my guts. She means it. She's not carrying an empty bag this time."

"If what I think counts," Sonny said, "I been thinking about everything you told me, Legree, and what I think is my man here is right. This truck guy has something on her. Yeah, she started out messing around and fucking people over for who knows why, but it seems to me the truck guy probably found out and it was *him* that pulled all the serious stuff and then, and then . . . awww, shit, just making it worse."

Quinn knew. His was the anonymous call the night of Tina's attack. He didn't witness the actual assault and couldn't make a positive identification, but the description he gave fit Deep Tread. Quinn saw him jump in Tina's car and drive away two minutes before Juice pulled up in Cassidy's rental and "found" the victim. Stan confirmed that Tread—his real name was Marion Langton—had been in the Blue Dog earlier. When he left, Stan ran after him for the bill and saw him get in the rental Juice was driving. The owner knew Juice well, or as well as he could know someone he'd fucked a couple of times in the beer-storage room, and could testify she was in the place frequently, hustling pool and, well, hustling.

After that night, Quinn stuck as close to Juice as he could, driving her wherever she wanted to go, the bar, the hotel, the Dowser's, was tailing her when the pottery shop caught fire and watched as she ran out, unburnt and with a full head of hair, and climbed into the monster truck. He hadn't witnessed the murder but had seen Juice and Monica together. Legree figured the kid was more than a little in love—Quinn had no answer to why he hadn't come forward sooner.

"So what are you saying, she's psycho? Running around the valley trying to destroy it and fucking men to help her and, and, and, insane? Literally insane? Random evil on the loose—is that how you explain it?"

"I can't explain any of it," Legree said. "I'm just telling you what happened. We know she was most recently in Vancouver, but it couldn't have been long, either that or she was running a clean line. Never arrested in the city, not even a speeding ticket, never paid a phone bill, power bill. The RCMP sent her jacket. A few minor scrapes in Saskatchewan and Manitoba over the years, but nothing like this. She's the only common thread, Langton's a stooge she recruited later on, and he can't be the killer—a hundred people saw him drive his truck into a hole in the ground the day of the earthquake, including you."

By then I was full to the brim. When the concierge desk sent someone up to inquire about what to do with the clothing they'd been holding since clearing out Juice's room—skirts and blouses and pants and jackets that had been hung in ensembles from the swag lamps and heating grates and disposed harmoniously over chairbacks and the bed—the second-tier evidence failed to provoke.

Legree followed me into the hall and started in, but I cut him off with: "Don't worry, I'll call." When he turned back to the room I added, "She's pregnant."

He looked like a man tired of the price to pay for his work. "The Dowser told me."

"Just go easy, okay?"

I left the hotel and walked up the palm-lined drive to the street.

CHAPTER 38

It didn't take me long to start upending what I'd heard in the Star Chamber.

They had it wrong. They knew facts but not Juice. Deep Tread was the orchestrator, any idiot could see that on even the most casual reflection. Striving too hard to leave her mark, shouting from atop a soapbox what my father muttered in his rye glass, Juice had gotten in so far over her head that she went out of it. Yes, her lies did harm and her truths hadn't all that great a track record either but it didn't matter—she was a meddler, not a demon.

I was so badly out of shape I had to cut the walk off before it could turn therapeutic. At a bend in the sidewalk I blundered into a jumping cholla, and while extricating myself fell into the rocks. Though freshly dumped and arranged they were old, most of them sporting a glossy coating of rock varnish.

Rock varnish needs the desert's diurnal temperature extremes to form. Condensation at night leaches out iron and manganese oxides, which stain the surface once the sun evaporates the moisture. At least, that's what I'd learned as a kid. Since then I've read that it forms from airborne particles settling on the surface, explaining why it takes years and years to accumulate a coating of varnish. Then again, I've come across information on the necessity of surface bacteria in glueing the particles together.

My Christmas gift from the Dowser had the same frosting. One day months ago while entering my notes I found myself playing with it, idly picking the surface with a fingernail, and the conflicting accounts of the coating's formation raised a flag. I left off my writing and spent the rest of the day and two after that scouring Internet sites, in the time I had to spare between worrying about what to do with the rest of my life and more important things such as whether Architectural (Subcommittee – appearance) would authorize a kiddy pool out back of the house for my feet. What I came up with were more discrepancies, each purporting to confute the last. Ultimately, the only totally accurate evaluation was that the formation of rock varnish is poorly understood.

That night on my trek from the hotel, examining landscape rocks that had spent umpteen years acquiring their veneer and now were sitting with their accumulated coating scored by the shovels and backhoes that had deposited them beside the walkway I thought . . . I thought, who cares? Maybe history is just a coating. And if so, it may also be a disguise.

Handfasting—even the Dowser wasn't sure that she and Sonny were married. Were Sonny and his wife? The gays pouring into Toronto and Massachusetts to put the stamp of acceptance on their love? Why does love have to be legislated in the first place and yadda yadda and fuck it, science and blind belief and sparks of emotion reduce to an identical beverage when mixed by the same blender, so trust neither scientist nor witch. But vagrant as my thoughts had become, my background was potent enough to convince me that when push comes to shove you burn the witch. Except, of course, for my English granny . . . and the neighborhood witch my mum brought home that time . . . and every old lady we had branded with witchdom as kids . . . and Juice, who'd turned into a witch, or who'd been one all along, and so don't burn the witch never burn the witch and fuck it again with the rocks and witches and everything. Burn no one.

Up ahead was our neighborhood. Was I going home or still coming from? The formation of Morty Cahoot is poorly understood.

I entered the compound like a colonial agent hoping his treaty with the local tribe was still being observed. Neighbors on their way to work drove past stonefaced, no friendly waves, no thermos-cup salutes. Who knew what and how much? Early. The slash of crayola on the horizon held no warmth, flowers and hummingbirds enticed and hovered with resignation.

When I finished relating the evidence, Roger delivered his verdict. I'd been hoping he'd take my side, but he had an angle all his own, turning the whole trial on its head by convicting Chas Cassidy. In his version, the reporter was the Vegas magician, Deep Tread the assistant providing diversion, and Juice the hapless volunteer pulled up on stage from the audience. It was going past the comfort of self-delusion and I told him so, repeating the evidence.

"Cassidy isn't even a suspect," I said. "He and Legree have been working together, or at least comparing notes. The most we can hope for is that Juice has been somehow coerced by DT. Total nonsense to pin it on the reporter. For that matter, I'm starting to think he's the only one on our side. Other than the fact his doggedness has been humping my leg, I trust the guy."

"He's had it in for you since he turned up," Roger said. "With his prying and hurting and shoving his filthy face into our lives. Your novel's a perfect example. He couldn't possibly have gotten it from Juice. Where did she get a copy? It's out of print, and more importantly she doesn't read, not even magazines or the paper. Think it through—a reporter who's lied since the beginning, who's known about you all along and refuses to go away, hiding in his hotel room with nobody to keep tabs on him. He's after you. It all revolves around you."

"Jesus, don't say that. I already think everything's about me."

"It isn't funny. He has to be stopped."

"They'll find them and learn the rest of it," I said. "To listen to the detective, circumstantial evidence is all they have so far. There must be physical evidence—blood, hair, DNA—but the cops can't be positive or Juice would have been arrested. Legree himself admitted he was just going to question her."

"Is this how you support the people you love?"

"We have to wait," I said. "At least till there's more to act on."

"I've been waiting my whole fucking life!"

A minute later I watched as the Neon slammed over the speedbump at a rate of knots that could have broken the springs. I hadn't tabled the best advice, certainly nothing I could use myself, and by the time I'd undressed I was already worked up again. Wait, I'd said. How the hell was I going to wait while screaming at the top of my mind?

The crash drew me still wet from the shower. Looked as though I wasn't the only one sick of hanging around for what the media were calling "further developments." In the sliding patio door was a head-sized hole, glass fanned out across the floor. I pulled on my hiking boots, and while I was removing the fragile canine teeth from the door frame, I saw the rock under the table. I'd been expecting some kind of reaction from our good neighbors, and there it was. The stone was wrapped with a note, transforming it from granite into a chestnut:

MURDERERS!

Pretty simple. I smoothed the paper and put it in the office then went outside to check for signs of additional vandalism. Nothing around back or between the houses, but there in the morning light, spray-painted across the garage door:

KillERS! And underneath in a different hand: SNOW NIGGERS!

The revelations in Cassidy's hotel room had vaccinated me against shock, and I called the police with no more emotion than reporting a lost budgie. Legree wasn't available so I left the report with the first cop I got on the line, who recognized my name and suggested Roger and I consider leaving for a while. I immediately thought of holing up at the Dowser's, but it would be too easy to get lost out there. I could spend a long time back in those hills forgetting all I've loved and lost and said and done, communing with nature by rejecting the human element and winnowing my heart in isolation, occasionally tramping in to help around the house for payment of a meal and a car to sleep in. The simplicity failed to arouse; I wasn't ready to forget. The cop had told me to keep my head up and my eyes open, superfluous advice I nonetheless employed as time passed and the shadows grew darker.

Inside a week the neighborhood had the feel of a brush-burn right at the point where it could rip loose at any moment and explode into the trees. Roger wasn't speaking to me. Half out of his skull with worrying about Juice, out the other half worrying about us being targets, he thought I was adding to the situation by being deliberately provocative, merely because I was, well, being deliberately provocative . . .

. . . I skulk, I lurk, I creep and crawl on my belly like a reptile. I hide in the shadows and spring out to terrify children and old people and leaf-blowing gardeners unable to detect my tread through their ear plugs. Captain British Columbia, camouflaged, indistinguishable from the plant life, I could be anywhere—watch out!—as I measure my victims and swoop under the radar to cause mischief in the land. . . . Well, not quite, but I was doing what I could. Once a day I marched every street in the compound right down the middle of the road singing vulgar rugby songs, finishing off with a dip in the pool and a walk home in my underwear; each night I slowly cruised the premises in the Neon, growling out the window while shining a flashlight on passersby, dogwalkers, front doors; the strand of barbed wire I'd strung knee-high along the back patio might have been a bit much, but there you have it. I was both angry and full of mischief and briefly considered hanging a carpet over the hole in the glass slider. When not occupied with juvenile defiance, I did a lot of pacing and waiting for the phone to ring. Head up, eyes open.

The administration had disintegrated, which made it all the more hilarious when we received the Board's last gasp, a penalty notice fining us for having unauthorized "decorations" on our garage door. Along with KillERS! and SNOW NIGGERS! we now had:

Sickos!
ANIMALS
KillERS! (again)
666
REPENT OR PERISH
Go Dodgers!

Roger didn't care. If it wasn't related to the case he was building against Cassidy, it was beneath his interest. He talked a lot—thinking out loud very loudly and prophesying the reporter's comeuppance—without addressing me directly. Other than that he snorkeled alone in his bedroom. Three days into the second week of the ferment Tina appeared at the front door, the first we'd seen of her since Juice's disappearance.

"Oh, hi. Hi, Tina. Great to see you. I thought you'd gone somewhere."

A quick backward glance. "Could we do this inside?"

As I hustled her through the doorway she handed me a newspaper, and I pretended to look at the front page.

"I want to say this right off the top, because you guys have been so good to me. I don't think Juice . . . I can't believe she did it, that's all. Sonny told me to wait till all the evidence is in, I knew that already, I owe her that much, to wait till it's all in. And I can't help thinking she probably tried to stop him, I mean, if one of us was in that position . . . it happens all the time, women getting abused and they still can't leave the abuser. Mentally as well as physically abused, especially mentally. My God, the thought of what he must have put her through . . ."

"We've come by a couple times," I said.

"I'm keeping out of sight," she said. "We have to go about this in a controlled way. Too much happened too quickly, so this time it has to be solid reform without all the grandstanding. The continuity of the HOA has been broken, but we have an obligation to keep up the fight, and if we have to stay underground till the moment's right then that's what we'll do. Don't you agree?"

"Tina, I'm glad you're not set against Juice. But as for the good of the neighborhood—this isn't the best time."

"There's been some trouble."

"Not that a Visigoth would notice."

"We've targeted certain individuals for surveillance," Tina said. "We're certain the gunshots weren't intended to do more than intimidate. Oh, that's right, you were outside the perimeter on the evening in question."

"Hey, Tina—I'm just Smith, you know? A couple of minutes ago I was so glad to see you and now all of a sudden you're talking like a CIA operative."

Roger entered the room and launched right in: "No one at the hotel can verify Cassidy's whereabouts on the night you were attacked. Also, he had ample opportunity to start the fire. And he's still here in town. Obviously, he has more up his sleeve."

I told Tina to ignore him and Roger looked at me with harm in his heart.

"I just had to tell you," Tina said. "The persecuted have to stick together, those with a common cause. There are people on your side who believe in you. Well, they don't actually believe in you, but they believe in everyone having a fair trial. Not everybody is out to get you, is what I'm saying. In the last poll, thirty-eight percent think you should be given the benefit of the doubt. Thirty-eight percent true lovers of freedom. Actually, that's the percent of people behind Juice, but you guys are right behind. Oh, we can accomplish so much all working together."

"Yeah, like fire ants."

"See what I get from him?" Roger said.

"Anyhow," Tina said, "I have to go before I'm late for the council court. I'm on the jury. It's one of our movement's innovations—establish who the lawbreakers are so they can be monitored and stopped before they violate the rules. If the plan had been in place two weeks ago we could have prevented the vandalism to your house."

"The garbage on the front walk is getting out of hand," Roger said. "I bet it's those slobs who used to hang out with Deep Tread. If you want to innovate, find a way to drive them out of the neighborhood."

"We can't," Tina said. "Once we consolidate our hold, we'll have to use people who know the system. Most of them just need re-indoctrinating."

"Tina," I said, rather harshly even to my own ear, "I love you. Roger and I love you. Thank you for coming. Now I'm going to leave you with a piece of advice I never thought I'd offer in a million years, okay?"

"Sure."

"Listen to Sonny."

Exit the Blonde Job. Fuck me.

"It was good to see Tina," Roger said.

"If that's who it was."

For a minute there I saw on his face the unadulterated Roger, until he shook his head and said, "All because of one man," and I knew I was still talking to the doctored version.

I finally looked at the paper Tina had given me, expecting the usual. Nope:

Dupe Dashes for Durango

A flick down the article picked up Juice's name five times, Marion Langton's about the same, and I read enough on my way to the coffee maker to wish I could extinguish our flaming desert experience and reclaim my old Roger, our old life, even for just an hour or two. He and I would repair to the Sylvia Hotel tap room in Vancouver and hunch our shoulders over the paper and maybe note the waiter's wrinkled shirt—explaining it with an invented story about his binge and sexual conquest of the night before—and we'd read the article together while rewriting it aloud and simply incorporate it into our day. But we were in a different place on a tortuous road in a torturous time.

The Dupe was in custody. Half-mad with dehydration, Deep Tread had been picked up staggering his way to the Mexico border in the Algodones Dunes west of Yuma. He claimed to have been abandoned and left for dead by the Duper, one Juice Smith, when he stopped his monster truck to take a whizz. Duper *and* murderer, by the way, because on the drive she'd confessed—no, bragged about—killing some showgirl model actress and stuffing her in a carpet, making the poor young thing the Dupee or something or at least dead, that's for sure. Anyhoo, good thing while he was almost dead himself after taking several whizzes on account of the box of Budweiser the Duper had bought and made him drink that he came across a cube van there in the middle of the desert, and wouldn't you know but after hearing people yelling inside he pulled up the latch handle and there was a bunch of Mexicans some guy had driven across the border and left there in the back of the truck. They were nearly as far gone as him but they set out together and finally made it to a road and got a lift from a grape farmer who took them all the way to El Centro. Then the Mexicans and him drank a whole lot of water from the hose at a gas station and the grape guy said they could stay at his place if they didn't mind sleeping outside and the rest of them said sure but the Dupe himself f***ed off because he was scared the police would blame him for that thing up-valley. So he borrowed a car from the street and went after the Duper, heading east on I-10 all over again, and wouldn't you know it the s***box car gave out so he made for the border again on foot and passed out pretty much near where he'd been dumped the first time, and maybe it was a mirage but he thought he could see the cube van in a hollow, and anyhoo that's when the Border Patrol found him and handed him over to the cops even though he hadn't broken any laws except maybe helping illegal aliens. But they're human beings too and probably the nicest most hard-working people around except for the stupid and lazy ones. Mexicans, that is, not all illegal aliens, like the ones who bombed that government building in Oklahoma, but like he always says, help your fellow man and forgive, it's about forgiveness like the Good Lord said himself, except when a woman sets out to make a man help her do wrong then she should probably be executed and the man should be put on probation and taught a trade for free so he can become a benefit to society.

As for Juice, nothing but rumors and snippets of information and a few sightings in New Mexico reported in UFO lingo. That anyone with a monster truck and an overload of kissmyass could still be at large had to be a record of sorts.

What had catalyzed her fantastic behavior? At what point had her foundation shifted? Even if history is not a disguise, it's unquestionably a preservative.

Oh, just for the record, the Durango in the article is northeast of Mazatlan, nowhere near the US-Mexico border. Not a bad headline all the same.

CHAPTER 39

No news may be good news briefly, but in the long run ignorance avails no one. I was glad to hear Juice had been spotted. Wait, that might be the wrong way to put it—she'd been sighted. I'll explain the difference shortly; in the meantime I must say things hadn't been going too well inside the walls of old Vista de las Pantalones.

We had a gang problem. Or, as the latest message on the notice board had it: ". . . a problem with members of the community who deny the basic rights and freedoms of other members of the community's right to basic rights and freedoms." Hardly a day went past without property or personal damage, a mishmash of mayhem—car windshields smashed, flowers ripped up, patio cover posts sawn through, women harassed, gays and other "mutants" assaulted.

Two rival groups had emerged from the HOA shambles and were locked in a turf war, the homelands apportioned roughly along the lines of the softball teams the day of the earthquake. The backing-onto-the-main-road area was the land of the Guardians—the incumbents, in a sense—followers of Juice and Deep Tread. Berets pulled down to their eartops, sweatshirts silk-screened with *Bunny's Bail Bonds and Pawn Shop*, they ranged their turf in vehicles painted to match DT's monster truck, sallying forth on punitive raids to beat anyone foolish enough to be walking alone or to capture an unleashed pet for ransom. The backing-onto-the-land-for-sale sector was claimed by the Tommys, so named for their Tommy Bahama uniforms, a questionable choice for a novice army in that every garment torn in combat hemorrhaged the quartermaster's fund over a hundred bucks.

I was the wild card. Geographically, I was on the Tommys' turf, though both factions operated under the assumption I was emotionally tied through Juice to the Guardians. Isolated amid the troubles, I laid low. I recall reading that on the return of the royal family from their attempted flight during the French Revolution, a sign was posted to the Paris crowds that read: "Anyone who applauds the king will be beaten, anyone who insults him will be hanged." I took much from that lesson on neutrality in difficult times. On the occasions I encountered a roving squad from either faction I played it off against the other, professing unbounded commitment to the cause, and it seemed to be working—the house had become a demilitarized pocket. The dumping of garbage out front had ceased, and in two weeks the only addition to the garage door was LEOPARDS! which I took to mean we were being compared to those unfortunates with rotting flesh, or maybe I had it wrong and the graffiti artist considered us social leopards.

The notice board by the mailboxes stood tall in a trash pile of paper as each side tore off the other's broadsides to make room for its own, saddling me with a new vice—stealing up when the coast was clear to read the latest salvos, vicious polemics larded with invective, excellent entertainment that broke only one rule of language, that it's meant to communicate.

So here we have our gangs: Led by Tina, the Tommys claimed to be peacelovers forced into defending themselves against the depredations of fanatics; the Guardians were operating without a leader for the time being, assuming the role of righteous custodians awaiting the return of DT and Juice. Mr. Tread was still in the jug, denied bail for jumping it the first time after only six hours and being tracked down and hauled back from Nevada with a hangdog expression and a dose of clap. As for my honey, the truck had been found abandoned in a small canyon on the other side of the valley not far from the Dowser's. The police and desert rescue experts were conducting an ongoing search of the hills. Detective Legree inferred Juice had immediately reversed course after dumping her partner in the Algodones dunes and returned to the approximate scene of the crime, or crimes.

With all the public interest in the case, small wonder there were reports of sightings, though what had the Guardians and a couple hundred others worked up was a vision of a more otherworldly character. In an industrial park a mile up the street toward the interstate was Bldg. 21. A square cinder-block warehouse, it was last in a row of attached structures bordering the local elementary school's football stadium. At the back was a loading area, on the front a sign reading AA-1 DETAILS, a company specializing in automotive accessories such as chrome coffee-cup holders, roof-mounted flags and mini-DVD players gyrostabilized for off-roading. Markedly nondescript, it had been spruced up by an epiphany—Juice's face on the side wall. Visible only in certain light, cameras were unable to descry its essence or even its existence. The owner of

AA-1 DETAILS had been happy to grant the Guardians overseer rights on the strip of weeds and gravel adjacent the manifestation in return for help manning the tables at the outdoor market he set up for the influx of potential customers. Many a pilgrim arrived bearing offerings and pictures of deceased loved ones for the shrine, and left laden with novelty license-plate holders and Bob-Hope-shaped air fresheners.

Initially, local churches fastened onto the manifestation as welcome publicity. But once it changed into a commercial enterprise in which they had no investment, they began denouncing it as the Devil incarnate, or the automotive industry incarnate, or something incarnate enough to suck parishioners from the fold, a stance that only added to the stream of geeks and penitents toting six-packs and candles who arrived each day to sit vigil.

Again I wished the old Roger was around. Actually, any Roger would have been good—he'd been gone since the end of May, almost two weeks ago. I hoped it was an overblown huff, outrage that would shrivel as our past transcended the moment and have him walking through the front door any day now, but it was hope absolute. Our breach happened right before the gangs formed, while the neighborhood disgruntlement was still in solution and hadn't yet crystallized into tribes. Roger and I were waiting for the scoop from Legree while keeping on our toes in case Juice was truly back in the area and chose to deliver the news in person. I knew Roger was angry, and mistakenly thought it was over my recent conduct, so I promised to stop my underwear swims and neighborhood-watch cruises and to take down the barbed wire.

But that wasn't it, and before I could try a different angle, past and present met head-on. Elbows on the table, no more than a fidget here, a glance there, as though all human touches—color, quirks, creative eccentricities—were impediments. We were taking the world in our own good hands and boiling it down to a kitchen-sink radio drama:

ROGER: . . . which comes as no surprise because that's the way you are. It doesn't help, is what I'm saying.

MORTY: Stay on the subject. We're talking about your preoccupation, how it's scaring me. And don't swallow your tongue—I'm genuinely concerned.

ROGER: What I hold to be true is built on something. It has a foundation.

MORTY: I need you right now. I admit it out of friendship and love. With Juice gone and . . . well, it's burdening you to an unfair degree, but I need you to be here for me.

ROGER: I am. If only you knew.

MORTY: You're not here at all. This fixation on Cassidy has transported you into the phantom zone.

ROGER: It's all for you.

MORTY: The way you were.

ROGER: The way I was?

MORTY: The way you were when she died.

ROGER: You never even say her name.

MORTY: The point is you were there for me. I'm not going to say something as dumb as "I couldn't have made it without you," but except for you, I would have come out of it altered for the worse.

ROGER: You did, you changed for the worse. Not from her death, from her life, your life together. I was there for you when she died because I wasn't when she was alive. Call it guilt, call it making up for failing to support you when you were married. That's why I came back to you—because I had left you to deal with it alone.

MORTY: I don't know Juice very well, that's part of the problem. You can't have basic understanding without halfway decent information, so what chance did I have of telling what she'd turn into?

ROGER: We're talking about your wife. Sheila, use her name.

MORTY: Not that you can control love. When Juice came along I ran with the moment so it's ridiculous in hindsight to say I should have . . . I mean, what was I supposed to do? Ask for credentials, her family photo album, school transcripts, interview her doctor?

ROGER: Sheila. I hated her.

MORTY: And now she's gone and I should have done more. Something or other or just shut up and let her tell me she loved me when she wanted and felt lucky.

ROGER: But I did come back, didn't I? You were so appreciative it almost made me forget how horrible I'd been.

MORTY: What do you mean? You'd never leave me.

ROGER: I'm not talking about Juice. Jesus Christ, Morty, aren't you listening to . . . I let you have your life together, which would have been good and noble if it hadn't been out of hate.

MORTY: You've always been there for me.

ROGER: That's what I'm saying, it's what I'm saying to you—I wasn't.

MORTY: She wanted you around more. She knew how much you meant to me.

ROGER: That's one thing I can let myself off the hook about. Sheila hated me as much as I did her.

MORTY: She loved you.

ROGER: She didn't even love you.

MORTY: She died too young.

ROGER: Yes, she did. Too young and with all the spite in the world in her heart. Have you never wondered why you lost all your friends when you got married? Isn't it strange that you never met a single member of her family?

MORTY: What's wrong with you—has this Cassidy obsession wiped out your memory? Her parents were dead and she was an only child.

ROGER: Oh, come on, you couldn't possibly believe that story. You received letters from them. Addressed to you, letters you opened and read.

MORTY: You know full well those were from the fiancé she jilted back home. Jealousy, revenge, all lies. People do that, if it's news to you.

ROGER: They were people, Morty. A real mother and father and sister.

MORTY: And you think that because . . . ?

ROGER: I know it for a fact because I met her mother. She came to town on the bus and showed up at the door, your door, right when I was on my way past. She couldn't even bring herself to knock. I introduced myself on the sidewalk—that's what you do when someone turns away from your best-friend's door—and we went for tea. She wanted afternoon tea in the big city, a poor substitute for seeing her daughter but that's what she wanted. And yes, it was her actual mother. The mess Sheila left behind her was scarcely believable, and I only got part of it. With all that, I failed. I promised her mum I'd do everything I could, told her I'd talk to you, warn you about her daughter, her very own daughter and your very own wife, and that I'd talk to Sheila, try to convince her that her family forgave, play the good guy who brings everyone together—a nice part to play, isn't it, a lifetime's worth of nothing saved with one beautiful act—but I didn't even try. Didn't tell you and lied to the mother. She loved her, loved her so much that giving her another chance was a phrase that didn't even come up. She would have given her a hundred more chances, a thousand, whatever it took. No checklist or program to follow for their angel to earn back her wings or any of that. Open. Open and open-ended. Gutless me, that's who she ended up with for a counselor, an ambassador of goodwill who didn't even go through the motions or stick on a bandaid. Weak and scared, off in my own faggy snit until she died and there I was—stalwart Roger showing up late to provide support, hypocritical asshole.

MORTY: You're in trouble. Seriously, Rog, you're sounding sick. You can't start rewriting history to justify a vendetta against some journalist.

ROGER: Listen to yourself. What you just said doesn't even make sense. How can you link what I think of Cassidy to my feelings for your wife? I wouldn't lie about her because . . . this is just stupid! Sheila was bad, a horrible person, and she treated you like dirt and ran you into the ground to everyone she talked to and you can spend the rest of your life lighting candles to her and go ahead and climb a mountain and open your veins and die with a tear in your eye, all romantic and grieving. Nothing's going to change the fact that you were in love with the wrong person, a bad woman.

MORTY: So now you're going to tell me who the right one was.

ROGER: I already said this isn't about me.

MORTY: I can't understand how you could hate her so much.

ROGER: I've only scratched the surface.

MORTY: You think she's been coerced into all this.

ROGER: Will you please, please quit coming back to Juice. Of course she's been used and abused and everything else, but we're talking about Sheila.

MORTY: My memory of her holds my whole past together.

ROGER: A breakthrough, wow. A minor one—your memory of her is bent—but it's a enough to make me pour a drink.

MORTY: That's not a drink, it's a bathtub.

ROGER: You have everything wrong, everything. Oh, look at me—I'm crying, you've made me cry when I wanted to be all logical and practical and stop always acting like . . . fuck!

MORTY: It's okay. Fine.

ROGER: It's nothing like fine.

MORTY: Let's start over from this—you think I'm being overly romantic about my wife.

ROGER: Not overly romantic, completely self-delusional.

MORTY: Like you're being about some poor reporter who read of piece of plagiarism that inspired him to write a story.

ROGER: He's rancid, a piece of pollution.

MORTY: Between you and me—

ROGER: —the way it's always been—

MORTY: —between you and me, you're the one living a fantasy.

ROGER: Really, oh really. That word you used—inspired. How many times have you driven into my brain that Sheila gave you the inspiration to write your novel? Time and time again and again. Inspiration, you say, as though the book required it.

MORTY: Don't be an ass. All books—no, not all books, all things—require inspiration.

ROGER: That?

MORTY: I know you're not the biggest fan of my writing, but I still don't like your tone.

ROGER: That piece of venom?

MORTY: That venom is what carried us in the slow times between your gigs for tax-dodgers.

ROGER: What a horrible thing to say, horrible and beneath you. Are you blocking what I told you outside Ralphs that day? It's been all on me since the reading world was able to see through the clever phrases and realize they had a slash-job in their hands. The book was ugly so of course it sold at first—sad people had a voice to tell them that other people had turned them into what they were, and angry people had an author to say it's okay to loathe their families. Hands clean, not their fault, home free. I've said one thing to you more times than I can count—no one in your novel ever learned a thing. One-dimensional characters you cut off every time they came close to resolving anything of importance. Mean losers with hate for the world.

MORTY: But I did it. A completed a novel that people read and despite what you say, loved. And she was the inspiration, my strength.

ROGER: Something's missing in your head. No, I don't mean to put it that way. What I mean is you have the ability to remove yourself.

MORTY: Maybe talent's missing, maybe that's it. Is that what you're saying?

ROGER: Oh, the talent is there. Very well-crafted, neat as a pin with all the right devices to turn on the waterworks. But it has nothing to do with what you think—put your finger down, I hate it when you do that—because there was nothing of you in the novel. All the praise for your grasp of human tragedy was out of sync with the person who wrote the book. You didn't create a story with a little bit of you and a dash of drama and a pinch of invention, all you did was use a device that didn't suit you, namely, writing in the first person with a woman's voice. Right. As if you know how women think.

MORTY: Your bathtub's empty. Pour me one while you're at it.

ROGER: I'm done crying. You don't have to pretend this is a party.

MORTY: All that's important here is for you to come down to earth and stop acting like Chas Cassidy is a war criminal.

ROGER: Evil people have to pay the price.

MORTY: Roger the Avenger.

ROGER: You're bad at irony, you know that?

MORTY: Anything I'm good at?

ROGER: I'm going to be quite calm and collected before I say this. See? Not even refilling my tub. Now. Okay. You're the most lovely man I've ever met in my life. Always thought so, always will.

MORTY: How long do I have to wait for the qualifier?

ROGER: You're no good on your own—not the finger again!—and if it makes me arrogant or domineering or motherly, too bad, because I'm going to tell you why.

MORTY: Say it and be done. I'm only listening once.

ROGER: You need help. It's what I've done almost my whole life for you. And I'm going to cry again but goddamn it I deserve to, and what I'm saying is professional help because I don't have the strength anymore. You forget, Morty. You invent, you make things up. You can't remember and it doesn't matter anyhow because you shape what's actually happened into what you need.

MORTY: Listen, Roger, listen to me. I'm aware of your support. All of it, all the way. If you could read my notes you'd know that. It's almost the first thing I acknowledge.

ROGER: Let me read them.

MORTY: You said this is about me.

ROGER: Easy enough. After all, we're sitting here in my mum's old place.

MORTY: What does the location have to do with anything?

ROGER: Not the physical location—who owned it.

MORTY: Your mum. Willa, your mum. So what?

ROGER: "Didn't know your mum had this kind of money." "Your mum never seemed to be afraid of anything."

MORTY: Talk sense.

ROGER: You said those things.

MORTY: Sure, okay. I don't remember but both are true enough. I might have.

ROGER: Years and years and years of the same denial, referring to her as if you loved her because she was my mum but you didn't know her all that well, blah blah . . .

MORTY: Sounds pretty accurate.

ROGER: You lived with us! How important is the time between fourteen and nineteen? Are they the "formative" years? I guess all years are, so it's a stupid term anyhow, yet for that period she was as much your mum as she was mine.

MORTY: What the fuck are you talking about?

ROGER: Fourteen, on your birthday, that's when your mum was killed. Two weeks later you moved in with us.

MORTY: Get off it. I spent a lot of time at your place but that's hardly living with you. My dad wanted to be alone. His depression and drinking after mum died. . . . "

ROGER: Your dad drank because *you* weren't there. Fifteen, sixteen, seventeen, eighteen and never after. That's why he drank.

MORTY: Now you're the one with the fingers.

ROGER: Four days, Morty. Four days you saw your father after your mum was killed and that was it. You went home every year on your birthday and came back with stories of how much of a drunk he was. Four days in five years, and I only say five years because that's when you quit talking about him completely and I stopped counting. You didn't spend a lot of time at our house— you lived with us. Your room, don't you remember your room? You had that old Albert Einstein poster on the wall, black and white, his hair all frizzy, and Mum used to tell you that you were a genius too, that everyone was, even your dad. Funny, isn't it? You say you need me while all along your dad needed you and you don't even remember that the only thing you did was piss in his face once a year on your birthday and laugh at him. Okay, he wasn't the strongest man, not the smartest or the kind of father a kid goes around bragging about, but he was nice. Just a nice man and there aren't many of them around.

MORTY: I've said that in my notes. How many times do I have to tell you I've learned since then?

ROGER: You haven't learned a thing. And now I'm going to finish what I was saying—your dad was a little lost, a little sad, and that's all. His wife was killed and his son ran away to live with people up the road on the other side of the school. Just for emphasis before you start talking about Juice or Sheila I'm going to say it again—your dad was a nice man. And you bitched it by moving to our place and leaving him to sit and drink by himself.

MORTY: So it was my fault. All me, a kid of fourteen—

ROGER: —Fifteen, sixteen, seventeen, eighteen and forever after—

MORTY: —Why didn't he find me? Come get me? Even if he'd just staggered up to your door with a bottle in his hand and sang an old folk song and pissed on the sidewalk. Fuck him.

ROGER: Fuck you. Fuck you for either pretending all this time that you never left or for actually believing it. Scariest is that I think you truly don't remember.

MORTY: You're asking me to recall things that didn't happen.

ROGER: Not things, years. Formative years. And no matter what you thought of him then, there's no explanation for ignoring him since. Worse than ignoring—sealing him off forever.

MORTY: Sure, I spent a lot of time at your place. I had an Einstein poster, big deal. It was a cool poster back then. Lenny Walagrocki had one and he couldn't even add, but he liked the way the frizzy hair looked behind his lava lamp.

ROGER: Your dad didn't piss on the sidewalk or show up drunk and singing. Your room was in the basement and when you'd hear him at the door you'd crawl through that tiny window at ground level. He'd wear a tie, Morty—like he was courting you or something—and my mum would let him in your room so he could see you weren't there. He never even loosened his tie, you know that? Always done up proper right to his Adam's apple. Visiting his son who ran away, ran away and kept running. The poor man probably hasn't worn a tie since.

MORTY: Your family wasn't perfect. Your dad left your mum for another man. You and I are way beyond the gay thing, but it obviously caused some kind of disruption in the old nuclear family.

ROGER: Mum handled it better than anyone in that situation I've ever heard of and still raised two boys. All those years of embracing you like one of her own. She loved you.

MORTY: She loved a lot of people

ROGER: Yes, she did.

MORTY: Actually, she just handled the accounting.

ROGER: What's that supposed to mean?

MORTY: Nothing, I don't know what I'm saying.

ROGER: Why not his birthdays?

MORTY: Eh?

ROGER: Your dad's. At least that would have shown some concern, a sign that he was on your mind. But it was *your* birthdays you went home on. You were a stripper, Morty, showing half a tit to a guy in the front row drooling for pussy.

MORTY: I recognize the importance of people in my life.

ROGER: Sure you do, you just can't act on it.

MORTY: Soon to be charged with murder and who knows how many other felonies—Juice is top priority.

ROGER: I agree. And the only way to clear her from top spot is to deal with the actual criminal.

MORTY: Not that again. You're going to give me the runs. I'm surprised you're not lying on a hill with your hat on backwards targeting Cassidy with a sniper rifle.

ROGER: I love Juice as much as you do—okay, that's dumb but you know what I mean—and here we are arguing when we could be working together.

MORTY: I'm not about to buy into your warped notions.

ROGER: We're supposed to be sharing.

MORTY: You're questioning everything I accept to be real.

ROGER: There's no questioning involved. I'm telling you straight out that you don't know what you're talking about.

MORTY: Nobody can be right or wrong all the time every time.

ROGER: You can start by not being so defensive.

MORTY: It's a natural reaction when under assault.

ROGER: I'm not against you.

MORTY: No, what you're doing, or at least trying to do, is purge. Purge me of my demons and baggage and misconceptions without realizing it's an attack. On top of that, you're trying to make me ignore the evidence against Juice.

ROGER: Quit twisting my words. I'm not claiming Juice is innocent.

MORTY: Yes you are.

ROGER: No I'm not.

MORTY: Yes you are.

ROGER: No I'm not.

MORTY: Yes you are.

ROGER: Touched you last.

MORTY: Ha, hahaha . . . you fucking guy. Ha, hahaha, I feel fourteen again.

ROGER: Sit down. We're not done yet. Heh.

MORTY: Laughing at your own pitiful joke.

ROGER: This isn't a joke—heh—okay, I'm all right now.

MORTY: You forget something.

ROGER: What? Heh, that was pretty funny.

MORTY: Let's not go overboard.

ROGER: Okay, what am I forgetting?

MORTY: You think I'm crazy about the past and crazy about the present. You think I'm delusional but come on, Rog, there must be something I'm not inventing . . . think hard . . . how long do I have to wait? . . . you're crying again . . . what about my mum?

ROGER: You got her right, what can I say? Your mum was great. She could be a pain in public but it was fun. That's why we loved being around her—we had a big kid to take the pressure off when we did some dumb little kid thing.

MORTY: So how come I never knew her? Why is it my dad is defined—even if you think I have him all wrong—and my mum is just . . .

ROGER: Someone you wanted to build a house for.

MORTY: Yeah.

ROGER: Remember how much she smoked?

MORTY: Ha. Unreal.

ROGER: Puff away while she was eating, blow smoke in your face while she was talking to you. That time Whitmeyer was in juvie court for throwing the cans of tomatoes from the school roof onto passing cars—your mum showed up as a character witness, hadn't even been asked to by Whitmeyer's parents or lawyer. And she lit up in front of the judge.

MORTY: And the judge didn't say anything!

ROGER: Let her smoke her brains out right in the courtroom while she rambled on and on, building up Whitmeyer as a saint, the judge covering his mouth—

MORTY: —so we couldn't see him laughing!

ROGER: There was something about her.

MORTY: How about your mum—do you have her straight?

ROGER: Yeah, I always had a feel for her. It was different with my dad. You'd think after he came out of the closet we could have shared that at least.

MORTY: Have we lost the intensity of children? Without that everything dribbles away. Especially for a liar.

ROGER: Oh, I'm so tired of that.

MORTY: Rough ass. Deal with it.

ROGER: You're no more a liar than anyone. Not now, anyway. Frankly, I'm bored to death with hearing you say that humans evolved as social animals, yet what gets through is that we have to be able to predict and manipulate so we can survive as individuals and reproduce. Which means we're selfish, Morty, selfish. We lie in nice ways so others don't take offense, we lie for personal gain or just to win at something and we use excuses that the rest of the world can see through like glass. Half-truths, illusions and, and . . . and actually, you're one of the more truthful people I know. You're not a liar. Except to yourself, that is—go ahead and take that as far as you can run with it because you know many things but not yourself. And now I'm tired. I've been trying to convince you that . . . I don't want to convince you of anything. Just talking, and if you still feel the need to pound me about Cassidy, it's wasted effort. I'll take the beating and do what I have to do. For once I'm going to do the right thing—what I have to do.

MORTY: So this is it? We're going to run around in circles, disputing what happened in the past until we both snap?

SNAP!!
That was the end of the conversation. The fan let go over our heads without so much as a wobble and auto-gyroed into the slider, hitting the broken glass and taking out the whole sheet. We looked up at the connection box in its ragged cavity, and Roger dragged the fan by its wires across the glass and put it on the table. No more disagreeing, no tapering off, we just went to our separate rooms and played the what-I-should-have-said game until conquered by sleep.

In the morning Roger was gone. Done, kaput. I heard him crying in the night, a full-blown symphony of drenching tears and mucus, and I failed to check on him, convincing myself he'd be better off without the intrusion. In the morning he was gone. In a spasm of worry I called to file a missing-person report with Legree, and he told me to wait forty-eight hours—I got the impression even three or four would make him happy—but the fit left me almost immediately and I let the report go the way of bad first guesses.

From outside came the sound of a loudspeaker touting the virtues of the Guardians and that's about it. The gangs were gearing up the summer campaign and I was alone. Bye for now, Rog. I know I'll see you soon, and whatever I'm culpable of, I hope like hell it's the end of the marks it leaves on you.

It's been a couple of weeks since Roger told me I wasn't me. Before taking off he left money—could I feel any more of a cowflop? I drank most of it away and the bills piled up and the fridge looked more tempting closed than open and I suppose I could have buggered off but there was too much left. Not to do—I wasn't doing anything anymore except dodging the gangs and waiting—but to see and hear.

I found myself thinking of getting a job, and if I hadn't been so sad the notion would have left me hysterical with laughter. Can't say I've ever had a real one. When my wife was alive I floated along with work. "What do you do?" people would say, and I couldn't say. "Found work," I'd tell my wife. "Great," she'd answer, "you got a job." I'd say, "Nope, no job, just got work," and she'd know I was filling time again with hourly labor, picking up this and that, picking up anything short of empty bottles roadside or lonely men curbside. The prairie people in my novel toiled endlessly, relentlessly, at jobs that were never done. The work was the same each year except that the folks got fewer cents on the bushel and gas prices for the vehicles kept going up and so did insurance; pig feed inflated and return on the piggies deflated and maybe this year was the time to rip up the barley and plant canola to cash in on the healthy-fat craze. Or something. They had a job, at least, didn't have to move to the city and start looking for one there. For a while, anyway.

Out of touch, that's what I am. Astray and excluded from the working world as much as I am from the literary. Long ago I decided not to lead a life of quiet desperation, though I figured the desperation was inevitable, so chose the loud version, and as usual turning up the volume obscured as much as amplified.

It's half June, and today Chas Cassidy called and left a voice message offering to help with anything, anything at all. I spied Sarah on the street and she ran away in a panic. Later, on the way to the mailboxes, I saw Martin. He looked forlorn, out of uniform and reasons and a daughter and options.

How many more duels will it take to achieve satisfaction? Roger Jeffcoate—more important to me than Juice is and Sheila was—is lost. And my only response is to wait for the next event. While foraging for food I found his mum's plaque—*Aqui se acaba la tristeza*—on top of the fridge and took small pleasure from smashing it for the lying bastard it was.

I'm willing to take the blame for a lot of things, though only if I suspect them to be true. If self-delusional, I have few alternatives other than throwing up my hands and blaming it on the bossa nova.

CHAPTER 40

The compound was approaching a state of total incoherence due to radical assholishness. Rumor had it Juice was exercising shadow control of the Guardians, who in an oligarchic thrust had upped the level of violence. The Tommys were responding in self-defense, a phrase much touted but disingenuous due to the gang's tendency to strike first to achieve it—"Advance justifiable preventive deterrence," as they had it on their leaflets. Whether or not Juice was pulling the strings was moot, though for a fact she wasn't idle; Chas Cassidy's hotel room had been broken into and trashed. It was Juice all right, identified by Cassidy's sister, who surprised her in the act and took a beating for the unfortunate timing. Missing were the copy of my novel Juice had given the reporter and one of his sister's teeth.

The local news channel worked their way into the jail for a LIVE! interview with Deep Tread, who belatedly recalled something he'd left out in his initial statement to the press—Juice had revealed the hotel-room-break-in plan right before she coyoted him in the desert, told him two or maybe three times and could hardly wait to do it again to someone else. Staring down the barrel of the lens, puffed up from the attention like a tainted sausage, he added so much drivel the anchor-biped cut him off to go LIVE! to a city-council meeting on how many snow-making machines would be needed to turn a section of bighorn sheep habitat into the Coachella Valley's first ski hill.

According to Detective Legree, Juice hadn't technically broken into the hotel room, rather she'd gained access through a maid by posing as an encyclopedia salesman. Yes, that's what he said. We were standing a short distance inside the front door.

"So what's the big deal about this book?" he said.

"The novel? She loaned it to him, that's all, probably wanted it back." Watch check. "Where is that nerd?"

"What's so important? You work alone all the time anyhow."

"How about that other book?" Legree said.

"Oh, man, if you knew how much I want to apologize for . . . Hey, don't look so interested, it isn't related to the case. I read something that got me worked up, that's all. I guess Roger would say it's about, well, it's about people dealing with stuff I've forgotten. Or made up. Or never learned. Whatever. Tragedy and loss and how selfishness and a lust for control hurts people who . . . sorry, your eyes are glazing. This isn't helping you much, is it?"

Saved by a car pulling up out front. Legree glanced at his watch again and yanked open the door. By the sound of the car I could already tell he'd be disappointed. It was still afterfiring, snorting and vibrating like an aggrieved pensioner as it struggled to shut down its vitals.

"Get out," the detective said. "This is a police site."

"So that's what you do," Sonny said.

Legree pulled an envelope from his inside breast pocket and passed it to me. "Warrant."

I ditched the envelope on the couch. "Did you think I was going to turn you away from the door?"

He checked his watch in reply. Sonny headed into the kitchen and poured himself a drink and we trailed him out onto the patio.

"How's Delilah?" I said.

"We had a service on Tuesday."

That stopped the clock right there.

"Jesus, Sonny, I'm sorry. I can't . . . I'm sorry. She went so fast. Not much more to say. Sorry, that's all."

"My condolences," the detective said.

"You shut up," Sonny said without malice.

"How's Saxon holding up?" I said.

"Good, really good, pretty strong that kid. Forgot about him sort of. All along, is what I'm saying. Quinn the squeaky wheel and Delilah the sad case, kind of didn't think about Saxon the little guy in the middle. Be okay, all of it. Money's okay soon, got some work coming in. Believe it or not, a reference from Quinn, got himself a job up the hill." His laugh was almost genuine. "Wish I was one of those guys who thinks everything happens for a reason."

Legree broke the pause. "I don't suppose you know anything about that developer who was assaulted Monday night?"

"Nice timing," I said. "You're a true professional."

Sonny didn't need my help. "The one who wants to build on my land?" He was talking to the detective without looking at him. "Just what

I saw on Channel 2. After I bumped into him in the Ralphs parking lot and stuffed him in the shopping cart and ran him into the cactuses, it was all over but the crying."

Legree broke that pause, too. "Sure. Don't even know why I asked."

Nice touch, though I wasn't about to say so.

Sonny wasn't listening to him anyway. "All those forests up in Canada, Smitty. Funny how when they clear-cut them down to stumps they still can't see where they're going. Hey, Legree, if I testify the developer guy's a criminal, like find something on him, in bed with the electricity guys who faked our big power trouble or that, you think I could get one of them witness protection things? Don't need much, a couple new pieces of ID and a few acres should do it."

"I'm sorry about your daughter. Don't talk like you and me are strangers."

"Yeah," Sonny said, "I guess you got some points stored up over the years."

A car entered the compound and Legree signaled the driver to pull over alongside the house. It was the computer nerd, mentioned on the warrant. On his way across the grass he swatted aside a hanging olive branch that would have been a foot over my head. Unshaven, with the look of an athlete transitioning from a life of pumping iron to pounding beer, if he was representative of what computer science schools were churning out these days, the field would soon have the choice between taking over the world through information technology or by frontal assault. I assured him there was nothing hidden on my computer, that I had to call tech support just to change the little clock in the corner of the screen, and he must have been another true professional because he took the comment as an insult to his craft. After a schoolyard staredown, I led him inside to the desk. Legree hunched behind his shoulder and told me to wait outside.

"How long they going to be?" Sonny said. "Thought we could catch a beer, you and me."

"I don't think I'm up to socializing," I said. "Oh, sorry, unless you want to talk."

"Delilah's something I got to get straight in my own head first," he said. "Thought we could have a beer, that's all. Might not be around much any more, me and the Blonde Job are looking for a place. She gets in too much trouble on her own so we better stick together and for sure not around here. High desert maybe, Quinn's up in Yucca Valley, could be time to climb the hill, see what there is to see."

"How did you talk Tina into abandoning the Cause?"

"Didn't lay nothing on the line or nothing, just told her what I thought. Feels funny, somebody listening to what you say. Me, I think she kind of forgot why she started with it in the first place. Who can explain what anyone does if they go through what she did."

Legree called from inside—I'd grown to loathe the sound of urgency—because the Special Forces tech-specialist needed my e-mail password. A snide remark about his lack of expertise paid nothing more than a flinty silence, and I replaced him in the chair.

"That thing play movies?" Sonny said.

"I told you to wait in the living room," Legree said.

"Told," Sonny said. "Show me in the warrant where it says you can tell a guy."

INBOX1(1 new)

Before I could click, the assistant put a large hand over the mouse and I had to duck through the opening under his arm. Sonny and I had been in the kitchen less than a minute when we heard the printer going. I hoped like hell it was from Roger.

"No good what they're doing in there," Sonny said. "Everybody needs secrets. Me, I always wanted to work the rides, at the fairs and Disneyland and all them, being in charge of kids having a hoot would be good. Funny, Delilah loved the rides but I never seen a kid so scared of them. Even those teacups with the seats that just go in circles and spin a little bit, they scared the shit right off her. Loving it and scared both."

When they came out, Legree stood in front of me with an enigmatic look that had a bit of all people in it; for a minute I didn't know whether I was being regarded by an inquisitor or a defender. He handed me one copy of the e-mail and kept the second. Then he stuck out his hand. The gesture took me by surprise, but after a second or two I reacted, pumping a jack to mask my hesitation.

Sonny waited till their cars were well clear of the house. "You should read that in private."

"You don't have to go."

"Just out to the Bonny for some tools," he said. "Fix that fan and the slider for good."

Sonny still talked a good story, but his walk couldn't sustain the fiction. The familiar cocky roll on the outside of his heels had turned into a flat-footed slap, his head bobbing in tired unison. It's hard enough to hold both love and death in your mind at one time, a level of magnitude more difficult when it's about the same person, and that person is your child.

The death of love—how does that happen? It can drain away but seems impervious to direct attack. Inconceivably, I still loved the messenger despite her message:

Dear Morton Hag Cahoot,

Whoa! I was blown away. I'd been struggling with how I related to the world, or at least fit in, and your book answered all my questions. Every one! I read and read through the night, which is quite a lot when you're only eleven. When I read it again a couple of years later it helped me in so many ways that it hadn't the first time. Like it made me understand why my dad wanted to sleep with me so much even though he told me I was starting to get old and pretty soon I'd look just like my wornout mum.

Whoa! It even explained her. All her crying and talking about my sister all the time. And why she hated me, hated my guts for sleeping with my dad and getting him sent away. She told me she didn't hate me, but how can you believe an adult when you're still a kid? You know where she told me he went? To the farm. I remember her telling me that he felt trapped and that he went to live on a farm so he could have space. I told her we already lived on a farm. And you know what? She started crying again and said that's something her mum used to tell her when they had to kill one of their dogs. She didn't even know the difference between when she was a kid and when I was.

Anyhow, I think I fell in love with you. Your book showed so much understanding. A lot of years later I built my own house all because you wrote about a woman who built one. I had fantasies about living in it with you, maybe because I was messed up with drugs and I was drinking too much, and anyhow we'd be the perfect couple, the kind the neighbours would all look up to. I know in your book you made her build the house for herself even though in real life I built it for my sister, except I guess writers are allowed to make some things up. Besides, it was silly of me to build a house for my sister right? Because by then it was after you made her kill herself. (Not in the book, because you left that part out—Ha!)

But the stuff you did write about was perfect. All the parts about my mum and dad, it was like you really knew them. Even me. It's hard to read about yourself and think it's you. That's not what I mean, what I mean is like have you ever heard your own voice on a tape recorder or something and you know it's your voice but it sounds all funny? Same thing with your book. It was my mum and dad and Sheila, I could tell it was them but it was weird reading all the bad things about me, not the bad things I did but what happened especially because there was so much in there that happened to me when I was real little, stuff I hardly remembered but did right away as soon as I read them.

And did you ever get my sister right! Okay, maybe I don't know for sure because she was older and everything and I wasn't even ten when she left but my mum told me lots about her. I wish I could have grown up with her more. When I read what you wrote about her and found out we both had so much in common, especially the stuff with dad and everything, it made me miss her. Anyhow, I'm not blaming you for that part except then she met you and fell all in love and never came home.

It really was an excellent book. Why don't you do a sequel? You could write about afterwards, after everyone read your book, the way people in town treated me and my mum. Like the time I was with her and she won $10 at BINGO and she wanted to celebrate but the coffee shop wouldn't serve us. That was pretty bad because we didn't even want to sit in their stupid place, Mum only wanted to get some Chinese food to take home. And you could have a whole chapter in there about the time some guy broke into our house when my dad was in jail and wrecked the place and smeared poop all over the mirror and hung my mum's best dress on a chair and cut it with a knife and nailed my dad's good suit to the wall and shot it with a rifle. That would be excellent adventure. And about the time the older boys from the high school held me down in the dirt and stuck

*a bottle up me. You have such a way with words it'd be hilarious!!!
I mean they'd stick their dinks in farm animals but they thought I
was too dirty for their stupid things—Ha!*

*Oh boy, I'm getting tired. I don't know how you can write so
much all the time. I guess it's easier on a big keyboard, this airport
thing is so cramped and you have to keep putting in quarters. I
guess I'll finish though. Then it's time. It's probably raining and
I'm looking forward to the smell when I get off the plane. I love
Vancouver.*

*I don't know if you can love a whole city, I sure do though. As
soon as I was done building the house I moved there. My sister was
dead except you weren't. It was great. Away from the farm at last
and nobody knew anything so I could do what I wanted. After you
made Sheila kill herself I wanted to do something right away except
I was only a teenager. But right after the last coat of paint went on
the house I burnt it down because who was it for, right? and
whammo! out to the coast.*

*I miss Vancouver and I miss seeing you and Roger. He's your true
blue friend and I'd never do anything to hurt him. Maybe I can't
help it a little bit because he loves you and so when I hurt you it
hurts him, right? But that's life, like they say.*

*I miss the old town too, I think. What do I mean "I think" when
I just wrote it? What it is, is that it was neat until your book came
out, even with my dad and everything. It was a pretty religious
place, all Bible belty, which isn't so bad if it helps someone but all
their talking about the rains and the children and infants and
plagues, I mean come on, you got to admit it's funny we lived
together in the desert when back home they used to say the desert is
where the sign of the beast'll be delivered. Kooky.*

*Anyhow, I fell in love with you except you'd already fallen in
love with my sister and then made her kill herself so what was I
supposed to do? After I moved to Vancouver I followed you around,
and of course Roger too and it was hard. I loved you but how could
a famous author respect anyone who couldn't even do anything after
what he did to her sister? I had no guts, and who loves someone like
that? So it's like I couldn't kill you but I could kill the stuff around
you. You're smart enough to understand that, right? You did it to me
and Mum and Dad in your book and you had the guts to do it to*

Sheila, about all the stuff she went through with our family. So you get it. (Besides, I had to wait till you went away because all those years in Vancouver you were already drunk and crazy all the time so how much more could you be punished—Ha??!!)

Okay, big confession time. Ready? I really feel bad about Alliyah. I know people can't help who they are, and she was just a slut, the pictures and magazine articles and all that. And maybe I should have empathized (I bet you like that word, Mr. Writer) because I was a slut too when I was little, that's what Dad said and later even Mum. But when it came down to it she was part of your world. Poor her had to go because her parents were too stupid to stay out of your life. Too bad, so sad. No, that's not it. I really feel bad about her.

Poor stupid people who got caught in the way. Like Sheila. Even at the end when she killed herself there was everyone feeling sorry for Smith instead of his dead wife. Oh yeah, you weren't Smith then. You stole her name and used it afterwards, after you drove her so nuts she took her own life (her own life, a precious thing, you can look it up anywhere) and you wonder why the people around you have to suffer? Maybe you're not so smart after all. And maybe I love you except I sure don't like you. If it was just you and me somewhere like it was with me and my sister I bet it'd be all love except that it isn't and somebody has to pay. Too bad, so sad, it's the horrible people around you who have to pay. Okay, Sonny's not horrible but that's life, like they say.

I don't hate them. I don't hate anyone. For an example, I love the man in your book. Not the one about my family and me but the one you stole from that man in Newfoundland. Love him. How anyone can do more than survive and actually end up feeling stronger is beyond me. Same with Sheila, she couldn't either.

I'm 5' 6" tall, have black hair, am well-proportioned (until the implants come out—Ha!), and like short walks in the rain and bad movies.

I love you but you have to pay. You did a very bad thing and that's all there is to it.

Sincerely,
Juice

p.s.: I'll see you again. It's in the cards, like Sheila used to say. Also, the love. Love conquers all, right?

p.p.s.: If you have to trust anyone except for Roger I guess you can trust me. A smart guy like you should be able to find out where I am. Oh, and you can trust Cassidy. There's a real gentleman for you, and you need somebody like him who's on your side.

Sonny returned from the Bonny laden with tools, took one look at me and turned around. I haven't seen him since, likely never will, and last I saw on my way out the door, the fan was still broken.

PART FIVE

CASCADE

CHAPTER 41

On my nineteenth birthday, my father had only himself to talk to. No excuse, no explanation for my taking a pass. Based on Roger's testimony, I'd been living with him and his mum for years; by the time I hit nineteen the father-son cord had unraveled and parted and I didn't even drop in for my dad's annual summation. I'm sure it would have run true to form. He would have swirled his glass of rye and said something such as: "It's a hard world out there so you have to be tough," and I would have replied along the lines of: "The reason the world's so hard is because everyone in it is trying to be tough."

Embracing one biological imperative while suppressing another—competitiveness vs. the ability to consider and choose—is so limiting that if there is a higher power She should confine the behavior to bacteria. But don't misinterpret. Although I truly believe that treating life in that manner is to be only partly human, the motivation for my answer would have been to get my father's goat, not to make a point. Then again, I may not have said anything of the kind. I was old enough, more or less, to act like a man, more or less, so maybe I would have realized my dad had run out of ingredients for a fresh batch of theories. Maybe I would have agreed just to make him feel good: "Yeah, I know what you mean, Dad," and let him have his annual moment with his kid.

He's still in the house, the one he did what he could to turn into a home. I spent many years disagreeing with the man, yet I must say that after skipping my nineteenth-birthday visit I've found it hard. Get that one—hard. Mewling isn't it, considered in the sweep of a life, as though we're born entitled to X years free of agitation? Yet I've found it a great deal more difficult nailing together a framework for my own life than tearing down my dad's.

Here's one from my father on my eighteenth birthday, the last time I saw him: "The apple never falls far from the tree." Sadly, he meant it as a warning.

I made the situation worse by saying, "Unless the tree's on a hill." After a moment to make myself feel like a wise man I added, "Also, the apple can get eaten by an animal and crapped out miles away." Another drink and a tear in the eye for him and one last trip out the door for me.

Now, again, I have to hit the road. Nothing left to wait for, time to book out.

Chas Cassidy hadn't disengaged. Although he wouldn't enter the compound due to the civil war, he'd been pelting me with alarmist messages. No details, he told me every day on the answering machine, no details unless we met in person; he was still at the Marriott and it would be in my best interests to contact him; he was worried for my safety, he had information, hard information, that could affect my life or even terminate it. As if I hadn't already opened Juice's grotesque gift pack. Ah well, he was trying, good for him.

The back slider was already agape, and I left the front door unlocked so the gang members and the curious and the wind could compete for homesteader rights, until remembering it wasn't my house and shutting it up tight as I could, locking the front door and nailing the carpet over the slider. The last few feet on my way to the gates I saw Martin and Sarah going the opposite direction in a replica-Hummer golf car, highly modified—winch, bush guard, six overcab flood halogens, a stereo speaker blaring "Ride of the Valkyries," sheet-metal armor riveted along the sides to the height of Martin's chin, His-and-Her golf bags holding a shotgun and a rifle apiece. I clapped them off. Clapped and waved one last time and shouted their names but they were on a mission and ignored me.

The final insult was the gate. I'd left the keys in the house so stood nose-to-grill with my knapsack full of meal-replacement bars and plastic Platypus water bags until someone entered and I made my escape. Only one more stop to make before beginning my forty days—I had to see Juice.

Past the elementary school's football stadium was the industrial park. Traversing the asphalt along front of the warehouses and workshops I came to Bldg. 21 and went round the side. Not a pilgrim. There was one guy picking through a pile of palm fronds and garbage, probably searching for the mate to the sandal in his hand, but the true believers had abandoned the site. I stood back and stared at my love. With the drop in attendance, AA-1 DETAILS had shifted the marketing machine into high gear by airbrushing Juice's image on the stucco, a facsimile that wouldn't have looked out of place on the side of a 1970s van—dark dark eyes the right color but slightly crossed, cowboy hat atop purplish hair, STP undershirt over enhanced tits. The Duchess of Hazzard. I toasted her with a bottle of Gatorade, but there was no lingering because it was time to walk.

I followed Highway 74, where in a series of savage switchbacks it strains for altitude up the pass splitting the San Jacinto and Santa Rosa mountains. Twenty miles and a full day later I stopped on the side of the road, ate seven sawdusty bars, washed them down with a gallon of water warmer than my core temperature and passed out in the ditch. As day was breaking I awoke filthy, footsore and confused to a vista of high chaparral and pinyon pine. Juniper, agave, prickly pear measled the earth. The massif of Toro Peak stood rampant in my line of sight as I jerked erect. The day before I'd thought vaguely about climbing to the top. The striking views from Toro parenthesize the San Jacinto and Santa Rosa ranges, the Coachella Valley down to the Salton Sea and the desert all the way to Mexico, but I could visualize the Marine Corps microwave station on the summit and wanted no reminder of anything two-legged. Up the way was Pinyon Flats, with its array of horse acreages beneath the pines, echelons of mailboxes indicating high-country retreats and breeding ranches but nix on that, too—already I'd been repeatedly sand-whipped on my ascent by a parade of motor homes and a scourge of luxury sport-utility vehicles. No people at all, please and thank you. I shouldered my gear, backtracked down the highway to the Sugarloaf Café, waited in the gravel parking lot till it opened, ate a proper breakfast, hid behind some bushes in an arroyo down the dirt road behind the place and passed out for another two hours.

On awakening I lanced my blisters and headed off with a will, working out the kinks and cramps, up-and-downing my way along the Santa Rosas. I hadn't planned on backtracking, but eventually found myself angling toward the Coachella Valley, until catching a glimpse of the suburban sprawl and regaining distance and altitude, keeping to the ridgeline.

For over a week I held roughly south. On reaching the first of only two predetermined destinations, I stopped and looked and smelled. The Santa Rosas were nearing their end, roughly paralleled the last few miles by the San Ysidros, the two ranges pinching a V of desert that held my town. There it was—Presidente. Nothing, no buildings, no people. A fantasy town destroyed by an imaginary earthquake. At least, I think that's where it was. My act of creation had involved nothing more than borrowing a pen from the barmaid at the Blue Dog and circling a spot on a map from a 7-Eleven.

Nice nostalgic visit, then it was down the mountains to the Salton Sea and around the north end and across the valley and through the Mecca Hills and up again, up north and west into the Little San Bernardinos, three weeks, four, the voices constant now and in my dehydration and fatigue I loudly responded to the man who was my father, the woman who was my wife, the stranger G.H. Nuttall—people I had robbed.

Juice had no voice. She was with me all right, every ankle-turning step of the way, but she didn't speak. Her e-mail was too recent to have acquired ghost status and confusing enough on its own to make hallucinations redundant. Much of her message was nonsense, too many omissions and contradictions to swallow. Juice had told me her dad went to jail for hitting a teacher, yet wrote it was for abusing his daughters; the story of being forced to adopt out her baby wasn't referenced in the e-mail, though she brought up less important details; the Dowser had gotten the scoop that Juice was pregnant, but not a jot of it in the message—was I a future father, or did that honor go to the babbling ass cooling his heels in the local jail, if there was a baby on the way in the first place? It would seem the only surety was her relation to my wife, but at least one major assumption was required to maintain it: Juice was telling the truth. Oh, come on—she'd shown cunning and master manipulation technique all along, so why couldn't she have investigated my wife's past and added a few details from the novel?

Her actions, though, hard to work around those. The main hangup was whether she'd arrived in the valley already twisted or had corkscrewed along the way. Which version of Juice to believe—Before or After? Either way meant I had fallen in love with a . . . well, sociopath is too harsh and nutcase too flippant, but either one will do. It's probable that my hallucinations started the way they always have, right from the giddyup. Juice's first e-mail:

> Whoa! I'm blown away. . . . Whoa! I haven't slept since. . . . I think I'm in love with you. . . . You show such understanding . . .

Had Juice truly been lying in wait all these years? Waiting for what? For me to become such an empty vessel, so starved for love, that I'd be easy to buffalo? If so, I couldn't fault her timing. The poor girl—after helping create the eleven-year-old Juice I'd moved on to permanently warping the adolescent before settling in for a short career of being the adult's pawn. As specter power I'd incited and as lover I'd abetted her every step, the ups downs and switchbacks of a spectacularly crazy walkabout.

I was well past denial so what was the glimmer? Was it physical deprivation making me think maybe, just maybe, there was a magical mystical wild-ass explanation, a monstrously filthy practical joke, a twist at the end, or . . . Juice's confession matched all evidence and testimony and I believed her totally and there was no chance of a good resolution beyond . . . a slim chance, a sliver, so I was doing myself no favor by . . . Light-addle-block-headed, I gulped water and wiggled my fingers to get the circulation going then set off walking as fast as I could, driving her out, physically ejecting her. I couldn't start thinking that way again, not a dram of it. Juice was guilty, done deal.

What was next? It was insane vengeance she'd taken—the wrong thing for the right reason—but still, guilt and repentance are punishments generally recognized as being insufficient. There was more coming, had to be, head up and eyes open. But you never know. Just as blind love is still love, blind hope is still—

—Fuck! that was the worst fall yet. It hadn't left me crippled under circling vultures, but I had to lie still awhile and catch my breath before picking the cactus spines and coarser bits of gravel out of my legs and forearms and digging the sand from my shorts.

I wasn't lost despite not knowing where I was. Two days back I cut downhill for supplies, hoping to fetch up near the Dowser's, but forced by weakness into taking the easiest route, I got off track and spilled out on the valley floor a short way from the Blue Dog. Distances were deceptive in the vicious land—heat waves and shimmers and shudders salted with blowing sand—and it took me two hours to reach the road. Very little strength by then, not enough to go inside and fight more of the truth despite the ache for solid food and a cold drink and a taste of air conditioning and anything else that would have satisfied many an ancient prophet with haranguing the authorities from atop a bar stool, devil take the desert. So I kept on keeping on, dragging along the shoulder past two intersections until reaching a beer joint advertising a pizza special. While waiting for my order I ducked a cannonade of jokes about my sunburn, and left the second I was done fueling. Gorged and heady, I threw up the pie in the parking lot on the Friday night spot reserved for it, and regained the mountains by walking up the street till it gave out. And now I'd fallen and didn't know whether I could get up, but did, because I had one more stop.

This time I kept to the lower slopes so I wouldn't miss the Dowser's place again. I recognized the side canyon where Sonny and the kids had camped, and followed it down to the property. I'd been planning to observe from afar, but unconsciously kept walking toward the house until realizing I could be spotted and pulling up. I flashed back to the old one-panel newspaper cartoons from when I was a kid, some prospector or cowboy or such dragging himself across the desert past a cattle skull and saying something humorous to an imaginary companion. Or talking to a vulture on a fencepost or struggling toward an oasis—I can't remember the details, and I don't remember laughing, but I was always running across them in the paper and in magazines, a minor artistic trend of the time, I guess.

Another thing from back then—Visible Man. I had an old set of encyclopedias with four or five volumes missing, a Christmas present from my dad he'd found in a used book store. I was so excited on opening the box I forgot to not thank him. Aside from the color pictures of rocks and minerals, what fascinated me most was Visible Man, a series of pages on the human anatomy. On the base page was a skeleton, cranium turned sideways, hands held palms-out. The preceding plates were acetate overlays that could be flipped down over the bones, each adding a collection of organs, the cardio-pulmonary system, neural network. The last sheet might have topped it off with a dermal covering—I can't be sure because there were pages missing among the volumes that weren't—but in any case, there I had it, Man in all his glory. I could grow a fully adult human from constituent parts and by reversing the process reduce him down to the bare bones. A few years later they came out with a Visible Man plastic model kit so I could perform the operation in 3-D, and there was also a Visible Woman version—by then society was giving tentative recognition to women as humans—but I found the sculpted forms of both men and women too complicated. I much preferred the flat layers of plastic in my book.

The geography around me had been flensed to the bone, yet could and surely some day would be outfitted as it was in the past, forest, sea, savanna or . . . or just like it was now. One peeled man can't record deep time, never mind predict it.

I snuck closer and threw a pebble at the back window. Tick! as though trying not to wake up the parents. Come out and play, Water Witch. Tick! Find me some water, find me some love, find me. Neither a face at the window nor a body at the door. As hot inside as out and about as inviting. The museum was abandoned, the Dowser's oddments and totems dust-covered and sad. Power off, cars in the yard over their rockers in sand, sleeping bags bunched under the window, a bag of granola I stuffed in my pack, a knife I used to puncture a can of spaghetti to drink the sauce. I went twice around the interior, in my unsound state wondering whether I'd find traces of lipstick or semen from the days of desert whoredom. I would have stayed awhile, but when the ground began to shake I ran outside.

Standing by the outhouse. Another one, very soon after the first, probably an aftershock but maybe the onset of the Big One. Quiet now, shhh! hide-and-seek. Hear and feel, be still and listen to the rock. Trembling in the knees as I fought to keep from puking the spaghetti sauce. It could be the earth-zipper opening along the right-lateral transverse fault. . . . never mind the geology, shut up and feel. Shhh! *Nada.* Just a couple of waves, the crust rolling over in its beds. What a neat way to end things that would have been—the Big One spilling the valley's guts as I was trying to discover my own. But no. Rumbleshake, pause, rumble, blah.

The water was shut off and I couldn't start a pump with my life on the line, which it almost was, so I scoured the yard until finding an old bucket and rope. It took over an hour of dredging the well to get enough gray slurry to fill my water bags, then I was off again for the hills. Before I hit the five-hundred-foot level—still in the Dowser's charmed circle—I was arrested by the squawking. The ravens had arrived, coursing through the air above the derelict property. Although many British Columbian and Pacific Northwest native tribes assign the bird spiritual status, the corvids around there were anything but god-like. For that matter, they seemed a different bird entirely, as though their collective behavior had been altered, only their fascination for shiny objects remaining. Let them have it all, act as they please. If I didn't keep moving they'd be picking my carcass before nightfall. I think I waved at them.

On my way southeast I tried to guess the location of Sonny's dream plot. It must have been close by but it didn't matter—it was out of his reach forever, the whole package recently purchased from the developer by a coalition of government and conservation forces, with the goal of leaving it be. Sonny probably wouldn't mind much now that it wasn't ticketed for thousands of houses and twelve golf courses. Neither deer nor antelope would play there, but something more important than a low-handicapper would.

Humidity and stench were creeping up-valley from the Salton Sea. August, and I figured that was about it, time to stretch out the legs for the finish line. After so long on uneven terrain the valley floor was a relief to cross, and a day later a burst of energy propelled me across the interstate and into Indio's north end. Couple of breaths with my hands on my knees, then down the street until reaching the bus station, its shabby building and dusty lot an exotic oasis.

Solicitous of the gringo in his precarious state, several Mexican workers and their families were quick to offer me a seat, fetch me water, lend me a freshly laundered bandanna for my flaming skull. Slightly recovered, I shuffled back up the street with almost the last of my— excuse me, Roger's—money, and returned from the Circle K with a load of sandwiches and refreshments, fixings for a bit of a fiesta with my friends against the fence out back.

They were impressed when I told them roughly where I'd been staying the past year. After much gesticulation, the help of several English/Spanish cognates and a lot of patience, an old man dug in his plastic bag, pulled out the English-language daily and thrust it at me, a wrinkled finger with no nail stabbing at a picture of police vehicles blockading a gate under the sign, Vista de las Pantalones.

Curious faces until I pursed my lips and nodded.

"*¡Ahí viene la bola!*" an old man cried gleefully.

I blocked out the voices to read the report.

The modest temblor I had felt split my old compound. Just a tiny crack that took all of two days to drain the pool, it was yet the final natural catalyst—View of the Pants turned on itself like a gut-shot wolf snapping at its own entrails to still the pain. Rival divisions within the Guardians and the Tommy Bahamas were battling each other and one another and one thing or another, a hash of undirected violence based on a catechism of fear.

All phone lines and cable connections were cut. No mention of Tina, so she and Sonny must have left by then, the best of a bad lot of news; Martin and Sarah Kolachuk were sequestered in their house directing semi-automatic gunfire at any and all trespassers; Deep Tread had escaped from jail again, but was apprehended seventeen minutes later after a swimwear-shop clerk on El Paseo Drive called in about a foul man who was refusing to leave unless she directed him to a store that sold disguises . . . er, costumes, that's it, costumes for like a party or something, with a fake beard, and get away from that phone; the owner of AA-1 DETAILS was dead, smothered by a Guardian with an Oakland Raiders flag as the auto-parts dealer was soliciting the neighborhood for funds to develop a TV series called "Saints on Paint—Miracles Where You Least Expect Them"; last night the police found at the foot of the wall a man bound and gagged, tarred and feathered, with a note pinned to his underwear—TRAITORS GET THIS. WHAT'S COMING TO THEM. JUST LIKE THIS. SEE? THAT'S WHAT THEY GET. THIS, WHAT THEY DESERVE—though on closer inspection at the Millard Fillmore Center, it wasn't tar on the man but chocolate, with partially melted Easter Bunny ears protruding from his sternum to prove it, and in lieu of feathers, a layer of old pee-stained goose down from a comforter, neither of which detracted from the intent.

The city police had been joined by the county cops and a special task force, and a group of residents had snuck out of the compound to appeal to the governor to send in the National Guard, though after the post-escape excitement they decided Sacramento was too far to go, and were arrested in Rancho Mirage while climbing the wall to get a look at Sinatra's old place. The adjoining compound had welded shut their gates, beefed up their private security force and sent the mayor a petition in three parts demanding, respectively, a city prayer meeting against violence, the cessation of police helicopter overflights during the traditional 4:00 to 6:00 happy hour and the immediate arrest and impressment of the Pants troublemakers into the occupation forces in Iraq.

The Mexicans had been waiting impatiently, and once I was done pelted me with questions I couldn't being to answer. Responding to the boarding call, they scraped together their roped-and-taped luggage, casting empathetic eyes at my disintegrating pack, and we lined up for the Hound. After a quick stop in Palm Springs, the bus took to the freeway. My companions were bound for points north—Monterey, Watsonville,

San Luis Obispo, Daly City, San Jose, Gorman, Woodland, Red Bluff, Bakersfield, Oakhurst, Clearlake, Benicia, San Rafael, and on up into Oregon and Washington, away, away from home. And me, the frostback, going home.

One of the old women cried when we said goodbye in Seattle. So far she was and so close I was, and I cried a bit myself. Just a tad, because by then I was looking forward to sealing some gaps with Roger, and Canada was so close, yet I was already missing the desert, and when we crossed the border it seemed like it wasn't one at all, and I debarked at the downtown station and got on the Skytrain and climbed to street level from the Waterfront station and it was comfortable, like the clothes you dig out from storage at the first cold snap of autumn, and I humped the pack through Gastown and up to Hastings and along to my apartment—so glad Roger had been sending up the rent—and opened the door and the windows to blow out the staleness and the smell of me when last I was there, and I wanted to go out and buy a lottery ticket and immediately use my winnings to treat the whole bloody town in my excitement, but instead unpacked my notes and put the paper and the disks beside the computer and went to sleep on the futon, anxious for the next day.

CHAPTER 42

The rain is beating down on the addicts. A dark night weighing heavy on dark futures. So tired but I should wrap this up, soldier on. Late as it is, I should be able to find a spare paper somewhere after I'm done, and I'll read the thing and save it to wrap a slice of pizza to bring home and that'll be that.

And after? The past year I've been a man of two minds, both unsound, an actor playing double roles, comfortable in neither. New starts gone wrong release paralyzing agents, and I have little interest in the future. And what a shame, because on getting home I felt charged and eager for the next day, but when I crashed on the futon—early, like a kid trying to rush the arrival of Christmas—I couldn't stop the chatter for two hours. Finally, I slid into more of a blackout than sleep. I wasn't awake five minutes the next morning when an RCMP officer banged on the door and told me the Mounties were in charge of the Canadian portion of the investigation due to the international connection, offering me immunity for turning Juice in.

"Pardon me?" I said.

"Yes," he said. "A full pardon."

Before it could descend fully into farce I stated that I had no clue as to her whereabouts and furthermore—on my toes and in his face—I wasn't looking because she was after me too and if he didn't believe me he could ask Detective Legree once he figured out how to work a phone and he accused me of obstruction and I called him a beautiful spring wildflower and that set him into such a rage he called me nine kinds of lying prick before leaving in a vortex of brain-dead suspicion. So much for my first happy morning back. On the good side, at least I was in tight now with the local constabulary.

Rigid with fatigue and contrariness, unable to think straight, I went downstairs to stand in the rain. Marking my doorway was another Horseman, undercover as a street person with $140 Nikes. I asked him point blank about Juice, and he replied as plainly that the California cops had traced her e-mail to an Internet kiosk at LAX, but there was a communications mixup, and by the time airport security responded her plane had already landed in Vancouver and she'd disappeared. That's all he'd been told, a claim I accepted. Seemed like a nice guy, and I said he was welcome to wait inside, an offer he declined.

Time for work, if I could calm down and concentrate, or more importantly if I couldn't. Amid arranging my journal and research material beside the computer, I pushed back the chair with such force I startled the dead jade plant in the corner. Computer? I didn't own one. Where the hell had it come from? There it sat, COMPAQ PRESARIO, the same model I'd been using in the desert. The continuity must have blinded me the night before and prevented it from registering and . . . checked all over, nope, no card or message, though obviously it had come from Roger. Boot—identical software. Even my files and folders, while empty, had been recreated and titled, awaiting a slip of a disk into the tower and a couple of clicks to be filled with desert memories. Roger for sure, the only explanation, confirmed when I found an envelope containing three hundred dollars sticking out of the user manual.

I went outside again and planted myself on the sidewalk, jerking my head at every movement as though expecting to catch him ducking into an alley like Jean Valjean. Had the Mountie still been around, I would have asked him to keep an eye out, but I guess he'd been recalled after blowing his cover. Ten minutes or so in the soothing rain and I picked up a coffee and a paper and returned to the apartment. The local and provincial news looked foreign, so I went straight to the junk-thought sections. Fingerlick, flip, toss, gloss, skip, scan—Oh.

Page E4, a column under the byline, Glenda Glitss:

> Well, readers, I have good news and bad. The bad news first: This is my last week. And now right onto the good news: Chas Cassidy is back.
>
> After a sabbatical in the California sun, our intrepid reporter returns to his regular spot on Saturday to take over the reigns of the weekend *You and Me* column. Some of our older readers might be familiar with the name Morty Cahoot, a transplanted prairie boy who wrote a novel called *Silent Life*. Even if you missed it, this is your chance to find out what happened to the man who penned the one-hit wonder. (The book wasn't really a "hit" but I've been told there were people who liked it.)

Chas has spent months in personal conversation with Mr. Cahoot, and assures me this is a heck of a story, his best yet. With all the rain we've had here in Lotus Land lately, you should read the weekend column about the desert just to dry out!

On a personal note, I want to thank each and every one of my loyal readers for tuning in while I've been trying to fill pretty big shoes. But there's a silver lining in every cloud, even the ones over the North Shore Mountains. I'm proud to announce that as of September, I'll be the new International Affairs Correspondent, and if you feel the same way as me, about our reader/writer relationship that is, I look forward to hearing from you on my website. Together, we can turn this Middle East thing around!

Shalom, Allahu Akhbar, and put your hands together and take them apart and put them together again for Chas Cassidy's return.

The smart thing would be to run, preferably to some place where the rain falls mainly on the plain instead of on my parade, which ruled out the Coachella Valley. And what a shame. I missed my walks and my talks and still don't know what had happened to the Dowser—with everything she did for me the least I could do in return was . . . well, anything she wanted. I'm truly aching for the natural part of the desert, I could sure stand to see Sonny again, running around Vancouver looking for Roger while half-expecting an attack by Juice isn't doing me any good. Yeah, get away and find the Dowser, have a beer with Sonny, maybe stay awhile, buy a plot of land backing onto the mountains and build a house. Right. That'd fix me up.

The world of my notes felt safer, or at least more familiar, than the one around me, so I tried to treat the computer as a pet instead of a parasite that had immigrated in the body hair of a smuggler, and spent the morning organizing the past year. In the afternoon, realizing I'd make no progress till the voices were expunged, I wrote them out of my head and by suppertime I'd covered the hike and was cutting and pasting the beginning of our road trip. My system must have adjusted to the vulture's eating habits I'd been keeping—not a growl all day until the assault of grilling meat from the apartment below awoke the scavenger within and propelled me from the desk onto the street in search of something burned and dead.

The next day I retraced the Hari Krishna parade route, recapturing nothing of what I had experienced the year before, so it was back home and back at it. And then, after hours on hours at the desk, I went out for the day's paper, figuring I was safe till the weekend. At the counter of a diner, coffee in hand, wet newsprint.

The Big One.

Allow me to yank this out from earlier in my notes:

> In California, as the Pacific Plate meets the North American Plate and rides northwest relative to it, great stresses build up, the ground bends and eventually snaps, creating or enlarging a fault, of which there are many intertwined, bent and braided for over eight-hundred miles along the San Andreas system.

The earth had struck the Coachella Valley a withering blow. It's unnecessary to go on at length about the destroyed buildings and rup-tured infrastructure because it stopped there. Not a life was lost. Much pulverized stucco in many heads of hair, bruises and sprains and charley horses, but shitless as the residents had been scared, they all walked away hale and hearty and eager to get to the carwash.

My new machine wasn't connected to the Internet, so no sense going home. After finishing the coffee, I splashed to a cybercafé up from Gastown to tap the news from down south. Same stories in all the regional papers, including those from the coast. Rock talk and damage estimates and much speculation on how much worse it could have been—with so many projections and extrapolations I could sense the disappointment—and interviews with the mayors of Palm Springs, Cathedral City, Rancho Mirage, Palm Desert, Indian Wells, La Quinta and the rest of the valley communities, and there must be more to it than that, come on, there had to be something about—Ahar, Matey!

The standoff at our old compound was over. The minor temblor of a few weeks ago had sent the citizens over the edge, and now a massive quake had pulled them back. The article stated the police were having difficulty gathering both evidence and testimony on the many criminal events during the civil disturbance. Several anonymous View of the Pants residents were quoted, saying in almost identical language that when the desert delivers the sign of the beast it is time for all humankind to band together. Men, women and children, Guardians and Tommy Bahamas,

Christians and renters—the whole menagerie had clammed up and was refusing to talk to the cops, schism healed, a united front. In a "Manifesto" carried by the *Desert Sun*, my old neighborhood asserted its right to self-determination. Before speaking further to the media or cooperating in any way with the authorities they would be repairing the houses, replanting the trees, fixing the pool. Every symbolic fence between neighbors would be torn down, while the actual one around the compound would be raised and fortified. Change was afoot in the 'hood. New times, boundless opportunity, a chicken in every Ralphs.

There would be holdouts, I'm sure, traditionalists nostalgic for the good old days when a man could proudly walk the streets with a sidearm recording Code violations and reporting leash-law transgressors, but that too would pass as the next generation was reared to appreciate that danger lay only outside the tribe. There was more but that would do. It was good enough that everyone had survived the disaster. Whew. Martin could be proud of his earthquake preparedness efforts, assuming he and Sarah hadn't been killed before the truce by incoming rounds. *Aqui se acaba la tristeza*—Here all sadness ends.

A flashing pop-up alerted me that I was running out of rented time on the computer, so I hastily did one more piece of googling: *¡Ahí viene la bola!* The cry from the lips of an old man at the Indio bus station.

The only direct reference I could find was in Spanish, and the translation program was inoperative. I printed the pages and carried them away. Back in front of my building was the undercover Horseman, in a T-shirt in the rain, shivering and looking devastatingly like a junkie, except for the *Maintiens le Droit* tattoo on his eighteen-inch upper arm.

As I came up to the door I said, "*Hola. ¿Como está?*"

"*Muy bien. ¿Y usted?*"

Out came the pages. Apparently, the phrase was popular in the early-twentieth-century during Mexico's revolutionary upheavals. *¡Ahí viene la bola!* —Here comes the mutiny! shouted with celebratory delight at the frequency of the rebellions. *¡Ahí viene la bola!* —Yeehaw! Do your worst, motherfuckers, I'm having another *cerveza*.

After that I worked hard on the notes, avoiding the paper for the rest of the week to buck up for my Saturday depantsing.

And Saturday it is. The paper's been waiting for me all day while I've been writing and dealing with the RCMP again—the first cop, still snarly, no details, this time looking for Roger instead of Juice—and now it's time. Shortly, I'll head out and test myself against Cassidy's story then improvise a reaction.

I'm fairly complete with the details of Juice's rampage, and while some of them escape me, that's okay, I don't need every question answered. At this stage most of them are irrelevant anyhow. If only I could stop wanting to climb inside her mind, the main component of my ache to see her again. A fascinating woman with black hair and dark dark eyes is still haunting a little boy operating under the fallacy of the central position. Although it can get buggered up, a whole life is too complicated to be one-hundred-percent ruined. My main concern is how much life I have left, because I suspect Juice won't be satisfied with destroying my world as I did hers. She can't possibly feel she's achieved redress. But she'll do what she'll do and I'm not afraid, not really.

G.H. Nuttall is another matter. Now *he* scares me. I finally got around to some elementary research, and discovered he's writing and teaching in St. John's. I'm in no possible emotional or financial shape to defend myself, but that's not what's important—retribution and exposure are piffles. He did it and I did not. G.H. Nuttall knitted past, present and future together. He had the strength to seek and find himself by tapping the source. Me? What source? The earth rumbles—hell, it hasn't taken a day off as far as I can tell—and I keep insisting it's too deep to investigate. For all my talk of diversity and complexity, you'd think I'd get it.

Life was easy when I met my future wife. Frustrating, maddening, and for someone like me with no sense of proportion, dangerous, but so easy. I loved her and she didn't love me. Simple. Knew where I stood. We were connected in no true sense, and while we often laughed and cried at the same time it was never at the same thing. The night I went down on one knee she answered my proposal of marriage with: "Sure," the shining moment of our relationship.

But I loved her, I think. I know for a fact I loved being in love, and though she didn't love me back, she must have been like me and needed the emotion around her, to inhale its scent and feel its tingle and contemplate the mystery of how it colors the air, because no one says "Sure" out of desperation. Wait a minute, let me . . . naw, I'll let that comment stand.

I had great ambitions at first, though they were well disguised, mainly because it was impossible to observe me in action—I wished mightily to leave my mark on the world while avoiding the required effort. Sheila couldn't understand why I wanted it in the first place. She was bogged in the past, a life of reliving, and worse was that she extended only the over-arching theme, none of the specifics. Her journal was variously her wor-rystone, comfort zone, safe space and nemesis. She'd write through day and night and smoke unfiltered Players and scream at her typewriter and shred what she'd written and rewrite it until there was no light left to make the shadows retreat. At times laughter would percolate through the door, but it was the kind prompted by Tarantino films, a baleful sound unrelated to humor.

It was autobiographical, of course, I could tell that much, a deduction unbolstered by evidence because I was never allowed to read a word. On countless days when she'd be sitting at the desk behind the closed door while I sat at the kitchen table with a dozen beer that wouldn't have time to warm to room temperature, I was given to fantasy, particularly after reading a book or watching a movie about an artist torn and disintegrat-ing yet bonded to a soulmate. I'd invent dialogues between us, hoping Sheila would come charging out of the room, manuscript pages in hand, to share the remembrances. It would have meant I was leaving her alone to find what needed finding, do what she had to do, and good enough if all I reaped was the turmoil.

Not much luck of that, though. She didn't even like my rock collec-tion. That's life, like they say, in the words of her sister.

And then she killed herself—nothing so mild as an overdose or an exhaust hose in the car, no, it wasn't a easy way she chose—and I was left alone. She had no family that I knew of and no friends and I'd lost most of mine. Roger was there, of course, the very morning after as though wired into my heart's security alarm, but that was it. So I sat. For many days I sat and relied on my best friend, who displayed the bedside man-ner of the truly wise by checking in with the right frequency and staying for the proper duration. For all the time alone I came to no conclusions, not even the trite observation that life is short. I didn't learn a thing, heightening the sense of isolation, though as a corollary effect of the soli-tude I came to a decision.

I had been madly in love with a woman who couldn't share anything but the most superficial aspects of her past, so now it was time to get right down to it on my own. I'd discover her in death, that's what I'd do, a dollar short and a day late—big deal. When shocked beyond despair, immediate reaction is all we can expect. So before my period of hyperso-cializing, of caterwauling around Vancouver swept up by and lost in one or another clot of people more experienced than I was in not giving a shit, I read.

I read at her desk. Notes and jottings and extended passages of youth and tragedy and anger and violation and many pages of good hard writing. Everything about my wife down to the color of her first dress I learned from her journal and diary and strung-together short stories. Then I read what had crystallized from the solution of failed starts and half attempts—her book. Solid, excellent. And I read it; I read it over and over.

Her dad. Mum. Younger sister. Dad again, much of him. Dogs on the farm. Rye whiskey and school and farm boys. More of her dad. And her mum. Hard nasty venomous writing mixed with truly beautiful passages marbled with love when she was just her and her dad hadn't slept with her for a while and the weather was fine and there was food in the house and about the time they won a raffle trip to the city to watch a CFL game and little Sheila didn't like football but the hotel had an indoor swimming pool and what a buffet in the hotel the next morning! and she thought it must be like Paris. Not many of those, though, and as for the rest, I didn't have to read between the lines to understand why she could never tell anyone because it was right there in plain English.

But I wasn't anyone, I was her husband. Why couldn't she tell me even when I cried because she was crying? She carried the past with her and revealed none; I spilled all of mine but my load was false. I would have loved for us to meet—it didn't have to be in the middle—but we never did. Pants on fire.

It wasn't intended for publication. Sheila Smith's story, that's all.

I copied her manuscript longhand with a few dozen Bic medium-point pens on tablets of yellow paper and paid a college kid to prepare the typescript. I enjoyed the painstaking process of transforming my wife's words into mine. I hand-copied every line including spelling mistakes, grammatical errors, peculiar punctuation. My editor—and after her the copy-editor—grew exhausted trying to convince me the submission should be cleaned up, until collapsing into a fan club and buying me drinks and treating me to dinners after noteworthy reviewers praised the publishing house for its courage in allowing the "essential nature" of the work to appear between covers.

On the cover—Morty Cahoot. If you were dumb enough to kill yourself and so stupid to marry someone like me you deserve . . . All you have to do is tell me, you stupid bitch wonderful love of my life, just tell me and your book will have been safe, sitting there forever on the desk or in a box on the closet floor. I won't tell, honest, cross my heart and hope to die. Whatever you think of me is accurate but I'm trying to help, stuck trying. I want your help, too, greedily suck it up if you offer. I tell you everything, don't I? But you're dumb, dumb as a bunny. Except you know exactly what I am. Pounding your typewriter and cursing the love your dad forced into you and your mother hadn't the strength to give you, and my love, the kind of love so strong that I want it to be mine alone—I love you but it's mine, gimme, get your own. Jesus, you're smart, you know my foundation can't support a house, not even one of cards.

But you were stupid to die, you sure were that. Stupid to die and to ... well, that's between us, the only thing between us.

Praise for the novel died quickly and the book soon went out of print. Good.

EPILOGUE

That was supposed to be it.

The End.

I wouldn't add another layer—my take on a reporter's exposure of what he thought of things I've already told you even if I'm wrong and he didn't know what was what or even if he knew more than me—because nobody should be expected to keep that straight. Surely, at that stage of remove the truth would be unrecognizable. Cassidy's article would mark the end of a bad piece of business, and with luck Roger and I would be able to rebuild.

The End.
Bye.

No such luck. The addict in the gumboots raised a hand in greeting. Word on the street has it the cops are after me, and the past few days the junkies on Hastings have been treating me as part of the collective, albeit one who must have money stashed, because I look as if I'd passed out in a tanning bed. I waved back at Gumboot and zigzagged my way to the West End.

The bars were letting out, which meant the Korean guy would be bracing for the surge of locals staggering in for rolling papers and the house specialty—a half-frozen wiener on a yellowish hot-dog bun with exactly seven sesame seeds set into the crust, a couple of condiment packets secreted alongside, the whole works wrapped in plastic that only a vampire's teeth were sharp enough to open. I picked up the pace to beat the rush.When I slid the newspaper onto the counter, the owner wouldn't even look at it. When I asked him what was wrong, he pretended not to hear, displaying the common sense required of convenience-store workers at that time of night.

"Come on," I said with bite, a little high on my street power as a police suspect.

"Sorry."

"What are you sorry about?"

"Read paper."

"That's what I'm going to do."

"Read paper outside."

"I've been coming in here for years," I said. "You and I, we get along don't we? We're friends."

"Read paper outside. Closing now."

"Before the Sylvia lets out?" I said. "And the Arms up the street? You're messing with your bread and butter."

"Take bread and butter for free. Read paper outside."

"We're friends, for fuck sake."

He looked down at the paper. "Very good man, your friend. Lend me money two times. Your friend, very good man."

I was getting nowhere, no surprise considering I didn't know where I was going. I needed an explanation, that's all, a straightforward explanation just once about anything without having to claw through a mile of cobwebs.

"Closing now," he said.

"Yeah, yeah." Inadvertently, I added to my badass rep by not having my wallet on me. The owner waved off the fifty cents, probably relieved I wasn't looking for protection money.

Paperboy, my first job. Show up on time in blowing snow and wind strong enough to lift your seventy-five pounds off the pavement, pick up your load, don't be late. The papers had to be individually folded—in thirds like a letter, loose right end tucked into the opening on the creased side and Bang! on the knee to seal the fold—and that's what I did at the counter before plowing my way to the door, parting a group of drunken West-Enders who veered to each side and began bouncing around the display racks like cattle with the blind staggers.

But I couldn't let it go. I wiped the rain from my face and went back in and from the doorway said, "What's your name? We're friends, and I don't even know your name."

But the owner was already out from behind the counter, yelling at a man in an Armani suit to put back the package of beef jerky he was stuffing down his pants. I detoured down to Beach Avenue. Rain-swept, litter-free. I took the route along the water to the Aquatic Centre before cutting up toward downtown and all the way home to read about myself.

ROCK VARNISH

Now it's early morning, greasy gray sky, street lights still on, and I'm back at the keyboard thinking through my fingertips. Entering notes is doing me no good so soon after the event but here goes, best as I can manage:

– as one of their own, Charles H. "Chas" Cassidy is given front-page coverage.

– he's in Vancouver General Hospital. Separated shoulder, broken nose, possible punctured lung, multiple cuts and contusions.

– Friday night, right before the Saturday edition is put to bed, Chas Cassidy, back in town to resume his post as weekend columnist of *You and Me*, leaves his favorite restaurant, Delilah's, in the West End. On reaching Denman Street he turns left toward the beach, planning to walk off his dinner on the seawall.

– a hundred meters short of the park, a Dodge Neon driven by one Roger Jeffcoate hurtles down the grassy slope toward him. Cassidy dives onto the rocks below just as the car veers right, slams sideways into the lip of the retaining wall and flips over, landing inverted on a boulder, steps from where Cassidy lays cradling his arm.

– two witnesses say it looked intentional, alleged attacker aimed for Cassidy at the corner of Denman and Davie, but spun out in the rain and had to reverse into an alley to get turned around before catching up to the reporter on the seawall.

– Cassidy points out that Jeffcoate could easily have killed him, but obviously changed his mind and swerved at the last minute. He refuses to press charges. The police inform him that attempted murder is a crime out of his hands.

– Jeffcoate is in the critical ward. Unconscious, sixty-forty, doctor hopeful if not confident.

I choose to believe Roger will come out of it okay. Afterward, I mean—the injuries and criminal charges have nothing to do with the Roger I'm talking about. Roger, my Roger, hasn't come to this from submerging his natural instincts until they surfaced on their own with a vengeance. Rather, it was an isolated instance of . . . Roger, what the fuck have you done, Rog? We talked about this, you and I, years and years ago, in the flush of young friendship, with time ahead to do it all, talking up the world and our parts in it, agreeing the greatest achievement in the sum of a life is a legacy of good will and doing no harm. But I'd already started twisting it, hadn't I? Already on the way. And now look what I've done to you. Be well, wake up and be well. I'm trying, working hard even though my chunk of time's eroding—getting old, need reading glasses even for my hindsight. Ha! That's a joke, man, wake up, the Moho's rumbling, you don't want to miss it. I believe you. I believe in you.

Hours to go. They'll let me in to see him, have to. *Fucking right I'm family, lady—his mum raised me since I was fourteen. Outta my way.*

The article picks up on p. 15:

> – Jeffcoate will be charged with attempted murder, though a prominent Vancouver attorney expresses the opinion that based on Cassidy's refusal to press charges and the unsound state of his attacker's mind, the charge will be reduced. When asked how an unconscious man's mind can be considered either sound or unsound, the lawyer replies that it's obvious from his actions. Questioned about what could prompt such actions, he states "An unsound mind," which is what his client has. When asked how an unconscious man with an unsound mind could have retained counsel, the lawyer responds that he's a prominent Vancouver attorney and is taking on the case pro bono, and that only someone with an unsound mind would turn down an offer like that. An unsound mind, he repeats, what his client has.

> – City Council is looking into possibly suggesting a provisional committee be formed to make inquiries into the chance of maybe releasing limited funds to finance an unofficial and nonbinding study on whether a resolution can be found to the increasing problem of people backing into alleys in high-traffic areas such as the West End.

– Canada Revenue Agency and the RCMP are considering filing exotic-species smuggling charges against Jeffcoate over a desert tortoise shell with a bullet hole found in his trunk.

– five mayoralty candidates are interviewed regarding the incident. Two declare war on crime; one proposes erecting a chainlink security fence along the seawall; one calls for a return to earlier closing times for bars and restaurants; the last claims something like this was bound to happen the minute marijuana laws were liberalized, hemp being a well-known suppresser of common sense that can lead to both reduced judgment and violent behavior, and though "Reefer Madness" is a myth, both reefers and madness exist and so can't logically be excluded as being in some way linked, even though there is no indication "Mary Jane" was involved in the actual incident, besides which, the attacker has been identified by several known homosexuals in the West End, and while they unanimously assert he's one of the least aggressive people they've ever met, their opinions are suspect, being homosexuals and all, so are likely biased toward protecting their way of life, which is a good thing to protect so long as it isn't a way that goes against God's will and you're not high on MJ.

What used to make Roger and me laugh isn't working. By the time I finally turn to Cassidy's article I'm either unruffled or numb, depending on who's in charge of the definitions. Fold the paper back and crease it to shut out the furniture ads.

Hold it, nothing here—*You and Me* isn't in its usual place. No column at all, for that matter. Shit, if I have to wait another day I might lose it entirely, keep looking, Morty. Oh, okay, here it is back on the front page below the fold. Front page, I'm on the front page.

And what do you know—Glenda Glitss is, too:

Well, loyal *You and Me* readers, I have good news and bad, and by now you know the bad. Chas Cassidy, one of the last truly great old-school journalists, was the victim of a hit-and-run last night, although the coward driving didn't run and Chas wasn't technically hit.

The good news is that your loyal columnist is mending well in the hospital and passes on his best wishes to each and every one of you. He told me that himself.

As the regular visitors to the column know, Chas is my brother. But he's more than that. Friend, supporter and mentor in the long and lonely climb to the top, I don't hesitate to say that our brother/sister relationship has nothing to do with the way I feel, that as a professional, I have never and will never measure up to his standard of excellence as an observer of the everyday person, Homer's "common man."

I was asked at the last minute to write this special weekend message. I'm afraid it's quite short, and I hope you understand. Chas's brush with death has moved me beyond movement.

You're probably asking yourself why we didn't just run Chas's column as I previously mentioned, and I'll tell you: Because this is the best news of all!

When he came back from the desert, Chas submitted a 25,000-word story to the editor. If you can't imagine how hard that is, try writing a simple word on a piece of paper and then copying it 24,999 times.

Unfortunately, there was only space for the usual column, and out of loyalty Chas agreed to let the editor cut his submission. Because of staff reductions, the editor's position is being temporarily filled by our food critic, who didn't have the time (who would, wearing two hats?) to go through such a lengthy essay. So he decided to run the small first draft that Chas wrote months ago.

I read it. I mean it. I wasn't above taking the time from my writing to read something else, and that's not just because of who the writer was. It was his usual excellent work, a story about the man I told you about, Morty Cahoot. Just an average man who wrote a book a long time ago and now hangs around golfing or something in the California desert. I actually met Mr. Cahoot when I went to visit my brother, but being a professional, I wouldn't even consider stealing a story. And I must admit, in Chas's hands, Cahoot comes alive on the page.

Remember now, I promised you really good news!

Here goes: As a tribute to an exceptional writer, loyal employee and a real spirit-picker-upper around the office, the paper has decided to print the whole story. That's right. Starting Monday and running through the week, the whole essay will appear in six parts, culminating next Saturday in amazing revelations. I know the whole story, and believe me, hoo-boy.

To show how much you shouldn't miss the series, the RCMP and the FBI and probably even NORAD seem quite interested in getting their hands on it. I can't really blame them, because there's some awful stuff in there.

But no way, José. They'll have to get in line with you, the people. This is what we're all about: Telling you, the people, what you have a right to know without government intervention. Journalistic freedom is as important as all the other kinds, and our lawyers agree. You can read the whole thing starting Monday, so stay tuned.

On a personal note, I'd like to issue a challenge. Tomorrow I am going to be down on the beach at English Bay. At exactly noon, I am going to pick up a stone and place it on the spot where my only brother almost met his end. I hereby challenge all his many, many fans to join me and add a stone to the pile. Years to come, we'll be able to take our kids down to the water and show them the monument, a testament to a career, a human being,
You and Me.

It's late morning and about as light out as it looks to get. Sure will be nice if the clouds part and a screw of sunshine bores through the condensation on my window and takes me square in the face. But it probably won't happen, and I'll be satisfied with just a tad less rain and a few sucker holes in the clouds to let me know the sun hasn't given up. No more than a few, though, please, because I can use the murky protection till my forehead's done peeling.

Almost done here, then it's over to Vancouver General. It's my turn, Roger, so buckle up and brace yourself—I've got this thing started, but it might take a while to figure out how to get it into gear, and for sure the steering's going to be a problem. Not to worry, put yourself in my hands. I feel good. Yeah, it's a strange time for that prairie dog to poke out its head, but there it is, Rog.

Here's a list of solid practical things I can do while I'm helping you recover: Stay off the booze, eat right, exercise, lose weight, dress well, get a job, start a savings account, and to avoid stress stop challenging everything. Excellent self-advice. How about this list: Apologize, hand out clean needles, renew my library card, rage at whatever I disagree with, start a novel of my own, save a witch. Much better.

Now no more delays. After the hospital, I'll come back to the apartment and start reading *And the Sea Shook the Rock* like a tourist instead of a pickpocket. As for Juice, what's there to do? I could use some help on this one, Rog. Tough times ahead until you're well enough to give me some advice, and it's advice I need right now.

I should phone my dad.

The End.
For real.